Meant
TO BE
Mine

LISA MARIE
PERRY

FOREVER

NEW YORK   BOSTON

Copyright © 2016 by Lisa Marie Perry
Excerpt from *Yours to Take* copyright © 2016 by Lisa Marie Perry

Cover design by Elizabeth Turner
Cover images copyright © Shutterstock
Cover copyright © 2016 by Hachette Book Group, Inc.

Forever
Hachette Book Group
1290 Avenue of the Americas
New York, NY 10104
forever-romance.com
twitter.com/foreverromance

First Edition: August 2016

Forever is an imprint of Grand Central Publishing.
The Forever name and logo are trademarks of Hachette Book Group, Inc.

The publisher is not responsible for websites (or their content) that are not owned by the publisher.

The Hachette Speakers Bureau provides a wide range of authors for speaking events. To find out more, go to www.hachettespeakersbureau.com or call (866) 376-6591.

ISBNs: 978-1-4555-9435-1 (mass market), 978-1-4555-9436-8 (ebook)

Printed in the United States of America

OPM

10 9 8 7 6 5 4 3 2 1

ATTENTION CORPORATIONS AND ORGANIZATIONS:

Most Hachette Book Group books are available at quantity discounts with bulk purchase for educational, business, or sales promotional use. For information, please call or write:

Special Markets Department, Hachette Book Group
1290 Avenue of the Americas, New York, NY 10104
Telephone: 1-800-222-6747 Fax: 1-800-477-5925

*To a little girl with a big dream who grew
up and turned her dream into a career.
Go have a cookie—you've earned it.*

Acknowledgments

My sincerest thanks to the phenomenal team at Grand Central Publishing/Forever, who believed the steamy romance between a scarred woman and a broken man was a story that should be told. A special note of appreciation goes to Lauren Plude for falling in love with my characters, and to my brilliant editors Dana Hamilton and Michele Bidelspach.

Heartfelt thanks and all the sexy-man GIFs to my amazingly talented and encouraging agent, Sarah Younger.

My gratitude to the American Heart Association, an organization whose research, dedication, and tireless efforts help save lives every day.

Finally, thanks to all who truly understand why I call my Facebook page "Dr. Jekyll" and my Twitter feed "Mr. Hyde."

Meant to Be Mine

CHAPTER 1

"Mother Nature's a tease."

A snap of lightning revealed itself, then vanished so quickly that it held no color, no discernible shape. There was no cry of thunder to punctuate it. Only a spark, there and gone in a blink.

So swiftly that the congregation of mourners, with their heads bent and expressions brushed with quiet grief, didn't glance up to acknowledge the bolt that had struck so low in the early-evening sky that it very well could've tasted the ocean.

Sofia Mercer couldn't argue with her friend/dry-humor dispenser's assessment. "The best tease there is." Her focus traveled past the hilltop cemetery and its canopy of trees—trees that offered no real protection from the elements and left everyone vulnerable to the assault of wind—to the deep gray water in the distance. Waves danced, swayed, collided. Her chest ached, not with the bite of mourning that had settled inside her the moment she'd gotten word of her great-aunt's sudden death but with the dull soreness that aggravated the dark mahogany north-to-south scar between her breasts. The sensation coincided with crappy weather—not that it was always accurate. And she certainly wasn't interested in convincing people, even her closest friend, that she prepared for storms based on whether her surgical scar was itchy and achy.

Which was the only reason she hadn't taken her umbrella when she and Joss Vail had left New York City this morning to drive to Cape Cod for the funeral. According to Joss, who swore by her trusted weather app, Barnstable County would be blessed with a sun-and-surf Memorial Day weekend. That had been hours ago, when they were loading suitcases and tote bags—mostly Joss's—into Sofia's all-the-extras SUV for an overnight stay on the Cape.

If the stab of lightning overhead and the warning ache of Sofia's scar were any indication, this edge of the county was due for rain and chaos before sun and surf. Now they were standing in a town that was as close to the Atlantic as one could get without taking a dip in the water, huddled against the wind with the other mourners. Most were strangers to Sofia. Maybe they'd been familiar—friends, even—before, but time had chipped away any connection. Some had responded with forced smiles when she caught their eye. A few had offered awkward hugs before escaping across the grass to fiddle with cell phones or spew gossip about her in whispers that rode the wind.

Sofia couldn't be comforted or consoled or insulted. She couldn't be forced to care about smiles or embraces or whispered gossip—not when she and her father had been forced to put Eaves, Massachusetts, in the rearview mirror.

Years in the past, she reminded herself again. It didn't matter, but it did.

It mattered that only death could compel Sofia to return to Eaves. It mattered that she felt like an outsider, an interloper, an intruder. Though logically she deserved to grieve among the people who, even if they'd never loved her, had respected Luz Azcárraga. Yet none of it should matter, because she was here today to lay an orchid on Aunt Luz's casket and say a prayer and good-bye.

Prepared to do just that, she took a bracing breath of sea-and-salt-scented air and ventured deeper into the gathering, toward the array of luscious spring blooms and gilded-framed photographs on easels that surrounded the six-foot-deep carving in the earth. The images reacquainted her with the Argentine woman Sofia remembered. Luz hadn't been much older than Sofia's mother. So vivacious and piss-and-vinegar, she'd resisted monogamous relationships, and to defy the conservatives who'd tried to shut down her erotic boutique she'd famously bicycled into a town hall meeting wearing nothing but tattoos, ass floss, and Not-Allowed-symbol pasties.

How many more crazy-wild stories would Luz have shared over the round of ice-cold beer Sofia had been promising her every birthday since she'd turned twenty-one? Maybe she'd broken that promise so many times that Luz eventually quit holding her to it. Maybe not. No way to tell—and, hell, she deserved the painful weight of that unknown. The casket was already inside the plot. Without apology or explanation, Aunt Luz was gone.

As the priest concluded his prayer, the guests began to disperse, murmuring words Sofia didn't register. Approaching the casket, she was vaguely aware of Joss trailing her. The next time she was annoyed with her friend for leaving dirty dishes in the sink or borrowing stuff without asking first, she'd recall that Joss had passed up the opportunity to cater pastries for an elite Upper East Side bazaar and sacrificed a Hamptons weekend with her man to moral-support Sofia through her great-aunt's funeral.

Kneeling, Sofia paused before whispering, "Bless you, Aunt. Good-bye." She reached down and let the orchid drop soundlessly onto the casket, then straightened to find her friend studying the frames.

"You look like her—especially in this pic here," Joss commented, glancing from Sofia to the photograph of a twentysomething Luz posed on an antique bicycle against a backdrop of a sandy Eaves street and the Atlantic Ocean. There were flowers stuffed in the bicycle's basket and decorating her hair.

Sofia considered her own features: the dense wavy hair, gently hooked nose, and smattering of freckles came from her father's Irish heritage and the full lips, the dark eyes, and the touch of warmth in her pale complexion were gifts from her Argentine American mother. She was proof that once upon a time nothing but love had existed between her parents, that no cultural or political differences could eclipse their need to be together. Nice fantasy, whenever she was in the mood to overlook the divorce and how she couldn't remember her mother even if she wanted to.

"When I was a kid, people would call me Luz's miniature. As the story goes, when I was born she insisted that even though I'm only a quarter Argentine, I would look like her." At the warning howl of wind, she crossed her arms to rub them. The high-necked black leather dress she wore was decently durable, but the garment was sleeveless and left her exposed from midthigh to the tops of her pink high heels. "Not even genetics could stop Aunt Luz from getting her way."

"A determined lady. Like you."

Determined, sure. But Aunt Luz had no hard limits when it came to family. Folks hurt her, abused her, walked away from her, but she refused to cut them off. Sofia's heart—the one that had failed, and the one that pumped life through her body now—could never be so forgiving... and that frightened her. "Shh, Joss. Don't let Aunt hear you," she said with a soft smile. "A lady she had no ambitions to be. She was a beer-drinking, card-playing firecracker who peddled lingerie and kinky sex toys for a living." She took another glance down at the casket as she began to walk away. "And I loved her."

"I know you did."

"It's complicated, Joss."

"I know," she said again, steering Sofia to the side, out of the way of a group of people approaching the plot with long-stemmed roses in tow.

"Miss Mercer? *Espere un momento*—Miss Mercer?"

Sofia halted. She hadn't been referred to as *miss* since before her thirtieth birthday, which had come and gone un-eventfully. At thirty-one, she was still in her twenties at heart. Literally. The female organ donor had been several years Sofia's junior.

A hulk of a man with sun-toasted olive skin, an angular face, and a gray-streaked braid about as long as Sofia's arm approached. Accompanying him was a cocktail of scents: leather from his jacket, tobacco on his breath, and some-thing earthy that had her thinking of the barefoot walks through the woods she'd loved before everything fell to shit.

A biker. He had to be one. He probably had tattoos, club patches, a road name, and stories that'd blind her mind's eye.

He traveled with steel between his thighs, with the sun

sitting on his brow and the wind fondling his hair. She just knew it—and was instantly jealous.

She lived in the safest New York City apartment she and her friend could afford, and the only reckless danger she dabbled in was scoring X-rated flicks for the monthly pizza-and-porn night she and her work friends gathered for after hours.

"Yes?" she said slowly, noticing one hand was hidden behind his back.

He muttered, *"Vamanos"* as he revealed a leash gripped in his fist. At the other end of it was a gray-coated, silver-eyed wolf.

"Holy shit cakes!" Joss yelped, then slapped her designer as-seen-on-the-red-carpet coin purse over her mouth. "Sorry—but what is that and why is it at a funeral?"

"Siento, señorita," the man said with a look that should've been patient but was instead pissed off. "You allergic?"

"To wolves?" Sofia and Joss asked in tandem.

At that he smiled, and he dropped a few notches on Sofia's asshole meter. "Tish is a purebred Siberian husky. Four years old. An award-winning show dog, before Luz took her out of the business. *Tu tía* found Tish to be a remarkable companion. Hold this, *por favor?"* He was already looping the leash over one of her wrists.

Sofia's scar began to ache again, and she rolled her eyes skyward. Twilight was falling, and overcast thickening. "You are...?"

"Javier Bautista." His handshake almost took her arm out of its socket.

"You're Aunt Luz's lawyer?" In the brief minutes they'd spoken on the phone, she'd imagined a suit-and-tie type of man. At least one who religiously used a razor.

"Got the card to prove it," he said, giving her a lengthy stare that danced the fragile line between rude and stranger-dangery. He held out an embossed business card between two fingers.

"Then you took care of her funeral."

"I took care of Luz."

"Luz didn't let anyone take care of her."

"No, Miss Mercer. I didn't let her stop me from taking care of her." Tangled up in his accent and hoarse baritone was a delicate strand of emotion. "Luz left clear instructions. But . . . *joder*! Neither of us expected an aneurism to take her out."

Sofia didn't know the intricacies of her great-aunt's life or death. But she wanted to learn every detail, including what really defined Luz's relationship with Javier Bautista—who, even ripened by the elements, appeared not much older than forty.

"I'm headed to the bar a coupla doors down from Luz's store. Going to have a beer in her honor. Join me?"

"I'm not going to do that."

"When do you want to settle the paperwork?"

"Paperwork?" She glanced to Joss, who gave her a look that said *What the hell you looking at* me *for?*

The lawyer's brows formed a tight V over cinnamon-brown eyes.

Joss took her cue without hesitation, stepping away to tour the gravestones peppered across the dense grass, seemingly relieved to escape the company of the Siberian husky, which now sat solemnly at Sofia's feet.

Sofia swung her wary gaze from the canine to the man. "Mr. Bautista—"

"Just Bautista."

"Okay. Bautista. All I know is that I'm here for my great-

aunt's funeral. I don't know why I'm holding a wolf's—
dog's—leash, and I definitely don't know what paperwork
you're talking about settling."

"Luz left it all to you," he said slowly. "The business.
Stock. Tish. Everything."

You've got to be fucking kidding. Sofia didn't say the
words. Paralyzed, she said nothing—simply stood with her
skinny pink heels sinking into the ground and Tish the wolf-
dog sitting vigil beside her as Javier Bautista invited her to
find him at the bar if she changed her mind and then walked
away...

Leaving Sofia wide-open to a sudden onslaught of rain
and questions.

Shrieking, Joss rushed back over as the crowd of guests
scattered and the cemetery crew began to cover Luz's grave.
For the first time Sofia noticed that almost everyone carried
umbrellas.

"I'll never trust that damn weather app again," she said,
rediscovering her ability to speak.

"Fair enough. And that man? Javier Bautista?"

"Just Bautista."

"*Mm-hmm.* Boyfriend. Boyfriend. Boyfriend."

"Why are you repeating that word?"

"To remind myself that I'm stamped. Otherwise I'll need
to change my panties. He's hot, don't you think?"

"I think, Joss, that he's old enough to be your father."

"You do not."

Relenting, Sofia said, "All right, I'm exaggerating. But I
think Aunt Luz might've been more to him than just a client.
And clearly he's much older than you and me." Not just
in age—he had the kind of wear and tear that didn't come
from coasting through the years, but from experience, brutal
knocks, hard living.

Joss paused, her blue eyes narrowed to long-lashed slits. "Why'd Bautista haul ass away from here without the dog?"

"She's my dog...now. Aunt Luz left her to me."

"What are you supposed to do? Take her back to Manhattan and hide her in the apartment? Which, by the way, isn't an option." Joss plastered her itty-bitty purse on top of her head, but it offered no shelter whatsoever for her ash-blond curls. "Let's get in the car. We both look like wet dogs, and we've got an actual wet dog to consider."

Sofia tugged the leash, met resistance, and gave Tish a pleading look. "I can't leave you here," she said to the dog, painfully aware that the beast wouldn't move if she didn't want to and could very competently snap off a limb if she felt threatened enough. "Come with me? Tish."

The dog's ears twitched, and a pink tongue darted out to lick across her nose. The movement gave Sofia a good enough look at her choppers. Hell.

Tish rose to all fours, power and sinew beneath the fur, and began walking.

"If you're going to try to keep this dog, you have to establish authority," Joss cautioned as they neared Sofia's SUV.

"First I have to establish that she's not looking at me and seeing Tish chow. Help me get her in the backseat." After some maneuvering, the dog was settled on one of the rear leather seats with Joss beside her and Sofia behind the wheel.

"Where's the reception being held again?" Joss inquired after a too-long stretch of silence.

"I'm not going," Sofia said, blinking drops of mascara-tinged rainwater out of her lashes. "I was just super-soaked out there, and...Joss, she left her world to me. Everything that made her Luz. She left it all to me."

"Everything?"

"Her dog, her business. Aunt Luz's attorney"—she fumbled for the business card—"said there are stocks."

"In what?"

"Don't know. God, I didn't know she had a pet. She left everything to me."

"You said that already," Joss reminded her carefully.

"I know. Just trying to see if repeating it helps me believe it. I wanted to be just like Aunt Luz—focused, a real go-getter. Now I find out she left her life to me."

"Believe it yet, Sof?"

"No." She turned the key in the ignition, and the V8 engine purred. She'd have to have the vehicle ridded of dog odor once they returned to New York. It had taken a decade of doing without designer clothes and restaurant dinners to save enough money to cash-buy the Lexus—the one gift she'd allowed herself since the fashion merchandising certificate she'd tacked onto her business degree. Parking, gasoline, and maintenance costs made owning a car in the city an impractical luxury, but the SUV was freedom, safety, and emotional comfort on four wheels.

"If we're not going to the reception, let's at least get some sandwiches to take back to the cottage," Joss said. "We need to find something to feed Tish in case she gets any bright ideas about gnawing on me or my possessions."

Fingers of fading sunlight now bled into the swirling blue-and-lavender horizon. The beautiful wash of red and gold and violet lounged over the sloping hills and a curtain of tangled trees. The rain had ceased, but Sofia didn't trust that a ten-minute downpour was the worst of the storm.

Navigating onto Eaves's main road, which would take them from the cemetery to what comprised the resort town's hub, Sofia saw that the perfect black pavement cut into a cave of overhanging trees. It was almost glorious enough to give her peace.

All too soon the trees gave way to a mishmash of buildings tucked here and there. Lowering the windows in hopes of drying her hair and neutralizing the stink of rain-drenched dog, she was greeted with charcoal- and seafood-accented air.

"When I was a kid, there was a gas station on this street...somewhere...that had a sandwich shop in it. The owner named sandwiches after his favorite customers."

"Get a sandwich named after you?"

"The Sick Pickle Sub. Your average sub sandwich, but with no mayo and extra mustard and double dill pickle." Sofia peeked into the rearview mirror to see an expression of horror on Joss's face. "Thought you liked mustard and pickles."

"*Sick pickle?*" Joss leaned forward to grip the front passenger seat's headrest. "That's hella insensitive, don't you think?"

"Gordie was my dad's friend, a very nice old guy. My bad ticker wasn't a secret, but a lot of folks had the idea that it was a taboo subject. Not Gordie. Naming my favorite sandwich what he did was his way of saying, 'Hey, she's ill and we all know it and this is her sandwich.' "

"Never would've thought of it that way. Think Gordie's still hanging around?"

Sofia shrugged. "I tried to stop thinking about Eaves some time ago. My dad and I moved when I was seventeen, the transplant happened when I was nineteen, and the rest is..."

"Your new life."

"Something like that. Ah—here we are!" She indicated a gas station tucked off the shoulder of the road to the right.

"Might as well squeeze a few gallons into the tank, in case the innkeepers boot us out for trying to smuggle a dog in and we have to drive around for a place that'll put us up."

Joss groaned as a fresh sheet of rain fell from the heavens. "I'm not going out in nature's shower again," she declared, settling back in her seat. "I want to eat, wash my hair, dry my clothes, and go to sleep. Just give me food. We haven't eaten since Mystic. That's just cruel."

"Sorry you signed up to be my friend?"

"Never. I'll even prove it." Joss exited the SUV, then came around to let the dog out. "See? I'm taking Tish out for a piss. This meal, though—and I'm talking sandwich, drink, *and* Fritos—is on you."

Sofia smiled all the way to the tiny convenience store, because it felt good to do something other than harp on the past and panic about the future.

She didn't know what inheriting her great-aunt's life *really* meant. She didn't know what kind of secrets hung between Luz and Bautista, didn't know how long Joss would stick around the Cape before her Wall Street lover called her back to New York. She didn't know what she was going to do with a former show dog that could kill her with a single strategic bite.

But she hadn't come out on the other side of heart failure, abandonment, and shelving her dreams of a Manhattan retail career just to crumple now.

Survive or get licked. For her there was only ever one option, and she'd survive this day rocking black leather and pink heels and eating a family-size bag of Chex Mix.

Sofia ducked inside before the rain-speckled glass door could swing shut behind the flannel-shirted guy in front of her.

Oh.

The shirt covered a pair of wide shoulders and a broad, muscled back. She'd never deny it—she appreciated a good male back. A sturdy, hard, solid-looking man tempted her with fantasies that he was strong enough to hold the weight of her baggage.

As the silver bell above the door jangled and more people shuffled in, the man continued his easy stride to the packaged-ice freezer and Sofia had to let him go. Wading into the cacophony of voices, rain drumming on the roof, and the squeak of busy footsteps on waxed tile, she searched the sparse pet needs offerings, recognized a dog food brand from its obnoxious get-stuck-in-your-head commercial jingle, grabbed a stack of cans, and let nostalgia draw her to the back of the store.

But there was no sandwich shop counter, and no Gordie. In their place were a gift card kiosk and a Redbox. The rigged old claw crane arcade machine that'd probably been hustling locals and tourists alike since the 1990s remained. Relief, as pure and unexpected as the rain that danced on the roof, made her ache to cry.

Quickly grabbing prepackaged sandwiches, cans of soda, Chex Mix, and Fritos, Sofia made her way to the end of the queue just before a family wearing damp I ♥ CAPE COD tees and carrying armfuls of touristy novelty stuff could squeeze in front of her.

Mmm, and there it was again. That impressive flannel-covered back. What if he smelled as fresh as clean cotton? Or, better yet, as comforting as hot chocolate? A tiny step forward and Sofia might be able to sniff this guy.

Sniffing strangers in gas station convenience stores was a social no-no. She shouldn't do it. She wouldn't…

She did. Jutting out her chin and closing her eyes, she inhaled the scent of…tangerine incense.

She smelled of tangerine incense. There'd been bundles of incense sticks burning during Luz's service.

"I'd let you stay there with your nose in my back, but I should get this ice to my boat, Sofia."

Sofia opened her eyes to find him watching her over his shoulder. Beyond the sexy scruff of a beard, mussed brown hair, and hard-edged gray eyes was—trouble. "*Burke?*"

She'd let Burke Wolf fade into her past years ago. She'd muted their teenage conversations in her memory, had convinced herself to ignore the sharp rush of heat that rode her at just the thought of him. So why couldn't she remember the reasons she'd walked away, instead of wanting something she shouldn't?

Be my Burke again—just for a second. Make me laugh. Touch me anywhere. I need something…

Burke didn't seem to register the pretty smile the blonde clerk had waiting for him as he took his receipt, stepped aside, and said, "I'm going to take some of the weight off."

Stunned, she said nothing as he transferred the snacks and dog food cans to the counter.

"I was at Luz's funeral," he murmured. "I hung back, left early…"

She nodded as though she understood, but she didn't.

"The last time we talked," he said, catching her eyes with a look so heavy it pinned her, "you were covered in spaghetti sauce."

It hadn't been her most charming moment. Or his. The man was as much a part of the best of her as he was the worst of her.

Which was exactly why she wouldn't launch herself into his arms. They weren't friends anymore.

"Now I'm covered in rain." Sofia focused on the clerk scanning and bagging her loot. The crunch of the ice as

Burke shifted the bag to one side didn't warn her. Nor did she notice him ease a step or two closer.

His fingers gently worked beneath her collar to grip the nape of her neck. They were cold from the ice, but she and her tightening nipples didn't care.

She was clinging to what she found in his touch, arching into it because he was comfort and arousal and danger swirled into one drugging combination.

"I'm sorry, Sofia."

"About Luz?"

"Yeah. Everything else—let it stay where we put the stuff we don't want to talk about."

Sofia pried her gaze off the clerk, stole a glance at him. "It's crowded there, you know?"

"*Fuck.*" The swear was soft, but apparently loud enough for the herd behind them to grunt in offense. Stroking her neck, he said, "I know, Sofia. Damn it, I know."

"Let me go."

She was sorry when he did. But she had to survive this day standing in her own two rain-soaked stilettos—not depending on Burke Wolf to hold her up, no matter how tempting trouble could be.

CHAPTER 2

*I*t struck suddenly. Anxiety gusted through Sofia, bringing with it fatigue and a sensation of painful cold.

Debit card in hand, she froze for only a second. Then, before her mind could register what was happening, before her thoughts could gather, the tremors started.

Damn it, not now. Not in Eaves. Not in front of Burke.

Burke should've taken his ice and left when she'd told him to let her go. He wasn't touching her now, but no, he hadn't let her go. Now he had an up-close view to her brokenness. And she couldn't even scream at him to leave her alone, because the panic attack had rendered her speechless.

"Sofia?"

She wanted to answer him, but the words were tossing around inside her. Trembling, she tried to accomplish two tasks: breathe, and keep the contents of her stomach from splashing onto the counter.

When the card tumbled from her fingers, the clerk asked, "Is something wrong?"

"Here—" Burke pulled out his wallet "—put it on my card. C'mon, Sofia."

Oh, *hell*, no. She wouldn't let him think he could charge in and rescue her. Sweating through the coldness, fighting through the tension in her muscles and the pressure on her chest, she spoke. "I got it." She picked up her card, held it out to the clerk with shaky fingers. "Add twenty to pump four, please. And I'm pretty sure the rain hasn't rinsed away all the bug residue, so a few squeegee swipes wouldn't hurt."

"Go nuts." The clerk hesitated. "As in help yourself to the squeegee."

"Wouldn't the attendant do that, after pumping the gas?"

"Um, you *do* realize we're no longer full-service, right? You can pay at the pump and squeegee bugs off your own windshield. Progress—an awesome thing, huh?"

"Sorry, I didn't realize that had changed." A swell of complaints from behind interrupted her. She twisted around. "I *said* I didn't realize it. My aunt died, I inherited her dog, I live in New York but I'm stuck here, I look like crap and feel worse. Would it hurt any of you to be a little patient?"

"I can pump and squeegee 'bout as good as the next guy," Burke said, shifting the ice bag from one thick, finely muscled arm to the other.

She stared—enjoyed, if she wanted to be honest. If she was a fool for a good male back, then she was a freaking idiot for strong male arms.

A man who was so ruthlessly sexy from the back shouldn't be even sexier from the front. Especially when he was Burke Wolf, someone she'd despised, then loved, then tried to despise again for both their sakes.

Fourteen years ago, he'd been lanky—borderline skinny. The marijuana had made him more haunted-looking than handsome. But the cocaine had split his personality in two, and both had battled for control of one vulnerable body. And she'd loved him despite his struggle...maybe even *because* of it.

At his worst, he'd been confused, volatile, frightening. *That* Burke was familiar. The man in front of her was fucking beautiful, but completely new territory, and she'd better tread with caution.

Muscle gave him bulk, but also made him appear capable. He was more tanned than she remembered, his gray eyes clearer yet harder, his face still angular but brushed with that scruff of a beard she wanted to nuzzle.

The bristly scrape against her skin would cause enough tingle to wake up her senses and remind her that she wasn't a hollow shell wandering around a strange town that had once been her home.

"Want me to help you out?" he offered.

"Thought you were done here." The animosity was weak. Time apart could dull anger, dilute pain. Their broken friendship had been inevitable. When two messed-up teenagers needed each other as much as they had, they were bound to hurt each other.

"Is that a yes or a no?"

"I'm a big girl. Know my way around a gas pump and a squeegee, thanks," she said, stuffing her card and receipt into her purse.

"Yet you couldn't get yourself out of the rain."

The laughter of eavesdroppers accosted her. Instantly, she was flushed with embarrassment. "Screw you, Burke." Naturally, he was already walking out the door and she felt like an idiot to be growling retorts at nobody.

"Whoa. When did you two break up?" the clerk asked.

Probably they'd be better off to have used each other for sex and kept friendship out of the equation. But nobody here—not the clerk or the shoppers gathered around—wanted that sort of truth. So she lied. "Years ago. We were stupid then. Stupider now."

Sofia made up her mind to take her bags and go straight to the Lexus, but her gaze stalled on that damn plaid flannel shirt when she stepped outside.

Leave it alone. Leave him alone. Leave the past the hell alone.

"I wasn't done talking, you know," she blurted through the rain.

Burke was headed toward a not-half-bad-looking truck, but he turned and stopped. The rain sank into his clothes and battered his gorgeous skin.

"'Screw you, Burke.' That's what you said. I heard it. You got the last word, Sofia. I'm done. Get out of the rain before you get sick, and you're golden."

Before you get sick. Right. Heart failure had made her life all about restrictions and fear and being so careful because she'd been vulnerable—dying.

The urge hit to show him just how very much alive she was. She could still feel his touch on her skin, but damn it, a memory wasn't enough. Silently she screamed for him to put his hands on her—now.

Drop the ice and grab me. Shove me against the side of your truck, pull up my dress, yank my panties out of the way. Find the part of me that's wet because of you and not the rain.

He wouldn't, but what if they could do what didn't make sense?

What if, just once, she let herself take something she wanted? What if she weren't lost and broken?

But she was both of those things, so, backpedaling, she wordlessly crossed to the pump where her SUV waited. Setting her bags onto the passenger seat, she said to Joss, "Got food."

"So, about you and...?"

"Burke Wolf."

"See no drama, hear no drama?"

"Please."

"Okay, except he's walking over here."

Sofia straightened, slammed the door, and watched him wait for a car to pass before he strode to her pump. "What do you want, Burke?"

He thrust out the ice bag. Too puzzled to react, she mutely took it and he started squeezing fuel into the tank. "What happened to you in there?" he demanded.

"Excuse me?"

"At the damn counter. Your face went blank, you were shaking. What was that?"

"A panic attack. A mild one. They happen sometimes."

"Since when?"

"The transplant."

He was silent as he took away the nozzle and returned it to the dispenser, then took a squeegee to the windshield, prying away the insect residue that'd withstood the rain. "I should've taken a gig this weekend, let you visit in peace. I should've sent something—flowers or a card—instead of being in the way and pissing you off."

"You cared about Luz," she said. "You have every right to be here grieving her, too. And I'm sick of cards. I work for Manhattan Greetings. It's an indie card company."

Burke's mouth quirked as he screwed on the gas cap. "Writer? Artist?"

"No, I'm on the marketing team." Suddenly, the burning cold of the ice penetrated her skin. "So are we going to talk about everything but the transplant?"

"I don't want to get sucked in again."

"I sucked you in before?"

"Calling me your best friend? Looking at me like I was your hero? Damn straight."

"Really, Burke? *I* saved *you*. And you know exactly how and when and why." The memory of that pale, terrorizing morning all those years ago gave her shivers. Or maybe that was from the pelting rain, the moaning thunder, or the mound of ice in her grip.

"Want thanks for that?"

"No," she said resignedly. "Just go to your truck. Good-bye, Burke. Let's do this again in another fourteen years."

Sofia climbed into her vehicle, dumped the freezing bundle she carried onto the floor beside her, and started driving.

"Um, Sof?"

"I remembered the Fritos, Joss."

"Good. But about Burke?"

"Don't tell me he's sexy, or fine, or screwable. I already know. And we're done."

Joss hummed, and behind Sofia, the dog grunted as she tried to contort to lick a hind paw. "Not sure I'd say *done*."

Through the rearview mirror, Sofia ignored her drippy-haired, makeup-smeared reflection to glance at Joss. "Why's that?"

"I think you stole the man's ice."

* * *

"She stole my fucking ice." Burke was already in his truck, radio blaring, adrenaline riding him hard, when it dawned on him that the reason he'd driven to the convenience store had disappeared in the opposite direction with the sexiest wreck he'd ever met.

Slamming the heel of his hand against the custom steering wheel, he swore and laughed at the damn shame of it. He'd hung back, lurking on the fringes of the gathering at Luz Azcárraga's funeral, precisely to avoid cutting into Sofia's path. Well, for that reason *and* because half the folks in this town didn't give two shits about him or Sofia or, hell, even Luz. Fucking phonies, getting all nice and close to the dearly departed and filling their heads with fodder for a rumor mill that was downright vicious for a town of only about three thousand souls.

When this town turned against you, it wouldn't be satisfied until you bled.

Burke had lived in Eaves until he was old enough to ride to freedom. He'd hit rock bottom on cocaine at the end of high school—hadn't even walked with his peers—and it'd taken him a few brutal years to trust his sobriety.

These days, he didn't even accept a blunt passed to him on the dock. Gigs sucked long hours out of his life, and any given day he could die on the job, but his career as a longshoreman and occasional seafarer was pretty much the only facet of his life now.

On call for emergencies but off assignments for the foreseeable future while his body recuperated and his mind recharged, he was on what some men called a *vacation*. He found little joy in time off. While others were glad to take off when the opportunity rolled around, Burke accepted breaks only when he was running on empty and knew he'd be shit on the job if he didn't step back. Eaves wasn't the ideal place to dock his boat, yet he couldn't complain when he got what satisfied him: willing women and sleep.

God, he treasured sleep. Even with the fucked-up dreams, he was grateful every time he could stretch out on something soft and shut himself down.

Any pleasure he'd found in casual sex, working on his boat, and sleeping had evaporated when he found out about Luz. He'd seen her the morning she died, though he hadn't given her more than a cordial wave and a routine "Hey, how you doing?" But he could imagine how it'd played out. She'd been running errands, so proud of her freaky little store, as she always was, bicycling around Eaves with *Screw you* in that pretty smirk of hers. By afternoon she and her bike were flat on the ground in front of the post office, and she was dead.

The last death that had hit Burke this close to home had been his father's. In death the old bastard had reached him in ways he hadn't been able to in life.

Luz was devilry and sweetness, and if there was something about him she didn't like she made sure he was the first to hear it. He appreciated her for that. Despite the hell Burke and Sofia had brought down on themselves, he'd wanted to say a proper good-bye to Luz.

A lot of goddamn good that did. His argument with Sofia at the gas pumps still rang in his ears. He turned up the volume on the radio and kept driving.

Sofia Mercer was twisted perfection. And as long as he had her image revving him up, as long as his warped judgment kept falling back to the sight of her hot, tight body dressed up in black leather and pink high heels, nothing would cool him.

So he wouldn't wait out this storm on his boat with a tumbler of something ice-cold, as he'd intended. Didn't matter all that much.

Accepting the change of plans, he turned onto a road that'd take him to the heart of town and away from his sanctuary on the water.

CHAPTER 3

*T*his was familiar, Sofia thought. Under the dusky gray billows that left soft trails against the darkening sky, the narrow side roads wove into town. She'd missed how at this time of year the spring cut itself short and yielded to summer.

In the backseat, Tish stretched across Joss to poke her head out the window. After a moment of letting the air whip against her face, she abruptly began to bark at anything in sight or hearing range—birds, rustling branches and leaves, the crunching sound of a twig being split beneath a tire.

"If you're strongly considering establishing some authority with this dog, now would be an excellent time to start," Joss suggested.

"Easy, Tish." Sofia snapped her fingers twice to coax the dog away from the window and then raised the glass. In turn Tish pressed her body against the door and howled fiercely. She either was restless from being confined to the car—good thing Sofia hadn't allowed Joss to strap a seat belt around the dog—or had gotten a whiff of a scent that agitated her. Or Tish, too, was mourning Luz. "Sorry, Tish, but I can't let you go."

At the next turn to her left was the town's showpiece, an enormous marble slab that was now surrounded by carefully tended landscaping. Engraved in calligraphy were the words *Welcome to Eaves. God Bless Our Town.*

A memory of voices as gentle as faraway whispers surfaced.

If I can't get a new heart…Burke, listen to me.

Stop it, Sofia. I don't want to talk about that.

Too fucking bad. If the transplant doesn't happen…if I die, you can't go back to being stupid, okay?

What are you talking about?

Getting high. You went the entire day without doing blow or smoking weed. That's cool. It's good.

Shit, Sofia. You've been in my face, that's why. When are you going to go home already?

I don't know. Dad's not looking for me, anyway.

Luz might be.

You're going to miss me in your face, Burke.

I told you to stop it.

Why? Tell me why you don't want to talk about it and I'll go home.

We're…we're cool, you and me. Friends, right? So I don't want to think about…Damn it.

We'll still be cool, Burke. Friends.

Sofia flexed her fingers over the steering wheel, chided herself for letting the memory win out over all the thoughts competing for priority. She'd lived, and so had he, but they hadn't stayed friends.

Shoving herself away from the past, she approached Shore Seasons. Advertised as five-star luxury for guests on a two-star budget, the group of cottages was tourist bait, plunked right in the center of an enormous, eclipsing forest.

At the entrance she hit the brakes and scanned the area. There was an office building and parking lot in the forefront, and nestled deeper into the trees were the cottages. Yellow light poured from the porch lamps, shining over cobblestone walkways, trimmed hedges, and flowers on the cusp of budding.

Their cottage boasted an elegant sitting room with a fireplace, a pair of large, inviting beds, and a claw-footed bathtub. They hadn't had time to absorb the details or do much more than claim beds, dump luggage, and change clothes before heading to the cemetery for the service.

Sofia could use a hot bath and hours of sleep. She wasn't accustomed to turning in so early, and doubted she would get much rest if she tried. Last night she had lain wide awake for hours, staring into darkness before eventually drifting into a shallow sleep.

A rap on the driver's-side window stole her attention.

"Don't lower that window," Joss warned.

"Joss, we're not in New York City."

"So? This might be a postcard-cute small town, but think of how many horror movies are set in small towns."

Sofia's hand shot away from the window control button. She turned to meet a man's dark eyes. She knew the car doors were locked, but Joss's logical advice infused her with paranoia and she glanced down to make sure.

Wind caressed the man's hair, nudging a dense brown lock over his brow. He didn't even blink. Instead he kept his gaze steady on hers and gestured for her to open the window. When she didn't he cupped his hands around his mouth and hollered through the glass, "Need help?"

She could clearly see the office building straight ahead,

its fancy logo glowing white over a green-and-beige awning. Firmly shaking her head, she drove past him to claim the available parking space nearest to the entrance.

"Phone," she muttered aloud, rifling through her purse. She found the smartphone and was relieved that it was getting decent reception. She shifted to look around for the man. He was gone, almost as if he'd vanished into the trees.

Moving quickly, they secured Tish's leash, let her out, locked the SUV, and then rushed into the office as though bats from the depths of hell were nipping their asses.

"Stop! Stop right there." Rising from a tufted armchair behind the reception desk and clutching a glossy fashion magazine was a dough-faced woman with round eyes that narrowed into slits as they stalled on the dog. "What is *that* doing inside my office?"

Frightened by the shrill shriek, Tish howled and rose to her hind legs. The receptionist startled, sending a pair of subscription postcards fluttering to the desk.

Damn it. This woman wasn't all warm smiles and sincere condolences, as the gal who'd greeted them at check-in had been. Getting permission to let Tish stay overnight was going to be hard enough to sell *without* the dog showing her ass.

Sofia quickly stroked Tish from the top of her head down the length of her back. Pressing down on the dog's posterior, she whispered, "Sit now. It's okay." *I'm lying. I'm lying to a dog and myself.* Tish plunked down on her rear end and began sniffing the scents of pine and honey. Sofia cleared her throat and turned to the receptionist. "Hi. I'm Sofia Mercer and this is Joss Vail."

"The New Yorkers, right?" the receptionist asked with a note of . . . derision?

"Uh, yup, that's us."

"Paget told me about you. She *didn't* tell me you intended to sneak a dog into your cottage. She has absolutely no authority to make these decisions, but I tend to follow up behind the summer help. She part-timed in Luz's sex store and I gave her more hours to help her out after, well, you know. But deception's a no-no. I doubt she'll last here through the Fourth of July."

Harsh. Sofia didn't want to be the reason for anyone losing a gig, especially since Paget had already lost the employment Luz had provided. "She didn't know about Tish. This isn't a plan to break rules. We drove in from Manhattan for Luz's funeral and someone gave me her dog. There wasn't an opportunity to figure out where she'd stay tonight—"

"No animals allowed." The woman—the nameplate on the desk said A. Oakley—gathered the postcards and tucked them into the magazine. "I can forgive the stench that...creature...brought into my office, but now you need to turn around and escort it outside."

Hostility, blazing red and raw, hit Sofia. The woman stood petite in a bronze-colored suit with hair the hue of strained carrots and eyes the color of dirty dishwater. "Ms. Oakley, please—"

"*Mrs.* Oakley." Indiscreetly she held up her hand so that the diamond on her ring reveled in the light. "But call me Anne. No harm in keeping things pleasant. You are paying guests after all."

"Anne?" Joss said. "No shit, Anne Oakley? *Annie* Oakley? People have a lot of fun with that, don't they?"

"*Joss!*"

Joss repented with a sheepish look and a solemn "Sorry about that."

Anne Oakley eyed them critically. "I won't claim to know how things usually work for a couple of hip New York twentysomethings, but here at Shore Seasons, our policies apply to everyone. No pets allowed means *no pets allowed—* especially Luz's bitch."

So this woman knew Aunt Luz. And from the tone she'd adopted, they hadn't been warm and fuzzy friends. Even though a female dog was technically a bitch, Sofia was thinking that right now it took a bitch like Anne to know one.

"Tish is a guest, too," Sofia tried.

"*Guest?*" Anne swung around, circling her chair to pluck a thick binder from a shelf. Slamming it down in front of her, she went on, "When potential guests book reservations, they're made fully aware of our policies. Pets of any kind, especially Luz Azcárraga's b—"

Sofia cut in. "If you call her 'bitch' again, we're going to have a problem."

"Consider getting in touch with the town animal shelter, look into boarding."

"It's only overnight. You know, we do have direct access to our cottage and could've sneaked this dog in. But we wanted to ask permission and negotiate this rationally."

"Each of our cottages is thoroughly inspected after guests check out. Signs of animals on our estate would not have served well for you."

"Tish is a well-behaved show dog." The *show dog* part was true. As for the *well-behaved* part, the jury was still out.

The door swung open and the man from the parking lot strode in. *Sharp.* No other word seemed capable of capturing the ironed-suit-and-expensive-shoes look of him. Dark, windswept hair framed a frowning face. His narrow-set eyes settled on Joss and his mouth curved beneath a thin mustache.

Joss, whose arms were crossed and expression tense, visibly tossed her small-town-horror-movie caution aside and smiled at him. Tish interrupted the trance, bouncing up on all fours and growling low.

Judge not, Sofia wanted to caution herself, but she couldn't help falling into agreement with the dog. There was something about this man that threw her defenses into panic mode.

"Get that mutt out of here," Anne advised, tugging Sofia back to the crisis at hand. To the man she said, "Mr. Strayer, this is a surprise. What can I do for you?"

Moving to the coffeepot, he said, "You're with someone now. I'll wait."

Anne addressed Sofia. "Have a good night."

"How can you be so callous? This dog's owner—my great-aunt—was buried today. I cannot and will not leave a living being in a car or on the street overnight."

"Then I'll allow a cancellation. Full refund. It's the best I can do. I need a copy of your identification, the reference number, and the credit card used. Expect your money in about three to five business days."

Joss's uttered "Oh, shit, now what?" weighed on Sofia.

The man moseyed to the door and slipped outside again.

"No refund, no cancellation, Anne," she decided, "because Joss is staying." Patting Joss's shoulder, she said, "You stay. Tish and I are taking off. I can't leave her alone. There's a motel that's been around for ages. Maybe we can get a room there. If not, I'll keep looking until I find someone who'll let us stay the night."

"Hey, wait," Joss said, her voice low, "who's going to put you and a dog up?"

"I don't know. People in this town loved Luz. Even if they don't like me, they'll take Tish as a solid to Luz."

"Why wouldn't anyone like you?"

"I said before. It's com—"

"Complicated." Joss nodded, as if she understood, but Sofia knew she didn't.

Guiding Tish out of the office, the three headed to the SUV. The man lurked nearby, holding his coffee in one hand and a cigarette in the other. Sofia discreetly wrapped her fingers around the small container of pepper spray she kept on her key chain.

Moving toward the car, she felt him watching them. Then she heard his footsteps on the ground. She wasn't fragile anymore. She could defend herself now. She was fully prepared to whirl around, blind him with the spray, and send a knee hard into his balls.

"It's not necessary to spray me in the face with that."

She and Joss turned quickly.

"I saw your hand fumble for it," he added, his mouth forming a slow smile. "My name's Aeneas Strayer. I paid my respects to your aunt, but it wasn't the best time to approach you."

"You knew Aunt Luz well enough to offer your respects. Anne Oakley in there seemed surprised to see you in her office. From the sound of things, you're a local. So I need to ask: Did you follow me here?"

The slow sip he took from the coffee cup afforded him too much time to devise an answer. "I only wanted an opportunity to talk, Sofia. Luz and I had an ongoing conversation. Business details. I was hoping you and I could continue that conversation."

Sofia didn't intend to discuss business with anyone but her great-aunt's attorney. "I'm sure if I need to get in touch I'll be able to find you, Mr. Strayer."

"Be sure that you do," he said after a moment of silent stillness. Carefully he considered the ash and smoke at the tip of the cigarette, then he let it fall to the pavement, screwed his shoe against it, and went back inside the office.

In a sixty-second time span, she and Joss hustled Tish into the car, got in, and made tracks for their cottage.

"Luz sure had a knack for surrounding herself with attractive men," Joss commented. "That guy, though. Hmm, can't put my finger on it."

"Because you have a boyfriend?"

"Ha. No, I mean I can't figure him out."

"Fortunately you won't have to. Whatever business stuff Luz had going with him, it's for me to untangle. As of tomorrow morning you're off the hook and will never have to set your pedicured feet in Eaves, Massachusetts, again."

"It's not a hardship, hanging in here with you. Friends stick together when things are great and when things are shitty. Neither of us has had many great days. I feel guilty about having the cottage to myself."

"Your guilt's no good here. You and Mr. Six-Figure Salary were probably going to phone-sex all night anyway, and God knows I don't want to overhear that."

At the cottage, Sofia freshened her makeup and combed her hair before repacking her overnight bag. So much for a hot bath in a claw-footed tub.

"What's the name of this motel you're headed to?" Joss asked, walking her to the door.

"White Anchor. It's a no-tell motel."

"No tell?"

"Cheating spouses, two-timing lovers. They come for a little discretion and don't tend to mind the thin walls, one-ply toilet paper, and drafty rooms. The unscrambled porn channels are a plus."

"If I were rude, I'd ask how you came to be so knowledgeable about a place like that."

"Funny thing about no-tell motels in tell-all towns—eventually everyone finds out."

"Oh. So you don't have firsthand experience?"

"Sorry, no dirty stories here." Not that she hadn't *wanted* some firsthand experience with Burke, the guy who in high school had pushed her past all her boundaries except that one.

"You'd endure a motel bursting with people fucking but not Peter and me phone-sexing? Not saying that we were going to."

"You were."

Joss cleared her throat. "What if your plans don't pan out?"

"I told you I'll search for a friendly face. Then there's the lawyer. Bautista. Maybe he can help."

"Know where to find him?"

"He said he was going to this bar near Aunt Luz's boutique. If he's not there I'll find him. I have his card."

"Be careful. Call me."

* * *

Sofia sat in her car as the White Anchor Motel's neon lettering shimmered over the rain-dotted hood. "Well, my darling Tish, it appears we're thoroughly screwed."

No pets allowed, the sleepy-eyed, whiskered man at the front desk had said when she mentioned Tish. His condolences about Luz—"Beautiful broad, she was"—and he'd smiled kindly to soften the disappointment, but policy was policy. She understood and respected that, but was stunned to find so many closed doors in a place that'd once been her home.

Not quite discouraged, though, she turned the key in the ignition and set out for Aunt Luz's boutique.

Blush, illustrating sensuality from its pale pink shake-

shingle siding to its brass accents to its tastefully but unmistakably erotic window displays, sat on a corner lot on
Society Street. Directly across and wedged together were a
stationery shop, an apothecary, and a laundromat and dry
cleaner—Suds when she'd known it, but now called The
Dirty Bastards.

Society Street was the heartbeat and lifeblood of Eaves—
or it had been, as Sofia recalled it. Not particularly pretty, but
like any living being's heart, its function was vital to keep all
else in good working order.

Here the streets were grimier, the buildings colored with
character, rusted iron, and washed-out brick veneers. The
residential neighborhoods tucked close to Society were
quaint and their curbs lined with vehicles. People lived hard,
worked hard, and played hard here. Everything outside of
this dim sphere belonged to what her great-aunt had none-
too-affectionately dubbed the Affluents—the wealthy who
liked to throw their dime around. They'd molded Eaves
into their kingdom—dominating the town with beachside
mansions and award-winning architecture, and one by one
devouring businesses that didn't jell with the image they
wanted the town to portray.

Luz, an Argentine immigrant who'd traveled the United
States before settling on the Cape, sparkled in the shadows.
Eaves was the only home she'd known in America—and she
didn't want another. Sofia had realized that the day she'd
suggested Luz move to New York with her and Luz had
turned her down cold.

Sofia stood on the sidewalk in front of Blush and allowed
Tish to trot up to the darkened window with a homesick
whimper. No one ever said losing someone would hurt like
this. She'd been a baby when her parents had divorced and
her mother fled to Europe. She'd never mourned her

mother—just accepted her as a void in Sofia's failed heart. Now she was a stranger, and the only motherly influence Sofia had known was Luz's.

Female influence, rather. Luz was far from motherly.

Sofia took in the sight of the building. It was all big windows, shake-shingle siding, and wrought-iron sconces. Above the boutique was Luz's apartment, which had been Sofia's apartment, too, for a time. It had been the darkest yet brightest time of her life.

Joining Tish at the storefront, Sofia reached up and drew her fingertips over the gold lettering on the glass. *Lingerie*, the word read. Sofia remembered helping Luz repaint these letters.

"Why'd you choose me, Aunt? Why me?" she asked, but the only answer was traffic on the road and wind in the trees. Tugging Tish's leash, she continued along the sidewalk, passing a vacant storefront—once a market called Cape Foods, she knew all too well—and arriving at the next building. With no apartment above it, the squat building boasted a sloping roof with atrium skylights. It was a shock of modern on the aged street.

A studio confronted her. AU NATUREL—CARO JAYNE, PHOTOGRAPHER.

The place was closed and it was the last one on the block, so Sofia was frustrated until she ventured around the corner and discovered a lit stairwell that apparently led down to a bar.

A bar called Bottoms Up.

No fanfare to it, just a glowing red sign... with the letter *B* shaped into a heart that looked suspiciously like a woman bent over ass-up. After much consideration about what to do with a tired and grieving dog, she escorted Tish inside.

Bottoms Up was larger than she could've guessed from

the street, but it was tight. It screamed sex. Not the posh, almost coy sensuality of Blush, but a rougher interpretation of the word. Dull overhead lights shone over a beaten pool table, chipped chairs, and benches carved from oak. A scratched bar stretched across the far wall, and every stool surrounding it was occupied. Gold, blue, and red beaded necklaces dangled from lights, swinging low over people's heads. The exposed beams were decorated with bras.

The smells of cigarette smoke and spilled liquor filled the air. Grunge music pumped through speakers and clashed with the 1980s love ballad moaning from a battered jukebox. The tables looked like overturned metal trash cans.

Quirky as all hell, but Sofia didn't hate it.

Men in worn jeans and T-shirts hovered over the pool table, turning up bottles and glasses in between shouts of conversation. Couples tried to sway together on the scruffy dance floor, but there wasn't room for anyone to do more than press close.

A man with toffee-colored skin ended up in front of her, looked into her face from beneath the bill of a Red Sox ball cap, and pointed at her. "I fuckin' know you!" When she hesitated, he laughed, yanking off his cap to reveal a smooth bald head. "Holy shit. You're some kind of babe."

"Tariq," she said, recognizing him now. She flung her arms around the guy, not caring that he was sweaty and smelled of beer. Somehow she had clung to the image of him as a gangly eight-year-old with a goofy grin and curly hair reined in to a springy puff. She'd babysat him off and on until she'd become too sick to manage her life and his.

"I'm insulted you didn't remember me," he said, squeezing tight.

"Sorry," she said when he set her free and accepted a beer a young woman in a short skirt pushed under his nose. He gulped half before handing it back and sending her away with an open-handed pop on her ass. Not at all used to this ass-slapping version of the young boy she knew, Sofia blinked. "Was that your girlfriend?"

Brows knit, he replied, "Naw." He hooked an arm around Sofia's waist and led her and Tish to the bar. She noticed a few stares and whispers as some of the patrons started to notice her. She perched on a stool as he moved behind the bar. "What'll it be?"

"Nothing, thanks. But I'm looking for someone. Javier Bautista. You seen him?"

He paused. "Sure you don't want a whiskey or something first? Bautista's not doing so good today."

"Neither am I, Tariq. She was *my* family."

"Yeah, she was. Sorry, Sofia. Just that you haven't been around in a while and, uh, anyway, let me find Bautista for you."

Tariq left the bar. A few moments later a woman with golden-brown skin and a mane of ringlets emerged. She rounded the bar, revealing herself to be dressed in a rum-colored halter top, tight jeans, and a Bottoms Up apron styled like a miniskirt.

Sofia rose off the bar stool. "The dog and I aren't staying. I'm searching for someone."

The woman silently lifted a hand. The silver bracelets on her wrist clinked together. She touched a man's shoulder and smiled, and he gave up his stool. Sitting beside Sofia now, she said, "Tish, Tish, Tish. This gorgeous pain in the arse is an institution in this town. She's welcome here. Especially today."

"Are you sure?"

"Tish and I are neighbors."

"Oh, this is your bar?"

"No. I love this place and help out down here when I can, but I own the studio upstairs."

Then she was Caro Jayne. "Au Naturel. What's that all about?"

"Portrait photography. I use only natural light and most of my clients book nudes."

Nudes. "You're a boudoir photographer?"

"And bloody proud of it."

"Aren't people nervous about posing in front of all those windows?"

"Only the front lobby windows are clear. The rest of the glass and the skylights are energy efficient with mirror film. This way the sun won't bake everyone inside and all the peepers on the street see are themselves trying to get a free show."

Sofia processed this with a nod, but her intrigue wasn't enough to compel her to give more commentary beyond a neutral "Oh."

"I keep a jar of dog treats behind the counter here," Caro said. "I'd quite like to spoil Tish." The woman sprang off the stool, retrieved said jar, and fed Tish two bone-shaped treats.

Stammering a thank-you, struck by the woman's kindness and the musical charm of her British accent, Sofia put out her hand. "I'm Luz's great-niece. Sofia Mercer."

"Assumed you were. Who else would be walking around obviously disoriented with Luz's dog in hand?" She smiled. "I owe plenty of gratitude to your aunt. She did more than pimp my business cards at her cash register. So, are you in the sexy wares business, too?"

"Um, no."

Caro shrugged as a patron waved her over to the end of the bar. "Pity. It'd be fucking awful to see the boutique die with Luz."

Even if Caro Jayne the au naturel photographer had stuck around to hear Sofia's response, she didn't have one prepared. And why should she? She was still digesting the fact that Luz had passed down her entire life. Sofia had inherited Luz's everything, damn near. Her boutique, her pet, her friendships and grudges...

Bautista carved a path through to the bar and took the stool Caro had vacated. Tobacco and leather scented his clothes; grief colored his eyes. In him she recognized her own need. She didn't know if it was comfort or a way to forget or someone to blame, but they were both missing something vital.

Except...

Wait, Luz didn't expect Sofia to inherit *everything* everything...did she?

"Change your mind about that drink?" Bautista hit a fist against the bar and someone brought him a bottle of Jim Beam. Making the sign of the cross, he said, "To Luz," and turned up the drink.

"You started without me anyway." When he offered the bottle and got off the stool to crouch and scratch Tish under the chin, Sofia drank the straight bourbon. "How are you?"

"*Todo bien.* No, that's a lie."

"Figured."

"What about you?"

"It turns out Tish doesn't have a place to stay tonight, Bautista. Since she's my responsibility now, that means *I* don't have anywhere to stay, either."

"Where's your friend?"

"Shore Seasons." Probably in a bathtub with her man groaning on speakerphone. "No dogs allowed."

"What about the White Anchor?" Caro suggested, going behind the bar to fill a glass with brandy. She grabbed her tip at the end of the bar, counted it, and stuffed the cash into her pocket. "Try them?"

"Same policy."

"Sorry, love." Caro was gone again, in a hip-swinging strut to customers. She moved fluidly, pouring in a dash of this, a drop of that, shaking concoctions while keeping a soft smile on her face, sliding beers across the bar, gathering empty bottles and glasses, and collecting her tips.

"Bautista, I'm not leaving Luz's dog—my dog—in the car all night. Honestly, as difficult as this day's been for you, I promise it's been twice as difficult for me. Tish and I need a place to stay."

"Meaning with me?"

"Would it be all right? We can talk about whatever paperwork needs settling, then Tish and I'll sleep and will be out first thing tomorrow."

"Got keys for you," he said, tugging a ring from his pocket and putting it in her palm. "Stay as long as you want."

Sofia was aware of activity around her, but for the most part her brain was tripping over assumptions and scenarios. She was asking for only one night, not *as long as you want*.

Did he think she wanted that? Did he think she *could* want that?

"Keys?" She shoved the word from her lips.

"To Blush."

Blush! "Good. I mean, thank you. Bautista, thanks."

"Apartment key's there, too. I was going to surrender everything when we go over the papers. Let somebody walk you over, in case you need something."

"Are you volunteering?"

Bautista crooked his fingers for her to hand over his bourbon. "I don't think I should, Sofia."

At least they were on the same page there.

"But him, over there—he needs to come up for air."

Sofia looked past a dozen or so people to see Burke Wolf at a table, alone, nursing a drink in a highball glass. She hoped it was a cold one, at least. Joss had shoved his bag of ice into the cottage's freezer.

"I don't need a keeper, Bautista."

"Maybe he does." Patting Tish's head, he said, "*Buenas noches.* Find me *mañana.*"

Sofia was aware of Bautista losing himself in the crowd, but she continued watching Burke. Clear liquid, ice, and slices of lime filled his glass. Vodka tonic? When she'd known him, he hit drugs and alcohol hard. Had he given up narcotics but remained faithful to what came from a bottle? How challenging was it for an addict to court that kind of temptation?

Just as she was beginning to feel like a voyeur, someone charged toward Tish with fascinated shrieks and several people tossed their attention her way.

Burke's face lifted and his gaze met hers in a silent collision.

"Burke." Not that he could hear her. Not that she'd been able to get her voice to utter the damn syllable. Her lips shaped the word and, understanding her, the man got up and crossed the room to her.

"You stole my ice."

"That's true. But I don't have it on me. Would you accept a bag of Chex Mix?"

"Nah. Let's just say you owe me."

"I thought we quit keeping score in high school."

"We did. Just screwing with you."

Any humor that might have been wrapped around the words was drowned in tension.

"I'm parched," she said, eyeing his glass. It wasn't her business to pry or give a damn but she *had* to know. "A sip?"

"Yeah." Burke held it to her lips, and apparently noticing her failed attempt at a subtle sniff, he murmured close, "It's tap water with lime."

The differences between lime-accented vodka and what he claimed was in his glass were practically indistinguishable through scent, so she boldly drank anyway. "Water with lime." So he hadn't lied.

He set the glass on the bar. "You could've asked me, Sofia."

And unleash what—the fact that she cared when she shouldn't?

"I have keys. To the boutique and the apartment." She clutched the keys. *Her* boutique and *her* apartment. "I'm taking Tish over. We—You and me, Burke. Can we talk for a sec—"

"Okay." He took the leash from her hand, leaving her to do nothing but hold her purse to her chest.

They didn't speak as they left the congestion of the bar and climbed upstairs to meet the emptiness on the sidewalk. When they'd been tight there hadn't always been a need to fill the space between them with conversation. Now awkwardness pushed them back as they walked forward.

Tish hung her head and Burke bent toward her. "Hey, honey," he said gently, squatting down and hooking an arm around the dog, bringing her in close. "C'mon, put your head up, because it's not always going to feel like hell. You got my word on that."

The dog nuzzled his shoulder and he didn't say anything for a moment. They seemed to understand each other. From one Wolf to the other, Sofia thought.

"Thanks," she told him as they resumed walking, telling

herself the smile teasing her lips was because of his com-
passion toward an animal—not because she appreciated the
amazing things his body did to flannel and denim. "For what
you said to Tish."

"Same goes for you. It won't always be tough like this."

"Uh…" she began at the same time that he said, "Yeah,
um…"

"Interesting," she commented, "I thought our conversation skills would've improved in fourteen years."

"We didn't give a damn about conversation skills back
then. We didn't care about anything but being us."

Sofia reached to touch his hand but instead grabbed the
leash. "I'm going to take her upstairs. Let's bring her around
the back. Remember the stairwell near the door?"

"I remember everything. If it's all the same to you, I'm
not going in Luz's sex shop."

"What, dildos and cock rings make you nervous, Burke?"

"Hold up. *You* were the one who didn't know what to do
with a condom."

Sofia came to a full stop. "I was fifteen and not expecting
a guy to toss one on my lunch tray in the cafeteria. How was
I supposed to know that was your stupid-ass way of asking
me out?"

"Yeah, fine. Anyway, you freaking out and reporting me
to the principal got me a day of in-school suspension." Burke
leaned toward her, his shirt brushing her bare arm. "But what
I did *was* stupid-ass. Shouldn't have stayed mad at you as
long as I did for that."

Sofia noticed his attention drift to something behind her.
Shit, she'd stopped in front of the old Cape Foods building.
Burke's father, Deacon Wolf, had owned the place for
decades and for a time Burke had bagged groceries after
school.

If not for his father's market and her great-aunt's boutique, would they have ever gotten past that condom-on-the-lunch-tray shitstorm? Would they have become friends? Would she have fallen in love with him?

"The old man died a few years back."

"I know. I called Luz up, but she said you'd gotten the hell out of town. You're a longshoreman, right?"

He nodded as Tish began a determined trot toward the boutique and urged them along. "Started casual out of high school. While I was doing that, I checked off mariner qualifications and got some onboard experience. A maintenance crew let me learn on the job. Painting, welding—I'm your man." His smile was quick and it belied his casual tone. He was proud of his work. Good for him. "Some guys wait years to be brought in. I got lucky and the hall called me in right away. I get on the water for fishing and cargo gigs and emergency aid, but I've been permanent on the dock though for almost ten years. Been clean for about that long, too."

So he'd continued using years after she left town? "Why'd you wait?" she asked, though it wasn't her right to pry.

"I tried to kick that shit on my own a couple of times, even tried rehab. I relapsed. This time the sobriety stuck but I don't take it for granted."

Questions flooded her mind, but she selected carefully. "So where do you live?"

"Wherever there's work. I keep myself on call, keep myself flexible. When there's not much action, I work out of Boston."

It sounded as if being a permanent longshoreman made it possible to maintain temporary everything else, from living situation to relationships. No real personal commitments, no real roots. Something about the realization hurt.

But equally troubling were the visions she had of tossed ships and hostage situations and other worst-case-scenario perils. "Burke, it's…"

"What?"

Dangerous. So damn dangerous.

"Nothing," she said, pushing it all aside.

Taking the stairs up to the apartment, they found a modest but efficient place that smelled of incense and herbs. A tiny kitchen covered in seaweed-colored wallpaper held a pantry, a stove, a refrigerator, and a white table and chairs. Sofia got a shock when she walked into the living room and discovered that Luz had kept it furnished with the pieces that'd been there during Sofia's teen years—from the lumpy sofa stitched together with patches to Luz's grandfather's willow chair to the elegant animal figurines from their glassblower relatives in Argentina.

Sofia unsnapped the leash and let Tish wander. It felt so strange to be in this place without her great-aunt.

But at least she wasn't alone.

"Just got this new door up for Luz a few weeks ago," Burke said, pointing to an interior door in the hall. "It fell right off its hinges, narrowly missed bopping her on the head when it went down."

"You helped her around the apartment?"

"Yeah, whenever she let me. Stubborn as fuck, Luz was." He scratched his temple, let his hands fall to his sides. "I'm sorry she's gone, Sofia."

"You told me that already." Sofia walked with him back through the kitchen to the stairs. "Burke?"

"Yeah?" He turned to look at her with eyes that were solemner than they'd been years ago.

"I know you must have questions…about things. Ask me."

"Fine." A sigh sawed through his lips. He came closer, and she couldn't distract herself with his strong back and muscled arms. The flicker of desperation and confusion in his gray eyes was all she could see. "The transplant. Did it save you?"

"I'm standing here."

"Sofia, are you whole again?"

"When was I ever whole, Burke? Growing up with a dad who was half-afraid and half-resentful of me? Or trying to be a normal kid in school when every week I ended up in the nurse's office or at the hospital? Or, what, living here and working downstairs and every day falling harder and harder for you? Was I *whole* then?"

Pain in his expression startled her. "Shit, I shouldn't've brought it up."

"We were like this toward the end, Burke," she said, though he likely didn't need to be reminded of how they'd bickered constantly before she and her father had left Eaves. "We forgot how to laugh together."

"Fuck that," he said, and somehow they weren't on the stairs anymore, but in the kitchen again, and remnants of incense and herbs tickled her senses. "Listen to me, Sofia. Fuck the past. What matters is what's staring you in the face today. You have panic attacks."

"That's not the only thing the surgery left behind." She glanced downward.

"A scar. It's between your breasts, right?" He drew a line down his sternum.

"What, Burke, you researched heart transplants?"

"Yeah, damn it, I did. Just like you researched drug addiction."

Pressing her lips together, she closed the kitchen door, rested her head against it. "You're right about the scar," she said quietly. Turning, she did what she'd wanted to do from the moment she spotted his flannel shirt at the convenience store. She gathered the fabric in her fists and buried her face in it.

The shirt smelled less of tangerine incense and more of wind and the blend of scents she'd encountered at Bottoms Up. Lime was on his breath and bourbon on hers.

Burke's arms folded around her, but she resisted sinking into his chest. She couldn't let him hold her up. She couldn't let herself enjoy something that would end tomorrow, when she put Eaves in the rearview mirror again.

She shouldn't dance with trouble, rocking against the man she'd loved back when they'd been two fucked-up teenagers staring death in the eye.

"Let me see it, Sofia."

Burke's arms went lax, and she watched her own hands slide up her breasts to the collar of her leather dress.

I can't blame this on grief. This is me. And I can't do it. None of the men she'd kissed, danced with, or dated had ever seen her naked. Outside of medical necessity, no man had seen her scar—her damage.

"Sofia?"

Shaking her head, she released her collar and resisted all urges to turn around so he could pull down the dress's zipper. "No. I...I'm not going to show you."

There was so much to say, but she didn't want words and thoughts and truth now. She wanted the comfort of his flannel shirt and his hands on her. Grappling for the fabric again, she made a frustrated noise and pressed her body tight to his.

If the past didn't make it impossible for them to be friends again, then the palpable and greedy want between them did.

A virgin spending the night above an erotic boutique and

in the arms of a man who could undoubtedly fuck her to for-getfulness. Was it appropriate to laugh or cry at that?

"The scar," she said, taking control of a situation that had her feeling as though she were disconnected from gravity, "is here." Taking his hand, she placed it between her breasts. The gnarled and knotted scar tissue tingled at his pressure and heat.

"Sofia... know what you're doing?"

Glancing up, she found him watching her. Closer than even his touch was his gaze on hers. It might've singed her, if she weren't so cold to begin with. "I'm showing you my scar. You're going to look with your hands, not your eyes. Okay?"

"Okay," he said solemnly, taking what she could spare.

"And it goes down, like this," she continued, guiding his hand along the path of the scar. Heat built, curling the edges of the old hurt they'd caused each other.

He put her arms at her side, said something against her ear.

"Full circle?" she echoed.

"We went from me just wanting to sleep with you, to be-ing friends, to hating each other."

Burke's hands skimmed her neck, found her shoulders, traced her scar. One hand, then the other, then—oh, God—his fingers splayed and he cupped her breasts.

Sofia felt her eyes slide shut as he squeezed her flesh, but they opened again when he teased her nipples and drew a moan from her bourbon-flavored lips. She'd never known trouble could touch her like this, make her feel like this. "You're back to *just* wanting to sleep with me? Is that all you're after, Burke? Because if it's not"—her arms swung out to hook around his neck—"then we haven't come full circle at all."

CHAPTER 4

*B*urke had been sober for more than a decade, but standing in a dead woman's kitchen with Sofia curled around him made him feel drugged. There was no thrill with this kind of high, though—there never had been. Just that thousand-mile-per-hour free fall to a place where reality crumbled like chalk and all that remained was a sensation of hollow existence in a world that seemed familiar but was somehow altered.

Sofia was his escape, his emergency exit, and being with her had once distorted his life to make things appear less shitty than they were. A savior was what she'd been, with those fearless big brown eyes and that smile. That damn crooked smile. How many opaque nights and pale mornings had he vomited handfuls of pills or set aside a loaded syringe or cried on the floor, shaking, because his addiction to some dying girl's smile was stronger than the quiet desperation to take his leave?

He was clean now, but he still carried his addiction. It was a disease he couldn't shake. Counseling, strength cobbled together from the fragments of his soul, and the grace of God that he doubted he'd ever been worthy of had all pulled him to his feet and continued to guide him. But his connection to Sofia had never been addressed or cured.

If he let himself get hooked on her again, let her shatter him again, what would save him?

"I told you I didn't want this." His words were a clipped, careful warning, and his voice the scrape of a blade against stone. "Don't draw me in, drag me down. Don't do that, Sofia."

"I'm not." Her hands remained linked behind his neck, her slender body pressing gently to him. "Blaming me won't change the fact that how you feel about me has everything to do with you. It's *your* fault that you want me. Hate yourself for it if it helps, but take responsibility. And you didn't answer my question."

You're back to just *wanting to sleep with me? Is that all you're after, Burke?*

Sofia was holding him close yet pushing him to confront that question. On some level she had to know the answer. Everything that had brought them together as a couple of scuffed-up kids was laid to rest—their school days, her illness and the monkey on his back, his old man and now her aunt.

Their friendship was ashes and dust. They had no sweet high school romance to resurrect.

Too damn bad. He'd never kissed her crooked smile or seen her naked. It was because she had been sick, he sometimes told himself. Or because she was too skinny and laughed too much. Or because she was his friend and he didn't go around fucking his friends.

Sofia was sacred, elevated to some brand of perfection he couldn't explain. And she was right; he had himself to blame for that.

It was a mistake he wouldn't make twice. Sofia was a mortal, same as him, and she could be frightened and angered and warned off.

"How's this for an answer, Sofia?" Burke pried her hands apart and stepped to the table as he yanked his wallet from his jeans pocket. He observed her as he opened the wallet and flipped something onto Luz Azcárraga's kitchen table.

"A condom?" Confusion slid into disappointment. "Real mature of you, Burke. So you're reverting to juvenile antics to ask me out?"

"Not even that. I just want a fuck." Was that even true? It needed to be, because he couldn't let her lead him to destruction again. That's all that caring about her and depending on her had amounted to, and he wouldn't sacrifice his soul twice in this lifetime. "Let's start by getting rid of that leather dress. Keep the shoes on. They'll look good when you're holding your ankles."

Her face contorted as if she'd been spoon-fed something damn bitter. "Stop."

"Why?"

"A guy who acts like a jackass to protect himself emotionally is a coward. I've had my fill of cowards." She picked up the condom. "So here. Take your king-size condom and—" She stopped, swallowed, stuttered. "Uh—um, k-king size…?"

Burke crossed his arms. Under different circumstances he might've found it cute that she was all flustered and flushing pink in the cheeks. Now he knew better than to be taken in by anything that might endear her to him. "Ribbed, too. You're welcome."

"Stop," she said again, on a breath of sadness. "I know you're being an asshole to prove something."

"Oh, yeah? Not 'cause I'm a coward?"

"It wasn't necessary to come up here with me if your aim was to push me away. All you had to do was tell me you don't care anymore."

He cared, and here she was pressuring him to confirm it. Why? For reassurance? For some twisted satisfaction to tide her over until she hit the road for New York?

"The mind games are wasted on me, babe," he said simply. "You want me to hold you and tell you how deeply I care, huh?"

"If it's true, then, yes, I want to know."

"You got a donor's heart, now you want mine, too?"

Sofia's heels scraped the floor as she drew back. "Bastard."

"You're starting to get it," he said, but the words instantly made him feel sick and seedy. "Now that we have an understanding, let's do something about that condom in your hand."

"This isn't you, Burke. You were never cruel."

"You don't know what time and sacrifice does to a man like me. I told you we're full circle here. I didn't care about you in the school cafeteria that day. I was going to do you and move on."

"That's not who you are anymore."

"You're so sure I'd give you another thought afterward. If I bent you over this table and took you dry tonight, do you think it'd be because I *care*?"

"Who says I would be dry?"

The quiet words shattered some part of his defense, sucked him into her quicksand, shackled him under her spell. "Yeah, Sofia?"

"Yeah."

Break free. He had to. "You think I'm going to call or send you flowers or take you out? Is that what you're used to—New Yorkers wining and dining you? Tell me, then, how much expensive liquor and how many fancy meals will it take to spread those legs?"

"Are you accusing me of prostituting myself? Is that from the Eaves rumor grapevine or did you think it up all on your own to try to insult me?"

"Does it matter?"

"No, actually. No matter where it originates, a lie's a lie."

"It originated from me, just now," he said, weary, quickly losing the momentum it'd take to break down someone as strong as Sofia. "But you don't look all that insulted."

"That would be because I'm *not* insulted. Food is a valid reason to prostitute yourself. My dad skipped out on me right after the transplant. I was nineteen, terrified, but I didn't run back here. There were times when I was desperate enough to entertain things I swore I'd never do. Pride and self-respect are nice enough novelties, but they can't feed me."

Was she saying she'd considered putting out to quiet a growling stomach? Had she honestly believed that she couldn't come home—come to him—for help? If the answer to either question was a loud, taunting *yes*, he couldn't fault her.

"I went hungry, Burke." She held the condom up by the corner. "Take this and leave."

With a casual shrug he walked over but didn't take it. "Remember this, Sofia. Next time you think about putting your arms around me, remember that I can be a vicious son of a bitch. I have that in me."

"You can be vulnerable and sweet," she challenged. "Gentle. Loving. Weak."

"Damn it—"

"Giving. Honorable. Afraid."

"Stop."

"You cried in my arms before. You used to laugh when we were together."

"I was a goddamn stoner."

"You were my friend. Asshole." She crunched the packet in her fist, flung it at him. It bounced off his chest to the floor between their feet. Then it crinkled under Burke's weight as he took a heavy booted step closer to Sofia.

The tight proximity and heightened awareness amplified the smallest details—the shine of her hair under the lights, the contrast of black pupils flaring at the center of gold-speckled brown irises, the subtle tremble of her plump, frowning mouth.

"*Were.* That word makes all the difference. I'm not your friend anymore."

Burke was supposed to turn and walk out of Luz Azcárraga's apartment, but he had the misfortune of being a dumb-ass at the most inopportune moments. This being one of them.

Reacting too quickly for good judgment to solidify or for common sense to penetrate the surge of need that had taunted him from the moment he'd seen Sofia appear at the cemetery, he didn't turn around but instead stepped forward.

Close now, he caught the perfume rising off her neck. The surprised hitch of her breath tickled his ears. He thought she'd put her arms around him again, but she didn't. He thought she'd shove him. She didn't do that, either.

She flicked open a button on his shirt.

You don't want to get into this, Sofia.

It was only a thought, and a slow, confused one at that. He couldn't string two words together.

All he could do was watch her pop the next button, then the one after that. Her fingers worked quickly and the plaid flannel began to part between them.

When her knuckles brushed down his body, he felt muscles constrict and veins tauten. Burke lunged and he landed—his mouth against her soft lips, his chest against her lush breasts.

He moved with her until she hit the wall with a grunt that opened her mouth to his. Her taste intruded and he groaned, so damn greedy for more.

This was what he'd passed up when they were teenagers, toward the end of them. Senior year for him, junior year for her. She hadn't been good at hiding her feelings and her crush on him had started to pick up momentum.

Would kissing her then have felt even a fraction as perfect as this, though? Hard to believe it might've—he'd been nothing more than a shell, all hollowed out inside, and she had been...

Dying.

He'd almost lost Sofia without kissing her.

The realization rattled him, and he hated that. Burdening her with his frustration—because she'd always been strong enough to cope with the intangible shit he couldn't handle— he changed the characteristics of their kiss, making it hostile, hard, unforgiving.

The woman met him at every turn, accepting the intensity of their contact. She scraped her nails against his exposed skin, moaned at the lash of his tongue, responded to the hard pinch of his teeth with bites of her own. A faint coppery taste was introduced as she let out a strangled whimper, the sound vibrating through him.

"Are we going to have sex or kill each other?" he said, easing back to catalogue the damage her nails had left on his torso. A few scratches, none scored deep enough to draw blood.

"I…oh my God…I'm sorry." Disbelief and devastation battled in her eyes. "I've *never*—"

"What? Kissed?"

"Attacked. Hey, I really am sorry."

"You're apologizing to me, but you're the one with the bleeding lip. You didn't do that to yourself."

Sofia touched her fingertips to her mouth, winced. "Don't act so satisfied."

"I'm not." In fact, he despised himself for what he'd invited to the surface. The only redemption was that they hadn't gone further than a kiss.

He buttoned his shirt as she went to the sink and soaked a cloth with water.

"What'd it prove, Burke? Kissing me like that?" She turned off the tap, dabbed herself with the dripping cloth.

"That there's no sweet friendliness between you and me. I'm no different from the next guy you'll raise your skirt for. And you're no different from the next woman I'll fuck against a wall. If you don't believe me, then you're hanging on to some crazy fantasy." Burke pointed to her chest, making sure he had her attention, then he spoke so quietly his voice was a gravelly whisper. "That's your second chance. The choice here is real easy. You can waste your second chance on a fairy tale or grow the hell up."

Crossing the cluttered and mismatched kitchen, she held open the door. "Get out."

"Gladly," he muttered, grateful for the chance to leave this destruction and get back to the marina where he belonged, "now that you know what kind of man I am and what I'm capable of."

There were no tears this time, no sting of her anger colliding with his, no marinara sauce sliding down her clothes, but he'd hurt her even more deeply than he had fourteen years ago.

'Cause he was every bit the coward she'd branded him. And yeah, he was a bastard. She was right about that, too.

* * *

"Where were you when I was being mauled against the wall?"

Sofia waited in the entryway to her great-aunt's bedroom, fully expecting some sort of response because apparently she'd lost her faculties.

Tish didn't lift her head off her front paws, just continued to lie like a muscled, furred statue on the rug at the foot of Luz's massive bed.

Beside the beast was a pair of slippers, a bit curled at the sole and frayed all around, probably from a few dozen too many washings. A braided throw blanket trailed off the end of the bed. It was an unmade mess from the wrinkled sheets to the misshapen pillows propped against the headboard. Clothes were laid across the comforter—all price-tagged dresses in shades of blue, gray, and black.

Elegant, muted, kind of somber. Funeral attire, and all completely wrong for Luz. She wasn't elegant or muted or somber. She wouldn't have wanted to be buried dressed as someone her spirit wouldn't recognize.

How could Bautista have allowed this? If he'd been the one to select her clothes, then how could he have bungled something significant for a woman he seemed to respect so deeply?

Unless he was just another man who chose when to really care and when to quit giving a shit. The only predictable thing about males was that they were utterly and heartbreakingly unpredictable.

"Some companion you are," she said to Tish, coming into the room and pretending that it didn't feel weird to be intruding in her great-aunt's private space. "The only protection I had in that kitchen was a condom. If you won't be a reliable guard dog, then how do you expect to earn your keep?"

She didn't mean what she was saying, and from the dog's soft, bored sigh, Tish could peer through her flimsy bluster and wasn't much impressed with what she found underneath.

Not that Sofia was much impressed with herself at the moment.

Burke Wolf kissed me, groped me, bit me.

And she'd relished it, which revealed how bent she was beneath her practicality and sensibleness. She could still feel the slide of his tongue against hers and the tingle on her skin where he'd touched her.

At least her teenage wonderings about making out with her best friend were finally granted closure. It'd taken fourteen years, but she'd experienced a dream perversely come true and her curiosity was sated.

Only...who knew he'd be so *expert* at kissing and groping. And biting.

Sofia met her reflection in the mirror above Luz's dresser. The bleeding had passed, and now there was a faint sliver of red where he'd marked her. She figured wherever he was now, he wore the markings her fingernails had left on his body.

That wall of muscle and warm skin had felt glorious under her hands, so glorious that she'd lost herself and it'd taken an almost pleasurable touch of pain to reintroduce reality.

Kissing him had been a fantasy, a nice, if dark, departure from sound judgment, but not the fairy tale he'd accused her of holding on to. Not once today had she looked at him and seen a vision of happily ever after.

She'd seen...sex. Lust. Arousal. Dangerous, impossible trouble.

She wanted him and he knew it—which had lent him the perfect ammo to use against her.

The Burke who'd been her friend ages ago wouldn't exact this degree of intimate hurt on someone he cared about—not even when he was high or twisted up in withdrawal or at his worst.

Had Luz known how fundamentally Burke had changed? Or had she accepted this version of him just as she'd accepted all his demons before?

Sofia's father had warned her off striking up a friendship with a pothead, but Luz had seen Burke as "the grocer's boy" and treated him neighborly. Her philosophy was that Sofia's life was hers to wreck if she wanted. It had been another point of contention between Finnegan Mercer and Luz Azcárraga...another issue to deepen the resentment that had begun when Finnegan's wife cut out on him and their baby girl and he'd blamed Luz for raising her niece, Ellen, to be a free spirit.

Luz was wise. Sofia's life was her own and even though she'd veered off track and let Burke kiss her today, she was far from a wreck. She didn't need him to get her through or to be her friend.

Unlike when she had been a teenager and sitting in doctor's offices while most kids her age were hanging out, she had plenty of friends now.

One of whom was right here in Eaves and likely wondering if Sofia was bunking with a Siberian husky in her car.

Grabbing her phone and dialing Joss, she waited in the living room and counted the rings to distract herself from letting her gaze drift across all the photographs. Luz was big on photos and on bringing the personalities of people she cared about into her home.

Had Sofia ever gotten around to hanging any pictures in her own apartment? She didn't think so. Joss had put up so many that it wasn't all that necessary for Sofia to carve out time to give décor any real thought.

"Where'd you end up?" Joss asked immediately.

"Aunt Luz's apartment over the boutique. I met up with her lawyer at this little bar on the corner and he gave me the keys." Sofia went to the sofa and started to smooth out a wrinkle from the blanket draped over the back. "It's a lot like how I remember it. I used to live here."

"Did you really? I thought you and your dad had a house."

"We did. I stayed with Luz for a while when I was in high school." Sofia didn't explain why she'd moved in at age sixteen and had stayed for over a year. That shame was best left in the past... or dredged up whenever the name Mercer came up in gossips' conversation, she imagined.

Remember that Mercer girl with the heart condition? Remember that father of hers? You know why they had to leave town, don't you?

"You lived above an erotic store. How jealous were your classmates?"

"It wasn't all that glamorous. Luz was all about self-sufficiency and a person making their own way, so she had me earn my keep by working in the store after hours. Cleaning and inventory and counting out the register—that sort of thing."

"Was there at least a discount on all that inventory?"

"I think I'll keep you guessing."

"Are you going to be all right tonight?" Joss asked. "I'm worried about you. You didn't cry. People are supposed to cry at funerals, aren't they? Isn't that the big selling point?"

"The tears just aren't there."

"Is that shock?"

"Can we put less energy into diagnosing what I'm feeling and...God, I don't know...just focus on what's next?"

"Yeah, but what *is* next? Do you know?"

"No," Sofia had to admit. "It's like this. A few days ago I was functioning in the light and could see everything fine. Then Luz's lawyer called me, and that call cut out the lights. Now I'm figuring out everything in the dark. It's scary."

"Being in the dark's not so scary if somebody's there with you. You're not alone in this, Sof. Okay?"

"Okay."

"Mean it?"

"Yeah." Sofia smiled. What had she done to deserve the friend she'd found in Joss? "It's kind of strange to be here without Aunt Luz. The dog misses her. I think she's depressed. She's lying on the floor in the bedroom."

"I had a cat when I was a kid. No matter what kind of awful mood he was in, he could always be soothed with a belly rub."

"There's a difference between rubbing the belly of a little cat and rubbing the belly of an enormous dog who judges you when she looks at you."

Joss hummed as if to say *Good point*.

"Maybe she'll perk up once I feed her. Then we're both going to sleep. I'm seeing Bautista in the morning, but afterward I'll swing by to pick you up. Unless you need to get out earlier?"

"This place is so amazingly cozy, I'll probably sleep in. But if I'm overcome with the urge to sightsee, I'll call a car service."

"All right."

"Too bad we're not staying through the holiday weekend. I just saw a flyer in the office advertising some Memorial Day barbecue. It's happening Monday. Know something? I've been looking for barbecue love in all the wrong places since that little place around the corner from our building shut down."

"You went back to the office?"

"Yeah, Peter didn't answer my call so I took a walk when the rain let up. I love the after-rain smell. Anyway, that guy from earlier fixed me a cup of tea and we chatted."

"Which guy from earlier?" There had been so many faces today that Sofia was scrambling to figure it out on her own. It *definitely* wasn't Burke—he'd been occupied doing carnal things to her in this very apartment.

"The one from Shore Seasons. Strayer."

A whisper of suspicion teased Sofia. "What'd he want?"

"To pour me a cup of tea. He was nice." A beat of silence passed. "Oh, sweetie, I have to go. But if something— anything—comes up, call me."

"I will. You be careful."

"I always am."

Hanging up and noting that the phone's battery had waned, Sofia remembered that her charger was in her car. She took a deep breath and went to shut Luz's bedroom door. "I'm just running downstairs to get my stuff," she told Tish, as if the dog might give a damn one way or the other. "Then I'll feed you and then we'll get some rest and then…well, I don't know what we'll do then."

Tish's silvery eyes held hers.

"I'm sorry, Tish. I wasn't prepared..." *For you.* But what fault of it was Tish's that she'd found herself suddenly abandoned? The details were different, but Sofia understood the dog's predicament. "I wasn't prepared for this."

She took the rear stairs and hurried past Blush's Dumpster and the deliveries door to the side of the building, where she'd parked her SUV in the single space reserved for the store owner. Where Luz's car and the bicycle she had been riding when the aneurism had erupted were parked was beyond Sofia.

Vehicles and people on foot competed for dominance on the street. When she'd lived in Eaves, the season had found most downtown streets overrun with tourists, particularly at night, when everyone wanted to be somewhere other than where they actually were.

Shop windows glimmered, voices brightened the darkness, and there was a teasing hint of summer in the air, yet she wasn't compelled to wander and take a look around—and definitely wouldn't risk returning to the bar and finding a grumpy longshoreman staring at the bottom of another drink.

Besides, she had plans to feed a grieving Siberian husky, and in case she hadn't dabbled in enough danger for one day she would try to rub Tish's belly.

Lugging her bags back to the alleyway, she glanced at the completely dark building beside Blush. So Cape Foods had been vacant since Burke's father's death. Curiously, no one had pounced on the property. Even odder? The town council allowed the eyesore of an orphaned commercial building on Society Street when for so many years Luz had battled to keep Blush's doors open.

She looked from the market to Blush and let herself drift to the secret moments she'd spent underground, creeping past storage containers and slipping to the narrow passage-way that connected Blush's basement to the market's.

Burke would be there, reeking of smoke or sneaking a beer or hiding out until he could disguise his intoxication enough to face his father.

They hadn't been friends until she found him in that claustrophobic hallway and threatened to narc on him. When he didn't respond, she ventured closer and realized he was listening to music and lost in a drawing as his scraped-knuckled hand coasted over a sketchpad.

"What the hell?" he'd said, startling her. He tugged an earphone free. "Are you gonna sit down or what?"

"I didn't know you knew I was here."

"Your shadow's on my paper, and I can smell you. That friggin' incense stuff."

"I can smell you, too," she'd said. "Weed."

Captivated was what she'd been, and somehow a condom on a lunch tray had seemed insignificant compared to her need to be near him and watch him draw.

It was a beautiful memory of a beautiful boy she loved. Burke wasn't that boy anymore, though. He was a man who kissed like a savage and talked like the devil, and now the memory seemed artificial somehow.

Leaving the empty market in the dark, Sofia ascended the stairs and reentered the apartment. She fed Tish and maintained her patience when after fifteen minutes of sniffing around outside the dog refused to go potty but decided to whimper the moment Sofia locked them up tight in the apartment. It was ridiculously late when finally Tish stretched out in front of Luz's bed.

Sofia showered and pulled on her pajamas, and though she wanted nothing more than to lie across a thick mattress, she hesitated.

The apartment contained two bedrooms: Luz's and one she used as a personal office. When Sofia had lived here, her aunt had bought a twin bed and put it in the office to accommodate her. There was no twin bed now. That half of the office held herbs and bottles of essential oils, apparently devoted to Luz's aromatherapy interests.

That left one bed in the place. Sofia was so weary and so wrung out that she went to it.

She set the brand-new dresses aside, peeled back the comforter, picked up a pillow to fluff—and found a long, spiraling strand of hair. It was a silken black thread between her fingers.

Luz had refused to let herself gray.

"God." Sofia returned the strand to the pillow and turned off the light. "This sucks, okay? It sucks and I hate this!"

The dog's spine rippled and Sofia snatched the braided blanket off the bed, toed the slippers aside, and sank to the floor beside Tish.

"I get to miss her, too," she explained, and felt equally stupid and comforted to be expressing her feelings to an animal. "I loved her. She was the only mom I had."

Curling up on the rug, covering herself with the blanket, Sofia cried. And Tish sighed and kept watch until they both fell asleep.

* * *

"Caroline, *vamanos*." Javier Bautista crooked a finger and the woman passed off her bottles to Tariq to deliver to a table. Javier moved behind the bar, grabbing a fresh beer and tucking himself into a nook where he could speak freely. Bottoms Up was his place. The regulars knew not to crowd him, and tourists caught on quick.

Caro Jayne joined him, wiping down the bar as beads twinkled over their heads. "Are you putting me in charge and finally going home?" she asked over the noise of music and voices.

Yes and no. "I'm making a change to the bar."

"A change? Oh—at last getting rid of that tired pool table so people can dance?"

"Caroline, hear me out. Did you see Luz's girl leave with Wolf?"

"Mm-hmm. He certainly is good-looking," she said. "It's not even just my opinion. It's a fact."

"Know where they're headed? Blush." He uncapped the beer, drank down half. "Sofia owns it now."

Caro searched his eyes. "Luz left her the store?"

"Yeah. She's probably going to sell it. That development firm that's been sniffing around these past few months? They might take it off her hands, and if they conquer her, they might conquer Burke Wolf and take his old man's building. Then the holdout on this block will be you."

"And you," she said, then paused. "The bar. This is yours."

"Not if you want it," he said quietly. Too much of his history with Luz was entwined with Bottoms Up. Too much love and too many lies. "I need to step away."

"Bautista, you can't walk away from this place. It's a part of you." She waved a hand. "This is your grief talking, a reaction to the funeral."

"It's a choice. A man stands by his choice."

"It's bollocks and I'll never forgive you for putting me in this position. I love this place as much as you do. I'll fight those developer bastards every step of the way. But I have a studio to manage. I have a son. I can't do it all alone." She put down the rag and squeezed his hand. "You and Luz promised to look after Evan and me. She can't anymore, but you're still here. I can't do this without you."

Caro was tougher than she allowed herself to believe, but fear blinded her. She still carried the ghosts she'd brought with her to Cape Cod when she popped up in this bar with a baby and without a plan.

"There's the option to sell to the firm, Caroline. You'll profit. I'll sell the bar to you cheap and you can turn around and bring home double—maybe triple—to your son."

"No." Anxiety raised her voice a few decibels, rippled over her words. "We're in this together. I'll join you in ownership, if a partner is what you need. But I'm not going to let Luz's death take you both away."

Bautista let the conversation end there, and when she blended into the fray he finished his beer in the pseudo-solitude of the nook. Bottoms Up was the possession he'd treasured most before he let Luz in. He'd thought they'd had an understanding. He'd thought he knew her.

Now? He had an urge to disappear, a friend who wouldn't let him, and the beer in his hands.

CHAPTER 5

*S*ofia woke up cranky. There was a twinge of pain from sleeping all night on the floor and a dog was lying on her hair. If she and Tish had battled each other for space on the thin rug—and, clearly, Tish had won—Sofia didn't remember it. Tugging herself free of the furry anvil, she sat up slowly and rubbed her eyes.

So this was real. Somehow she'd thought it wouldn't be, that things would be different, brighter, in the morning. Only the sky was bright now, as sunlight bombarded the room and warmed her. Everything else still carried the smoky hue of devastation.

She hadn't even dreamed. Or if she had, she remembered nothing now. Feeling cheated, because dreams had always let her escape when she needed to, she got to her feet slowly and figured her subconscious was in limbo with the rest of her. Which was sad, because sometimes things that didn't make sense in reality were so vividly clear in dreams.

"Get up, Tish." She went to the mirror to inspect the severity of her cried-out, puffy eyes and to pluck animal fur from her hair, but none of that seemed to penetrate as important when in the glass she saw the dog rise and slink toward her.

Tish stopped beside her, still standing at attention, and gently bumped Sofia with her dewy nose. It wasn't precisely an act of obedience. Instead it seemed, oddly, a gesture of respect.

"Oh…" Turning and kneeling, she grabbed the dog into an awkward embrace. "I don't really care if you're listening to me only because you think I'm pathetic. I'll take what I can get."

A growl vibrated through Tish's body and Sofia quickly let go. "Okay—too soon. I get it. Sorry."

They made it out of the apartment without event, but only one of them emerged ready to approach the day on a well-fed stomach. Sofia had slept on her aunt's floor, had showered in her bathroom, and had been kissed in her kitchen, but she couldn't bring herself to rummage through the cupboards for food.

Hungry and a bit disoriented from a night of hollow, restless sleep, she let Tish trot a few paces ahead—

Then she almost lost her arm when a piercing whistle compelled the dog to sharply dash around the side of the building and the leash pulled taut.

"Wait! *Damn it, stop!*"

The leash escaped Sofia's grip and she stumbled to the ground in a clatter of jingling bracelets and a helpless yelp as Tish took off at a fierce, unapologetic gallop.

So much for obedience or respect.

Sofia got up, grabbed her purse, and started running, sacrificing no time to brush dirt and debris from her clothes. Damn that dog for slipping the leash. And just wait until she found the source of that hellish whistle.

Rounding the side of the store, she confronted a quiet street with no trace of a rambunctious wolf of a dog terrorizing it.

"Has anyone seen a dog? She's a husky with a gray coat. Anyone?"

Foot traffic continued to flow, which aggravated her to no end—hadn't she left the big-city hustle and bustle in New York?—and she popped into the path of a teenager on Rollerblades skating circles on the sidewalk in front of the market. A streak of electric pink stood out in his ebony hair and the frown already in place deepened when he saw her closing in.

"If I seen your dog, I would've said so," he said dismissively.

"Saw."

"Huh?"

" 'If I *saw* your dog.' Or 'if *I'd seen* your dog.' "

"Seriously?" The kid shook his head and when he shrugged his shoulders, she noticed the tip of an aerosol can poking out of his hoodie. From the blue smeared across the nozzle, she didn't have to twist her brain to figure out it was spray paint. There were only so many reasons a kid with an attitude would be loitering in front of a vacant building armed with a can of spray paint, and all of them said *vandalism.* "If you ever find it, leash it."

"It's collared and leashed. The dog pulled the leash off my wrist when she ran away."

"Oh. Then that probably sucks for you."

"Yeah. Probably." Sofia bit back a remark, then had to do it again and once more, as if she were struggling to maintain her grasp on a kite tail on a blustery day. As if she were struggling to maintain her grasp on a leash when a Siberian husky on the other end of it had different ideas. "Give me the spray paint."

"What spray paint?"

She put out her hand. "You don't seem to give a damn about helping me, but I'm going to help you by taking the paint so I don't have to report to the cops that I saw you skating around outside this building with a can in your hoodie."

Fear and defiance struggled on his face, as though the possibility of being caught both scared and appealed to him. Was that what he wanted? To confront the consequences of vandalism?

She could leave him to self-destruct, or she could insert her help where it wasn't wanted. "I'm looking out for you. The can, please?"

When he surrendered it, she put herself back in motion, trashing the spray paint, then combing through the threads of people who'd chosen these precise moments to clog Eaves's answer to small-town America's Main Street. No Tish. The only animal she could see was a Pomeranian that was barely larger than a hedgehog and was gleefully pissing on the bottom of an artificial glitter-sprinkled tree at the end of the block.

This can't be my Saturday. This can't be my life. I can't be running around terrified that I lost a dog who ditched me the second somebody whistled.

Denial never did her any favors, so she kept charging forward, past the peeing Pomeranian—at closer range it looked cute enough to cuddle—then stepped into the street at a careless moment and had to do some fancy footwork to dodge a pair of cars.

The blaring of horns and shouts of profanity followed her as she made it to the other side and dashed into The Dirty Bastards.

A pair of men dropped their tasks and leaned on the counter, their gazes licking her up and then down as machines rumbled and laundry detergent perfumed the air. One smiled, then, as if remembering something, twisted the band on his finger and muttered, "I've got a wife. Ain't going down *that* road again," before tossing up a broom and stepping away from the counter.

Sofia doubted she was the picture of temptation. Panic had her glistening with perspiration. Gravel embellished the knees of her leggings. Sweat acted as an adhesive, gluing her white eyelet tank to her skin. She probably looked so filthy that no one would fault her if she marched over to one of those top-of-the-line front-loaders and crawled inside.

The other guy didn't have a smile at the ready, or a ring. What he did have was copper-red hair that fell past his shoulders, and a dark auburn beard. He lifted a thick set of brows over steel-blue eyes. "You were in one mighty hell of a hurry to get over here. If that Honda was going a mile faster, I'd be waiting for EMTs to scrape you off the road right now."

She crossed her arms. "I'm looking for a dog. Big, gray, hungry-looking."

"What's the name?" He grabbed a pen, twirled his hair around it, and locked the bun into place. The flow of movement caused all sorts of muscles to flex.

Joss, Joss, Joss. You're going to hate me when I tell you what you missed.

"Her name's Tish."

"I was asking for *your* name." The guy didn't have to smile; interest rode his lips anyway. "Tish, though. That's Luz's—"

Say "bitch" and I swear I'll—

"—husky. A real beauty, that one."

"A purebred."

"Her beauty's deeper than the coat, though. She's got intelligent eyes. Count on Luz to see what's special about her. She figured she'd get herself a dog and found the cleverest one in Massachusetts."

"Tish ran off. She's not clever. She's in danger, and I'm really worried about her."

He came around the counter and nodded a greeting to a woman who stepped in with a laundry bag. "Why didn't you put her on a leash?"

"Does no one even suspect I have the brains to do that? Attention, everyone. Tish was on a leash but someone blew a whistle and she bolted and nearly tugged off my arm in the process."

The man with the broom paused and chuckled. "McGuinty, you can either help her out now or deal with her when somebody leaves the dog on your doorstep. My advice—don't delay the inevitable." Then he went back to sweeping.

Bearded McGuinty pushed open the door. "After you." When she hesitated, he added, "This is as close to a gentleman as I know how to be."

"Holding open a door for someone so you can stare at her fanny when she walks out is your impression of gentlemanly?"

McGuinty's response to that was to stride out ahead of her and let the door swing shut.

"Hey!" She rushed out and caught up with him fast. "If you're going to bounce from one extreme to another, go back to the laundromat and let me handle this myself. And what'd that guy mean, anyway, about someone leaving Tish on your doorstep?"

"That guy's my brother, Abram. He owns the laundromat. And he was referring to the animal shelter. I run that with our grandpa and help Abe out when he needs it."

Sofia had begun calling Tish's name but halted. "The animal shelter? Is your last name Slattery?"

"Yup."

"I remember your grandpa. He and my dad were friends, did you know? A couple of Irish-blooded guys hanging out." She might've smiled if she weren't so nervous about Tish. "He'd bring me over to the shelter to play with the kittens and pups. For a long time I wanted one, but after so many years of 'Next time we see the Slatterys, I'll pick you out a pet' I gave up on that wish."

"Guess the wish didn't give up on you. Once we find Tish, you'll be good to go."

She would've been more likely to choose a cuddly Pomeranian or a cat that enjoyed belly rubs, but she said nothing as she continued to search the sidewalk.

"I remember you and your dad, by the way," McGuinty said. "When you said your missing dog's name is Tish, I placed you, Sofia. I was a grade ahead, ran with Burke Wolf and his crowd."

What had peers and teachers and gossips around town called them? Riffraff, druggies, badasses.

"Oh," she said, ready to bring his full attention to their search of Society Street and away from an unwanted trip down memory lane. "Tish? Tish! Here, girl!"

"And you, Sofia, were the do-gooder."

"Do-gooder?" She swallowed. If her heart condition hadn't made her isolated enough, spying on her classmates and reporting their every infraction to the principal's office sure had.

"It was the nicest way to put it. You thought telling on us was right, and it didn't seem to matter how many enemies you collected or who said you weren't cool. Back then, the crowd had a special set of pet names for you."

"Enlighten me."

"No," he said emphatically. "What'd be the point of hurting you now?"

"I want to know."

McGuinty looked straight at her. "Tattler."

"That's harmless."

"Brat."

"Still doesn't hurt."

"Ass-kisser. Prude. Bitch."

Well. Whereas sweat beaded on her skin and began to trickle, those words sank in—deep. "Do-gooder's the most musical of the bunch," she said, concealing pain with sarcasm. "Something tells me it was the least used."

He had the decency to appear ashamed. "Kids can be assholes, especially when that's exactly what they aspire to be. We were on a fast track to hell, all of us, and we thought we were having the time of our lives. You kept getting in the way."

"Then you must've been relieved when I moved out of your way." She doubted a group of badass teenagers had been the only ones pleased to see the Mercers go.

McGuinty clasped her shoulder. "Let's cross."

On the other side of the street, they stood in front of the Au Naturel photography studio.

"I looked up and down this side before," she told him as panic started to rise. If she wasn't careful, she'd succumb to another attack. Panic attacks had been sporadic in New York, and here in Eaves she was close to experiencing two within twenty-four hours.

"You didn't look closely enough." McGuinty pointed at the window, and she'd be damned: Tish stood on the other side of the glass.

"*Tish!*" The word was part question, part sob. She tapped

her eyes, warding off tears that resisted her control. Yesterday she hadn't managed to squeeze out any emotion during Luz's funeral, but she was about to bawl with joy at the sight of her inherited dog inside a boudoir photographer's studio. "But...How..."

"Folks who like Tish sometimes bend the rules for her."

McGuinty lifted a hand to casually wave as the studio's door opened and Caro Jayne joined them. "Sofia, do tell. The hottest guy to climb off a ship walked you home last night. Now Paul Bunyan himself is escorting you 'round the block at the top of the morning. Whatever *je ne sais quoi* you've got, I want it."

"You don't need *je ne sais quoi* to get this," McGuinty said to Caro, his voice low and frank. "You know that."

"So you say, but another woman's on your arm."

"Just helping a girl from school find her dog. Why don't you bring Evan to the 'mat today? Abram's got the vending machines loaded up. *Star Wars* stickers, bottle caps, gum balls."

"I don't have enough change for all of that."

"I'll cover it." McGuinty fished a roll of quarters from a pocket and handed it to her.

"Ah, so *that's* what that was."

"Not quite. There's a real easy way for you to find out for yourself."

The heat behind his words was directed at Caro, but Sofia was standing so close that she was brushed with it, too. Both women's gazes slid south to the front of his jeans. Was he a king-size condom carrier, too?

"Stickers are messy," Caro said, tossing him the quarter roll. "A bottle cap is literally the most useless toy in the entire history of useless toys."

"I don't hear any objections to the gum balls."

"Gum balls aren't healthy."

"Sugar-free. My brother's not too keen on contributing to the rotting of anyone's teeth. So, what do you say?"

"We're here only because my sitter is sick, my assistant's out of town, and clients are stopping by to pick up albums. Some other time, maybe, McGuinty."

"One of these days, you'll run out of excuses and either let me take you out or tell me to move along." It sounded like a promise but carried the weight of a warning, as though he and Caro had been indulging in a game for a while and he was growing weary enough to quit.

Sofia knifed through the tension. "Thanks, McGuinty, for finding Tish."

"Glad she's all right." He started for his side of the street. "Just so we're clear, there's not a fucking thing wrong with being a do-gooder."

"Then we're okay?" she checked.

"We're okay. If you decide Tish isn't enough of a handful, stop by the animal shelter. Just know that Grandpa will probably talk you into a card game. It's been a while since he played with a Mercer."

Sofia laughed, appreciating the gesture. "I might do that someday."

"What's a bloody mountain man doing on Cape Cod, anyway?" Caro murmured as they watched him return to The Dirty Bastards. "He should be in a forest someplace, splitting logs with an ax."

"The most unlikely people end up in the most unlikely places. What's a New York marketing executive doing here?"

"Or a black British ballerina?" Caro slid her hands into her jeans pockets. "Past life. Little-girl ambition was what it was. I thought I'd be a dancer."

"Now you're a boudoir photographer and a bartender."

"To be quite fair," the woman said with a sly smirk, "I wasn't aware of boudoir photography and bars when I was a little girl. If I knew then what I know now, I would've chosen the right path from the beginning and spared myself plenty of heartache and uncertainty. Anyway, let's reunite you with Tish."

She led the way inside to the lobby, where the dog now lay peacefully on a polished walnut floor. The place was decorated in a neutral palette, but rustic accents and pops of color gave it personality. Simple landscapes graced the walls, and above the wide reception desk was a photograph of Caro Jayne herself in a soft on-the-beach-at-sunset image that implied sensuality and suggested nudity but avoided explicit impropriety through careful posing and a few clever props—one being an old-fashioned camera held strategically in front of her.

"Hi, Tish. I don't suppose you came here to be photographed with your collar off, so it'd be great if someone explained how this happened." She faced Caro. "Her leash is gone. I had it in hand, then someone blew a whistle and she made a run for it."

"A whistle? Hell." Caro rubbed a finger between her brows. "The lead's on the desk. Now this whole thing makes sense. Apparently I've been lied to." She held up that finger and Sofia's attention was lured to a tattoo across the woman's wrist. Inked into her skin in bold midnight typewriter print was the word *breathe*. "Evan, come here."

From the recesses of the studio came a boy Sofia guessed to be four or five years old. His mop of curly hickory hair was long enough to fall over his brow and it shined under the lobby lights as he cradled a partially finished model watercraft. Hanging from a lanyard around his neck was a red whistle.

"Evan, this is Sofia. Say hi."

"No," he decided, and Sofia might've been offended by his instant aversion to her if his glower hadn't been so irresistibly adorable. "Mommy, I'm building a fighter boat for Luz."

"Fighter boat?" Sofia echoed.

"It's a naval watercraft," Caro clarified. She took it from the boy and set it on a table. "Very sweet of you, honey. It's coming along nicely."

Sofia's knowledge of model transportation—naval watercraft in particular—was limited, but she was more than a little startled that a child as young as Evan appeared to be so invested in constructing a "fighter boat."

And he intended it to be a gift for a woman who'd passed on. "That's for Luz?"

"Uh-huh. I'm gonna give it to her when she comes back for Tish."

Confused, Sofia looked to Caro. Why was she hiding Luz's death from her kid?

"The whistle's for his safety. He should use it if he feels he's in danger, but he treats it as a toy. I guess whenever Tish hears it, she knows he's nearby." Caro turned to her son. "Evan, you told me you saw Tish outside the door and let her in."

"Which isn't true," Sofia insisted. "She and I were behind Blush and headed to my car. The second she heard that whistle she went around the side of the boutique."

Shyly, the boy glanced from his mother to Sofia. "Sorry."

"You're not supposed to leave this studio by yourself," Caro reprimanded. "Then, on top of it, you lied. Never, ever lie to me."

"I'm sorry, Mommy." He slinked over to Tish and looped his gangly arms around the dog's neck.

Be careful, she'll growl, Sofia wanted to say, but Tish's tail began to thump.

She was...*happy*?

"Tish belongs to Luz," the boy said. "I can take care of her until Luz comes back. Please?"

Sofia moved closer to Caro, dropping her voice. "You've got to tell him the truth. Kids have a tendency to lie when they're being lied to."

"Evan's fragile." Caro picked up the model watercraft, then, seeming at a loss for what to do with it, she hugged it close. "The hardest thing to do sometimes is lie to your child. You only do it then because it's also the easiest thing to do, or the only option. When you're a parent, the easy ways out and last resorts can be blessings."

Sofia wanted to say she understood, but she could only empathize.

"Mommy, are you mad at me?" The boy's small voice had them both turning their heads. Evan still held Tish protectively. "Am I in trouble?"

Caro unwrapped her son's arms from the dog. "Sofia is Luz's family. She's in charge of Tish now."

"But Mommy—"

"I'd like her to stay," Sofia blurted, and everyone looked confused. Even Tish cocked her head curiously. "For a couple of hours. I have a meeting and I don't want to make her sit through it when she could be hanging out with Evan. So would that be fine?"

Caro's smile created a sparkle in her brown eyes. "We'd love it. Evan, why don't you put your boat away and then get the foam ball for Tish?"

The kid bounced up and started to zip out of the lobby.

"Not so fast," his mother interrupted, summoning him back. "Say thank you to Sofia for being so kind."

Evan charged, throwing his thin arms around her waist. "Thank you!" He looked up at her through his too-long curls. "Tish loves me. I'm her best friend. Does she love you, too?"

"Oh, of course," she said, because Caro was right. Sometimes it was easier to lie.

The response seemed to satisfy Evan and he released her to speed off again.

"Thanks," Caro said. "It's been Evan and me for his entire life. He's the sensitive sort and he's not quick to make friends. When he met Tish, it was as if he'd found his kindred spirit, if you put stock in that sort of thing. They've gotten on from day one. He'll miss her when you take her away to New York."

"When you're as close as Evan and Tish are, distance doesn't matter so much. I can bring her back sometimes."

"You'd do that for Evan?"

Sofia nodded. Weekend visits weren't out of the question, particularly when there were so many details left to settle in Eaves. "For Tish, too. Besides, I have *that* to figure out." She pointed in the direction of Blush. "I'm sort of your neighbor."

"Bautista told me. Do you think we'll be neighbors for a while? Are you going to hold on to Blush?"

"I might. It's an option," Sofia said optimistically, but Caro wasn't as easy to convince as her son. "Another option is accepting it for what it is—great commercial real estate."

"Oh." She seemed deflated. "You're inclined to sell. Society Street's its own community, kind of independent of the rest of Eaves. I love that about this street. But things are changing and I'm desperate to keep them the same. Is that selfish?"

"No, I get it. And I'm sorry I can't ease your concerns, Caro, but the truth is I'm confused." That nugget of honesty brought her relief. So she shared another. "I was born and raised here. I feel like a stranger now."

Caro nodded as if in agreement. "This isn't a remedy, but I'm here for you. I know what it's like to no longer feel you belong in your own home."

"Thanks." Sofia went to the desk and scribbled on the guestbook. "Here's my cell. Call me if anything comes up."

"Okay." Caro hesitated before adding, "It could be that part of the reason I don't want to tell Evan about your aunt is because I don't really want to believe it myself. Instead of going to her service, I took a shift at Bottoms Up. I say I want to protect my son, but maybe I'm only shielding myself. I loved that damn woman. She was my friend."

Sofia nodded. But she had to think—she'd loved Luz, too, yet had they been friends in the end? Or had time and distance let Sofia become as much of a stranger to Luz as she was to the rest of Eaves?

Escaping the question, she left the studio and tried to tell herself it didn't matter now.

Even though it did.

CHAPTER 6

$\mathscr{B}$autista wasn't a man who made snap judgments about folks—rarely was he interested in mustering the give-a-damn to try, and a low tolerance for boredom was partly why he turned away more clients than he accepted and was viciously selective when it came to the company he kept—but the moment he put Luz's dog's leash on Sofia Mercer's wrist, he could see the ugliness of fear twisting beneath all that beauty.

She wasn't his responsibility; she'd get no soothing words or reassuring smiles from him. As a matter of fact, the sooner she made up her mind to cash out the assets Luz left behind—and he suspected she would—the better his life would be.

His life, such as it was.

Every night since her death he'd slept here in his office, because his woman had despised the place. *Too corporate*, she'd criticized, rolling up the word in the thick blanket of her Argentine accent and whipping it out in such a way that he still didn't know whether she'd meant to tease or attack him. When it came to confusing him, Luz Azcárraga hit her target with the masterful precision of an expert markswoman.

Holing up in this place was taking its toll on him. It'd backfired, whatever plan he'd had to sleep and work here and then climb on his bike when it all came to a head.

His chopper waited in the shared parking lot of Eaves's East and West Millennium Towers, a pair of tinted glass-walled executive buildings that jutted out from the Cape like two rods in a cock-measuring contest. If he went to the window he'd be able to see his bike glinting up at him as if it were a lighthouse's beam slicing through a foggy night, but the ache behind his eyes and the thready sensation of weariness skittering along his nerves warned him away from direct morning sunlight. He wasn't a morning kind of man, yet he'd claimed an east-facing office—screwed-up planning on his part, and he was reminded of it each time he followed up a hard-liquor night with early client appointments and had to cope with the sun rising outside his windows.

The only client he'd booked today, the only person who could so much as tempt him to deal with anyone on the morning after Luz's funeral, was Sofia. And she was a no-show.

It was already after eleven—practically midday, which made it perfectly acceptable to yank a beer from the minifridge without hearing his legal secretary complain about him washing down his breakfast with alcohol.

Avoiding the keepsake trunk containing folders of paperwork, electronic storage backup devices, and boxes of trinkets he'd rummaged through only once, when he and Luz had been preparing her will, Bautista stood up and stretched. He had forty-five years on him and could still move with agility that didn't make his bones creak painfully or draw a labored grunt from his gut, but he'd been sitting too long preparing himself for Luz's niece to waltz in and take over everything that had belonged to the woman he loved.

God, he loved her…as deeply as he hated the lies she'd told him.

His shirt and pants were creased, but a pressed corporate image wouldn't matter one damn bit the second he threw his leg over his bike and revved it to a roar that'd quiet the thoughts tumbling through him.

Bautista put his hand on the door lever, ready to heads-up Nessa that he was grabbing an ice-cold, but it jammed on the first attempt. Adding force and throwing open the door, he watched Sofia all but stumble into the office.

Christ, it was eerie how closely she resembled Luz. There were some differences, obviously, but the similarities grabbed him so tightly that for a merciless moment he couldn't breathe.

"What if I said you kept me waiting too long and need to set up something with my secretary?" Bautista began to move around her.

"Please don't." Sofia's fingers latched onto his rolled shirtsleeve.

If Luz were here…If she could reach out easily and touch him…If he could be this close to her one more time and tell her…

"Take your hand off me, Sofia."

She let him go. "Sorry. But I'm asking you not to leave. I would've been here much sooner, but I lost Tish—"

Fuck, already? "That didn't take long, did it?"

"I found her, Bautista, but searching for her ate up some

time. Then I had to change my clothes, and these aren't even my clothes"—she pinched the front of her green top to illustrate that it was baggy across the breasts—"but mine were so dirty after I'd fallen and I didn't want to show up here looking sloppy and I had to go all the way to Shore Seasons to borrow an outfit from my roommate. After all that it made sense to check out, since we're heading back to New York today, anyway." Finally she stopped talking. "What are you thinking?"

"That you're boring me and wasting more of my time. People generally don't get a second opportunity to waste my time."

Sofia slid directly into his path. "You don't scare me."

"Yes, I do." As desperately as he wanted nothing more to do with the woman, he just as desperately wanted her close for the exact same reason: She was familiar. Hurting Sofia would be like hurting Luz.

Nothing had eased him into the idea of losing his woman. One morning she'd woken him up by playing with his hair and they'd had slow, easy sex, then they'd fought in his kitchen about coffee beans and she'd slammed his door because she knew he couldn't stand slamming doors. The next time he saw her, she was on a white-sheeted gurney at the hospital—an empty body.

The funeral had been his burden. Nessa tried to help, but he wouldn't allow her or anyone else's intrusion. Now there was Sofia, a woman who looked so much like Luz but could never be her.

"You want this to be wrapped up and over with, don't you?" Sofia tried, her voice closer. "Me, too. If you give me some time, we can settle this and you can go on with your life."

"She didn't tell you, did she?" he asked, turning around

and knowing damn well that Nessa now stood at her office door, riveted. "Luz didn't tell you that she *was* my life?"

"She—uh—no, she didn't say she was seeing anyone seriously. At the funeral you didn't make it all that clear, either."

"I'd figured out by then what I really meant to her."

"What does that mean?"

"You want to do this?" He pointed to his office and her gaze flew to the tattoos stretching down to his wrist—a flock of crows. "Go in, take a seat. Do it fast, before I change my mind."

Her glare was frosty, and that flare of instant anger made her startlingly different from her great-aunt. Luz wasn't the type to let anyone know the precise moment she became pissed. She'd held him at arm's length, always keeping some part of herself out of his reach when all he'd wanted to do was love her the only way a man like him knew how—protectively, greedily, selfishly.

"I keep comparing you to her," he said flatly, once Sofia sat in front of his desk and he came around to stand beside her. "I hate that I'm doing it, but that's what's happening."

"And I'm falling short of a woman you just described as being your life?"

"I didn't say you fell short. You're different. You're scared, *querida*. She wasn't."

"You don't know me."

"I know Ellen skipped out. I know Finnegan waited until you got a new heart before he did the same thing. I know that Luz had pride in her voice when she talked about her Sofia."

"Pride?"

"She loved you."

Her expression hovered somewhere between grateful and

skeptical. Whatever number her parents had done on her wasn't his problem to fix. He had to remember that.

"Luz told me nothing about you, Javier Bautista." She looked at her hands, her fingers curling and uncurling on his desk. "She was your life and you were her... what?"

"Lawyer." He went to the other side of the desk but didn't sit. He was damn tired of sitting, of being still. "A breakdown of her estate is here."

She opened the folder he put down in front of her and started to scan the spreadsheets. He was almost impressed that she continued to review instead of immediately shutting the folder and complaining of a headache. "Debts are itemized in section four. Her funeral expenses, in the second subsection, have already been resolved, paid from a dedicated bank account."

"All those dresses left on her bed. When those are returned, will the credit go back into this account?" She set down the open folder. "They were all—"

"Wrong for her," he muttered as the exact words drifted from her.

"If you knew they were wrong, why did you buy them?" she asked.

"I didn't. My secretary, Nessa, bought them at one of those high-end joints in Boston. The credit's going back to her."

"What was she wearing yesterday?" The casket had been closed, as per Luz's rigid instructions.

When I go out, I don't want anybody to see me with my eyes closed.

She'd wanted to be remembered by her smile and the way her stare could be so serious that it made folks uncomfortable. In death, she appeared vulnerable, but nothing would ever hurt her again—not even his love.

MEANT TO BE MINE

"She was wearing a black dress with flowers all over it. Lotuses. She'd wear it to the beach sometimes. That dress and a pair of sunglasses with white frames. I couldn't find the sunglasses but wouldn't have let her wear them, anyway. I wouldn't let anyone hide her face that way. I had them put her cross around her neck and her rosary in her hand."

"And her hair?"

"Loose. She'd want to be comfortable, right?"

"Yeah."

"Back to the paperwork. The debts are minimal—she didn't live all that extravagantly and kept her finances in good shape. Her computer hasn't been cleaned, but that'll happen soon. Her CPA surrendered tax records, and those are all here." He indicated a box inside the open trunk. "If you have trouble sleeping at night, dig in."

"This doesn't bore me. I have a business degree and I studied fashion merchandising. I don't come from glamour and fluff."

"And a motivation to get the most out of liquidation might keep you really interested," he said, though he'd meant the cruelty to stay in his head and not get out in the air where she could hear it.

Snapping the folder shut, she said, "I didn't come to Eaves because of an inheritance. I came to say good-bye to Luz."

He'd refrained from telling her about the inheritance over the phone specifically to find out if her moral compass was bent. So he was inclined to believe her. "Assets," he went on, ignoring his instinct to apologize when he'd offended unjustly. "She drove a Bug. It's at my place, along with her bicycle. The building on Society—the apartment and the store—are free and clear. Luz had two employees. One took off for Sandwich and the other works at Shore Seasons. You might've met her already."

"Paget. She checked me in. She seems nice."

"Blush's activity has been suspended and will remain that way until you decide if you want to sell or dissolve the store," he continued. "I canceled a shipment of condoms that tried to come through a couple of days ago, but you'll need to get involved and close out the open accounts. Again, it's detailed in the files."

"Slow down," she said. "God, this is too fast. Yesterday you tell me that everything of hers belongs to me now, and today you're telling me how to get rid of it all."

"Isn't that what you want? You've got a setup in Manhattan."

"Yes. A job and an apartment and a great car."

"Greeting cards are a long way from vibrators and rope. Whatever apartment you've got, I'm almost sure its landlord won't be all right with a Siberian husky. And something tells me you're going to get tired of putting New York to Cape Cod miles on that great car of yours. I was Luz's advisor, but I'm going to give you some advice and hope you'll accept it for your own good. You can't continue your life *and* try to hold on to the one she gave you. We both know it'd be most convenient for you to cash out, so don't pretend you aren't in a hurry to do just that."

She lashed out with an obscenity and then a whimper. "You're wrong. I'm not in a hurry to let Aunt Luz go."

"Time's going to move without you. My role in this is to transfer what was hers to you, not to give you sympathy or hold your hand. If that's what you're after, go to Burke Wolf. He went to the apartment with you, and I heard he took his time leaving."

She smiled recklessly and he noticed a dash of dusky pink

on her bottom lip. A tiny nick, a fresh one. "There's stuff between Burke and me that you'll never understand. For the record, he didn't hold my hand and wasn't all that sympathetic after we left the bar."

Luz had told him Burke and Sofia had once been friends but had fallen out when the Mercers left Cape Cod. Ask him, a couple of kids had no business getting all tangled up in each other the way folks said they'd been. Burke kept himself mobile and could be a mean son of a bitch—how he'd ever gotten along with a delicate type like Sofia, Bautista couldn't guess.

"It's too bad you've got nobody who'll let you cry. Ellen and Finnegan made sure to stay away."

"You know where my mother is?"

"Luz knew. I found Ellen's information in her address book. I contacted her and Finnegan because I wanted to know how they'd react. From the way Luz told it, she raised you when Ellen wouldn't and Finnegan couldn't. Know what he said when I told him? 'Okay.' That's all. And Ellen, she was Luz's best friend, wasn't she? They cut up in this town and had big plans, right? Well, Ellen said to me, 'I'm sorry for your loss, but I can't think about them.' That included you, *querida*."

She pushed away from the desk, dropped her face into her hands. "They know she died and won't come back at all? I haven't seen Finnegan since he dropped me after the transplant and I wouldn't know *her* if I passed her on the street, but I thought…"

Bautista started talking again, discussing Luz's stock—decades ago she'd acquired shares of an energy conservation start-up that was now a leader in high-efficiency fuel and automation, and more recently she'd bought in on a paraben-free hypoallergenic lube gel manufacturer—but eventually he stopped again, because Sofia wasn't paying attention.

He set a box of tissues in front of her, but that was as far as she'd milk this sympathy thing. When she wiped her face and got up to find a wastebasket, he saw a glimpse of scar tissue exposed by the gaping neckline of the shirt.

Aw, hell.

Life was hard, but that wasn't his lesson to teach, because she already knew. A surgeon had taken out her heart and put in a donor's, and that was how she lived to stand here in his office and remind him of his woman.

"This is yours, too, Sofia," he said simply, taking something from a desk drawer, placing it in her palm, and wrapping her fingers around it.

She nodded, but gasped when she opened her hand. A colorless diamond on a gold band. "A ring? You and Luz were *engaged*?"

"When I last saw her, the morning she died, she had this on her finger." When she'd pulled his hair, touched his body, and later flown into a cussing tirade about coffee beans, the ring had been in place. "She wasn't wearing it when she died. It was in her purse. She didn't want this. I thought she did. So what I told you before is true. She was my life, and I was just her lawyer."

"I can't take this."

"Sell it, give it to charity. Just take it."

Unlike Caro, who'd put up a tireless fight when he'd tried to walk away from the bar, Sofia raised no argument and slipped the ring into her purse.

"I'm sorry."

He nodded but didn't tell her the words mattered not at all. They finished quickly after that and he carried the trunk to the lobby, where a couple of suits surrounding a self-serve espresso bar ogled a woman lounging on a sofa browsing a magazine.

Whether she was oblivious to the attention or basking in it, he couldn't tell.

She closed the magazine, and when she popped up, something magical happened. Her blond curls bounced in unison with the jiggle of her lush, full tits. "All set, Sof?"

Closer now, he recognized her from the funeral.

"This is my roomie, Joss," Sofia introduced her. "Joss, you remember Bautista."

Joss automatically stretched out her hand for a shake, but seeing that his arms were full, she instead squeezed his biceps and smiled. "You saved a woman and her dog from a night of homelessness. Thanks."

She was as far from Luz as a woman could be. Luz was sixty and Joss might not be even half of that, but the contrast wasn't about age. Luz was friendly yet savvy and stoic; Joss was...careless.

Alluring as all hell.

He needed to ride, get his mind right again, maybe take a breather from his practice and check in with the club, who'd called him home to the circle when they'd heard about Luz's death.

"What's New York doing for you?" he asked Joss when she didn't seem to be in a hurry to release him.

"I'm a chef's assistant. I bake."

"She's an artist," Sofia added as they exited the building and met the sunshine that taunted his budding headache. "She made a replica of Monet's *Bridge Over a Pond of Water Lilies* with cupcakes."

"Impressive," he said, "but it sounds safe."

Joss frowned. "What credentials do you have that'd make your opinion at all important? *Bridge Over a Pond of Water*

Lilies wasn't safe. It was tedious and the art museum thought it was awesome and I'm proud of it. It's in my book."

"Portfolio," Sofia provided. "There's my car."

Bautista put the trunk in and caught a faint whiff of Tish. "Where's the dog? You said you'd lost her but found her, so where is she now?"

"At the photography studio over the bar. Caro and her kid are having a last hurrah with Tish before we take off."

Joss still looked offended. "I don't think I like you all that much, Bautista."

Whoa. Point-blank honesty. She didn't pull back. That shouldn't compel him to crack a smile through the hell inside him, but it did. "You're in the majority. Good luck with your cupcakes."

"Good luck being a dick."

"Joss!" Sofia pointed to the passenger side. "Let's get the dog and go."

The blonde strutted around him to get in the SUV. When she glanced back he saw darkness in her blue eyes that had nothing to do with shadow. It intrigued, lured him close, but she slammed the door.

Another slamming door. This one was a reminder that things could go south real quick if he wasn't careful, and even though Luz had taken off his ring and "Fuck you" had been the last words she'd said to him, he needed to let himself grieve before moving on to his next mistake.

"Thanks, Bautista, for handling the arrangements," Sofia said. "Joss is…well, she can be defensive about her career. Accusing her of playing things safe, it stabs a nerve."

"What will you do with Luz's life?"

"Don't know yet. I go back to work on Tuesday and maybe things will start to make sense again," she said, and got into her car.

Bautista was heading into the East Millennium Tower when he saw the SUV join traffic on the street. Getting a final look at Sofia Mercer, seeing the woman Luz had raised and loved like a daughter, he muttered, "*Mi corazón*, if your girl ever comes back, I'll look after her. I'll do that for you."

CHAPTER 7

*N*ew York was supposed to make sense. It was Friday again, a full week after the funeral—no, Sofia realized, squinting at the glowing white digits on her bedside clock, it was technically Saturday—but she was still struggling. Flailing. Falling to pieces.

She tried to sit up. An anvil pinned her legs. *Tish.* Harboring an unauthorized pet was a daily roll of the dice, but couldn't the dog at least show some gratitude by staying on her own side of the bed? It was as if Tish held her down nightly, lying on Sofia's legs or her stomach or her hair, as she had that first night in the apartment in Eaves, in an effort to stop her from going away.

The way Luz had gone away. Intelligent Tish may be— she didn't bark and expose Sofia and Joss for the rule-breaking tenants they were—but some things even she couldn't understand.

"You're bad for my circulation," she mumbled to the dog, going to extremes to slide one leg and then the other out from beneath the coverlet. The struggle caused her joggers to twist around her ass and her undies to wedge between her cheeks.

Making adjustments, she padded to the door. She hoped a middle-of-the-night pee and a glass of water would help her get back to sleep. Ever since her return to the city she'd felt strange, and she had a suspicion her colleagues figured she'd gone to Cape Cod and been replaced with a pod person.

At Manhattan Greetings brainstorming sessions, she'd been preoccupied pondering what exactly made a paraben-free hypoallergenic personal lubricant so attractive that her great-aunt had been compelled to buy stock. During presentations her mind wandered and she found herself doodling a boutique with shake-shingle siding and fancy lettering on the storefront. Among the handful of staff who got together once a month to hang out over pizza, beer, and porn, she'd picked at her food and daydreamed through the flick as everyone else chatted and joked around. That night she'd come home, escaped to the shower, and cupped her breasts, imagining Burke Wolf touching her there.

Which was why she'd accepted a coffee shop date with a guy she met on a subway platform. Nathan Swanson seemed nice enough—sweet, even—and carried around a cello as if it weighed nothing. If things went well, they would kiss. If things went *really* well, that kiss would erase Burke's and she could quit reliving the taste of him and obsessing about all the might-have-beens that weren't meant to be.

She needed this weekend to clear away the confusion. Her job was suffering because she was distracted by an inheritance she didn't deserve but had likely earned by default. Aunt Luz had no one else to bestow her life upon, that's all. Sofia's grandparents had died from cancer only months apart when their daughter, Ellen, was still a girl. Barely an adult herself, Luz had picked up where they'd left off, taking on the role of parent and friend to her niece. And when Ellen had gotten pregnant and married Finnegan Mercer and then abandoned them both practically the minute the umbilical cord was severed, Luz had stepped in once again, helping to raise Sofia.

And Sofia had repaid that kindness by starting over in New York and leaving all of Eaves, her great-aunt included, deep in the past.

No, she didn't deserve Luz's business and stocks and Siberian husky.

But she had it all anyway. Soon Bautista would need answers and she'd have to make decisions that she couldn't undo in the future.

God, she'd never get back to sleep when all she wanted to do now was open Aunt Luz's trunk and pore over every document inside.

Tish started to stretch, and Sofia thought the dog might get up and follow her to the bathroom, but Tish twisted her massive furry body and now lay in the exact spot Sofia had just vacated.

"Nice, Tish. Just nice." She tiptoed to the toilet, not wanting to disturb her roomie in case she'd already returned from her date and was asleep. Joss might be the world's lightest— possibly most paranoid—sleeper. The paranoia was something she couldn't be persuaded to discuss, and Sofia accepted that, even though on any given night Joss could slip out of her room with a weapon ranging from a lamp to a stiletto and then mumble the same explanation: "Oh, sorry, I thought you were somebody else."

Leaving the bathroom as quietly as she had approached, she went to the kitchen, filled a glass with ice, and poured a bottle of Evian over it. Expensive water wasn't a part of her normal diet—neither was pizza, since she would monitor her cholesterol and glucose levels for the rest of her new life—but she'd taken home leftovers from pizza-and-porn night and Joss hadn't been around to demolish the freebies.

She slowly backed herself up against the nearest wall and touched the glass to her neck. Hard to imagine being kissed in this kitchen. It was too immaculate, though before last week she'd considered that something to brag about.

No one would press her against this wall or toss a condom onto that table. This was a kitchen made for entertaining friends with Joss-prepared appetizers and Sofia-mixed cocktails before outings to Broadway shows or late-night concerts. It was her roommate's creative space whenever she got her confidence up enough to attempt recipes that might break her out as more than just a chef's assistant.

Sofia wanted more for herself, and for Joss. For the first time since they'd been pulled from a waitlist for this building, she was less than satisfied with the home she'd made here.

Grief. That had to be the reason she was so disconnected. It didn't help that the guy who'd been her closest friend and the love of her teenage life had stunned her with a kiss and then confused her with asshole behavior.

"Step one foot in here and I will cut you, God damn it, I swear I will!"

Sofia lunged out of the kitchen to see Joss flinging herself into the apartment and trying her damnedest to shut the door on the male arm poking through.

"Stop being so dramatic," a man shouted. "Damn it, Joss!"

"What the hell?" Sofia ran to the door as Peter Bernard burst through and Joss started slapping him with her handbag. "Joss! What's going on?"

"Call the police. Have them carry out this creep in hand-cuffs. I'll Instagram the shit out of the whole thing." She jumped onto a leather chair and sobbed.

"What happened?" Sofia demanded, noting Peter's di-sheveled hair and rumpled clothes. "What did you do to her?"

"I didn't touch her."

Joss's head popped up. "Oh, but you touched someone, didn't you? We were at your parents' social. How disgusting can you be?" She turned to Sofia. "The second I went to the ladies' room, he got balls-deep in one of the caterers."

Oh, no. "Get out, Peter."

"Not until Joss stops acting like a bitch and talks to me."

"Get out," Sofia said again.

"I have nothing else to say to you!" Joss screamed. "You cheated on me, and you humiliated me."

"Leave. Now." Sofia intervened in the calmest voice she could manage. "Or I will get the cops out here."

"Hey, this isn't your business," he barked, grabbing her arm and causing the ice water to rise up like an angry wave and crash over the front of her.

"That's it," Joss announced. "I'm calling."

Peter dropped Sofia's arm and backed away, palms out. "I—I didn't mean to do that. I'm sorry. Joss, come on, you know I never mean it. This thing with Emily, it's over now. I swear to you."

Joss's response was to brandish her cell phone and start dialing.

"I fucked up. I made a mistake," he allowed, going to the door. Sofia put herself in front of Joss, shielding her, but his glare pierced her straight through. "But I'm not going to apologize again, Joss. Cut me off and you'll be cutting off the connections and the money and the gifts. You're just an-other Emily—nothing special."

He left, banging the door shut with angry force that disturbed the wall art.

Visibly rattled, Joss rushed to the door and locked it after him. "Sofia, I'm sorry. He had no right to put his hands on you."

"He's got no right to put his hands on you, either. I heard him when he said he 'never' means it. Joss, you're stronger than this."

"That's the thing, though. I'm not. The connections are . . . they're everything in my industry. The woman he was with probably opened herself not because he's a prince in stockbroker's clothing, but because he's just an opportunity or some friggin' bridge to better opportunities. The sex isn't all that great. He's too fast."

"Or too rough? And I don't mean just sex. He grabbed me and he wouldn't leave when we told him to. Call the cops. I want to report this."

"Wait. I can't do that—call and report him."

"Give me the phone, then. I'll do it."

"Please don't, Sof."

Sofia's throat tightened as all sorts of warning bells chimed. "Why not? Don't let him abuse you."

"He will take away every good thing that's happened to me. He has the money and the ability to do it. You know that."

"If you buckle, he'll win. He cheated on you. He hurts you. Don't let him win."

Joss handed over a blanket and Sofia dabbed it to her dripping face and soaked T-shirt, then dropped it to the floor and began to mop up the mess.

"If he takes away my contacts and opportunities, I lose. This is New York. No matter how many times I bite into the Big Apple, I always end up with a mouthful of worm. I can't get ahead without using someone and letting him use me. That's just what my reality is. In this city you can throw a rock and hit somebody trying to turn a cupcake into a profitable business or a few good recipes into a legit career. I'm…I'm just another Emily."

"What if New York isn't the apple you're meant to bite, Joss?"

Her friend sat down again, sniffling softly. "Huh?"

"Manhattanites aren't the only ones who enjoy a good pastry."

Joss shook her head. "If this has anything to do with the baggage your aunt dumped on you, I'm not interested. It's bad enough we're violating our rental agreement by hiding Tish here."

"I have a store and a home out there."

"Listen to yourself, Sofia! *This* is your home."

"It's not," she blurted before she even realized what she was saying. "It never truly was. Manhattan Greetings is fun and crazy and wonderful, but it isn't a career—not the one I want. It's just a job. This apartment is just a place to sleep. I've hung a grand total of zero pictures on the walls. Yes, I counted."

"You're confused."

"You came home pissed that Peter cheated on you and the moment he reminded you that he can buy and sell you, you spun a one-eighty—and *I'm* the one who's confused?"

"Peter and I are in a relationship."

"Abuse is what turns a relationship into a crisis. He's hurt you before. You don't have to admit it, but I'm your friend and I love you and the next time I see him I only hope Tish is around to use his cock as a chew toy."

Joss shut down, withdrawing from the conversation and from Sofia's concern. "I'm not going to drop everything I've built here just because you went to Cape Cod for a funeral and got hit with a little nostalgia."

"Okay." With that word, Sofia felt them pull apart and their friendship all but snap under duress. "I'm going to do it, though."

"Sofia."

"I have to." She pushed her damp hair out of her eyes. "I have to try to use the tools Luz left me before I liquidate."

"Liquidate now and start the business you want to run. Fashion and accessories. That's your dream, isn't it? Be smart about this. Yeah, you worked at Blush once upon a time, but would you be fine with immersing yourself in erotic retail?"

"I have to try," she repeated.

"What do you know about kink?"

"Enough." Not from personal experience, but what did that detail really matter now? "Porn night featured wax play."

Joss's sharp ring of laughter was startling. "God. That's like saying you can become a surgeon just because you watched someone play a game of Operation."

"There's a successful business, lucrative stocks, and an apartment in Eaves. They belong to me."

"You were like a broken record for so long. 'I'll never go back.' What changed?"

"I went back. I came home," she whispered, and she began to shake because it was so startlingly clear. Eaves was her home, though she had no family left. Her past was ingrained in the sand and sidewalk, her memory on the lips of people who still lived there. She wouldn't be anonymous there, but perhaps now she was strong enough to appreciate that. "Maybe it won't pan out. I might fail."

"You won't fail. You're too stubborn to fail." Joss came

over and folded her into a perfumed hug. "I'm going to miss you."

"So that's an official no, you won't come with me?"

"It's an official no. I don't have a rich aunt or a hefty financial cushion. I have a stand mixer and some talent and a man who's going to open doors for me if I'm patient enough." Joss's phone began to chirp before she stopped speaking. She went totally still. "That'd be Peter," she said, the words bundled in uncertainty.

"Guess what? I'm not leaving New York if you're still bothering with that guy."

"Then I won't bother with him."

Sofia leaned back. "Seriously? Just like that."

"Yeah." She shrugged and ignored the call. "I'm not going to stand in the way of your doing what's vital to you. Go to Eaves and make us proud."

"Us?"

"Luz and me. I'm gonna go to bed." Joss started toward the hall but turned. Her mouth tightened, then after a moment relaxed into a wistful smile. "Good-bye, Sofia."

"Good night, you mean?"

"Uh-uh. Good-bye. I won't want to say it when it's actually time for you and that canine beast of yours to go."

Alone in the quiet, Sofia exhaled. She could change her mind. It wasn't as if she'd packed or made arrangements or told a soul other than Joss what she was contemplating.

She could stay put and continue the fight she'd begun when her father had left her here with a freshly transplanted heart.

Or she could go home again.

* * *

"Suppertime, men!"

Burke cursed, profane words marching out one after the next like railcars. He stilled the handsaw and slung off his goggles. "Abe, you and the wifey seem to want this extension built before next summer, so how about letting us work?"

Abram Slattery tugged off a pair of work gloves and stuffed them into a back pocket as he trekked to where the guys had set up sawhorses and stacks of lumber. Orange extension cords snaked through the grass. Frames had yet to be raised and attached. Cigarette stubs and flattened beer cans filled the wastebasket swiped from Hannah Slattery's pretty little powder room. The yard might resemble a war zone more than a worksite now, but the added square footage—a nursery for the twins baking in Hannah's oven, and a craft room for the mama-to-be—would be finished with care.

If all the interruptions ceased for just one damn day. Car after car contained at least one woman who'd poke her head out the window and stare at the spectacle. One claimed she was lost and needed directions. Another brought a six-pack and in return got Burke's solemn promise that he'd give her a call. He wasn't all that interested, but she had a sense of humor he liked and the other guys had all but threatened to clobber him if he didn't secure the beer for them.

Burke was on a vacation of sorts for the next several weeks, but time on his boat was precious and he wasn't cutting into that time just to piss away the day at someone else's house. Abram had recruited a half dozen men to help realize his wish to give his wife a haven—and in the process make up for whatever transgression had nearly busted up his marriage not too long ago. Burke had joined the fray because Hannah was kind of extraordinary, if unrelentingly nosy, and he figured anyone who was as tiny as she and actually happy about the idea of pushing out two babies deserved a reward. And though Abram hadn't said it before and likely never would, Burke owed him.

Abram, who'd helped his younger brother, McGuinty, detox in high school, had stepped in as Burke's sponsor after his previous attempts at rehab and sobriety had failed violently. Once Burke had hooked up with a port, he'd left Eaves, but Abram's line was always open.

That didn't mean Burke would spend the summer hanging out at the side of the Slatterys' house and playing eye candy for women with a sweet tooth to satisfy.

"The sun's gonna drop soon. Besides, we're moving at a good pace," Abram said. The other guys had taken "Suppertime, men," as a cue to strip off safety gear and were heading inside to start tracking dirt on the floors and filling the air with the stench of sweat and cigarette smoke.

"The walls aren't finished." Burke glanced at his forearm, where a yellow jacket had pierced him deep. "A big rain's gonna hit in the next few days, so where do you want to be in this project when that happens? You call this a good pace, but if we keep getting visits from hot women carrying cold beer, you're gonna need to have your twins pitch in to get this done."

"Fuck, you're in a bad mood." Abram whistled. "Well, then you'll thank me for this warning. Hannah's gone ahead and invited a friend over for dinner. A single friend, on the rebound."

"Please tell me the friend's for McGuinty or somebody else."

"Nah, you're in the hot seat. Hannah's worried about you. She says it's not natural for a grown-ass man to live out of a boat with nobody at home who cares about him."

"She said that? Nobody who cares about me?"

"She said *companionship*, but that word makes me friggin' itchy. I told her you get plenty of pussy all on your own, and she said if I ever said that to her again, I wouldn't get any until our kids went off to college."

"So you pushed me under the bus for tail?"

"Hell, yes." Abram shrugged. "The friend's easy on the eyes. She's kind of new, used to work at that sex shop across from the laundromat. She's pulling a check from the cottages for the season."

For the season meant through the summer, which meant she might be temporary. "And she has no plans to stick around?"

"Doesn't appear that way, but you know Hannah. She thinks she's an ambassador for Eaves and it's her mission to have folks put down their stakes here." The man squinted. "Hey, you gonna put something on that sting? It's not looking all that pretty."

"It's fine." It annoyed more than it actually hurt. "What's the friend's name?"

"Peggy or Petra or something like that. You interested?"

"In sitting at your table and having everybody watch us knowing good and damn well it's one of your wife's matchmaking experiments? Not really." Burke laid down the saw. "So thank Hannah for giving it a shot, but I'm not sticking around for that."

Abram chuckled. "Ahead of you there. I tried to tell Hannah you'd pass this up, but she wasn't hearing it. I'll have her wrap a plate for you to take to the boat. Freezer shit's convenient, but something home-cooked now and then is good for a man."

"If you're about to try to sell the perks of marriage, take your pitch somewhere else. I'm not in the market for a wife."

"Not at all. Just letting you know mine whipped up a

damn tasty roast with potatoes and she's gonna wrap a plate. Grab it before you make your Houdini escape."

Left alone, Burke neatened his workspace and brushed dust and slivers of wood off his T-shirt. Eventually the addition would be complete and it'd look good. When Abram had approached him asking for a pair of hands, he'd had a glint of real excitement in his eyes—the look of a man passionate about a dream. A nursery for his kids and a craft room for his wife weren't extravagant things, but listening to the guy ramble on about the project, you'd think he was making plans to give her a piece of heaven itself.

He couldn't imagine wanting to bring somebody that kind of happiness, investing all of himself in a relationship, building any kind of life for a family of his own.

The house was noisy and already glowing bright even though the sun hadn't begun its quiet departure. This was permanence, and it wasn't for him. The closest to permanent that he could allow was the two-grand-a-month slip he'd leased at the Eaves Marina.

His boat, *Colossians 1:14*, which he'd named for his mother's favorite Bible verse, wasn't a home. It was the only possession that mattered. He lent it his labor and his heart, and he trusted it more than he'd let himself trust any friend, advisor, or lover. The vessel was the only family he had left, and the only connection to his mother, who'd folded from complications of chicken pox—a virus Burke had brought home from kindergarten the same way he'd brought a worm from the playground that he hoped to keep forever or a drawing he'd colored and was so proud of.

In whom we have redemption, the forgiveness of sins.

She must've known how her son would turn out...who he'd become. He was sin and destruction, and redemption was a dream. Kind of like these new walls, yet they were part of a dream that stood to be accomplished eventually.

He entered the house through the mudroom, ready to stomp the dirt from his work boots on the mat, but came to a sharp stop when he saw Abram and Hannah pressed together with a tipped-over laundry basket at their feet and nothing between them but her round belly.

"Oh—sorry, bro," Abram said, setting his wife aside as pink filled her pale cheeks. "She was giving me a clean shirt. I sweated through the other."

"No explanation necessary," Burke told them. "It's your house. I'm just going to grab my plate and cut out of here."

"Stay, Burke. Grab a chair and eat with all of us, please?" Hannah said in a sweet-as-syrup tone that'd probably persuaded legions of men to change their minds.

"No," he said. Tiny word, *no*. But dressed in the right tone—firm, nonnegotiable—it was profoundly effective.

Hannah squeaked and looked to her husband, who only shook his head and somehow caught the shirt she suddenly yanked from the knocked-over basket and tried to fling at him.

"What are the odds that she'll spit on my roast or salt the ever-loving fuck out of my helping of the potatoes?" Burke asked as she marched out of the mudroom.

Abram slugged him on the shoulder, laughing. "She'd never sabotage you like that. The bad press might take a star from the restaurant, and that'd *really* get her hackles up."

Hannah was an internationally trained chef, and ran an upscale place where Burke's worn plaid shirts and skull caps weren't welcome.

"I had to ask. Weren't you the one who told me she threatened to withhold sex from you for the next eighteen years? How am I supposed to know what she's capable of?"

"Oh, yeah?" Hannah had appeared at his side carrying a platter piled generously with roast, potatoes, a thick dinner roll, and macaroni and cheese—damn, how could Abram call himself a friend and not mention there'd be mac and cheese? "I'm capable of sending your plate home with my friend. She's polite and sincere, and at least she'll appreciate my intentions."

Shit. Now he'd lost his right to homemade mac and cheese—with the crumbly crust on top, too. "I didn't mean to piss you off."

"But you did. Both of you."

"Fine. I'm going to take off and think of appropriate penance. There's a silver lining here, though. Your friend won't waste her time on a man who's impolite and insincere."

"Know what your problem is, Burke?"

"That plate in your hand's gonna get nice and cold if you mean to stand here and run down all my problems."

"I was only going to say you try too hard to be an abrasive bastard." With nothing more to add, she bristled when her husband tried to soothe her and then marched away again.

Burke turned around on the mat. "Sorry, Abe."

"She'll forget about it. That's her way."

"Glad to hear it. But she's mistaken about one thing. I don't try too hard. Being an abrasive bastard comes real damn easy for me."

On his boat he showered and then rummaged for food. He had a Hungry-Man rotating in the microwave, half-done, when he stopped the timer and trashed the tray. He considered calling the ginger who'd brought the six-pack to the Slatterys' but wasn't in the mood to figure out somebody new. Identifying a woman's motives—from the questions she asked to the way she touched him as they fucked—was ordinarily as thrilling of a high as anything else. Tonight, though, he wasn't in the frame of mind to play.

The fish-and-chips joint downtown was the exact definition of a dive, and Burke fit seamlessly into the milieu when he straddled a chair at a table near the pickup counter and nursed a ginger ale while he waited for the waitress to put through his shrimp and slaw basket order.

"It'll be a minute," she warned him, tossing her gaze from one end of the packed place to the other. "Summer crowd."

"Tourists gotta eat, too," he said neutrally. This place offered damn decent seafood at prices that were easy on the wallet, but it was standing room only most nights, since the owners had extracted seating and replaced it with a jukebox and plenty of floor space to dance.

There were places to dance in Eaves, but church basements, family-friendly halls, and the glass-walled ballroom studio weren't where people ended up when they wanted to grind. Grinding dirty in a dive with fish in the air wasn't ideal, either, but Burke knew better than most that everything in life demanded sacrifice.

So he wasn't particularly empathetic that couples dry-humping their way to a hookup might be inconvenienced by the scent of fried fish on their hair or would have to squeeze into the underground bar on Society Street for a no-hassle good time in a place that had cleaner air but no room to gyrate.

He flipped over the paper place mat in front of him and grabbed a pencil from the Solo cup that held "Rate Our Service" tickets. He began a maintenance list for the boat—living aboard, even practically, meant constant repair—but for no clear reason he stopped tuning out the racket around him and put down the pencil.

"Just because you offered me a fish fillet doesn't mean I'm obligated to eat it," someone complained.

Swinging up his drink, he looked through the dancing, laughing, good-timing patrons toward the pickup counter.

The bottle almost slipped out of his grasp. What the hell was she doing here?

Word was Sofia Mercer had turned right back around to New York the day after her aunt's funeral. That'd been a few weeks ago—Memorial Day weekend—and since then he'd worked damned hard to forget the impact of their crazy, destructive encounter in Luz's apartment.

He hadn't tripped out since McGuinty had scored some fucked-up hallucinogens in high school and one of their buddies had almost flung himself off a plank bridge. So the woman stirring up a scene wasn't a creation of a drug.

Wrapped in tight jeans, drenched in some silky little high-necked, short-sleeved shirt, she was real.

And oblivious to everything but the crisis on her hands.

"I ordered a chicken fillet sandwich. Grilled. I don't want fried cod."

"Are you allergic to seafood?" a cook on the other side of the counter asked.

"I prefer not to eat it. Why didn't anyone let me know you were out of chicken? My number's on the order."

"Sorry about that. As you can see, we've got a full house tonight," the cook hollered out over the crash of music and the sizzle of frying food. "Fifty-minute wait on the chicken, or you can get a full refund. But seafood's kind of a thing on the Cape. You did call a fish-and-chips restaurant."

"Grilled chicken sandwiches are on the menu. People say they're the best around."

"Experiment a little. Would that kill you?"

"I'm not allergic, but if I ignore my diet in the name of experimentation and start eating copious amounts of greasy fried foods, then yeah, it will kill me."

The cook planted his hands on the counter. "Hey, look, princess—" Another man tapped him on the shoulder, said something while gesturing up and down his sternum, and then the cook took on a pained expression and went to the register. "Ah, jeez, I'm sorry. I didn't know. Here's your refund. The grilled chicken order's on the house and we'll even have it run out to you, but it's still on a fifty-minute wait."

Burke didn't have to work too hard to guess what the other guy had told the cook, and judging by the self-consciousness that took over her body language, neither did Sofia.

"Fine, okay. I'm at Blush on Society. The sign says closed, so just knock." She squeezed her way out of the restaurant.

Fifty minutes was ample time to collect groceries and fix a multicourse dinner with trimmings from scratch. Maybe not that, but if he were in her position he wouldn't put off a hungry stomach for the promise of a sandwich nearly an hour past its original wait time simply because it was free.

Burke relinquished his table and went to the counter to cancel her chicken sandwich and his shrimp basket—making this his third failed attempt at dinner tonight. When he pointed his truck toward the market and thought up the ingredients he'd bring to Sofia's door, he told himself he was being practical.

Not at all dangerous.

CHAPTER 8

For the first time since Luz's death, the sex shop's lights burned.

- BLUSH -
LINGERIE & EROTIC VICES

But something else was different, too. Was it the naughty gold letters across the windows? The displays against smoky black backdrops had changed. Gold mannequins, all but one naked as the day they were assembled, lounged over a velvet chair, posed so that their hands covered each other's genitals. The clothed mannequin was propped on the chair dressed in a fuzzy white robe that gaped open, revealing a line of fiber-glass flesh. The scene looked like...

An orgy.

On the other side of the door, a line of similar man-nequins with their backs to the street wore pale panties accented with bows at the ass crack and appeared to be linked together by a long shimmery scarf loosely looped around their bodies.

Holy hell. In the past the place hadn't been permitted to flaunt X-rated images within street view. In an effort to be fair, Burke supposed the window displays weren't straight-up X-rated, but they were suggestive if not deliberately sexual. He had a mind as deep in the gutter as the next man's, but he wasn't so perverted that he walked around seeing orgies where there were none.

Sofia had done this? The possibility was like a woman's tongue down his body—hot, naughty, unbelievably sexy.

And something he had no business thinking about. His truck was angle parked at the end of the block and if he had a sudden attack of nice guy's remorse he could leave the groceries in front of the door, knock, and take off.

The thing about that was he hadn't driven to the grocery store and brought the food here to be nice. Guilt over the way he'd left things with her the night of the funeral was wearing him down, and he wanted to know why she was back and filling her aunt's store windows with mannequins that'd put the town council in a panic.

The fading sunlight drew slanting shadows on his T-shirt as he tucked a loaded paper bag to one side, spun his baseball cap backward, and then knocked on the door.

Through the door he watched her appear from the rear of the store and navigate around product displays and clothing racks. Only when she was directly on the other side of the door did she recognize him behind his sunglasses.

"*Burke.*" He liked that, the shape her lips took on when she said his name.

She opened the door. "What—Um, why are you here?"

"I brought you something to eat."

"Why?"

"Can I come in and tell you all about it?"

Her face twisted in a frown. "Tell me now, because the way you talked to me the last time we were together is still fresh and I'm not sure I want you to come in."

"I was at the fish-and-chips place. Couldn't see any point in letting you wait another hour for a sandwich, so I canceled my order and yours."

"Oh? How very high-handed of you."

He put out his hand so she could read his watch. "See that? Food to your door a half hour early."

"It wasn't as if I was sitting in this boutique twiddling my thumbs. I'm meeting one of Luz's employees later and then I'll be up all night reviewing the books. So you're not coming to my rescue, Burke."

"That wasn't my intent. I can turn around and give this bag to the next person who walks by, if that's what you want."

Sofia appeared to waffle, drawing back to shut the door before she flung it wide and reached for him. "Wait, Burke. Can we not do this? Can we not be like this?"

"I don't know how to be anything else, Sofia."

A resigned sigh gusted from that pink, glossy mouth. He wanted to swallow that sigh, breathe her air, surround himself with the miracle it was that she was alive to stand in front of him glaring cautiously.

"No arguing tonight," she said. "Let's agree on that, and you can come in. I want food."

"Your call."

"It's not, though, is it?" Once he stepped inside she shut the door and engaged the locks. "You kicked addiction by being persistent, and you were going to manipulate me into letting you in by the same means."

He came to a stop. "Want me out? Say 'Get the hell out' and I'm gone."

She raised her eyebrows, as though he'd called her out on a dare. She advanced on him, her chin tipped up. "Get the—" Drifting toward him, she all but stuck her nose in his neck, sniffed around, and then sighed. "You can stay."

If she came any closer, they'd be touching and he'd have to drop the grocery bag and fill his arms with her. "What changed your mind, Sofia?"

"You. You smell so fucking good."

Neither expected that. Her eyes turned into saucers and she awkwardly wrested the bag from him. "Um...Anyway. C'mon in back. There's a kitchenette. Small space, but I don't want to go upstairs and rile up Tish."

So they weren't going to examine that *You smell so fucking good*?

Burke didn't press, just hooked his sunglasses onto his shirt and followed—more than a little intrigued. He'd never breached Blush's entrance. His father and his cronies had laughed and leered about the place, but Burke's block would've been knocked clean off his shoulders if he'd been caught sneaking in underage. By the time he was old enough to legally enter Luz Azcárraga's "porn palace," he hadn't wanted to buy his rubbers there because it would hurt Sofia to know what he was doing with someone else. He hadn't wanted to break what was left of her heart.

Now he let her lead him past racks of lingerie and tables of stripper shoes to a separate section of the store. They were no longer in the land of pink wallpaper, oversize chairs, aphrodisiacs, and a fancy hotel-esque atmosphere.

All around them were windowless walls, gray with a silver damask pattern. There was shelf after shelf of pornography DVDs and books, vibrators, strap-ons, lube, bondage accessories, dolls, games, costumes, novelty items—

"Candles categorized under kink?" he asked, picking up a taper.

"For wax play."

What?

"You know, melting a candle down and pouring it on someone's body. People tend to assume it's a Dom/sub interest, but anyone can enjoy it. These candles are paraffin, so they're quite safe and don't contain irritants that you'd encounter with dyed or fragranced ones." She shook her head at his continued dismay. "Wax play's a powerful stimulant, really wakes up the nerves, and it can create some amazing art. You were an artist. So imagine if it were you and me. We'd get a few candles in different colors, and as the artist you could stay dressed as you are or however you felt most comfortable, and I'd take everything off because I'd be your canvas."

No way was this a real conversation. She had to be screwing with him.

"Sofia—"

"Wait, I didn't get to the core of this. It's about respect but especially trust, so if I were to agree to be your canvas, it would mean that I trusted you not to hurt me. You'd test the heat, then hold the candle up high enough so that the wax wouldn't burn me. By increasing the distance of the drip, you'd increase the time it had to cool before it reached my skin."

"Wouldn't it be hell to peel wax off body hair?"

"It would," she agreed, "on moderately hairy parts of the body. Depending on the person, you'd avoid certain areas. No one's sensitivity to it is the same."

"You said imagine if it were you and me."

"Oh. Okay, well, if I was untied and hadn't been whipped and I felt safe, then I'd say not on my face, on my scar, or inside me. Other than that, my entire body would be your canvas." She gestured to the candle display. "So that's an intro to wax play. Care to buy a bundle of the paraffins?"

Mirrors revealed the effect that being literally locked in a sex shop with Sofia was beginning to have on his body. She had to notice it, too, yet she stood there trying to sell him candles.

"What?" It was the most coherent word he could manage.

"I'm kidding. The boutique's not up and running, as you can see," she said in a dramatized whisper. "But you seem to be...as I can see."

Her gaze stroked his cock, and she might as well have unzipped him and reached right in, because he hardened up and couldn't disguise it.

As if guided by some silent fascination, she edged closer. She neither retreated nor pushed him away. "What brought that on?"

"Ignore it," he said. *Pleaded.*

"I can't. It means something." God, was that *hope* shimmering in her brown eyes? Did she want him this way? Aroused body. Confused mind. Weakened control. "Is this because of the merchandise...?"

"None of the tricks you've got on the shelf matter when you're looking at me like that and telling me to imagine getting you naked."

She searched his eyes, but if she saw the heat there she opted not to trust it. "We lost control of the conversation. It's my fault—sorry." She turned and ushered the grocery bag through a pair of swinging doors that almost slapped him backward.

Burke trailed after her to a utilitarian kitchen, saying nothing until she put the bag down and they were facing off with an island between them. "That was one hell of an insincere apology."

"It's all I've got. It's all you and your insincere erection deserve."

Insincere? Did she want him to prop her against this island and show her how sincerely he ached to bury himself inside her?

"Sofia, you're in my head." He jabbed his temple. "Playing around in there the way you used to. You're getting to me again."

"I got to you before? Refresh my memory, because back then you never had *this* kind of reaction to me. We didn't even kiss until...uh, until that day in the apartment." She glanced upward, swallowed. "So this is different. New."

"Yeah, it's different, and it's going in the wrong direction," he said, logic prevailing as he grasped for control. Maybe they could reclaim friendship—maybe they wouldn't get even that far. They could get hot but go nowhere. They'd dead-end or spin out.

"So let's talk about something else."

Shoving his hands into his jeans pockets to adjust, he said, "Those mannequins in the window. Did they come from the triple-X room?"

"No, from basement storage."

"Town hall call you in yet?"

"As a matter of fact, they did. It wasn't pleasant and someone gave me a card for a psychologist, because clearly my choice to change up a couple of window displays with something that better reflects the boutique means I'm cracking under grief."

What was she doing, then? Sprucing up Blush to unload it? On a corner lot on Society Street, it was prime real estate. He didn't doubt the vultures were circling, raining down business cards and pelting her with offers.

"It might not be worth the headache to battle the town all

that aggressively, if you want my take," he advised. "Compromise. Eventually both sides will get what they want."

"Well, I *did* compromise. They asked me to repaint the mannequins. Apparently the alabaster color was too explicit, but gold is fine."

He reached over to assist as she started emptying the bag. "Town hall's all right with a gold mannequin orgy and bondage?"

"It's not an orgy. It's…" She shrugged, and as he watched the heat rush to her cheeks, he felt his own heat rush in the opposite direction. "An awakening."

There was something strangely private about the way she held that word: *awakening*.

"The other scene is *playful* bondage, so you're not completely inept at interpreting erotic window displays." She smiled, then for the first time noticed what she'd unpacked. French rolls, lettuce, a plump tomato, mustard, dill pickles, and—

"That turkey's low sodium," he said, coming around to her side of the counter. "So's the cheese."

She turned those big, luminous brown eyes on him. "These are ingredients for a Sick Pickle Sub."

"It was your sandwich. You used to like it."

"I did." She reached, almost touched him in what could've become a hug, but she caught herself. "I do. Thanks."

"Since old Gordie's gone—"

"Did he pass away?" she asked, taking knives from a drawer and sheets from a roll of paper towels.

"Nah, his kids grew up and called him out to California, I heard. He didn't like me enough to name a sandwich after me, but he was all right." They assembled a matching pair of subs, then she grabbed a couple of waters from the fridge and they sat side by side on the floor in the Erotic Vices section of the shop.

Realization rang through him. "You changed a word on the front window. It used to say erotic *treasures*, not *vices*."

She nodded, sipping her water. "Yeah. Take a look at the product around us, Burke." She reached up and plucked an item from a hook above her. It looked like a stout purple dildo. "An ass plug isn't a treasure. It's an orgasm enhancer."

"Plenty of people might treasure something that enhances an orgasm. Isn't *vice* considered a negative thing?"

"No, not for me and not for this boutique. I'm rejecting the negative connotations and turning the word on its head, because I can."

"Getting town hall's drawers in a twist, tweaking the name of this section, it seems like unnecessary effort for Luz's place."

She put the plug back. "Burke, it's not Aunt Luz's boutique anymore. It's mine. She left it to me, along with Tish and all her other possessions."

Whoa. "You live in New York, so what're you going to do? Sell it all?"

"I'm selling none of it. It's mine, Burke, and I'm keeping it. Tish is my dog now. The apartment upstairs is my home. This is my boutique."

"Hold up, Sofia. Does inheriting something really make it yours?"

"Aunt Luz trusted me to do as I see fit with what she left me. Tish and I are still figuring each other out, but I'm getting used to her lying on me every night. And even though the apartment needs some changes to make it my own, I'm in no hurry to erase Luz."

"What about New York?"

"I quit my job there and agreed to help cover a few months' rent until my roommate can replace me."

He wasn't buying for a minute that dropping her life there to pick up where her great-aunt had left off here wasn't scaring her shitless. "Is that all you had going there—a job and rent?"

Now she picked at her sandwich. She'd eaten only half of it, while he'd demolished his and guzzled down the water without ceremony. "It's all the commitment I had, yeah."

"What about a man? Who'd you leave high and dry at the drop of Luz's will?"

"I don't have a man. But I'm figuring out what I like," she hastened to tack on. "A couple of weeks ago I went out with a cellist. He had great muscles from carrying around his big instrument."

Burke snorted. "Sofia, what's going on in that filthy mind of yours? You comparing my instrument to his when you haven't even seen mine?"

"I'm saying I have a nice, well-rounded life. Sooner or later I'll settle down with a guy who's nice and well rounded and stable."

"I thought you had that already." A second floated by before he realized he'd spoken aloud. He found her studying him, puzzled.

"What do you mean?"

"Over the years...I, uh, I thought about you once or twice." A dozen times. Hundreds. Even that might be a conservative guess. It'd been next to impossible to carve her out when she was rooted so deeply in every element of his existence. "I didn't ask Luz. I put a picture together of you with some good guy."

"A good guy?"

"Somebody who'd keep you safe. Somebody who didn't make you cry—who got you to laugh or at least smile. You've got a crooked smile. And I, uh, I figured that good guy would get to see your smile every night. I've hated him for years."

"You've been hating someone who doesn't exist." There was her familiar, sweet smile, peeking out of hiding for him. "I dated. I have exes—*lots* of exes. But a good guy didn't come along, Burke."

"What about your cellist?"

She hesitated, and her smile disappeared. The brightness between them dimmed. It was as if a jealous cloud had obscured the sun. "He's nice. Uncomplicated. He took my mind off you."

"Were you thinking about him when you told me to imagine pouring wax on your naked body?"

She started to get up and he thought she might stomp off in a fit. But she put her sandwich on a paper towel and set it aside, then crawled in front of him. "He kissed me, after our date."

"Okay. Did you want more?"

"What?"

"When he kissed you, did you want more?"

Defiance slid across her eyes, then uncertainty and regret in quick succession. "I don't remember."

"Then he didn't do it right. He didn't kiss you right. If he had, you'd remember what you felt and what you wanted, and for damn sure you wouldn't be alone in this place with me." And the dumbass that he was, Burke spread out his legs and folded his hands on her arms to draw her closer. "C'mere and let me show you."

"You're not going to kiss me."

"You already know what to say to get me to back off.

Don't forget, though, the last time you thought about telling me to leave, you said I smell *so fucking good*." He barely touched her now. "But if you want me to walk, I will."

Sofia's tempting lips slid against each other like two lush, slick bodies. "I taste like mustard."

"So do I. It was a good sandwich." He leaned forward, not kissing her but coasting his hand down the line of her back to grab her ass. "Put your hands on me, baby."

"I'm not your baby. I'm not yours."

"You will be." It was neither a request nor a threat. It was fact—naked, bold, and yet vulnerable. "When I touch you and all you care about is how my mouth and hands are making you feel? You're mine."

A squeeze of his hand and she planted her palms on his shoulders and seemed to collapse into him, her mouth settling on his.

Finding Sofia's flavor beneath the spice of mustard and the tang of dill was a game for his tongue. They were tangled, with her kneeling between his thighs and his hands working into the silk of her hair.

"If I'm kissing you right, you should want me to lift your hair and lick down your neck," he said. "You want that?"

"Yeah."

He complied, stopping at the high collar of her tank top. "If I'm still doing this right, you should want me to taste these goose bumps on your arms. Do you?"

"I do."

He bunched her hair, giving it a firm enough tug to have her opening her eyes straight into his. "Who do you want to taste you, Sofia?"

"You."

"Who am I?"

"I know who you are, what we're doing." Her voice

teetered. She was on the edge of something and he was just as shaken to know he'd led her to that place. "You're doing it right, Burke."

"Then you'll like it if I do this?" He started at her shoulder, sampling her skin and gently abrading her with his whiskers, and worked his way down to her fingers. Taking two into his mouth, he heard her moan.

She was his in this moment, except it was she who had him caught. They were sitting alone in a sex shop but all he wanted was her.

"Still right?" he asked, letting her digits slide free of his heat. As her mouth returned to his, he edged his hands beneath her shirt and traveled up until two lace-covered mounds greeted him. He knuckled her nipples until they puckered to his satisfaction.

God, yes.

"If I'm working you right, Sofia, you're gonna want me to unhook this bra and taste you here." He pinched her, tugged the bra, and freed her breasts. "Say it's right."

"It is. It's right," she urged him on as he smoothed his palms over her tits. Then his thumb slipped, encountering the tight line of scar tissue in the valley. "Stop! Let me go— now."

His hands dropped immediately. What the hell had he done to trigger a one-eighty so fast that his head spun as he sat sprawled on the floor with a hard dick and hands that ached to be reunited with her body?

She crawled backward, fixing her clothes, then rubbed her scar.

The scar.

"Did I hurt you? Is it sensitive there?"

"I'm sorry if this looks like I led you on or something," she said, ignoring his questions, "but the kiss was a stupid idea. I'm not going to let you fuck me on the floor just because you brought me a sandwich."

She stood up and so did he, sweeping up his baseball cap, which had fallen off while they kissed. "Is that what the hot and cold is about? Then let me tell you I'm sorry for being harsh with you in the apartment that day."

"What if I don't believe it? Maybe you did too good a job of convincing me that you're a cruel bastard."

There was more, something she was hiding, but the truth was he'd hurt her with hateful words and he owed her the respect of a decent apology.

"It's up to you to believe me or not. I'm sorry, though. That's part of the reason I came here tonight—guilt."

"What's the other part?"

"I couldn't stay at the restaurant and go on with my night. I couldn't head back to the marina and call up a woman who came to me earlier today with nothing but sex in her eyes. I couldn't do any of that, 'cause I couldn't think past the crazy instinct or whatever it was that kept putting me right in front of you when we were kids."

"We're not kids now. We can't blame what we do on being young or on coming from wrecked homes."

"What happened to no arguing?"

Sofia picked up the remains of her sandwich. "We're not arguing, are we?"

"I'm apologizing."

She closed her eyes. "Burke, you threw the question out there—how many dinners would it take to spread my legs? I told you I went hungry, and that's true. But there were times when it would've been easier to eat."

He didn't want to know, for damn sure didn't want to let his mind go wild imagining what she might've done for a meal.

"After my dad left, I was trying to catch a break—trying to catch my breath, really. Luz wired money when I had nothing left, and that was great. But she told me to prove I could make it without her support. I wanted that, too. That's why I wrote the bucket list."

"You made a bucket list?"

"Yeah. The transplant gave me a second shot, but eventually my time's gonna run out. I started to picture what I wanted my future to look like and I figured it's not too late to accomplish stuff I'd missed out on, being sick all the time."

"What's on it? The list."

"The most important goal is to own a business. I wanted to be Luz's miniature for real. I wanted to be like her, but to do that I had to find my way without her. It was so hard when sometimes there wasn't enough money in my account for food." She started to move past him but somehow their hands brushed, then tangled, and in a moment he was holding her. It felt as right as the sun yawning awake over his boat in the morning, or the slide of his favorite cold drink down his throat. "When you implied that I screw for food... well, at least I could've gotten all *this* over with if that were true."

"Sofia, I'm listening. I'm working damn hard to understand. But I can't read your mind. Don't ask me to try."

She retreated, and even though his hands felt useless without her heat under them, he didn't reach for her again. "It's not clear? Do you think I have sex with my shirt on the entire time?"

She was throwing out dots and leaving it up to him to catch and connect them. "Are you saying you like to cover up during sex?" he asked gently. "Need the lights off? That's not strange. I've been with women who're the same way. One time it wasn't about that—she just wanted me to be in her and couldn't wait. Another had implants and was still sore. She didn't want me to touch them. It happens."

"It's not about being caught up in the moment and forgetting to take off all my clothes, and it's not that my scar's so sore that it can't be touched." She shrugged, offering a flat, contrite smile. "I'm different."

"I know."

"You don't, though." In her gaze was a plea—no, a demand. So he shut up and listened. "Burke, in high school, when kids were hooking up, testing the waters, experiencing stuff, where was I?"

"With me."

"We got together when we could, but we weren't the kind of friends who hooked up. You wouldn't allow it."

Because she was different, as she'd said.

"Sometimes I was with friends, but what about all those after-school doctor's appointments and being bounced from Boston to Providence to New York for lab tests and scans? The opportunity to experience stuff passed me by. After the transplant, the panic attacks began. I'm trying to get past that, but it hasn't happened yet." The strength in her voice broke, and she had to take a second to regroup. "No one's hung around long enough to wait for me to be ready. Now I figure that if a guy sees my ugliness, he won't be able to handle it."

It hasn't happened yet . . .

No one's hung around long enough to wait for me to be ready . . .

If a guy sees my ugliness, he won't be able to handle it . . .

Was she saying—

"Burke, I'm a virgin."

*   *   *

Sofia hadn't taken off a stitch of clothing, but she felt naked in front of Burke. Because she'd let her secret slip, and now it circled them in a teasing, predatory way that made her wish she'd shown him the door instead of rambling until she broke.

Until she freed herself.

The truth hadn't set her free at all—it'd stripped her bare. Burke had been revved and ready to uncover her, and in a way he'd accomplished that.

"You've never had sex, Sofia?"

"That's my interpretation of *virgin* in this context." She was uncomfortable—not from the conversation necessarily, but her bra was crooked and she wouldn't dare go about fixing it in front of the man who'd been set to rip it off her body.

Or maybe he wouldn't have handled her like that. She didn't know how he was with a woman, just that he was a listener and seemed...considerate.

He'd worried that he had hurt her when he touched her scar.

"What I said to you in the apartment. I didn't know I was talking to a virgin." He took a few steps back, as though preparing to flee the scene of a crime.

"You were talking to *me*, Burke. You wanted to hurt *my* feelings. So you did. What difference would it make?"

"Every difference. All the damn difference." He put out a hand to maybe stroke down her hair, but changed direction and adjusted his cap.

She called him on it. "You were about to touch me but you didn't."

One step and he was close—filling her view and all her senses completely. And yes, he did smell so fucking good. The clean, basic scent of some practical soap was nothing special, but there was a bite of citrus and it tickled and tortured her at the same time.

"What's the difference?" she asked. "What difference does it make whether I'm a virgin or a whore? What if I'm both? Would that turn you off or would you keep wanting me anyway?"

"You're not the whore in this room," he said roughly. "I have that title and I'm not sharing."

"A man who admits he's a whore—that's rare."

"I like sex, and coming back for seconds from the same person gets messy. People'd call a woman a whore or a slut or whatever might make her feel ashamed about it, but I'm not above all that just because I have a dick. If folks want to jabber, let them." Casually he patted a pocket, which held his wallet, which held a condom—maybe more than one. "I'm protected, clean, and not breaking any laws. That's good enough for me."

"Then I'm part of an endless parade of one-night stands?"

"We didn't have sex, so you're not part of the parade. The women I hook up with aren't interested in commitment. A few lie, but most agree that being clear on what we want from each other cuts down on unrealistic expectations." He looked at her closely. "Tonight we stood in this place talking about wax play. You put a mannequin orgy in the store window. You called it an awakening. Is that supposed to be *your* awakening? Like a fantasy or something?"

"I think I won't answer that."

"Be straight with me, Sofia."

"Again, what's the difference? I'd prefer to chat about my fantasies with someone who won't escape on a cargo ship at a moment's notice. I don't have to talk about this any more than I have to show you my scar."

"Who's had the honor, then? The cellist? It doesn't sound

like he's the type to escape on a cargo ship. Has he seen the scar?"

Nathan Swanson was a nice enough guy, but after their coffeehouse kiss she'd let him know there wouldn't be a second date because she was leaving New York and figured he wouldn't want the hassle of a long-distance anything. Quick, neat, no unrealistic expectations.

"Doctors have seen it. Maybe a peeping somebody in a dressing room."

"You're holding yourself back because of an imperfection?"

"It's not only that, Burke. It's the reason for it. Sex is strenuous on the heart. Organ rejection or failure in the first year can happen more often than you'd guess. I didn't want to take chances. When year one passed, I focused on surviving past year five."

Burke did touch her, finally, and she sighed. His hands felt ridiculously strong and capable. "Now it's, what, year twelve? When are you going to trust that this heart is yours?"

"It's difficult to accept that or get over it when every day I take medication and monitor my diet. Every day I'm reminded that because someone—a fourteen-year-old girl—lost her life, I get to live mine. I don't want to be careless with her heart."

"It's not hers anymore, though, Sofia. It's yours. The transplant happened so you can live *your* life."

"I hear you, Burke. I'm just not there yet, okay?"

"Am I making this worse for you?" he asked. "Because I don't want to do that. If hashing out the past and dealing with whatever's sitting here between us is harmful to your heart, then I can..."

"What, stay away?"

"It's an option." He couldn't. Physically he couldn't stay away. She'd known it when she unpacked the groceries he'd brought her and realized he remembered her favorite sandwich and had taken the care to choose heart-considerate ingredients.

Their friendship *wasn't* dead. It had been abused and brutally neglected, but it still pulsed with life.

"I'm waiting for you to tell me what to do," he said softly, releasing her. "Damn it, do I pretend you don't exist or do I keep coming to you and…"

"Kissing me?" she supplied. "We've been alone twice since the funeral, and each time you kissed me. Each time we were headed for more." She meant to cross her arms but ended up hugging herself as if to protect herself from his rejection. "I'm not sorry. I liked it."

Burke steepled his hands in an unspoken plea. "Sofia, you stopped me when I touched your scar. You said you want someone who won't leave on a ship."

"So no more kissing."

"We can't handle kissing."

Then where are we? Her arms uncurled, fell limp to her sides. She was exposed again, so desperate to let the question tumble out, but equally afraid.

Burke turned away from her, bracing his hands on the counter and dropping his head. "Sofia, kissing you is the best and worst thing I've ever done, and I don't know what to do with that."

Fourteen years ago she would've been thrilled to her toes to hear these words, to hear him admit that he felt something more than friendship and the strange dependency between them. Standing here, her skin still tingling from his exploration, she was lost.

"So we'll do nothing," she offered, settling a hand on his

back and pressing against the warm, hard muscle. "We'll co-exist. You have your work and I have Blush. Shouldn't that keep us from jumping at each other?"

"I'll find another laundromat," he said, glancing at her with a wry smile. "Ain't any sense in hanging out at The Dirty Bastards if all I'm going to do is look across the street and imagine what you're doing in here."

"You and McGuinty are still friends, then?"

"Yeah. His brother's my sponsor. Good people."

"Don't change your routine on my account. Once I re-open this place, feel free to stop in for condoms. We carry king size." She patted his back. "No need to sneak to a gas station so my feelings aren't hurt. I'm not a girl with a crush anymore."

He straightened and gestured around him. "How long do you think you'll be able to manage this store without being tempted to really test-drive your heart?"

"Running a boutique means moving product. If I get to a place where I want to test-drive my new ticker, then it'll happen. One doesn't influence the other." She started for the front room and almost smiled at the sparkle of the street outside the side window. "There are a few hurdles, but I'm doing this."

"What kind of hurdles?" he asked, close behind.

"The gloomy vacant building next door, for one. It's an eye-sore. I'd take it and expand Blush if it meant improving my street appeal." She turned, expecting an answer but finding only silence. "Sorry, I guess your father's store isn't something you want to think about. Anyway, I don't need the extra square footage. At the same time, I don't want to babysit a vacant building, and I'm sure Caro Jayne doesn't, either."

"If it starts to weigh you down, all this stuff that Luz left you with, don't be too proud to pack and go."

"Was that advice or a warning?"

"You decide," he said as someone knocked on the door.

"Hold that extremely confusing thought." Sofia peered through the glass, saw a pale slip of a woman topped with hair as white and smooth-looking as a dove's wing, and hurried to let Paget Mulligan in.

"I'm early, I know, but I brought food." Paget jostled a patchwork knapsack and a plate of something that seduced Sofia's stomach to purr even though she'd just eaten. "Oh, and I see you brought muscle. Is he here to help haul up all that furniture you were talking about?"

Her gaze had landed on Burke, and Sofia whirled. He stood out of earshot, frowning at an oil painting propped against a wall. It wasn't meant for boutique décor, but she couldn't lug it upstairs alone. The piece was a not-so-abstract titled *Fellatio*, and Joss was the artist. "Him? No. The furniture hasn't shipped yet, and he's…um…" *He's the guy who was ready to do me in Vices.* "Funny thing, he also brought food. Is it going around town that I'm in need of nourishment?"

Paget's smile touched every corner of her face. Amber-green eyes narrowed playfully under dark brows, and twin citrine gems twinkled in her dimples. Facial piercings and tats weren't permitted among Shore Seasons staff, so the cheek bling had been missing and the gothic images inked into the woman's entire left arm covered with makeup when Sofia had first met her at the inn. Meeting the real Paget had been a charming surprise. According to her, Luz had respected self-expression and only asked that everyone follow a simple and straightforward code of conduct: Don't be an asshole.

"The only gossip I've caught is that you're rebooting this place. Someone at Seasons isn't giddy about it." Meaning

Anne Oakley, Sofia would bet. She'd done a crappy job of concealing whatever conflict she and Luz shared. "On this plate is a delicious meal prepared by a bona fide restaurant chef. My friend Hannah invited me over, tried to fix me up with some guy. He stood me up, and here is the yumminess he missed out on." Paget handed Sofia the plate.

"Oh, no, I'm sorry that happened." Though she was glad the yumminess in question ended up in her possession. The food smelled delicious.

"It's fine." Paget's voice dipped conspiratorially. "That guy over there completely makes up for it. He's sex in blue jeans."

Giggling, Sofia gestured for Paget to follow her. "Paget, this is Burke Wolf. He and I went to school together. Burke, this is Paget Mulligan. She was one of Luz's assistants and I'm promptly stealing her away from Shore Seasons."

Paget's already white face paled further. "Well, hi, Burke. Hannah Slattery wasn't exaggerating when she said you're hot…and that you're an incurable ass." She turned to Sofia. "Your school chum is the man who stood me up."

"Really, Burke?" Sofia stepped over to him and whispered, "Don't let me interfere with your regularly scheduled whoring. Go with her, I don't care."

"I told my well-meaning, annoying-as-hell friends that I didn't want to be set up," he said. "But that response of yours—proof that you *do* care." He addressed Paget. "I'm sorry you got caught in Hannah's matchmaking crap. Is that plate mine?"

"It's mine," Sofia said. "I'm claiming it. Unless you two are thinking about going forward with your date after all, Paget and I need to talk shop."

Shaking his head, Burke left the boutique. And Sofia wanted to call him back inside, into her arms, because there were more questions to be asked and confessions to be made and mistakes to atone for.

"Hmm, hot guy," Paget said, "but he looks like trouble. Who needs trouble?"

"It's not always need," Sofia murmured. Sometimes it was want. A helpless craving. A fatal flaw of attraction.

Her attention drifted to the window display featuring the panty-clad female bodies, and what hadn't clicked before about the mannequins' arrangement now shifted soundlessly into place as a new vision took shape in her mind.

Beautiful bondage.

CHAPTER 9

I thought this place was supposed to be a knickers and
kink shop, not a storage unit."

Sofia, speckled with gold and smeared with white, sat
atop a ladder with a file folder open on her lap. The goal was
to flip the sign from CLOSED to OPEN before the tourist flood
ebbed at the end of the summer, so she was multitasking,
working from sunup to sundown and then some, refreshing
the boutique's front room with a bolder color palette and
ripping out carpeting in favor of the shop's beautifully battered wood floors—all while processing every document her
great-aunt's lawyer had relinquished.

She hadn't heard the bell jingle over the door. Snapping
to attention, she closed the folder. Beyond the maze of furniture and shipping boxes that were left in front of Blush this
morning—no walk-up delivery, the movers had stubbornly
said after she begged, bribed, and pathetically threatened
them to haul the pieces up to the apartment—was a curly-
haired blessing.

"Caro! Please say you have nothing important going on and can use your ballerina strength to help me lug a few hundred pounds of furniture."

"Oooh, I can't, love. I have a date."

"And you came here to rub it in. Did McGuinty Slattery get to you?"

"Ha, ha, ha. No. The date's with my little boy. I promised him we'd fly kites at the beach and he wants Tish to come along. That's why I'm here. Evan colored a picture for you to soften you up. Hopefully you like Captain America."

"Fine, but don't tell Tish I traded her for a picture of a superhero. She's upstairs." She plucked her keys from her overalls and pitched them near the door. "Got them?"

"Got them."

"I wish Captain America and his big muscles were here to move all this stuff. It's hard to maneuver a ladder around it all."

"I can imagine. What's under all this tarp and plastic? It looks like Pottery Barn threw up in here."

"Stuff from my place in New York. Bed, dresser, bookcases, craft desk, sewing equipment, odds and ends."

"Is this an armoire?" There was a rustle of plastic being pulled aside. "Hello, lovely."

"That's an antique, from Ireland. It's one of the few things my father didn't sell when money was tight. He knew I loved it." Of course, the piece was profanely imposing and heavy and he would've had a devil of a time putting it in hock without her catching him. The little things of so much value—jewelry, art, the iPod from Burke that he'd insisted Sofia keep when she claimed to never want to see him again—had been sacrificed quickly to buy food and put off bill collectors.

That was Finnegan Mercer, always willing to make the

difficult decisions to serve a greater purpose. He'd liquidated her small luxuries for her nourishment and well-being. Too bad he couldn't be the father she deserved, so he'd left, leaving a handwritten letter taped to the very armoire Caro touched now.

Finnegan's smudged, narrow script called his abandonment an act of honor and proof of ultimate love, but Aunt Luz had said it was cowardice and then growled something foreign about castration.

Sofia knew that her father had started anew in Wisconsin, was on a financial upswing, and was remarried with three school-age children who didn't know her. She was forbidden to contact her half siblings. Finnegan had asked her to stop calling him *Dad*, as if the first nineteen years of her life hadn't mattered. Her feelings toward him were someplace between forgiveness and stubborn anger.

"You're not just scarred," Caro said to her, thoughtfully. "You're scuffed, as if life's tossed you around a bit."

"Scuffs give a person character." Though she despised her own. Everything that was broken about her made her feel dirty, and she wanted to scrub it all away. This might be her new life, but her slate was far from clean.

"That's a naïve way to look at it, but all right."

Sofia shrugged. "I prefer *optimistic*."

"Optimism without conviction to hold it up is sort of pointless, isn't it?" Caro chuckled. "There's something very hidden and completely interesting about you, Sofia, behind that America's-darling façade."

"Who's calling me a darling?"

"Oh, that's drunken rubbish I overhear at the bar. Supposedly you're cute and sweet and need some good solid therapy so you can turn around and go back to being a nice girl in New York. I think you're naughty and corrupting, and

I'm glad I'm not the only one on this block who fits the description."

"Corrupting." Okay, so what if she was flattered by the word? "How's that?"

"Your window displays look like *Kama Sutra* demonstrations. Honestly, since you nested here, every time I stroll past this shop I get inspiration to find a man and shag him stupid."

This time Sofia chuckled. "So why don't you?"

"It's not practical. I have a child and his well-being matters more than my libido."

"Single moms date."

"Not me."

"So at the ripe been-everywhere, seen-everything age of thirtysomething you're on the shelf for good?"

"Twenty-seven, and I wouldn't say for good. More like indefinitely."

Treading carefully—tiptoeing, really—Sofia asked, "Want to tell me why?"

"I won't expose Evan to a carousel of men walking in and out of his life. That's what would happen if I dated, because I'm not searching for anything serious."

"So you require casual, but Evan needs stability."

"Yeah, and his needs will always be what matter most. He saved my life, Sofia, and I owe it to him to be the best mum that I can."

What did that mean, *he saved my life*?

"What'd McGuinty say when you told him? He must not hold any hard feelings, since just this morning I saw him swaggering to your studio with daffodils." Hating to see Aunt Luz's powder-blue-and-chrome bicycle retired in basement storage, Sofia used it to run light errands in town. Pedaling down Society, she sometimes noticed McGuinty bringing flowers to the photography studio. It was old-fashioned and unexpectedly sweet of him to court Caro with flowers at her door and friendly waves from his brother's laundromat across the street.

"I haven't told him, not in so many words," Caro finally said. "The flowers are nice. I grew up in a little village in Kent and on weekends my brothers and sisters and I used to go to the countryside and pick flowers for our mummy. He knows I miss that and clearly he's using it to wear me down."

"To me it seems charming."

"Charm's a device people use to achieve an ulterior motive."

"That may be. I knew McGuinty in high school and only vaguely then. But what I also know is that he runs the animal shelter with his grandpa and that place is across town. It seems unlikely that he'd be spending so much time at The Dirty Bastards because he really enjoys his brother's company."

"I'm nothing but a challenge, and he'll get bored soon enough."

Sofia recalled the seriousness in McGuinty's voice the morning he'd helped her find Tish at Caro's studio. "Are you sure he's okay with hanging in limbo like that?"

Caro cleared her throat. "Evan's waiting. I'll get Tish now. Good luck clearing out all of this, and the paint looks phenomenal."

"Does it really?" Anxious, Sofia gave the front room a critical glance. It was a distinct, bold move to paint the pink front room in alternating thick vertical stripes of white and gold. A pink, soft Blush was too coy; a striped and damasked Blush was committed to owning what it was.

"If it looked ghastly, I'd tell you. Example, those Farmer in the Dell overalls? Ghastly."

"Whatever. Go get the dog before I change my mind."

"Where do you want me to leave Captain America?" Caro waved a rolled-up piece of paper in the air. "Evan wouldn't forgive me if I let paint get on it."

"The armoire's empty. Put it on a shelf in there. After you grab Tish, toss the keys in there, too. I'll get them when I dig myself out of the rubble."

"Honestly, I don't know how you're not claustrophobic in here with all this furniture. There's no way in hell you're going to be able to finish painting."

"There'd be even more, but the apartment upstairs is furnished and I felt bad about leaving my roomie with a naked home."

"Well, if you can make it outside, go to Bottoms Up and get Bautista over here to help. I'm sure he'll do it."

Sofia began a descent down the ladder and lost her visual on Caro. The woman was by no means petite, but everything had been stacked so high. She began to rearrange boxes, asking, "Why would he be at the bar so early in the afternoon?"

"He stops in sometimes to check on things, usually stays in his office. Tariq's tending, so just go down there and tell him you need the owner."

"Wait, what are you talking about?"

"Bautista owns the place, though he's trying to convince me to take it over."

"He owns Bottoms Up but wants to sell it to you?"

"That's right. But I can't run it alone, so he's sticking around...even though he acts as if he wants nothing more than to motor out of this town." Caro cleared her throat. "Sofia, are you really putting down your roots here?"

She peeked around a tower of boxes. "They've always been here."

"The circumstance is this. I don't want to hold Bautista

here if he needs to get away for a while, but I can't run Bottoms Up alone. Tariq's a bartender only—he's made that plain and won't change his mind. Luz and Bautista, they watched over Society Street. Blush and Bottoms Up are their legacies, you see. I'd need help keeping the bar open. So would you consider claiming a slice?"

Would she go in on ownership of a bar with Caro? "That's a ton to think about. I'm not saying no. But I'm still processing that it's Bautista's place. What do you know about that?"

"Rumors have it he bought it and sealed the basement entry to the building next door so his motorcycle club could meet there, but they moved the location again after he retired."

Sofia's mind twisted, she was so confused. Blush and the Cape Foods building shared a basement passageway, so she wasn't surprised that all three basements connected. It was the only thing Caro had said that made sense. "Why did you say *retired* like that, as if you used air quotes and I couldn't see them?"

"Because I'm skeptical. I like Bautista. He and Luz took care of Evan and me. All that aside, he might have money and he might be a fucking brilliant lawyer, but under that suit is a roughneck."

"You mean there's an actual motorcycle club in Eaves?" Sofia had somehow instinctively known the moment she saw Javier Bautista at Luz's funeral that he was from the underbelly of some harsh society.

"The Dead Men. An outlaw club that the police thought they busted up years before I moved here. As the story goes, some guy locked up for homicide or something in Boston beat Death Row and became chummy with some work release convicts. There were all kinds of money and high-society connections to capitalize on here on the Cape. That was, oh, about forty years ago. If you grew up here and had no idea, I'd say your family did a fantastic job sheltering you from it all."

Her father had kept her cocooned in a nanny's care while he worked his way to manager of Eaves Bank. Then, when she was in high school and her medical costs had exceeded his salary, the cocoon had begun to fall away until he'd lost everything that had once defined him as a man and a pillar of this little town and he'd left her to Luz.

Bautista's bar hadn't existed when Sofia lived here before. The space that now housed Caro's studio had been a wine and cheese shop, so whatever club traffic the Dead Men had going then had been far from Sofia's stomping grounds.

"Since the move, the bar doesn't see any action," Caro said, "but I've seen jackets, heard conversations, know about the violence."

"What kind of violence?"

"Territory disputes. Fights. Shootings."

Aunt Luz had been in a relationship with Bautista— engaged to marry him. She must've known…must've accepted his lifestyle. Pedaling a ten-speed around town and selling sex toys didn't make a woman oblivious.

"What if I told you I was joking about the whole thing?" Caro offered. "Would that erase the fear from your voice?"

"I'm not afraid." In fact, she felt oddly detached. Perhaps it was the satisfaction of confirming that her first impression had been right, and she hadn't been unfair to judge him on the spot. Or it could be that on some level she was intrigued. "And you're not joking. This is for real. Bautista really is an outlaw motorcycle gang member."

"Retired. Sort of. They call him Judge."

"Semiretired." Sofia's mouth felt dry as she mentally

flung herself at every TV portrayal and fictional interpretation of outlaw clubs. The men were beasts riding steel. "A semiretired motorcycle gang member who probably carries a gun and forced Aunt Luz to live in disgusting misogyny."

"Oh, oh, oh, hold on a moment, okay? Sofia, listen, I realize these types of…brotherhoods, if you will…aren't known for their gentlemanly nature, but Bautista treated Luz like a queen. I think he really did love her, and she was too much of a spitfire to let him own her."

Was that why Luz had taken off her engagement ring, because it symbolized ownership?

"He's not a demanding man. If he trusts you, he'll protect you. That goes a long way with me. This isn't something I commonly get into with people, because it's difficult to go there, but since I rather like you it should make things easy." Caro paused, allowing a tight silence. "After I left Kent, I bounced around the States a lot. When I had Evan, I knew he'd need a home. He was an infant who kept the craziest hours and the only place that seemed to accommodate us was Bautista's bar. He paid me, the tips were decent on top of it, and Luz helped manage Evan while I figured myself out."

"I'm glad they rescued you," Sofia finally said.

"They didn't. I told you before. Evan saved me. He's my world. That should tell you how safe I felt with Luz and Bautista. I'll go get Tish now."

"Caro, wait. You told me all this, and what am I supposed to do with it? How am I supposed to feel?"

Another silence, inflating like a balloon until Caro's melodious British voice popped it with "Aren't you glad he's on your side?"

* * *

Bautista sat in his fat, beat-up leather chair. It was all he needed. It was almost as old as his bike—and more valuable. It knew his secrets, the weariness of his body, the burdens he stored inside himself. Luz had straddled him here, whispering to him as he rocked inside her. The chair knew her secrets, too.

Ice clinked the inside of his glass as it began to melt in his whiskey. The bartender manning things today had put it in his hand when he'd come through, laser focused on going straight to his office.

On the way Bautista had passed a group of young folks gathered in front of the johns—if he found out they were under twenty-one he'd haul their asses out and give the watchman hell for letting them slip through. They were split into two groups—men in front of the Gents door and women in front of the Ladies door—and pens were being passed around as they took turns autographing the wood. Each door boasted a full-size drawing of a naked body—courtesy of Rooster, one of Bautista's club brothers, and the man deserved points for anatomical correctness and realism. When Rooster had drawn on the doors, he'd labeled them Cocks and Cunts, but Bautista had threatened to slice open his tires unless he changed the names. And because he thought he was funny, Rooster had signed his name on the genitals, and that's how the tradition of signing the john doors had started.

Bautista had never added his signature, nor would he. It wasn't important that he put his name on everything that belonged to him. It was why he hadn't asked Luz to tattoo his initials into her soft golden skin. His club brothers and their forefathers had their women inked—a few branded—but some customs wanted to suffocate his morality and he always followed his morality, whether it went against the law or against the outlaws he regarded as family.

With one foot in the club and one out, Bautista knew the Dead Men had an allegiance to him, yet they were making plans that didn't include him.

He hadn't ridden with them in months, but that had been his choice, to withdraw slowly as he started to realize a different type of life—one that saw him in his East Millennium Tower office during the day, wrapped up with Luz at night, and keeping an eye on Bottoms Up on the weekend. Now there was no Luz, and if he reaffirmed his loyalty to the club he would be welcomed back into the fold.

If he did that, his brothers would be obligated to tell him what Luz had been planning behind his back. What he knew was enough to hurt him—she'd lied to him about needing money to buy the Cape Foods building so she could expand her boutique—but he didn't have the full truth yet. He wouldn't act until he did.

Bautista heard voices outside his door and looked at his watch. Rooster was early... That didn't seem right. He was never early for a talk.

The door opened harshly, slamming the stop, but Bautista remained relaxed in his chair as Sofia invaded his office. Paint dotted her hair and skin.

The bartender, Tariq, said, "I told her not to come back here, but she lied about going to the ladies' room."

"I didn't lie," she said. "I do have to pee, but I can hold it until I say what I need to say to Bautista."

Signaling for Tariq to leave, Bautista considered her. It had to be a crime to put dungarees on this woman. She'd been blessed with beauty, and folks in this town were paying attention. To look the way she did and hole herself up in a sex shop was starting to draw the kind of interest that had women whispering and men lurking around for more than an eyeful of mannequins simulating sex.

He had to ask. "What the hell are you wearing?"

"Overalls. Is Eaves united in some hatred for overalls? I was painting."

"Why don't you finish that up? Come back here when you don't look like a ten-year-old and I can take you seriously."

"No, we do this now." The flare of courage and insult was organic, not practiced, and at last he sat up straight and nodded.

"What do you want?"

"The truth would be a great place to start, Bautista." She leaned in, resting her fists on his desk. "Or would you prefer that I call you Judge?"

So she knew. It'd taken longer than he expected for the gossip to circulate. How had he been described to her—as a monstrous thug who let his gun do the talking for him and pillaged and ravaged just because he could, or as some damaged vigilante hero to be idolized and imitated because TV motorcycle outlaws were so goddamn cool?

"When we first met, I told you to call me Bautista."

"I know about the Dead Men."

He couldn't help but smile. She'd heard about his club, but she didn't know. He'd destroy hell itself before he let that world touch Luz's girl.

She was his woman's flesh and blood, and she'd come back to live Luz's legacy—that made her his girl, too. She was his responsibility, his to watch over.

Sofia would repel the thought of it. She was independent. She had a mighty chip on her shoulder and secrets inside her that he didn't want to carry. His conscience and this chair could hold only so much.

"Who *are* you?" she cried. "I've been here for weeks and never knew you owned Bottoms Up."

He shrugged. "Gossip's traveling slower than usual. The tourists must be distracting everyone."

"The gang. You're all outlaws." She glanced around and he wasn't altogether sure she wasn't looking for weapons on the walls or a shrine to his club's patch. "You're killers."

"Pipe down."

"No, I won't!"

"If you thought I was a killer or some evil monster, you wouldn't be in here disrespecting my office." He pointed to a chair near the door. "Sit down. On second thought, don't. Wet paint on my furniture's just going to piss me off."

"It should've dried by now."

"Go ahead." He waited for her to drag the chair over and perch on the very edge of it. Even upset with him, she was considerate. Some kid his Luz had raised. "I'm not a killer. I'm a protector."

"This isn't *tomayto, tomahto*. I heard your club's been involved in territory disputes and shootings. Blood's on your hands."

"I haven't killed anyone," he maintained.

Her slim throat worked as she swallowed the realization. "You didn't deny that blood's on your hands. You didn't say you weren't involved in the territory disputes and the shootings." She spied him. They were caught in the middle of Eaves's first heat wave of the year, so he'd pushed up his sleeves and wound his braid at the back of his head. The tattoos running down his forearms were exposed. "Luz never told me about you. She wasn't wearing your ring when she died. Maybe you invented a relationship to soothe your ego or something, and she was too afraid to tell you where things stood."

"Your aunt wasn't afraid of me. She pushed me and she tested me, wanted to see how far she could go before I snapped against her. But it never happened. I loved her from the night she came to this bar and tied a cherry stem in her mouth."

Sofia softened with a smile. "The cherry thing. That's Luz, all right. I've seen her do it before."

"I never hurt Luz."

"Did you ever hit her?"

Bautista trapped her attention, as if he held her face between his hands. "Never without her consent, and she never hit me without mine. We respected each other's safe words."

Color rose on her cheeks. The woman who'd posed mannequins in positions he didn't think were possible was blushing about sex play?

"Okay, I don't think I needed to know *that* about Luz."

"You asked if I hit her, and I wanted to make it clear that this isn't a game of *tomayto, tomahto*. So if you can handle the answers to your questions without turning the color of a tomato, then we can keep talking."

"Sorry, but I'd rather not know the details of my great-aunt's sex life, thanks." Yet even as she said the words Sofia absently stroked her arm with her fingernails and rocked on the edge of the seat.

There was a delicate line between repulsion and captivation, and the living proof of that was a woman with the face of an innocent and the mind of a debauchee who sat in front of his desk at the halfway point between turned off and turned on.

Bautista rose, followed the perimeter of his desk, and stopped behind her chair. "Who're you thinking about, *querida*?"

"What... ? No one."

"Liar." Someone had gotten to her. He knew what attraction looked like, knew what lust smelled like, and knew that someone who worked for a sentimental greeting card company didn't dive into arranging hot-as-hell window displays unless she had some specific inspiration in her head.

He had a guess, but he'd keep it to himself. He didn't need her secrets, didn't want them. His duty was to fulfill his promise to Luz. He'd protect Sofia and guide her as if she were his own—but as for anything else, it was up to her to open her eyes.

"All you've shared is that you and Aunt Luz had an…uh…adventurous sexual relationship. It doesn't sound like a happy, great love to me."

"Great loves aren't happy. They're torture and they drag you through hell, and if you make it to the other side you think it was so hard-won that you just go with it."

"That makes it sound as if love's about winning or taking what's in front of you just because it was hard to get and not necessarily because it's with the right person."

"Then maybe all that matters for you is what *you* think love ought to be. For me, love was confronting that I'd give up everything I thought was important to me for the benefit of my woman. That woman was Luz. I put my bar on the line for her."

Sofia coiled her body in the chair. "Excuse me?"

"I offered to mortgage the bar to get her the money I thought she needed to buy the Cape Foods building between us."

"So she wanted to grow Blush and, what, carry more product?"

"That's what I believed, that she wanted the building for Blush." The documents her CPA had turned over after her death had exposed that lie. "To get her the money to make an offer on the property, I geared up to sell this bar—"

"And give up the place where your meetings were held? Or might *still* be held?"

"My club doesn't meet here." His comrades sought counsel here; people came here for money and requests for favors. But she hadn't asked him that. "I was going to sell Bottoms Up to help my future wife grow her business."

"What stopped you?"

"A few things. The property owner refused to sell, my future wife died, and I found out she was so damn well off that she didn't need the proceeds from the sale of this bar."

"Maybe she wanted you to sell the bar to end the chapter of your past that involved the club. You're retired...or partially retired. I can't blame her if she wanted you to be truly done with that life."

He couldn't have blamed Luz, either, had that been true. But it wasn't.

Bautista returned to his chair, easily imagining that if he didn't, the thing would erupt without his weight to press down the secrets it held.

"Your disagreement about this bar is a moot point, isn't it?" she asked. "You want Caro to take it on. She asked if I'd go in on it with her."

"What'd you say?"

"I didn't say no. The way you talked about this bar makes me believe you don't want to let it go completely. So don't. Let Caro have a slice and let her help. I'll help, too, but I can't be associated with your club. If I take a piece of this, I'm taking a piece of a bar and nothing else."

So she was asking him to make a choice. Retired or not? In or out?

"Noted, Sofia."

She exhaled, as though finally free to release a pent-up breath. "Okay." She relaxed a little. "Why'd the property owner refuse to sell the Cape Foods building anyway? Suppose I want to purchase it. If I can't get my furniture hauled up to the apartment I'll need the extra space for storage."

"Always have a plan, Sofia. If there's one thing I can teach you, it's that."

"I'm sure I can learn plenty if I'm privy to half of what Caro's overheard." She winced.

So Caroline Jayne had filled in a few blanks for her. It didn't bother him. He held Caro in the highest regard. Anyone who could survive her trauma and be an unquestionably devoted mother deserved his respect. She was also a gifted bartender and whenever he left his place in her hands, he needn't worry about a damn thing. "Caroline's been keeping you entertained with stories?"

"I have no reason to doubt what she says. Don't be upset with her."

"I'm not. I protect her, the same as I protect Slattery across the street and the stationery folks, the same as I protected Luz and Old Man Wolf—" Though years before the man's death Bautista's instincts had warned him to take a closer look at the grocer. He might've if Wolf's kid had come back, but Burke had kept himself scarce until after his father died. "Society Street's *my* street, Sofia. I'm invested in the safety of everyone on this strip. Think of me as a neighborhood watchman." Checking the time, he saw that Rooster would arrive any minute, and he didn't want the two crossing paths—not today. "Are we finished here?"

"Yes, but would you give me a hand moving up some furniture?"

"I have a meeting."

"A meeting." Her eyes narrowed momentarily, then she stood and started for the door. "Fine, then I really will shove it all into the building next door."

Bautista resumed his relaxed posture in his chair and breathed in the smell of aged leather. "I think the owner of that property might not appreciate it if you do. But if you're a believer in 'it's easier to beg forgiveness than to ask permission,' then go for it."

"Who's the owner?"

And so it begins.

"Burke Wolf."

CHAPTER 10

*S*ofia paused, wasn't sure she so much as blinked for several seconds, as Bautista's words registered. Burke owned the old market building, and he'd consciously ignored opportunities to tell her. The vacant real estate diminishing the street appeal of both Caro's and her businesses was his responsibility. On top of that, Luz had approached him about purchasing and he'd refused to sell.

The chirp of her phone cut Sofia off from dashing out of the bar, hopping into her SUV, and driving to the Eaves Marina while still wearing the overalls that were apparently more offensive than the mannequin sex in Blush's windows.

She would find him later, after she showered off the paint and traded the overalls for something...sexy. She could do that, amp up her appeal for the singular purpose of charming the truth out of him. So Caro *was* right—charm was a device, and Sofia intended to use it for all it was worth.

Retrieving the phone from the apron pocket of the overalls, she saw Joss's name paired with a headshot of her wearing whiskers. That had been snapped at a Halloween party last year when Joss had squeezed herself into patent leather, put on cat ears and a tail, and called herself a sex kitten. Sofia had sewn her own lingerie-inspired costume to achieve sex appeal while covering her scar, and had accessorized with long ears and a fluffy tail and called herself a Playboy bunny. "Hey, Joss," she said into the phone, turning to leave Bautista's office when he threw his hand forward as a signal to get out *now*. "I'm going already!"

"What?" her friend squeaked.

"Not you," she assured. "That was meant for the grumpy tattooed man currently throwing me out of his office."

"Where are you, Sof? I wanted to surprise you, but the store's locked up tight."

"The store? Joss...are you here, in Eaves?"

"Yeah. I wanted to go to the beach. Surprise," she said, though her next breath was shaky and the enthusiasm in her voice had waned. "I'm sitting out front, but people walking past keep giving me change. If you'll be much longer, I'm going someplace to buy a scone. Some guy gave me a buck and told me to get a scone, so I might."

Sofia was immediately alarmed at her friend's erratic babbling and that she'd up and driven to the Cape on a weekday without so much as a *Heads up, I'm on my way!* "Something's wrong, Joss. Tell me." She heard movement behind her and turned as Bautista rounded his desk.

"What happened to her?" he demanded.

"I—I don't know." Returning to the call, she said, "Joss, just wait there. I'm down the block but on my way."

"Okay. Sof? I'm sorry." Then she disconnected.

No, that didn't sound good at all. "Joss is in front of Blush and people think she's homeless. I need to get to her before she runs off to buy a scone."

"What?" Bautista asked, opening the door and guiding her out. "You gotta know that last part makes zero sense."

"Joss is a pastry snob—her words. She prefers to eat homemade pastries, her own creations. It's all part of perfecting her craft, as she says." Sofia noticed him walking out with her and shutting the office door as the noise of the bar enveloped them. "I thought you had a meeting. That's why you can't help me move my stuff upstairs, isn't it?"

"Change of agenda," he said, not expounding. As they passed the bar, he cuffed a patron on the shoulder. "Hold it down till I get back."

Sofia was occupied with making her way to the exit and didn't pry. Sunshine and heat fell over them as they reached the sidewalk, then turned the corner.

Joss stood up, dusting the seat of her jeans. Luggage barricaded the boutique. She wasn't the world's most practical packer, but not even she would bring a dozen cases and bags for a day trip to the beach.

"Hi!" The false perkiness was further alarming—so was the way she winced when Sofia hugged her.

"Are you hurt?" Sofia asked, and fell speechless when Bautista reached forward and took away Joss's sunglasses.

"*Hey*—" Joss gasped, snatching them back and putting them on.

But Sofia had already seen what her friend was trying to hide.

A bluish-gray bruise edged with a yellowish tinge ringed her right eye. There was a dash of red where the skin had split. The bruise was sickeningly beautiful, and Sofia's heart hurt. "Oh, God. Who did this?" In her gut she knew, but she needed to hear the name.

Joss shook her head at first. "I'm sorry. I shouldn't have come here like this. I'm functioning on emotion."

"Who touched you?" Bautista's voice was quiet yet firm enough to garner an immediate response. Joss's crisis didn't involve him, but his presence was strangely a comfort.

"Peter." Joss sobbed into her hand. "I was going to stay away from him, but he was so persistent. He apologized for cheating and then he set up an interview for a pastry chef gig at a restaurant on Park Avenue. But the interviewer was an ass and I walked out. Peter found out, said I embarrassed him, and we fought about it. He hit me, shoved me down."

"Please tell me you reported him," Sofia said.

"I called the cops, and his parents got him sprung five minutes later. The word of an upstanding heir to New York royalty versus the word of New Jersey trash, right? When he got out, he dumped me."

"That son of a bitch." Sofia looked at the luggage lined up along Blush's storefront. "You're not going back to New York, are you?"

"My name's shit now. Peter took away every good thing he made happen. I'm like Cinderella at midnight." She wiped her nose on the sleeve of her shirt. "The rest of my clothes are in my rental car. It's parked across the street."

In tandem Sofia and Bautista looked from the collection in front of them to Joss. There was no way it'd all fit in the apartment's bedroom closet.

"Sof, I'm sorry I didn't hear you out when you suggested I join you here. I thought I could play Peter Bernard's game and win." She shrugged and turned to gaze at the store. The display in front of her featured a teddy-clad female mannequin straddling the lap of a nude male. A black cloth covered their hips to add mystery and suggestion. The male's hands were secured behind the female's back with silk ribbon. "Mannequin porn. I'm standing on the street looking at mannequin porn. Your Aunt Luz must've been some kind of talented pervert. I would've liked her."

"Oh. Aunt Luz didn't set these up."

"You?" Joss smiled. "Then I'm proud to be the friend of a talented pervert."

Bautista stood watching Joss, his eyes hooded, his jaw tight with tension Sofia couldn't name. Finally he spoke. "You can handle this from here, *querida*?"

"Yeah, but I thought you were going to help with the furniture—"

"Can't do that. Got to take care of something."

"Where are you going?"

"I told you, I have a meeting." Bautista lost himself in the stream of passersby, leaving Sofia with a bruised Joss and an assemblage of designer luggage that hadn't a chance in hell of fitting in her apartment.

* * *

Only half of Joss's things fit upstairs. The clothes—"That's a Prada. It can't be left scrunched in a suitcase!" "Can't we unpack the stilettos *and* the kitten heels? What about sandals for the beach?"—crowded the bedroom, and the cosmetics and toiletries made the bathroom look like a department store makeup counter. Everything else they carted downstairs to basement storage.

The process went slowly because of frequent interruptions. Caro had returned Tish, who straightaway whined to be taken out to pee. Then Joss had concealed her bruise with makeup and they'd had dinner at a dock restaurant. While Joss dug into her buttered lobster, Sofia ate a grilled chicken salad and endured other diners flitting past to murmur belated condolences for her loss.

"It's a shame Luz hadn't any family around in her last days," a woman commented with a condemning *tsk.* "She had a man, but a man ain't necessarily family. And it's not hard to figure just what she was doing with a younger fellow like that."

Sofia had dropped her fork and when she reached for it, Joss stopped her with, "If you pick that up, there's a high likelihood you'll stab someone with it. Leave it, and let's take the rest of this food back to the apartment."

The apartment, she'd said, as though nothing had fundamentally changed and they were still a pair of go-getting New Yorkers dreaming about futures that seemed so far away.

What *hadn't* changed?

Sofia continued to wonder as she tried to sleep with Tish stretched across her legs. Eventually she got up and slipped out of the bedroom for a drink, but the living room lamps blazed and she poked her head around the corner to find Joss standing and appearing to study nothing in particular.

"Can't sleep, kid?"

Joss smiled. "In a few months I'll be thirty. At that point you're forbidden to call me *kid* ever again."

"Deal." She went to the kitchen, drank water from the tap, and returned to the living room. Joss hadn't asked for company, but Sofia sat on a chair anyway. "Does it hurt? Your face?"

"Not really. It looks bad."

"It *is* bad. What Peter did...you didn't deserve it—"

"Please don't, Sof. NYPD gave me numbers. The hospital dumped all kinds of pamphlets on me. I don't need anyone else to remind me that I'm a textbook example of a victim of domestic violence." She began to pace, the dark shimmer varnish on her toes contrasting with her pale skin and the white area rug. "The thing that really sucks? The system that's drilling into my head the importance of protecting myself and seeking help is the same one that released the bastard who hurt me."

"It's not fair."

"No, it's not. Accountability's a one-way street. Men can lie and devastate and what happens? Nothing—certainly not justice."

"I know you're hurting, Joss, but there is justice. It happens in big and small ways. Sometimes it takes a while and waiting for wrongs to be fixed is painful."

"So forgive and forget what Peter did to me? Are you seriously saying that, or am I just overtired?"

"Not all men are jackasses."

Joss snorted. "Just the ones I keep running into."

"I'm for damn sure not saying forgive and forget what Peter did, but don't write off everyone else." She didn't say anything more but let her friend continue to pace the rug and wander the room.

"So they were engaged. Bautista and your Aunt Luz," Joss said, picking up a silver frame. It was a private moment between lovers frozen in time—Bautista kissing Luz's neck. Their long dark hair was tangled and there was nothing but water and sky and driftwood behind them.

After Sofia had digested what she'd learned in Bautista's law office, she'd shared the major points with Joss. "Yeah. He says he loved her. I think I believe him."

"Hmm, sure. *Love*. What does love mean to a guy, anyway?"

"Depends on the guy," she replied, recalling her chat with Bautista earlier. For him, love was sacrificing what was personally important to realize the best interests of his fiancée. He'd sacrificed in grand and intimate ways.

Did Burke believe love comprised sacrifice and compromise? Why in hell was she even wondering?

"I came here because I don't want to wallow," Joss said on a sigh, putting down the frame. She stretched out on the sofa, shook out her blond curls, and hugged a pillow. "I intend to make myself useful, the same as you said you did when you lived here with Luz."

"Meaning what? Work at Blush?"

"Sure. You know I worked retail in the past."

"Yeah, for Teavana and upscale, platinum-cards-only stores in the city. Blush and its clientele are different."

"Different's good. Different is what I need until I'm ready for plan B of my life."

"What's plan B?"

"I haven't figured it out yet. But I'll help out with the shop however I can. It's summer and something's in the air."

"Salt."

Joss laughed. "No, something else. Not a scent but a really subtle alert that this might be it for me—my second chance." She squeezed the pillow. "Okay, so here it is. Your new life started when you got the transplant, but mine hasn't yet and I've been waiting. Well, now I think it's happening. Coming here because things went to shit again...Maybe Eaves, Massachusetts, is my second chance."

"For what? This isn't your dream. You told me your dream is to run in celebrity circles. You want a pastry business. You want to be your own boss, not my employee. I'd be happy to sell your sweets in Blush, but the customers are expecting treats in the form of flavored lube and edible underwear."

"Dreams always look different when you wake up." Joss shrugged. "So will you think about it?"

"I don't have to. Of course you're welcome to help out at Blush. But it's only temporary."

"Oh?"

"Yes, because you're going to have your own business to run someday and can't be helping me sell erotic stuff on the side."

"Aww, but I like erotic stuff." She pointed across the room to the painting Sofia had lugged up to the apartment the night she and Burke had kissed inside the boutique. "Exhibit *Fellatio*. You should sell it. It might rake in a bundle, and I'm not just saying that because I'm the artist."

"I'm not selling that piece. I'm having too much fun unnerving people with it. My assistant, Paget, refers to it as *Blow Job*. Burke stared and I wasn't sure if he was weirded out or horny."

"Burke, as in the hot guy from the gas station? That man's shoulders alone are the reason God made flannel." Joss fanned herself with the pillow. "I've been waiting for all the backstory between you and him since the funeral. The fact that you've been keeping your mouth shut says volumes."

Though Joss had asked for details, it seemed somehow cruel to launch into whatever was brewing between Sofia and Burke. It was probably nothing...or it might be everything.

They hadn't spoken since that night in Blush, yet they breathed the same air and slept under the same Cape Cod moon. In her dreams she let him stroke her to awareness. Awake and alone, she touched herself with his sulky, unforgettable face in her mind.

He'd inspired the window display downstairs that Joss called "mannequin porn."

"Try to get some sleep, Joss," she said, getting up. "Want to keep all these lights on?"

"Yeah," her friend said, turning and feeling under the

edge of the sofa until the end of a narrow object poked out. An umbrella. A weapon.

Sofia supposed tonight more than most nights, Joss needed the assurance that she wasn't helpless. "Hey, Joss, what if Tish slept out here in the living room tonight? She's furry and her breath smells like Milk-Bone, but she's sort of a dreamcatcher for me."

"I don't need a dreamcatcher, Sof." But as Sofia began to quietly slip down the hall, she said, "She can sleep out here tonight, though, if she wants."

Saying nothing more, Sofia guided Tish to the living room and brought out a blanket. Joss and Tish stared at one another—a woman and a dog both wary and both hurt, but open to finding an ally in each other.

When Joss hesitantly patted Tish's neck and the dog lay in front of the sofa, Sofia smiled and went to her room.

God bless Tish. Count on a dog to hold things together when they wanted to fall apart. Tish was Sofia's courage, Joss's safety, and little Evan Jayne's kindred spirit.

That night, Sofia couldn't sleep. But she thought about Joss and Caro and the gruff protector who watched over Society Street from an underground dive bar. She daydreamed about the friendship she'd forged with Burke in the secret hallways under their families' stores. And she researched and made plans, and by morning she'd conceived an idea that was a crazy, wicked risk and might not work. But she hadn't moved back to Eaves to half-ass her way through life.

First things first, though—she needed to see Burke.

* * *

"You going to head on home?" Nessa Pare folded her wide frame into the captain chair in front of Bautista's desk. The finger wave pattern of her close-cropped hair shone under the light as she straightened her shoulders and banded her arms underneath the ledge of what had to be a specialty-cup rack. "Or am I babysitting your grown ass all the way to sunup?"

"Take off if you need to, Nessa," he said to his secretary. "Court's at nine."

"We both know that if I take off, you lose an alibi." She crossed her cheetah-print-booted feet on his desk, and because it was Nessa, who made up for his every deficiency and could throw back more drinks than any man who'd drifted into his bar, he didn't put her on the other side of his law office door. Nessa could shake down the entire damn building with the booming vibrato of her yell, and in the late hour there was still more business to be done before he stepped away tonight. "Don't bullshit a bull-shitter."

"Thanks for the advice. If I ever need more, I know who to come to."

"I saw Rooster stroll through the lobby."

"Corporate investors stroll through this lobby all the time. It's late, Nessa. Sleep on your crazy-ass accusations, fix your attitude, and approach me differently in the morning."

"Uh-uh-uh." The points of her boots arced back and forth. "You sent me off to file papers and didn't count on me doubling back to get my tablet. I don't know where you met up with Rooster, but I'll bet my new Fendi bag you did meet him and something's about to go down."

"What needs to go down is your blood pressure, Nessa. Quit getting worked up over assumptions. Ain't no room for overactive imaginations here. Save that for court."

"Don't try to dance around me," she warned. "I'll stomp your toes and keep on struttin'." She put her feet on the floor and steepled thick ringed fingers. "So how am I going to be spending the next hours? Shredding documents? Securing new phones? Filtering email?"

"None of that. Clean hands." The same couldn't be said for his conscience, but as for his hands, only holy water would make them cleaner. He'd built his success with clean hands, engineered it with a callous conscience. "We're not the only ones keeping this building lit."

"Yeah. Alibis all over the building. Maybe you don't need me here after all, and I can go have a martini someplace."

"We *are* still prepping for court. But as I said, if you have to take off, *vete a casa*." Bautista fanned folders across the desk. His office burned bright and neighbors passed in the halls. They would notice him here with Nessa, their heads bent over papers.

This was a precaution, should questions surface. He couldn't mend Joss Vail's broken spirit or return the bloom to her rose or heal her bruises, but justice was his forte. Justice outside the lines of the law was a specialty, and one he didn't dabble in often.

"Whatever you're orchestrating, I hope it's for a friggin' good cause." Nessa held him in a skeptical look. "Is it?"

Retribution. Was that a good cause? "Yeah, Nessa. It is."

Joss didn't like him, but a woman needn't be agreeable to deserve fairness. A system that allowed a man to tear down the world of a woman he victimized and walk free was cracked. Bautista wanted to modestly convey that after beating his girlfriend, Peter Bernard would've been safer behind bars than roaming the streets.

Humble man that he was, Bautista found no particular satisfaction in seeing his *orchestrations*, as Nessa called them, played out. He didn't need to have his visual, auditory, and olfactory senses engaged. All he required was confirmation that a conversation occurred. The conversations, though, usually involved very little discussion.

So he worked in his office with his legal secretary and they prepared for a high-impact morning. And when, at the agreed-upon time, he put in a call to an all-night pizzeria and a familiar voice told him what he'd expected to hear, he ended the connection and told Nessa, "Put through the usual midnight-oil order." Half pepperoni, for Nessa, and half green peppers, for him. "Come with me to pick up or call it a night and go home. Up to you."

"Are you riding with them again?" she asked flatly. "What about retirement? I believe that when folks pass on, they get a viewfinder on the ones left here. Luz ain't going to like what she sees if you get it in your head to re-up with...them."

Bautista *was* banking on another ride—the final ride with his brothers. If Luz did have a viewfinder, she would see what motivated him now. He wasn't seeking her approval or understanding. Both were immaterial and no way in hell would she have given him either.

But all those plans were put on a short hold. Joss Vail's catastrophe had demanded immediate intervention. She wouldn't thank him for it—likely would hate him for playing Robin Hood when she hadn't asked for a hero who followed an unconventional protocol of law. The legal system was a fickle lover—sometimes it was in sync with him, but other times, such as when it allowed social status to set free an abuser, it turned its back on him. So he improvised, guided only by his keen sense of judgment. It was so keen that his club brothers didn't doubt his directives, but only men with seniority were trusted with his instructions.

"I'm going, soon as I draft this memo." Nessa, as brown and soft as oven-toasted bread, turned her voice into granite.

"I'm concerned about you, Bautista. Losing her's twisting you up."

"Concern's no good here." He strode to the door. "Cut the lights out when you leave. I don't want to get another angry note from night maintenance. I'm going to pay for what I ordered."

The pizza and the trip his brothers took to New York City tonight.

CHAPTER 11

$\mathcal{D}$aybreak lazed over the ocean and the water undulated gently, relishing the teasing stroke of it. Warm wind puffed softly, like a yawn falling over Sofia's skin, but she didn't pedal a U-turn on Society to change her clothes. She had a specific part to play, and the black suit, so tight that the short jacket and cropped pants hugged her possessively, was the outfit to shove her into character. Even her hair, twisted into a chignon and denied the chance to whip the air as the bicycle bulleted down the sleepy street, contributed to her costume.

The white knuckles, clammy palms, and microscopic perspiration pebbled across her nose revealed anxiety.

She was bicycling to the marina to propose a business deal, not to ask for a favor. Yet she was nervous underneath her clothes, and hot, too. Her wardrobe was meant for air-conditioned offices, posh dinners, and nightclub hopping—not cross-town jaunts on a chrome bike. She'd chosen the bike over her SUV because it was the less conspicuous of the two. A Lexus's engine announcing its presence at sunrise was bound to draw people from their boats. A woman bicycling barefoot in a business suit with high heels in the basket might look peculiar, but not many would notice, and that was good enough.

This was about business, nothing more. Okay, so she'd have a rare opportunity to catch Burke first thing in the morning. And *fine*, she was excited about that. Would his hair be mussed and his shirt rumpled—if he slept in anything at all? Would he be all warm and gravel-voiced?

Redirecting her thoughts, she pictured Cape Foods. Once Eaves's practical neighborhood market and the downtown hub where kids hung out in front of vending machines while adult conversations carried through the aisles, it was now a shell of itself—a dark, empty place.

Shopping there had been awkward, downright dreaded, when she was in high school and on the outs with the grocer's son. Whether it was stacking cans of tomato paste on top of eggs or giving her a bag with a hole in it, Burke found ways to retaliate against her compulsion to sniff out his secrets and expose him far and wide. She'd been lonely in those early years, losing her junior high friends to cliques that demanded loyalty and conformity she couldn't spare. Medical appointments defined her social life, and after too many declined invitations and missed sleepovers the girls had left her on her own in the strange cutthroat world that was high school. Without friends, she'd made enemies. At least then someone knew her name—even if they preferred to call her something else.

Brat. Prude. Bitch.

Had Burke used those words before they'd become friends and he had started carrying her groceries for her and slipping sketches into her bags? What about after she'd stabbed him in the heart before going to New York to get a new one for herself? What had he called her then?

Now she wasn't hot—she was frigid underneath her skin as she jammed her feet on the pedals and commanded herself to go faster. So fast that she couldn't identify the occasional person taking to the street to start their day. So fast that she could no longer detect the aromas of baked bread and fresh coffee in the thick June breeze. Faster still, until she might escape the past, because she didn't want to think about that anymore.

And then, when it seemed her lungs might deflate from the exertion, she could see the marina.

A man on a boat, that's all Burke Wolf was. She couldn't hold the memory of him as the complicated, wrecked soul who'd hurt and healed her in those hard growing-up years.

Sofia dismounted and paused on the dock. An array of vessels tucked in slips lay before her, lined up on the deep gray water that twinkled as the sun continued to indolently arc through the sky.

Was Burke's home the robust yacht on the far end, which glistened and made her see luxurious sunset suppers and hear Andrea Bocelli? That didn't fit the man who ate sandwiches on the floor and said dirty, rough things in her ear. Did he live in the narrow, battered craft that couldn't be more than twenty feet? She doubted it accommodated his height and wingspan...height that shadowed her nicely and wingspan made up of sinewy arms, large hands, and long fingers that knew exactly how to stroke her nipples until she was tight and aching for—

And then she was hot again. Just that suddenly, and for no reason that could lead to anything good.

Well, there *was* one thing it could lead to, and if what

they'd begun in Blush was any indication, it'd be incredibly good—of that she had no doubt.

Sofia's gaze bounced from one boat to the next as she proceeded on the dock, too absorbed in her search to let the heat of the wood on her feet clue her in that she'd left her confidence-boosting Gucci heels in the bicycle basket.

She'd known live-aboards before, friends of Luz's who floated off the grid most of the year. Their craft had been cramped but they lived off essentials only and craved a mobile, minimalistic lifestyle—playing gin rummy with Luz and other Cape Cod locals one evening, then sailing off to the Caribbean the next.

What did Burke crave out of this life that he devoted so much of himself to handling cargo on ships but in his downtime kept himself on the water and ready to sail away at a moment's notice?

As though he was here, but not really. As though he was with her, but not quite.

"I think you lost your way, Sofia."

"*Gah!*" She gasped, spinning around and stumbling. If she fell to the left she'd pitch herself off the dock. If she fell to the right she'd land against a hard, taut body. Glimpsing Burke's easy smirk as she reclaimed her balance, she decided it was a toss-up which option was more dangerous. "I was supposed to catch *you* off guard."

"Huh?"

"Forget it." She countered his smirk—oh, when had he learned to perfect that half-sulky, half-amused twist of his mouth?—with neutrality. Blank expression, straight posture, steady breathing. Which was complete bullshit, because his proximity penetrated her resolve, seducing her without touches or words—only nearness. Euphoria surged, coasting along her skin and quickening her heartbeat. "You didn't try to stop me from falling." She adjusted the strap of her cross-body purse and pointed to the foam cups in his hands. "At least you kept hold of what's important."

"Wasn't the plan to avoid touching each other?" Burke said tensely, as if he regretted everything about that plan. He walked past her, then stopped. "Coming?"

"Uh…"

"You get yourself up at the ass crack of dawn and creep around the marina for any reason other than finding me?"

Smartass. And damn him for being so astute—and sexy while he was at it.

"I didn't know which boat was yours."

"C'mon, then. I'll introduce you." He began walking but when she didn't follow, he turned, confused. "Sofia?"

Clouds kissed and parted overhead, and a sheet of filmy light was cast across the dock, spotlighting them. He wasn't just out of bed and lazy and sleepy. He was totally alert, in faded jeans and a gray tee that was streaked with—

"It's oil," he supplied, because she'd been staring and he must've figured the smears preoccupied her. The truth was she wanted to know what he'd look like if he put down those cups and peeled off the shirt.

"Oil," she repeated. The kind of oil she'd appreciate wouldn't be swiped across his shirt but dripped onto his sun-golden skin, and she'd be the one to massage it into him, trailing a stream up his abs, then fanning her palms over his pecs…

"Yeah, oil. For the boat. I change it myself." A note of curiosity relaxed his face for the briefest of moments, and something inside her sighed. Then a frown took up residence, creating shadows where there was once light and openness. "Change your mind about the stalking?"

"I wasn't stalking." She'd simply shown up on the dock

unannounced and was creeping around hoping to catch him off guard to lay down a business proposal.

"No?" He eased into a spread-legged stance, apparently getting comfortable for whatever explanation she might throw out there. He drank from one of the cups. "Let's hear it, then. The Tremaines in the fifty-footer at the end, they get up early for breakfast at the general store. They can get an earful, too."

Dropping her volume, she said urgently, "I came to speak to you about something important, but I don't know which one's yours. I'm not going to cause a scene for your neighbors' entertainment. I can leave." But she didn't want to leave.

Don't let me leave, Burke. I want to stay. I want you to want me to stay.

"Don't go," he said. "You seemed pretty determined to get to me. The marina's not exactly next door to your sex shop, is it?"

No, but your father's building—your building—is, and we need to talk. "You're holding two cups of coffee." An assumption registered. "Maybe you want to send whoever's in your bed on her way before I get on board?"

Burke's eyes were assessing, measuring. "Two cups of coffee's all it takes to make you jealous?"

"I'm not jealous. I'm being considerate of your one-night wonder in there." God, she was lying, because the prickling on top of her veins had nothing to do with consideration and everything to do with envy that wound green and possessively through her like climbing ivy. "So. Yes. I'll leave. Now."

"Sofia."

She pivoted, and something bit into her sole, but she could respond to nothing but his voice. "What?"

"There's no one on board. I got out of bed at four something to knock out chores. Got a full day ahead over at Abram and Hannah Slattery's house. The two cups are for me. Piping hot even through these damn sleeves, but the general store makes it good." He winked and it almost felled her. "Since you got all dressed up for me, I can share."

Sofia bristled at his teasing. It really came much too effortlessly for him, considering the canyon-deep hell between them. Either that or he wore a mask and was as torn and confused as she. "I'll take one. What are you doing at the Slatterys' place?"

"They've got a couple of babies on the way. Abram wants a nursery for the kids and a craft room for Hannah. I'm helping out."

"That's nice of you."

"Nah, I'm just keeping busy." Burke walked over and handed her the cup he hadn't drunk from, and she felt slighted somehow. She wanted to put her lips where his had been. Cheap thrill, she knew. It also happened to be a safe one. The attraction was trouble, but could either of them ignore it entirely?

"Mmm...oh, there's mint in this?" *Yum.* She went for another taste, taking a slurping sip that lacked any hint of grace. Giggling, she commented, "That wasn't cute, was it?"

"I think it was," he said, so gently she felt as if he was coaxing her out of hiding somehow. Not even touching her, he drew her along after him.

As they walked, a pinch of pain flared in the bottom of her foot to the point that she limped the final few steps onto the cockpit of a boat that gleamed white save for the cobalt lower half. *Colossians 1:14.*

"Didn't you go to P-town and have Colossians 1:14 tattooed on your arm back in high school?" Belatedly, she groaned at the faux pas. It was the equivalent of *Didn't your dad chastise you in front of the entire school for getting that tattooed on? Didn't you kick a hole in Principal Whaler's door because your dad went postal about that tattoo? Did you ever forgive me for telling your dad you sneaked up to P-town to get a tattoo?*

"That was the first. The consequences of that didn't stop me from getting more."

"Oh. I didn't know."

"I made sure you didn't." For a time he'd worn one long-sleeved shirt after another. She wouldn't admit now that she'd noticed. "When I wanted the old man to find out, I showed him. You should've been busy enough tipping over everyone else's secrets. Why add all my fuckups to your burden?"

Somehow they'd made it past all that and they were here, together. What kind of miracle, or prank of fate, was this?

"This here's a forty-footer. A beast, but I can handle her on the water all right." Pride tinged his voice as he listed the restoration and upgrades he'd applied since laying down almost two hundred grand and having the boat shipped from Louisiana. "The bottom paint's fresh. I took care of that and had the rigging checked out practically the minute I walked off the site in Boston."

"Since you're permanent there, at the harbor, how often do you go out to sea?"

"As often as possible. I try to put my name at the top of disaster aid lists, but I can usually find a cargo ship or a gig with a fishing crew. I got myself sent to Alaska last winter. Can't say I was enthusiastic to come back here. On the other end of that, Eaves wasn't all that enthusiastic to welcome me home."

Sofia adamantly denied that the churning in her stomach

had anything to do with the touch of longing coloring the matter-of-factness in his voice. "Forgetting someone's fuck-ups can be impossible, but people are equipped to forgive. Redemption and forgiveness, they happen. Reacquaint yourself with Colossians." On the cockpit the water's coolness and the sun's heat engaged the breeze in tug-of-war, but she didn't sit and bask in the competition. "The drugs, the acting out, that doesn't define who you are."

"There you go with your fantasies again." Contrition dulled the sharp delivery of each word. "This place pinned me a long time ago. Some part of me is anchored here."

Me, too.

"Want a below-deck tour? And I don't mean that in a pervy way—unless that does something for you."

A smile defied her resolve to be opaque, to give away nothing. She started to keep up with his casual speed, but her foot hurt and she was done putting up a façade. "Ouch," she complained at last, holding out the foam cup. "Take this. I might've cut my foot on a plank."

"Not surprised. That can happen when you go stomping around on a dock barefoot. Seems a woman would wear some kind of shoes with a getup like that."

"They're in the basket. Of the bike. I bicycled here."

"*Bicycled?* Look, Sofia, I know Eaves is a mighty small town, but it's not so small that somebody like you can pedal from one end to the other like it's nothing."

"My heart is fine. As soon as the docs gave me the all-clear, I started building my endurance. A year post-transplant I was sprinting. This was nothing."

"You seemed out of breath when I came up behind you."

"That's because I was thinking about—" She swallowed the rest of that sentence, that single damning word: *you.* "Forget it."

Burke disappeared belowdecks and returned empty-handed, but straightaway helped her down a column of steep steps and carried her to his living quarters. "You say that a lot. 'Forget it.' Every time you do, it makes me even more eager to know your secrets."

He set her down on something firm yet cushiony...a mattress...his bed. He'd brought her to a cabin that was more spacious than she'd imagined, even on a boat this size. Portholes allowed sunshine voyeuristic entry. The cabin smelled of teak and clean laundry, spiced with the tang of lemon from the galley. She hadn't absorbed that she was being spirited someplace infinitely private.

"The purse, the jacket—get rid of them. If you're gonna give me your secrets, you might as well be comfortable when you do."

The jacket was the crucial article of her businesswoman ensemble. Without it she'd be a woman with a scar on her chest sitting in front of a man who had something she wanted. It was the critical thread in the image she'd stitched together. All else would unravel with mortifying ease.

"Air conditioner's not cranked up yet," he said. "You're hot in all those clothes, and I'm hot looking at you."

"That'll certainly change once I take this jacket off."

"So test your theory." Burke crouched before her, watching her as he opened the jacket button by button. Stripping away the fabric, he let his hands skate along the skin he uncovered. Testing her, he gauged what she'd allow and what might compel her to retreat. "I see the edge of your scar, a dark slash between your breasts. That's not scaring me off." He leaned close, kissed her neck. "You're so damn soft, right here. I didn't kiss you here the last time."

Sofia edged back. "Motor oil. I don't want it on my clothes." Her borrowed heart *thump, thump, thumped* inside her. The jacket, her shield, lay discarded on the bed some-where behind her, and she was only Sofia and he was only Burke. "Can you make sure that doesn't happen?"

The sheets rustled as she scooted toward the center of the bed, farther from the edge . . . farther from the door. His scent lifted from the linens, stroking her lightly, pulling her down gently until she lay on her back.

She was lying in a man's bed. *This* was new. If he stretched out beside her, would lying with him feel strange? They'd lain side by side before, sharing a pair of earbuds as they listened to music, sharing a blanket as they watched fireworks explode over the beach, sharing tears the morning she'd found him shaking and weak and made the 911 call that had saved his life.

They'd never been together this way.

"I'm going to take a look at that foot," he said, and stepped out of the cabin.

She was lying on an extremely sexy man's bed and the best she could get out of it was splinter removal. Embar-rassed, Sofia debated: Feign nonchalance or jet out as fast as her hobble would allow?

But he came back before she could decide. He'd traded his oil-stained shirt for a white one and held up a first aid kit. "Clean shirt, scrubbed hands, and whatever's bothering you should be remedied with something in here."

"Okay." It wasn't okay. She was clawing toward some-thing but afraid to gain purchase. So she let him pick up her foot. "Is it bleeding? Did I track blood on the pier?"

"Nope and nope. You've got a splinter. I'm going to tweeze the bastard out, then clean you up. Is that a plan?"

"Sure . . . it's a plan."

"It shouldn't hurt, unless I have to do a little digging to get a grip. If it pinches too much—"

"Scream?"

"At this hour, try not to. Marina folks like to let the sun and gulls wake them up, not screams. How about tapping me with the other foot? Whatever you do, don't squirm while I'm aiming the pointy end of these tweezers at you. You might end up with worse than a splinter."

Sofia waited, twisting her fists in the sheets in anticipation of pain and squeezing her eyes shut to brace herself for the sting.

"Hey, Sofia?"

Was he . . . laughing? She opened her eyes, unclenched her fists.

"It's out already. A little disinfectant and a Band-Aid should tide you over until you get some shoes on."

It was over, and so painlessly? He'd handled her carefully, capably. "You weren't as barbaric as I thought you'd be," she said as he applied the slim bandage. "I keep thinking the worst when it comes to you, and I don't want to do that anymore."

"Don't worry about it."

"Burke, thanks for patching me up." His smile startled her, comforted her, and she realized the compassionate, attentive side of him was nothing new. "And for remembering my sub sandwich and cleaning my windshield and being my friend when no one else would take the job."

"That stuff . . . I didn't do it for gratitude."

"I know. It's just that"—she wiggled her foot, still in his grip—"you reminded me that you're kind of good at taking care of me, so I shouldn't have worried about the splinter."

"I don't want to see you hurt, Sofia." His gaze found hers and held it . . . cradled it, like he cradled her foot. Then he raised it and laid a kiss on her heel . . . then another on her instep . . . then another on each toe.

Oh my hell. Oh. My. Hell.

"You owe me a secret," he reminded her, too serious to be called gentle. "What were you thinking about on the dock?"

"You." Sofia took her foot from his grasp and slid it down the stony terrain of his abdomen. When she'd asked him not to get oil on her shirt, she hadn't meant for him to change into another. She poked her toes into his muscles. It was so hard there—did he even feel the pressure? "Let me see you."

Burke swept off his shirt and it joined her jacket somewhere on the bed.

Well, damn.

One arm was inked from the curve of the shoulder to the top of the elbow. The bicep was completely covered. Words were written into his skin, images drawn into his flesh. Patterns and messages blended and competed, and he was so beautiful in front of her that he stole her breath like an unrepentant thief.

It was the sort of tragic, painful beauty that you could either treasure or forsake.

Sofia allowed her foot to slip farther, and she rested it firmly against his crotch. That was hard, too—unmistakably so.

"You've been thinking about this? Thinking about how I'd feel in your hands? How I'd feel in your mouth?" Burke covered her foot with his hand and moved it up and down the front of his jeans. "Tell me. I want to hear every word. Every little moan you've got. Every nasty wish you're hiding in that sweet mouth of yours. That's what you're going to do for me, Sofia."

She wanted to speak, but a trembling sigh tumbled out. Trying again, she said, "Oh, yeah?"

"Yeah." The whisper was so coarse she thought it scraped her. "My bed, Sofia. My fucking rules."

Egged on by his bossy, dirty words, she said, "Unzip your jeans."

"Then what?"

"The cock. I want to see it." As soon as the words sprang free, she wanted to roll over and slither off the bed. She settled for tapping her palm to her forehead. "That sounded much sexier in my mind."

"Hey..." His voice came softly to her, and then he was on the bed, lying with her, rolling her so that she draped on top of him. "This bed's built to take a lot. Don't hold back here, not with me."

"I really do want to see your cock."

Burke kissed her then, sampling her lips and twirling his tongue around hers. She heard his zipper surrender and then she turned her attention to what lay beneath it.

Denim and boxer briefs were concealing...

Mercy.

Sofia wasn't altogether certain how to best approach him. But she didn't need to be. They were learning, becoming familiar with each other. The uncertainties amplified the excitement.

Experimentally, she curled against him. Engorged from root to mushroom-shaped tip, his cock jutted from a patch of dark hair and arrowed toward his stomach. Veins threaded beneath the delicate-looking skin. She wrapped her hand around his flesh, then watched him move in her grip.

Burke groaned and she wanted to taste it, remember it forever. So she kissed him as she stroked, locking away the memory. No questions were needed, no instructions necessary, but the muscles in his abdomen flexed and clear fluid beaded at the tip of him, and she couldn't help but speak.

"You're so responsive to me. The sounds you make, and how your body reacts when I touch you…I don't want to quit touching you."

"Then keep doing it. Go ahead." His hand massaged into her nape, then she felt her hair unspooling down her back and soon he was guiding her. "Wet your lips. You can take me easier that way."

Stretching over him, she painted kisses across his pelvic bones before swiping her tongue across her lips and taking his hard flesh into her mouth. Relishing their unhurried rhythm, she explored, letting him engage her senses. She was eager to know all the ways they could fit together, all the ways she could get him to keep groaning for her like this. But to rush would strip away some of the pleasure, and she wouldn't deprive herself of a single opportunity to get her fill of this man.

Sliding a hand up from hip to stomach, she was warmed throughout when he took that hand and entwined his fingers with hers. And she let him in deeper.

It was right, natural, as though all the glances and the laughter and the hurt and lust had led to this singular moment—when they were joined somehow.

Burke's hand cruised down her spine to burrow underneath her tight black pants and trace down the seam of her ass. Bare skin on bare skin. "C'mere. Lift up."

When she rose to her knees and one of his fingers breached her slit, she gasped. "Sorry. I'm wet, I can feel it. But I wasn't prepared for that."

"You're not ready," he said, taking his hand out of her pants and sucking her moisture from his finger. "Not for me. Not yet. That's okay."

"What you just did," she whispered, "did you like it? How I taste?"

"Hell, yes." Burke leaned forward and kissed her, sharing the flavor of her arousal. "Do you?"

She smiled. "Yes. And I like how you taste." She returned to him, but their steady rhythm was sacrificed as the tempo picked up. Faster, harder, she took him, until he clutched her tight to him as he shattered in her mouth. A succession of spurts introduced his flavor to her tongue, coated her with his heat, and created a raw, messy layer of closeness between them.

She lay tangled with him until his breathing stabilized and he could manage to right his jeans. "I made you sweat," she said, laughing delicately as she peppered kisses up his shoulder until she could nip his ear. She couldn't stop touching him, couldn't silence the want for more. She was satisfied yet somehow deprived of intimacy that was deeper than even this. "So this was okay?"

"Incredibly." His mouth met hers, and they indulged and shared until one of them needed to breathe. "Is this okay for you? For your heart?"

Sofia didn't feel any discomfort, but her pulse rushed, and the more she focused on the rhythm the more convinced she was that it pounded quicker moment by moment. "It's good—we're good," she said, reassuring him even as she scooted off the bed and tried to stave off panic.

Breathe . . . in and out. Breathe . . . in and out. The thought consumed her mind, playing in a continuous loop.

"Hey." Burke was in front of her, holding her hands. "Can I have a listen?"

His question distracted her, and the mounting anxiety cracked. When he bent and rested an ear on her chest, she wrapped her arms around him because this was the single most vulnerable moment she'd experienced with a man and some part of her was glad that the man was Burke Wolf.

"Strong heartbeat," he said, slipping an arm around her and swaying her right where they stood. "What about your head? You looked like you were thinking a billion thoughts all at once."

"I was trying to fix a problem that didn't exist." She hummed with relief, so content that they were holding each other, getting closer, and were actually letting it happen. "Everything's okay."

"So do you need to be someplace else right now?"

"Nope."

"Good answer. Next question—have you ever eaten breakfast on a boat?"

"Hmm, I grew up in a fishing town, so it might've happened. *But* a sexy longshoreman has never fixed me breakfast before." She squeezed his shoulders, looked up at him. "Think you'd like to be my first, Burke?"

A simple question, packed with meaning, and his only response was, "Go ahead to the galley, Sofia. I'll be right there."

While he gathered the sheets she went to the galley to wash her hands. So narrow, the interior space was, but thankfully things appeared to be in their rightful places.

He wasn't messy, but then, Deacon Wolf had been a military vet who'd instilled his code into his son. The Wolfs' house had been clean—almost sterile, anyone could say.

When he joined her in the galley, he stood perfectly still, studying her face. "I'd kiss you hard every day if it meant your mouth would be this sexy when I let you go."

Kiss you hard every day. The words isolated themselves from the rest, hit her boldly, pressured her to pretend just for a second that they were part of a promise. "Oh?"

"See for yourself."

Burke directed her to the head and she popped right back out with "My lips look like they got stuck in a Shop-Vac."

The comment drew a startled laugh. The humor and euphoria were contagious but much too short-lived. "The last time we were together we agreed to coexist. What we did in my bed, that's more than coexisting. That's irrevocable. I'm not done with you, Sofia."

But how much time lay between now and the day when he *would* be done with her? He was going to leave again, whether reporting to some port for work or steering this very boat to his next faraway adventure.

"We should be clear that this isn't the sort of thing that lasts," she said, resting her hands on his chest. "You're going to take off whenever the urge strikes. I'm going to love someone who'll stay."

"For practical reasons we don't work."

"We don't," she confirmed, but that didn't mean she was happy about it. "The practical thing to do is to keep things platonic."

"And realistically, what'll we do?"

"Be together. Hang out, have fun, kiss when we want to...Eventually we're going to have to be practical."

He nodded his agreement, pointed toward the main saloon. "Eventually isn't today, so have a seat. I'll whip up some breakfast and you'll tell me about the agenda you brought to the marina."

Oh. Right. She *had* come here for a reason that didn't involve naughty naked things. "What are you fixing?"

"Pancakes. Is that all right with you?"

"You never have to ask. Who doesn't like pancakes anyway?"

"My mom. She was a French toast person. I remember she was stubborn as hell about it. Deacon made pancakes, taught me how when I got older."

As though the mere mention of his father's name could

change everything, Burke became churlish. He didn't offer much conversation as he mixed the batter and flipped the flapjacks in a skillet. The stack of pancakes he set between them on the varnished mahogany table was high and leaned precariously.

"The Cape Foods building," Sofia blurted after a maple-syrup-drizzled pancake.

A slight headshake answered her, then, "What about it?"

"It's neglected, Burke. I don't know the interior condition, but my guess is it still has great bones." Still he volunteered nothing—not information, not a question, not a demand to know why she brought the topic to his breakfast table. "Javier Bautista told me you own the building."

"Wasn't his duty."

"It was *yours*. You let me talk about how the state of it's affecting Blush and you said nothing. I would've appreciated for you to be up front."

"It is mine," he confirmed. "Deacon left it and some debts. I took care of things."

"What are your plans for it?"

"No plans."

Then he intended to leave it in limbo, connected to him but somehow not? "It used to be the social hub. It meant something. Now it's a ghost."

"Change's to blame. It was bound to happen. A supermarket came in, new ideas and people and places cropped up. Deacon's death laid ownership of his property in my hands and I'm managing it how I see fit."

"It's abandoned."

"There you're wrong. I pay the taxes, check up on it when I'm in town."

"And when you're gone?" Which was how often? Half a year, most of the year, years at a time? The man could stake his claim on something, make it his, and leave it anytime the whim hit. A building handed down, a woman who cared—it didn't matter.

"The property's insured, and it's not violating any codes. Taking Luz's place, tying yourself to her store, that's your choice and I'm respecting that. So respect mine."

"Someone gave me a second shot when I needed one. I'm paying it forward." She slid her plate aside and reached to cover his hand, but he moved out of her path. "Burke, please listen. I chose to put life back into Blush. I'd like to do the same for Cape Foods. Sell it to me. I'm prepared to negotiate a fair purchase."

"Greeting card business pays well if you're ready to put money on a building."

"Luz's estate was...substantial. The money's mine to spend."

"Dozens of offers have come through. None swayed me to lay down that store. Even Luz tried to buy it." He chewed deliberately, his voice so calm that it made her nervous. "What makes you any more worthy than the rest of them?"

"It doesn't need to be about worthiness. It doesn't have to be personal. Me and you and friendship or attraction, or whatever name you'd like to put on it? Forget it for a moment. I have money, you have a building, and I'd like to work out a deal."

"For what?"

"For Joss. Joss Vail. She and I were roomies in the city." Again she reached for him, although she'd clarified that this wasn't personal. How could it *not* be, when careers, friendships, the past and future depended on it? "She gave me that second shot. Dad didn't leave me with any prospects. I hunted high and low for work and then a girl offering samples in front of a Teavana took a chance on me. She was holding down two jobs and college, but she helped me get a gig delivering pastries. She shared her crappy apartment, let me figure out my life. We worked our asses off for better everything. Better educations, a better apartment, better clothes—all of it. I'm telling you she dusted me off when I hit the bottom. Now she's at the bottom and I want to offer her a second shot here in Eaves."

"How does my building factor in?"

"I want to convert it into an erotic bakery."

"An erotic *bakery*?"

"Yes. Chocolate cocks, sexual party cakes, aphrodisiac pastries." The pitch wasn't going precisely as planned, but that was the gist of it. Joss was a pastry genius and an artist with affection for the erotic. Sandwiched between a sex shop and a boudoir photography studio, she'd have built-in clientele, damn near. "Those are examples of what she can do if she had the opportunity."

"You said this wasn't personal, but your friend recruited you as the go-between."

"Joss doesn't know. This is on me." She'd left Joss sleeping, with Tish appearing deceptively relaxed in front of the sofa but on alert from nose to tail. Sofia hadn't wanted to build up her friend's excitement only to tear it down should Burke reject the offer. "I had a professional presentation planned."

"Before my penis sidetracked you." Matter-of-factly spoken, with only an indication of the start of a smirk.

Or maybe she was hoping for lightness to relieve the friction of this moment.

"Pretty much, yes."

Burke reclined in his seat and folded his arms, and the muscles leaped. *God.* "Enjoy that pancake?"

She nodded. "Delicious."

"Good. That's all you're getting from me. The building's not for sale."

Hadn't he been listening? Didn't he care? He'd let her go on, welcomed her to reveal what she and Joss had lived through—knowing he'd turn her down flat.

But Sofia didn't protest. She ransacked the galley, combing cupboards and drawers until she found a plastic container and lid.

"What're you doing?" he demanded.

"Taking all the pancakes. I can't give my friend the Cape Foods building, so I'm giving her breakfast. Not quite the same, but she'll value the gesture." Swiping the maple syrup, too, she marched off Burke's boat and to her bicycle on the dock.

It would've felt like a triumph had he not flown down the pier after her and had she not slowed so he could catch up.

Pier traffic seemed to bottleneck where she stopped walking and others interrupted their business to pry into hers. A barefoot woman holding Tupperware and syrup must look strange, so she didn't fault their curiosity.

Besides, she was more interested in the reason Burke was chasing her down after shutting the door on her business proposition.

"Sofia, wait." He was close enough to touch but she wouldn't reach out and watch him evade her again. "I was a dick to dismiss you like that. I'm sorry."

"I really am keeping the pancakes."

"And I'm not putting up a fight for 'em." He stretched out an arm, bringing her to his hard muscled frame and the clean scent of his white shirt. She struggled to compartmentalize, wanting two things: the vacant building he owned and for him to be out of that shirt and holding her tight again. "The building conversation—that was business, right? Let's make this personal again."

"Your marina mates are watching."

"Screw that. I'm thinking about you, Sofia. That harrowing splinter incident isn't forgotten"—he paused and the hint of teasing worked loose the tension in his frown—"and I don't like the thought of you bicycling home barefoot. Let me drive you back."

"Another act of heroism, Burke? What happened to not wanting to get sucked in again?"

"I'm in this with you. It's already done. Giving you a ride back is the right thing to do, so just let me do it."

Let him take care of you. Let him reveal that he cares.

In minutes Burke had loaded the bicycle into the bed of his turbo diesel Ford and they were headed to her side of town. When they turned onto Society Street and he parked in front of Blush, she finally killed the quiet. "This isn't coming from a place of hurt, or entitlement, but I'm asking you to reconsider. Maybe Joss won't want a bakery, and she has the right to say no thanks. But even if that's the case, I'd still want the Cape Foods building."

"To do what with it?"

"Expand Blush, rent the other apartment out. And there's the basement." She looked at his profile, willed him to at least glance at her. "Bautista wants Caro Jayne to take the bar. She asked if I'd go in on it, and I think I might. We talked about opening the space. All three basements connect. There's more down there than just a passageway for two kids to hide from the world."

His gaze searched hers then. "Blush isn't enough to hold you down?"

"I don't see it that way. You were right before—this is my choice. I'm choosing to put my stamp on Eaves. I'm choosing roots and a home and an opportunity to make the most of my life."

"Sofia." Burke unsnapped his seat belt and lunged to kiss her. Once, then again, intense enough to draw a deep moan. "You think I *want* the goddamn building? I don't. But I can't sell it."

Can't and *won't* weren't interchangeable, but he didn't owe her further explanation any more than she owed him proof that she deserved the chance to purchase the building. "Okay," she said, slipping out of the truck.

She remained on the sidewalk holding the bicycle's handlebars, watching him depart. It wasn't until his truck vanished around the corner that she realized her jacket was still on his boat.

She'd hurt him years ago, and today she'd swiped his pancakes.

He refused to sell a vacant building he didn't want, and now he had her jacket.

Did that make them even?

CHAPTER 12

$\mathcal{H}$ ate to be the bearer of bad news," Paget hollered into the boutique, where both Sofia and Joss were carting ladders and paint supplies through the labyrinth the furniture created in the front room, "but we're screwed."

Please, no more awful surprises. Yesterday morning the air system had gone on the fritz, leaving them all cranky and sweaty. Kotts & Sons had put off their service call until seven p.m., then charged Sofia the after-hours rate.

"How screwed?" Joss replied, lugging a ladder carefully around the tarp-draped armoire as Sofia followed with two five-gallon containers of paint—Communion White and Tears of Midas Gold—and stir sticks from the paint store. "Soft bed or hard floor?"

"Hard floor"—Paget paused, and cutting through the street noise was the grumble of an engine idling and then the foreboding whoosh of air brakes—"with no lubrication."

The *oh, shit* alarm clanging inside Sofia depleted her energy and she let gravity claim the paint containers. They hit the paper-covered floor with identical thuds and she wormed her way to the door.

Square in front of the shop and dominating the street was a shipping truck. One man approached with a clipboard in tow; his partner raised the rear door of the twenty-something-foot roadblock. He pointed the clipboard at Sofia. "You Joss Vail?"

"I am," Joss called from inside. She propped the ladder and it proceeded to slide and clatter to the floor, yet another obstruction, but she didn't stop to clear the path. Climbing over Sofia's dresser and bouncing across to where Paget leaned against the open door, she grabbed the clipboard. "I want to check the fragiles before I sign this," she said. "And I want to inspect the sofas and chairs and the mattress for rips."

"Ma'am, we're on a tight schedule and it's hotter than the devil's armpits out here," the man griped, but Paget's snicker seemed to diminish his bluster. "Check the glass for shatters, but anything else you'll need to look over later and file a report with the company. Everything's here—hold the door open and we'll bring it in."

"And put it where?" Sofia cried. Blush was beyond capacity with product shipments and what she and Joss had already carried over from New York—and not even all of that fit in the boutique. Caro Jayne and her assistant had stored some of the overflow in the back rooms of Au Naturel, but generosity, and pity, had limits. Sofia beckoned her friend back into the store. "Joss, I thought you were selling off this stuff."

"The consignment places want over fifty percent of the sale, so *that* wasn't going to happen. Flea market shoppers mind-game too much and care more about winning than bargain-hunting. I'd rather hoard all of this than accept pen-

nies for it." She'd worked hard for years to afford her ne-
cessities and luxuries alike. "The piano sold. Cool two hundred." Her smile was anything but joyful.

"I'm sorry." Neither of them played the instrument—it'd
belonged to Joss's grandmother, and was worth much more
to Joss than even its multithousand-dollar appraised value.
That was the one possession Sofia had expected Joss to keep.
"Can you buy it back?"

"No. My cousin has it, and it's a no-take-backsies situation. He's always wanted it, was pissed when Granny left it
to me."

"He sounds like a prick."

"Oh, he is. But you can't choose your family."

"You can pick your friends, though, and as your best
friend I have to tell you that Paget's right. We really are
screwed. There's nowhere to cram yet another truckload of
furniture in this store." Especially not if they planned to re-
open the boutique next month. Blush needed to function as
a "knickers and kink shop, not a storage unit," as Caro had
said. "Let's see if the deliverymen will haul some of it up to
the apartment."

No walk-ups. Fifteen minutes later, Joss, Sofia, and Paget
stood on the sidewalk assessing the collection of furniture
and boxes purged from the truck. It rumbled down the street,
and if Sofia had hopped on her bicycle she might have been
able to catch the deliverymen at a traffic light and beg them
to reconsider, but pride glued her flip-flops to the brick.

"We're three intelligent, strong women," she said to the
others. "We can figure this out."

"Make that four." Caro trotted to them. "I just drove in
from a location shoot in Nantucket and can use a good
stretch after sitting on my arse in the car for three hours. I'm
intelligent and strong, if I do say so myself." Flexing her bi-

ceps caused her stacks of beaded bracelets to slide down, exposing both wrists. The *breathe* tattoo Sofia had seen before. She'd never noticed the pattern inked into the other wrist.

"That's an electrocardiogram," she said. She was far too intimately familiar with ECGs.

"Evan's first heartbeat. Guess I'm a sentimental mum." The others attempted to lean in for closer inspection, but her arms dropped so fast it was as if she'd zapped them to her sides. "Let's clear this area before one of those brown-nosing committee bastards tattles to town hall that you're posing a safety hazard. Fines are hell."

"Wouldn't it be less aggravation to hire a crew specifically for this?" Paget eyed the memory foam mattress that was roughly quadruple her size and leaning against the shop front.

"Called up a few local companies," Sofia reported. "No one's excited about the walk-ups. There are plenty of commercial-building apartments around here, and somehow people move in and out, but no one wants to bite this time."

"Did you offer them extra money?" Joss asked. "I know you're used to holding tight to the purse strings, but I'd say this is an emergency. Let me pay the extra."

"Nope. Aunt Luz collected her assets by being financially prudent. I'm doing the same thing. That's why I'm not hiring an interior designer or outsourcing anything I can't do myself."

"What if we can't do this ourselves?" Paget queried, worrying the ends of her hair. Today it hung in a white waterfall down her back. "I'll give it my damnedest, but just saying."

"Don't think about defeat." Sofia went to the leather chair where she had sometimes slept while watching TV back in New York. She latched onto it first because she'd secretly missed it like crazy. "Caro and I can carry this piece. Paget and Joss, you ladies can team up."

Working in pairs, they brought up the chair and some lamps but hit a snag with the overstuffed sofa. Literally.

"It's torn," Paget called down to Caro and Sofia as they muscled a vanity across the rear lot.

"I can fix it," Sofia assured. She'd just need to dig out her sewing materials, wherever the hell they were boxed away inside Blush. Signaling for Caro to set down her end of the vanity, she announced, "Yeah, we can't do this."

"No crap," Joss said, her arms quivering under the sofa's weight. Halfway up the staircase, Paget *tsk*ed at the damage.

Caro's ass began to ring. She pried her phone from a back pocket and paced circles around the lot. "Girls, I'm sorry, but my sitter has to take off and Evan hasn't had lunch yet. I've got to get home and feed him."

"Take me with you!" Paget screeched, but she laughed as she and Joss brought the sofa down the stairs. "I'm kidding. But I am hungry. Someone at the Seasons called off so Anne Oakley put me on housekeeping. I changed and drove straight here." That explained the makeup on her arms and the simple pearl dots in each earlobe.

"Go feed the kiddo, Caro," Sofia said. When Caro wished them all good luck and scurried off, Sofia turned to Paget next as she fished her keys from her jeans. The woman had proven trustworthy in the brief time they'd known each other. Before Joss had moved in, Paget had pet-sat Tish while Sofia visited New York to tie up loose ends. "You go raid the fridge."

"And you and I are going out for groceries," Joss said brightly.

Paget frowned. "I wasn't planning on scarfing down the entire kitchen."

"What I mean is, I have an idea to get us some manual labor for cheap. That involves a bit of shopping. Are you fine with patrolling our stuff for a little while, Paget?"

"Sure. Bring back some Fritos, though."

Joss raised her tapered brows at Sofia. "Oh, Paget and I are definitely going to get along. We'll bond over our weakness for chips."

They took Joss's car to the supermarket. Though Joss had a specific checklist in mind, they found a distraction in every aisle. "Oh, there're the chips. Grab the Fritos." "Aren't we low on ginger ale? Let's get a bottle." "There's a sale on cereal. I'm getting Kashi—what do you want?"

When the shopping cart was half-full and they stood waffling between carb-smart frozen yogurt and Ben & Jerry's everything, Sofia asked, "What, exactly, is this plan of yours?"

Joss opened the freezer door and reached in for a third contender: a gallon of cookie dough and vanilla. "Immediate plan for solving our furniture-moving crisis? I'm going to bake cupcakes and we're going to take them to the laundromat."

The Dirty Bastards? "Not following."

Joss tossed her blond hair. The bruise had taken on a grayish-yellow hue and the tiny scratch had scabbed. "It's one of the prime spots to find a gathering of able-bodied men. From what I've seen it can be feast or famine, but we're heading into the afternoon and business picks up in the afternoons. The owner seems easygoing, and his brother's good for my eyes, but he puts my womanly needs in a tizzy." She tossed the cookie dough ice cream into the cart. "Ice cream, cold showers, they help neutralize the pent-up horniness."

"You've been staring at the neighbors?"

"I rode the subway for a decade—I'm observant."

"There's observant, Joss, and then there's on-the-prowl." Pinpricks of apprehension spread through Sofia. Joss's face hadn't yet healed and she was already scoping out men. Now she intended to bake cupcakes for them? "Where do the sweets come in?"

"We're going to take cupcakes over and ask to borrow some muscle."

"And that's it?" Sofia opted for the frozen yogurt but stared longingly at the ice cream selection. Slow-churn, flavors with candy bar bits added, gallons and quarts and itty-bitty pints. So many options, so much temptation, but giving in could be only a rare indulgence. "I just want you to be careful."

"That's it." Joss winked her bruise-framed eye, then opened the freezer to trade the cookie dough for fudge brownie. "This is a furniture-moving mission. And, all right, maybe someone will be so wowed by my baking that they'll remember where to get a tasty treat. People on Cape Cod have birthdays and weddings and get-togethers, don't they?"

Sofia discreetly looked around them for eavesdropping shoppers and wanted to whisper but doubted her friend would be able to hear her over Tom Petty and the Heartbreakers' "American Girl" blaring through the supermarket PA system. "That was the plan, for people to come to you for treats. It's why I went to the marina that morning."

The freezer door whined shut. "I don't understand."

"The empty building next door. I thought it'd make a great brick-and-mortar space for an erotic bakery—your bakery."

Joss dashed over to hug her. "Oh, God, that's *genius*! Yes, yes, let's get on that. I'm in." She leaned back. "How come you look like you're about to cry?"

"It's not going to happen. I went to Burke, then his penis

distracted me and we went back and forth about the property but he won't budge."

"Wait. You had sex with Burke?"

"Variations of it. We didn't do everything...but we did enough."

Joss appeared ready to fire off questions, but an elderly woman across the aisle had bumped her cart into a shelf and knocked over boxes of ice cream cones. They went to her, Sofia plucking the boxes off the floor and Joss reaching up high to grab the caramel shell topping the woman was after.

"Thank you, girls," the elderly shopper enthused, straightening the cart. "Y'all just as sweet as y'all want to be. Bless you."

She rounded the corner, her flat shoes squeaking on the floor, and when the squeaking faded, Joss folded her hands over Sofia's shoulders. "About the fucking. Details, please."

"I'm really glad you waited for that cute old lady to leave first. She thinks we're sweet. Not many have that opinion."

"Notoriety's an occupational hazard when you take over a sex shop." Joss sounded proud. "Part of the territory. Speaking of, did Burke mark his? I don't see any whisker burn or hickeys."

Sofia stepped back. "I'm mixed up when it comes to him. Of course the heat is real and I want to be with him like that, but he's not for me."

"Because of the building? Sof, don't let that bust up a relationship."

"It's that he shut down when I brought up the subject. He's standing in the way of a career plan, and it's like Luz taught me—never let a man crush your dream." She began needlessly organizing the contents of their cart, grouping like items together. As she sorted, she briefly explained Caro's business invitation and their idea to reimagine the bar. "Society Street is my life, mine to protect, and Burke's working against that. Am I attracted to him and do I care about him? Completely."

"But not at the expense of a dream."

Sofia nodded. "Luz prioritized. She was smart."

"She agreed to marry a man but took off her ring behind his back," Joss reasoned. "Isn't that what you told me?"

"Yes, but he's a biker. He leaves. He's going to leave again—that's why he wants the bar off his hands. Burke doesn't have a motorcycle, but he's got a boat and he'll leave," Sofia said. She hadn't rationally thought any of this through before acting on lust and emotion. Intuition led her to Burke's arms every damn time they were together. Their hands wouldn't behave; their logic abandoned them. "So to protect myself, I need to put everything I'll still have when he sails away first."

"What if the stars line up or something crazy like that, and you two end up in love? Would he leave if he loved you?"

"I don't know."

"Are you afraid to find out?" Joss eventually sighed sympathetically, because Sofia's silence was a clear answer. "Oh...Sof, it's okay. Let's just keep shopping. But tell me— what's his D situation?"

Sofia might not have as many notches on her bedpost as a tree had rings—okay, she had *zero* notches, or maybe a half notch if lavishing Burke with oral attention counted— but she'd seen lots of naked men. "Damn spectacular."

Joss was the first to snort a giggle. Then they looked at each other and broke out in loud, free laughter. The sound magnetized customers who peered at them, recognized Luz Azcárraga's great-niece, and exchanged long-suffering glances as they moved along.

* * *

Joss baked two dozen cupcakes. Paget was more than happy to assist, and their chatter, blended with rock music, pulsed from the kitchen as Sofia inventoried the apartment, listing furniture to donate to charity. Tish shadowed her, observing her methodically describing the pieces in a spiral-bound notebook and following up with neon-pink sticky notes on each item. Some things she wouldn't part with, such as the antique writing desk Luz's grandfather had built, but others were so personal and intimately Luz—her bed, for one—that Sofia didn't want to continue to cling to them.

Gradually, in cautious tiptoeing steps, she would make this apartment her own. She'd do nothing drastic like change the wall colors, as she and her friends were doing with Blush. Sofia and Joss had discussed converting the bedroom-turned-office back into a bedroom so Joss wouldn't be a perpetual couch-crasher. The aromatherapy paraphernalia would be moved to the kitchen, and they would turn one of Blush's back rooms into a legitimate office.

Electronics would be donated; so would most of the living room furniture.

"You didn't put a Post-it on the table and chairs, Sof," Joss said from the kitchen entryway. Ganache smeared her apron. "I'll clean them and shine them up, but don't forget to tag them."

"I'm keeping them," Sofia said, pressing a pink sticky note to a floor lamp.

"But...they're *white*," her friend sputtered. "You dragged me to Buffalo to purchase the set we had in our old apartment. What are we supposed to do with that?"

"We can keep it, too. We'll put it in basement storage."

"Heat exhaustion, that must be why you're taking a vacay from sanity right now. But fine, keep the old set." She disappeared into the kitchen.

The chairs were chipped and could make your ass go numb if you sat too long, but the table was white-painted pine. Why let a perfectly sturdy piece of handcrafted furniture go unnecessarily?

Sofia drifted to the entryway and gazed at the table. A memory kissed her, begged her to remember a sad day and a coarse man who'd lobbed a condom onto that very table. She wanted to hold on to that heartbeat in time, a sexually charged moment between two messed-up people who lashed out because it was easier to do that than forgive and trust again.

She'd called him a coward. One coward could always spot another, though. Even if he wanted her, Burke would be no part of her future. He knew too much about her family and too many of her secrets. Someday, when she was ready, she'd love someone else—someone who hadn't known her when she was broken, someone who hadn't been burdened with her complications. She would invest her love in someone who wouldn't leave her to start a new life far away, as each of her parents had. She wouldn't exploit a man's weaknesses until she absorbed his dependency, as she had with Burke.

And if there was no way to love without hurting at the same time, then she could do without. She had a business, a pet, friends...a gift inside her chest that didn't need the agony.

"I changed my mind about the white set," she said, and the other women looked at her. Tish pressed her snout into Sofia's thigh and whimpered. Was that sorrow, or had Sofia let herself imagine it? "It can go."

But she'd cry when it did.

When the cupcakes—half red velvet topped with ganache and the other half lemon—were cooled and decorated, Joss explained, "We're taking only a dozen across the street. As you can see, three lemon and three red velvet have the word *NO* on them. The other six have *YES* on them. Once we ask for the favor, all the guys have to do is pick up a cupcake. Even if they grab a 'no,' once they eat it they'll come on over. Trust me."

Downstairs, Paget waited in front of Blush to watch the spectacle, leaving the others to screw up the nerve to try to cupcake-bribe a laundromat full of men.

Sofia grabbed the old shopping cart Luz had used to transport her laundry, wheeled it around the side of the building, and said to Joss, "Beep! Beep! Hop in."

"Oh my God. You're crazy." But she handed Sofia the cupcakes and climbed into the cart. Then she folded her legs and stacked the cupcakes on her lap.

Traffic flowed but seemed to slow as drivers rubber-necked to get a look at a woman pushing another in a shopping cart on the sidewalk.

Horns began to blare and catcalls for their attention rang through the air when Joss started to sing.

"Really, Joss? 'American Girl'?"

"It's stuck in my head. Blame that supermarket. It res-onates, somehow." She went back to singing, practically shouting and swinging her hair through the chorus—and Sofia joined in, with a less musical voice by far, but she didn't care.

They crossed the street as drivers smirked and hands held phones out windows to capture the moment.

Sofia and Joss would probably appear on the Internet somewhere, might even receive a stern talking-to once the

PD got wind of their peace disturbance, but still, she just didn't care.

In front of The Dirty Bastards, they laughed when men jostled one another at the entrance as they competed for the glory of holding open the door for a pair of women toting cupcakes.

"Ladies, c'mon," Abram Slattery said on a groan, as though torn between telling them to leave and pleading with them to stay. "I'm running a business here." He threw out his hand to the people peering in through the door and clustering at the windows. "Ma'am, all that frosting in your lap can't mean good things for the clean clothes in here. I don't see any dirty laundry in that basket, so why don't y'all—"

"I can be a very dirty girl," Joss contradicted, and the room at large seemed to tense up in tight fascination.

What a flirt. It was seamless, effortless, as natural as breathing to Joss.

Sofia, meanwhile, could say nothing. Handfuls of customers lounged on the vinyl modular seating, transferred clothing from washers to dryers, hung out around the reception desk—but she could see only one man.

Burke. She hadn't known he'd be here, though Abram was his friend and sponsor. If she'd seen his truck parked at the curb, she might've asked Paget to switch places with her.

Taken the coward's way out.

Swinging her gaze around the room, though the only face that penetrated was Burke's, she identified at least five people who didn't appear to be actively sorting laundry or waiting for a machine to announce its cycle completion.

"We're in a predicament," she told Abram. "Joss has moved in with me and our stuff from New York won't fit into Luz's apartment. On top of that, a lot of the pieces are too heavy for us to carry up and down the stairs in the back."

Joss rose up in the cart, offering the cupcakes. "So if anyone here could spare some time, we want to ask if you'll help us out. Yes or no?"

Customers murmured and everyone seemed to wait for Abram Slattery to select a cupcake. Lemon or red velvet. Yes or no.

"Hell." Abram went to the window and scanned the street, pausing when he saw Paget standing in front of Blush with Tish at her side, looking like an *American Gothic* parody. Furniture was piled up on either side of them. "Looks like a GD sidewalk sale."

His brother separated from the crowd and swept up a lemon cupcake. *Yes.*

Stunned that McGuinty was the first to volunteer, Sofia said, "Caro was helping us earlier, but she had to leave."

People grunted and chuckled. Evidently his interest in Caro wasn't under wraps.

"Caro's not asking for the favor. You are, so I'm helping you out." He took a big bite and Joss just about preened in self-satisfaction when his resolute frown melted into surprised pleasure. "Fuck, this is good. Who made this?"

"Me! Joss Vail. I was a baker's assistant in New York."

"She's a phenomenal pastry chef." Pointedly, Sofia looked to Burke. "Imagine what she could do with her own space."

His face hardened. All right, so she pushed too far too soon. When he started walking, she expected him to bypass her and the shopping cart, but instead he followed his friend's lead and took a cupcake. Red velvet, but it, too, was a Yes.

"Folks should help each other out around here," he said simply. "I'm heading over there."

Other men descended on the cart, reaching for the treats. McGuinty picked up another lemon, this one a No.

Crestfallen, Joss watched him devour it and suck frosting from his thumb. "Did you change your decision from yes to no?"

"Nah. I just wanted another. I'm not even a cupcake kind of guy."

"Well," she said, all perky afternoon sunshine again as she passed the nearly empty container to Sofia so she could alight from the cart, "there's more in the apartment. Shall we?"

Sofia watched them leave the laundromat and turned to follow, but Abram, who was doling out instructions to his crew, called her back.

He took a plastic-draped garment from a rolling rack and laid it over the reception counter. "Your jacket's ready. No charge."

"My…" She peeled away the plastic. It was the black jacket she'd worn the morning she pedaled to the marina. "Wh-where'd you get this?"

Please say anywhere but the one place that would make sense.

"Balled up in Burke Wolf's laundry. With my own eyes I saw him standing right over there a few days ago throwing sheets in a washer. And what do you know, this here came tumbling out of his bag." His voice was low. "My wife saw it, too."

Hannah Slattery, who ran the Hot Dish restaurant near the bank building where Sofia's father had worked before disgrace ended his tenure and turned him loose.

On a few occasions Sofia had come into the laundromat and found Hannah manning the counter with her husband. Hannah was hospitality personified—she liked to engage and accommodate, and her smile was infectious.

"Ladies' fashion know-it-all that she is," Abram said in

that easy, ain't-no-rush tone of his, "she brought the thing over for dry cleaning and said it was the perfect match to a pair of black pants dropped off that morning."

Every fluid inside Sofia seemed to turn to ice. If she attempted to cry, the tears would be icicle daggers. If she tried to pee, it'd come out in frozen cubes.

"A pair of pants *you* dropped off." Abram scratched his chin as she took the jacket. "Now, Burke's my friend and what he does isn't always my business. But there's only one reason I can think of that'd explain why a man would head out first thing in the morning to wash a load of sheets—and that'd be because someone was rolling around in them the night before."

"What are you trying to ask me, Abram?"

The man chuckled. "Well, I'd thought you'd at least appreciate that your jacket's been all spruced up and returned to you safely."

"You don't need to be crude."

"Crude? Sofia, *crude* would be pointing out the extra care we took in cleaning semen out of the shirt you brought in with those pants. But I didn't point that out, so I'm not crude after all, am I?"

Heat rushed up from her toes and settled in her cheeks. The nerve of Abram—he didn't appear fazed and might in fact be amused by her discomfiture. The Dirty Bastards was, indeed, a fitting name.

"If this is such a crisis, talk to Burke about it."

They faced off, pupil to pupil, frown to frown. Abram was the first to blink. "One, thanks for confirming the suspicion. Now I know for certain what's up."

Damn it! Why hadn't she taken her jacket and bopped out of there? Allowing this man to bait her had rendered no benefit.

"Two, I did talk to him. He said he'd kick my ass if I said a word against you."

Burke had defended her honor? Confusion tossed her into a tailspin and she clutched the jacket to maintain some composure. "Abram, did you and Hannah tell anyone?"

"Nope. But people talk about how y'all used to be, you and Burke, and my wife's got it in her head that you're meant to be."

"It's not like that. We're not together. He hasn't even seen me naked."

It was Abram who blushed next, a ruddy pink color that touched the tops of his cheeks above his full beard. "Christ, Sofia, I didn't ask for specifics. I just want to tell you that I look out for Burke as if he were my own kid brother. Women have come through wanting to change him or needing him to be a man he can't be. It never ends well, and then he's got my own wife playing matchmaker no matter how many times he tells her to back off. You and your sexy window displays might be catching his attention now, but the thing he cares about most is his sobriety. I can't stand by and let you jeopardize that."

"How would I jeopardize his sobriety? In case you're not aware, I have my own health to think about and don't smoke or shoot to take the edge off."

"That's not what I meant." He opened the door and led her outside. The other volunteers were already scattered in front of Blush. "You live clean, and that's great. Burke, on the other hand, is battling a disease that can take hold of him at any time. Addiction's a motherfucker."

"I know that, Abram. I saw him at his worst, in high school."

His grunt of laughter lacked humor. "High school wasn't his worst. That happened after you left."

The last sentence carried the impact of a freight train, as though *after you left* meant *because you left.*

Leaving hadn't been her choice to make. Finnegan Mercer's opportunities on the Cape had dried up after his release from police custody. She'd been a minor and he the only parent who wanted her. She thought her father needed her, that if she survived she would have the chance to pull her weight and take care of him the way he'd worked so hard to take care of her in spite of how difficult she'd made his life.

Sofia could give all of her commitment to one person only, and she'd chosen her father.

She and Finnegan were family. She and Burke were friends. Friendships became untethered; sometimes they snapped. It was tragic but not unnatural. When she left, Burke had lost only a friend—not someone who was a part of him.

It wasn't as if he'd loved her the way she'd loved him.

"Burke and I haven't talked about that...what happened after I left Eaves."

"Well, maybe y'all might want to the next time you think about getting frisky."

It wasn't Abram's business to advise her. He wasn't her sponsor and she didn't require any big-brotherly wisdom.

"I told you," she reaffirmed as they crossed the street, "we're not together."

"And I'm telling you that before you and your shopping buggy full of trouble showed up, Burke was talking about heading to the supplies store and gearing up to check safety lines. Now he's over at your place moving furniture." His bear paw of a hand clapped her shoulder and it was a pleasantly friendly touch. "I don't think that's exclusively because of a red velvet cupcake."

CHAPTER 13

$\mathcal{B}$urke didn't pretend to know all there was to know about art, but he'd stake his boat he was standing in Sofia's living room and staring at a blow job.

"Hey, McGuinty"—he tapped a knuckle against his friend's arm—"the painting over there. What's that look like to you?"

The man scratched his chin, and there was the scraping sound of fingernails against whiskers. "Some lucky bastard living the dream."

That's what he'd thought when he'd first confronted the painting in Blush. It fit into the fabric of a sex shop, but hanging on Sofia's wall, front and center, it gave him chills.

No, not chills—the opposite. A vengeful heat traveled through him from the roots of his hair to the tips of his toes.

Quentin from the Eaves Historical Museum, who'd tucked at least three cupcakes into his corpulent stomach and might lose a button on his straining shirt if he took down another, came over to heft one end of Luz's frayed sofa. "Luz was a legend, but I think Sofia's picking up where she left off at double speed. Mannequin coitus downstairs, now *that*?"

All three men turned back to the painting. Sure enough, a pair of plump pink female lips wrapped around a staff jutting from a rug of pubes. The lines weren't all that defined and the colors of the oils were muted, but come the hell on!

"Sofia's friend, the cupcake fairy. You know she's the one who painted that oil, don't you? J.V." Quentin shook his graying head. "They didn't make 'em like that in my day." The oldest person standing in the apartment, he had a solid thirty years on the others. But if he and Sofia's roommate hit it off, theirs wouldn't be the first May-December pairing in this town.

Burke tried to keep his head down and focus on preventing his life from jumping the rails again, yet some talk wouldn't fizzle. The bored older women—not all of them single—who amused themselves with college-aged summer help, and the men with deep pockets who leisure-sailed and splurged on sugar babies eager to be spoiled? Yup, the folks of Eaves hunted secrets and exposed them loudly. They breathed one another's confidences the way smokers shared hookahs in a lounge.

People were still polluting the air with talk about Luz, who'd taken up with a man fifteen or so years her junior. Stir in the fact that she owned a sex shop and he rode a motorcycle, and the speculations seemed to generate themselves. Hers was the most recent death in Eaves—her name would remain in mouths until the next person knocked off.

That was how it worked, and why Burke rescued himself every time he got on a cargo ship or took his boat out of its slip. His friends and the memory of his mom weren't enough to compel him to call Eaves his home anymore. If he stayed, this place and all those who held his past like a knife behind the back would break his spirit and leave him hollow.

The men took the sofa to the alleyway behind the shop, and while a quickly winded Quentin gave himself some time to recover from the exertion, Burke went around to the front and found Sofia among the trio of women hauling an enormous cabinet from the store.

"What is that?" he asked.

Sofia grunted, "An armoire. It needs to go up."

"Let me take over." He was already going to her side and nudging her.

"I've got it, Burke. I thought you were on the removal crew anyway."

"Couch is in the alley, ready to be loaded up in McGuinty's truck. You shouldn't be handling something this heavy. Go on and take it easy."

"Burke!" She glared at him, and he doubted her fingertips had gone white from the strain of the heavy piece. The other women made "uh-oh" humming noises. "If you're here to help, then help. Don't boss me around, and don't dictate what's good for me."

"If I could jump in," Joss the cupcake fairy/erotic artist said, "we can get this armoire around the back, Burke, thanks. But may we borrow your truck? I think we're going to end up with two donation loads, and it'd save time to drive two trucks over instead of doing a back-and-forth with just the one."

"I'll drop off a haul, and do it with a smile on my face, if Sofia steps away from this before she hurts herself."

The profanity that passed her sweet lips wasn't unexpected. The angrily whispered "Nothing's changed" as she retreated and stomped out of the shop was.

Nothing's changed. In what context had she meant that?

Motivated to personally see the armoire upstairs and placed where she wanted, he recruited Abram and they carried it up.

"Anybody seen Sofia?" he asked when he'd walked through the apartment and couldn't locate her orange-striped gray shirt or her soft brown hair, which was braided around her head like a halo.

The apartment was transforming quickly as all the pink-labeled items were removed and some of the furniture rescued from the sidewalk or extricated from inside the sex shop was brought up.

"Check the store," the white-haired firecracker—Paget—suggested as she passed around cups of iced lemonade. "Or the basement."

The basement. He remembered it well. He'd never sneaked into the porn palace when he was a kid, but he had spent time in the space below it with Sofia. Sometimes they hung out in the Cape Foods basement, and other times in the hall that connected the two.

To some it might sound lame as fuck, but he was mellow and felt in control of himself when he was underground with her and it was just the two of them literally in their own world. On occasions when he was high on some shit or she was low in the dumps, they sat together but said nothing. On good days she'd watch him sketch and he would help her study history, her weakest subject.

They'd provoked each other's tempers down there, too. When he came to her all bruised up, she'd lecture him about picking fights. When she came to him with labored breathing, he'd lecture her about overtaxing herself cleaning her aunt's shop.

Each argument and battle had been derived from friendship. She'd told him once that she loved him, probably because then she hadn't known any better. And she was an imperfect fantasy to him, one that he'd fought hard to shake in the years after she had left Massachusetts.

There was no going back. Never again would he be the boy she thought she loved. She said nothing had changed, but she was wrong.

He'd changed. If he hadn't, he would've died a long time ago.

Burke didn't find her in the shop, and unless she'd taken off on foot and left her car and the bicycle, she was still on the premises someplace.

Taking the stairs next to the shop's kitchenette, he arrived in the basement. A tug of a chain and the room illuminated. Boxes crowded the space, as did furniture and a cast of flexible mannequins.

"Sofia?" he said into the immediate silence. Above was the muffle of footsteps. "You down here?"

He turned to the plywood-covered wall. A precisely cut rectangle, looking as though someone had carved it with a razor blade, was out of place. A similar rectangle was cut into the Cape Foods basement wall, and he'd have to lift it with his nails to pry it away and expose the door. Underneath this door was a shaft of light.

Sofia was on the other side, sitting on the floor, her back flush with the concrete wall. Her head drooped to one side and her shoulders were slumped.

"Hey, Sofia…" Stepping closer, lowering to his knees, he realized her chest wasn't rising and falling in a normal rhythm. "Sofia!"

Her eyes began to close as her hands weakly reached out toward him. "I—I can't…Can't…breathe…" Gasping, she crumpled and a tear slipped down one cheek.

"Jesus." He shot forward, taking her wrist in one hand to

gauge her pulse and using his other hand to pat his pockets. "My phone. Where ... where the hell did I put it?"

He'd left it in his truck, plugged into the dash. If he'd gone directly to get his ride when her roommate had mentioned carting a load to the charity lot, he would've grabbed the phone then. He would have it now and could dial for help.

Was it safe to move her? He didn't altogether know what was ailing her, but if she couldn't breathe it might not be a smart idea to do anything that would further restrict her lungs.

And if the problem had to do with her heart ...

"I have to get you some help." He squeezed her hand, wavering between getting up and taking the stairs three at a time and staying here with her hand in his because he was so fucking afraid of what might happen if he let her go.

Her head shot from side to side. "Uh-uh. Stay."

How could he sit here and watch her struggle? But if he were to leave her and she lost consciousness—lost her life— alone in a tunnel, he'd die, too. Her pain was his. Hadn't it always been that way?

"I'm going to carry you upstairs and get 911 on the phone. You stay with me, all right, baby?"

"Not ... your baby." The spark of defiance was carried out on a trembling exhale. She pressed one hand below her stomach and the other to her sternum. Another exhale, then those beautiful brown eyes opened again and found him.

She inhaled through her nose and her stomach expanded, then came another shallow sigh. Her body appeared to relax then and her breathing grew stronger.

A panic attack. She'd had one at the gas station convenience store the day of Luz's funeral, but she had been able to stay on her feet and speak through it.

"I'm getting you to the ER," he told her.

"No," she protested, and seemed to test herself with a deep breath. "I'll be okay. It was just a panic attack."

"*Just* a panic attack?" he repeated incredulously. "You were underground and alone and couldn't breathe!" It had to be a jackass idea to raise his voice, but he couldn't believe his ears. "I thought you were sitting here dying."

"I'm not." As if to prove her strength, she started to get up but wobbled and promptly slid down with a thud.

"Come here." Burke sat beside her and scooped her off the floor, cradling her on his lap. She didn't slap him or otherwise protest. She nuzzled her face against his neck and twisted her fingers in his hair. "I don't think many people know this space exists down here. Who would've found you, if I hadn't felt like a douche and gone searching for you so I could apologize?"

"You can still apologize."

"I changed my mind. I don't regret worrying about you. Never did." She felt light on his lap, but his concern exaggerated her fragility. She was slim but strong, could be perceived as shy but was a cache of boldness. "Why'd you come down here?"

"To think about you. You came down here to think about me."

"I went looking for you to say I was sorry for interfering with the armoire."

She was silent so long that he tipped her face up to make sure she was still okay.

"I didn't want anyone to see me fall apart, Burke. I hide them, the panic attacks. Joss knows, and she turns into a mother hen when they occur. But I can handle that. I don't think I can handle being the sick, pathetic Mercer girl again."

"Fuck all that, Sofia." When she sighed, he insisted, "No, no, listen. Say 'Fuck it.' Say it and mean it."

"Burke..."

"Say it. There's no one here but you and me. I won't tell."

"Exactly how many more secrets do we want between us?" she said, and when her fingers slipped from his hair they detoured to his jaw and drew circle patterns across his scruff. "Abram and Hannah Slattery know about us. They think I've been rocking your boat."

Damn Abram. Burke had told him to mind his own business when it came to Sofia, but the man had been dogged. Losing her fourteen years ago had sent Burke to a unique level of hell on earth, and it'd been the cruelest fight of his life to tear himself free.

"You didn't laugh at my joke," she pointed out.

"Make light of this all you want, Sofia, but it's not a funny situation. I asked Abram and his wife to leave it alone, and if either of them hassles you I need you to tell me."

"Don't lose friends over me. He said you threatened to kick his ass if he talked against me. That's some crooked chivalry."

"I meant what I told him. What's between us isn't their business. So, as I said before, repeat after me: Fuck it."

"Fuck it." Her laughter felt like cool raindrops on a hot night. "Fuck it, I'm going to do what I think is best for me."

"You catch on fast."

"That includes taking a stand against you. Upstairs you acted as if you don't trust me to know what is and isn't good for my heart. It was mortifying."

"Hold up. Did I cause the panic attack?" Had his interference caused her harm? The notion made him feel suddenly queasy.

Her hand drifted again, massaging into his neck and then settling on his chest. "No, it was Aunt Luz's kitchen table. I knew I'd be sad to see it go, but when McGuinty and Abram put it on the truck, I lost my shit. The attack hit full force when I came to the hall...then you were here and I remembered to breathe."

"How can someone forget to breathe?"

"I follow a set of breathing exercises to help me manage the more severe attacks. I'd blanked and then I was able to concentrate and recall the instructions. So thanks for having a guilty conscience and hunting me down." She brought her face forward, her lips millimeters from his. "Meet me halfway here. I want to kiss you for helping me through."

"I want to make sure you're okay before I start getting your pulse up again. I'm driving you to the hospital."

"Damn it, you're doing it yet again. *I* know that I can handle how you make me feel. *I* know that I want to kiss you right now. Do you want me to kiss you?"

"Hell, yes."

"Then let's do this and be done with it."

"I swear, Sofia, that's about as sexy as a sandpaper condom."

"The kiss will be much sexier," she said, shifting on his lap, "I promise." She covered his mouth with hers. Those full, tasty lips—and what he knew they could do for him—melted his strongest defenses.

"Let me touch you," he groaned into her, gliding a hand under her shirt and finding the graceful arc of her spine. He brought his palm around, skating on smooth skin and venturing north. "I want to feel your heartbeat."

"Feel me," she agreed, "but don't look. I don't want you to see the scar."

Her scar. She'd referred to it as her "ugliness," but how the hell could something that had saved her life be ugly?

She didn't try to guide him, but let him explore—and he let himself get lost, plumping one breast and then the other before he worked her bra down and could leave invisible fingerprints on her naked flesh.

Sofia responded to his every maneuver, grinding her ass on his lap as he teased her nipples and kissed her lips. "Whatever you're doing, I really like it."

"Some folks call it foreplay. I call it getting the most out of the moment. I want you to feel good when you're with me, Sofia." He felt good, that was for friggin' sure. But he'd taken too much from her that morning on his boat, and now he had a mission to help her experience for herself the pleasure she intended to sell in a sex shop.

I care about you, he almost said. In execution it'd sound like a cheap line that she wouldn't believe. The attraction writhing between them was legitimate and he needed to let that be enough.

For now.

She hid her scar behind her clothes, hid her sexual hunger behind mannequins in a window, but eventually, he would bring Sofia Mercer out of hiding.

Their lips parted and he traced a finger between her breasts, up the jagged trail of thick, knotted scar tissue. He wanted to see it, assure her it wasn't ugly, but he'd given his word that he wouldn't look, and he would kick his own ass before he violated that trust.

"It doesn't feel ugly," he said plainly. "I've got scars, too."

"From fighting. This is different."

What had she been imagining, all these years? Schoolyard brawls? A teenage fight club? Did she define him as someone so out of control that he'd gone searching for split lips, black eyes, and fractured ribs?

Yeah, it was different. Her scar was a result of a lifesaving medical procedure...not violence.

Laying his hand flat, he felt her heart pound quick and

strong. Caught up in the moment, caught up in her, he whispered, "Losing you would've killed me."

He felt her slip away from him before she moved a single muscle. When she did retreat, sliding off his lap, fixing her clothes, and raking an arm across her mouth, she said, "I told Abram we weren't together. Was that a lie? *Can* we be together, Burke?"

"Casually, yeah. As friends, of course. But don't rope me into more. It wouldn't be good for you."

"That's not your call."

"It is, though. Tell me something and be truthful about it. How many panic attacks have you had since coming back to town?"

"A few."

"Uh-huh. And how many came on when I wasn't near you?"

"Uh…"

"Sofia."

"None."

"That's my point. Think it's a coincidence that your health teeters when I'm around? I'm harmful to you. I've known for a long time that I'm no good." She didn't know all the hell he carried. He'd do anything to spare her heart the burden of his skeletons.

"Stop it," she whispered, getting to her feet. "You'd never hurt me."

"Not intentionally, but the fact is I trigger something in you that you can't physically handle. I meant what I said earlier—it would kill me to lose you. As much as I want you, and damn it, you know I do, I can't keep putting you at risk."

"Are you sure my health isn't your excuse to justify walking away?" she challenged. "Hold me off, resist what's good and real and permanent, then take off on your boat. That's your plan, right?"

"It's worked out nicely for years. You wouldn't be the first woman to step back because she can't handle my career. It's dangerous, the hours can be shitty, and sometimes I can be on the water for weeks. I'd never ask you or anyone else to shut up and like it. If you want to bail now, I won't hold it against you."

"That *does* terrify me, but I'm not bailing. A career is one thing. Escape is something else altogether. I don't think I can love you halfway—either I'm all in or I fold."

Love. That word sank him. "Don't lay down some all-or-nothing ultimatum, Sofia. You might not like the answer you get."

"It's not an ultimatum," she said, turning to leave. "At the end, this road we're on is going to split. We'll go in the same direction or separate. We don't need to choose now, but we've got to be prepared to deal with both scenarios."

"Every time we try to be apart, you end up in my arms," he said, standing and leaving the hall on her heels. "I'm saying this, okay? I care about you so fucking much, and that's why I'm telling you that when it comes to me, if you've got to choose all or nothing, let it be nothing."

"Message received." But she sounded hurt, and that wasn't what he'd intended to inflict on her. "To reiterate, though, you don't dictate what I can and can't handle. Don't use my medical situation as your excuse to backpedal. Get your truck, haul a load, and you'll be done with your good deed."

Burke let her jog up the stairs, hanging back because he had no response scratching to get out. There was too damn much truth in what she said. This *was* just a good deed. Even the worst class of man was capable of a rare selfless act.

Burke would never be more than what he'd always been. A killer.

* * *

"Thank-you notes go a long way in interpersonal relationships." Joss sealed the last envelope and placed it on top of the short stack on their distressed pedestal dining table.

It was the day after their impromptu furniture-moving party. Paget had the day off at Shore Seasons and would unwind in the best way she knew how: headbanging at an indie rock festival at an amphitheater outside Boston. This morning Caro and her son had collected Joss for one of those hokey town tours as a crash course in Eaves 101. It had culminated in a whale-watching expedition, during which, Evan Jayne gleefully reported, Joss had heaved up a thirty-two-ounce grape soda and he'd lent her his LeapFrog learning tablet to cheer her up.

Tish had kept Sofia company, her harness loops jingling as they walked through town on errands. Sofia worried that the dog might feel disoriented with so much sudden change, now that most of Luz's furniture was gone. But when she tried to comfort the beast with hugs and smooches, Tish released guttural growls that spurred the thought *Please don't bite me.*

It might not be normal for someone to fear their own pet, but Tish's assessing eyes rarely conveyed her temperament and Sofia was usually left guessing. Stranger than that, the Siberian husky was nonetheless a comfort...a friend.

Now that Joss was home to keep an eye on Tish, Sofia could tackle the last of her errands: trips to the post office and the taffy shop.

"Joss," she said, for the first time realizing that her friend had placed custom seals bearing Blush's logo on the backs of the envelopes, "where did you find these? They look great."

"I didn't. I had them made across the street at the stationery store. I wanted to pop some business cards inside for a bit more publicity oomph, but you haven't finalized the design yet."

"That's still on my epic to-do list." She gathered the envelopes, addressed to the individuals who'd come to help them out. Whether out of pity or kindness or a craving for sweets—or raw curiosity to see what a couple of newcomers living over a sex shop might be about—they'd saved Sofia time and money.

"If we finish painting and restocking merch by next week, we're looking at opening before the Fourth of July." Excited, Sofia swooped down to touch her nose to Tish's. "Can you believe it, you canine mean girl? This is happening!"

Tish's eyes were silver orbs that conveyed, *Nothing would please me more than to piss on your floor right now.*

Sofia straightened and tucked the envelopes into her tote bag. "Joss, thank you. The cupcakes were a hit yesterday."

"What can I say?" She pretended to pop her collar. "I'm good at what I do."

"You are. Seriously. You're helping me with the boutique and being the friend I need right now. I wish I could help you kick-start your dream."

"It'll happen one day. I haven't given up hope."

"*One day* might've come a lot sooner if my plan had panned out." Sofia sat on the parson chair across from her friend. "As thrilled as I am to have you helping me out at Blush, I think you're meant for something else—your own dream. I wanted you to have the opportunity."

"Thanks, Sof." Joss patted her hand. "Burke may be hotter than any guy's got a right to be, but when it comes to getting to know him, he really makes you work for it. Yesterday I tried to make small talk with him, but he couldn't leave fast enough."

"Learning him's not easy," Sofia agreed. "But yesterday wasn't something personal against you. He and I had a run-in."

"A run-in?" Joss repeated, as if the term was synonymous with *sex*. "Oh? Similar to the one you had on his boat?"

"No." She paused, reflecting. "Come with me. I want to show you something." She led the way, and Joss and Tish followed her to the stairwell off Blush's kitchenette.

"I've been down here before, carrying extremely large boxes," Joss said. "It's a wonder I didn't do a Jack-and-Jill tumble down these stairs."

"You haven't seen this." Sofia pried away paneling to reveal concrete and a steel door. "Remember, Caro and I figured out that all three basements on this strip are connected. Caro says Bautista had the bar sealed off, but the connection's still there, just blocked. Years ago Burke and I used to sneak downstairs and hang out under the market or in this little passageway here."

Sofia and Joss crept into the hall but Tish wouldn't follow. The air was cool, stale. It lacked the refrigerant scent of the air system that serviced the boutique and apartment. Concrete, cinder blocks, joists, and lumber—the space must look unimpressive to Joss. But to Sofia, it was purely beautiful.

"No one caught you and Burke down here?"

"Not once. Guess Burke's dad and Luz didn't look past the paneling." She went to the spot where she'd sunk at the pinnacle of her panic attack. "Burke found me here yesterday. I had an episode."

"An episode. An attack? Oh, God—"

"I'm fine now, promise."

"You haven't had one of those in almost a year, I think, right?"

"Joss, I've had a few since I came back to Eaves."

Joss lugged a cinder block over and sat. "Talk to me, Sof. Is this wearing on you—losing your aunt and gaining Blush? What about Tish? And Burke?"

Change had assaulted her, hitting her without warning and at full velocity. But she wasn't shielding herself from it—she was absorbing it, taking hold of it with open arms. "Getting rid of Luz's things yesterday underlined that she's gone, for good. It hurts and it scares me that she left it up to me to continue this life. But, my God, Joss, I really want this—the store, the apartment, and the dog."

"And the man? What about Burke? From what I hear, he's *complicated*, and that's an understatement. His issues run deep. Then there's the wanderlust."

"Am I being stupid or reckless to show up for the challenge? Cardiomyopathy didn't stop me from being his friend when we were young. What's there to stop me now?"

"Friendship isn't friendship once you guys introduce sex and future-planning. I know you, Sofia. You're not going to settle for being his friend if you straight up fall in love with him. Look around." Joss spread her arms wide. "*This* is where he found you."

"It used to be a happy place, when I was sick and lonely and he was yo-yoing on drugs and getting into fights." It seemed every week he would appear with a fresh laceration or bruise. "We'd just be together."

"A guy and a girl in a private dungeon-like sanctuary... just hanging out?"

Sofia nodded. "Mm-hmm."

"No dry sex?"

"Nope."

"Kissing?"

"Uh-uh."

"Flirting?"

"Hmm, I smuggled a porn magazine down here once, but we ended up laughing and eating chips. What *wasn't* funny, though, was all the sex he was having with other girls. Condoms in his backpack, girls pressing against him at school. With me, he was hands-off. Saying 'I love you' only made things weird."

Joss leaned back. "Whoa. Weird how?"

"He ran. Literally, he bolted. It sucks to put yourself out there and watch the guy take off as if the devil swatted his ass." Sofia walked across to the door that led to the market's basement. Stroking the steel slab, she imagined the emptiness and darkness on the other side. "Anyway."

"Anyway," her friend said consolingly, "you and Burke are adults now and better equipped to handle this stuff. You won't slap a porno in front of him trying to flirt. He won't sprint off to parts unknown if you let him know you're in love with him…At least, he *shouldn't*."

"Sure."

"People cope with stress in different ways, I guess. You have panic attacks. He runs. You put that stress and fear on yourselves." She hesitated but eventually got up and returned the cinder block to its stack. "Know what I see? Two people who share an epically fucked-up past and are making themselves crazy trying to protect each other and their own interests at the same time. Maybe the *love* part of this whole thing is really there, and all that's left is the *fall in* part."

Sofia denied it with a headshake, refusing to consider that

possibly, maybe, *probably*... "I'll just watch my step, make sure I don't fall."

* * *

Upstairs, Joss began painting the trim along Blush's front room, while Sofia settled the dog in the apartment, then put her tote in the bicycle basket and took off for the post office.

Turning into the parking lot, passing a pair of mail trucks, she claimed a space near the flagpole, under stars and stripes that flapped in the summer wind. "Afternoon, Gretchen," she said to the gray-haired postal clerk leaning against the brick building with a sunny grin waiting and a cigarette pinched between her fingers.

"Hi, honey." Gretchen Pruitt *tsk*ed as Sofia dismounted and grabbed her tote. "If you don't find yourself a helmet, I'm going to go to the general store and buy one for you."

"I'll get a helmet if you'll quit smoking."

"Buzzing around town without a helmet is dangerous."

"Smoking's dangerous." Sofia awaited a rebuttal.

"Luz wouldn't want her great-niece to risk her health."

"Luz wouldn't want her friend to risk hers."

Gretchen harrumphed, her chestnut-colored eyes narrowing on a golden-brown face, then she made a production of mashing the cigarette on the trash can's ashtray. Fluffing her short silver bob, she waved Sofia over for a crushing hug. "You win this round, smartass. You're as insufferable as my hubby."

Gretchen's hugs were the best. The first time Sofia had visited the post office, Gretchen had come around the counter and enveloped her in one of those hearty, you're-not-too-fragile-to-be-hugged-properly embraces and recited a blessing for Luz right there in the lobby. No one liked

Luz—you either respected her, despised her with a passion, or loved her fiercely. And Gretchen Pruitt, who hugged with all her might and was years into weaning herself off cigarettes, had indeed loved Luz.

"The next time you strong-arm me into wasting a square, you'd better be packing some penny candy. I need something to get through the rest of my shift." Gretchen jerked her head in the direction of the post office entrance. "Renee Abernathy's closing with me. Grrr."

Sofia had met Renee, who looked to be in the same age bracket as Sofia's parents, only once. The woman had put her through the wringer for improperly filling out a shipping label. It'd been an error, but Renee had castigated Sofia in front of the queue. She wasn't looking forward to another encounter but refused to ask Gretchen to cut her break short.

"I'm going in," Sofia said, patting Gretchen's doughy arm. "Wish me luck."

"Good luck with that, honey."

Joining the queue, Sofia didn't have to wait long before Renee signaled her to the window. Taking the envelopes Sofia proffered, Renee twisted her lips in distaste at the name on top.

Burke Wolf.

"Are you carrying on with that one again?" Renee thumped the envelope. "Bad seeds don't simply stop being bad seeds."

Sofia smiled through her reluctance to respond to the woman at all. "Me and my roommate are reopening Blush and needed helping hands moving furniture. These are thank-you cards. One isn't any more special than the others."

Renee gave her a skeptical glare and began keying codes onto her touch screen. "I'm glad I got my daughter away from him and his crowd."

"Who's your daughter?"

"Courtney. She's in a PhD program out west. Political science."

Kindness begets kindness, right? "If she's happy, then I'm happy."

"Quite happy, despite that band of degenerates. Thugs, the lot of them."

Courtney Abernathy had reigned as head of student government, smoked pot in the girls' room, and—as Sofia had unfortunately witnessed once—had no qualms about sticking her hand behind Burke's Cape Foods grocer apron. "Mrs. Abernathy, Courtney and I didn't cross paths much. But Burke was my friend. He never tried to persuade me to do *anything* I didn't want to do."

The woman bristled in offense and went about stamping each envelope with scrunched eyebrows and forceful movements. "You'd feel differently if you had a mother who cared about you. With a thief for a father and a porn dealer for an aunt, it's really no wonder."

"How much is the postage?" Sofia interrupted. The post office, a quaint and rustic structure that might be called cozy under brighter circumstances, was tomblike as customers observed in rapt intrusiveness.

Gretchen came inside and took away the NEXT WINDOW PLEASE desk sign from her station. "Everything all right?" she murmured, signaling for the next customer.

"Young ladies calling on *troubled* young men? Oh, that's not 'all right' to me, but what do I know?" Conspiratorially, Renee Abernathy tossed her head toward Gretchen. "Burke Wolf."

"Oh," Gretchen said, but there was approval in her tone. "Cute as corn, and he pitched right in to winterize the cottage when Richard was on crutches."

"That old dump," Renee muttered. "No one lives there. Cut your losses already."

Sofia had visited the Pruitts' cottage—a tiny bungalow they'd intended to flip but then kept as a weekend house because they couldn't part with the place's view. Cramped and derelict, it wasn't pretty by any definition, but to call it a *dump* was spiteful as fuck.

"And Burke Wolf's no saint," Renee insisted, circling back to her original gripe.

"No, ma'am, but a saint's never sat at my dinner table. Burke's welcome anytime. So are you, Sofia." She winked, a smile pulled across her lined face. "Bring him sometime."

"Total's on the screen," Renee snapped. "Swipe your card and key in your PIN or hit the red *X* for credit."

Sofia took her receipt and strode out, feeling every set of eyes in the place escort her. She thought she heard the word *slut*, but it might've been the whisper of the door swinging shut.

Either way, she figured, hopping onto the bicycle, what did it really matter? As with *Vices*, freshly painted gold on Blush's storefront, she could turn the term on its head. She could manipulate it, dust away its hurtful connotations, and own it if she wanted. That was her right.

No one was without sin. It wasn't the duty of her neighbors to pick and choose which sins were worthy of condemnation and which deserved redemption.

Luz had stripped down and ridden her bike to town hall, making a statement to defend her boutique and the woman she'd chosen to be. For the first time Sofia thought she might be close to understanding her great-aunt in a way she never had before.

Proud, inspired, Sofia slid the ribbon from her ponytail, let her hair lash through the salty air, and pedaled to the taffy shop with a smile on her face.

CHAPTER 14

*B*urke hooked a finger around the neck of a bottle and laid some cash on the beaten bar. The week had been jammed with hard labor—hauling furniture at Sofia's, construction at the Slatterys' place, strenuous chores, and complex upgrades to his boat—and he figured Saturday was as good a day as any to sit still and goddamn breathe.

Caro slid a malt whiskey to another customer and counted the bills Burke had put down. "Mineral water's not *this* pricey. I'll get your change."

"Nah, I was hoping for your time instead."

"In that case"—she counted again—"this isn't enough of a gratuity."

"Give him some time, Caro." Burke half turned as his friend McGuinty approached with a bundle of camellias, which he draped on the bar. "Then you can tell me what you think of these flowers and join me at Grandpa's place. Football, fire pit, and poker. Abe and Hannah'll be there. Burke, too. The girls from Blush. Other great folks."

Caro stood with cash in her hand, side-eyeing McGuinty. "The last time a man insisted on pursuing me with flowers, my daddy frightened him off during a pheasant hunt in the countryside."

Patrons spied them. Now they ribbed McGuinty for his fail, and someone pitched peanuts at the flowers. He distributed threats, shook peanuts off the camellias and waited until Caro had signaled for someone to man the bar before he said plainly, "Camellias are your favorite. That's what you told me. You tell me plenty of shit when nobody else is around. You never said I ought to move along. Goddammit, that's what I'm going to do."

Burke thought she might finally discharge McGuinty. Not even the most patient soul could endure this ongoing game of catch and release.

Caro glided a hand up his arm. "Listen, love. Your grandpa invited me already, but I gave him my apologies. After my shift I'm reading Evan a story and tucking him into bed. But I desperately adore camellias."

Aw, Jesus. And just like that Caro freshened the bait and hooked McGuinty again. The ribbing ceased, but apparently so had his resolve to "move along." He stared at her hand on his arm, then his hands were on her hips and Burke thanked God he wasn't standing close enough to overhear their whispers.

Leaving the camellias, McGuinty tossed to Burke "See you at Grandpa's" and hollered a few words to friends he passed on his way out of the bar.

"What are y'all doing, Caro?" Burke couldn't help but demand when they found a vacant piece of sidewalk on the side street. She sat cross-legged, cradling the camellias. "You and McGuinty."

"Playing it by ear."

"Respect him. A man should know when he's not wanted."

"Who said I don't want him?" She clutched the flowers tighter. "I'm in a delicate position and all I ask is for him to let me breathe while I figure out where things stand."

"Yeah. Good." He wasn't buying it, but it wasn't his place to push. "I want to talk about Bottoms Up."

Finally she set the flowers down. When she turned toward him and pushed locks of springy dark hair off her face, sunlight slanted over her, illuminating all the enthusiasm in her eyes. She launched into a one-sided discussion, rambling about coownership and creative plans and "developer vulture tossers" until her earnest honeyed voice and animated gesturing ran out of steam. "So you see, Burke, it's quite perfect."

"Caro," he said at the first opportunity, "if you're worried about the developers edging you out, don't be." A representative from Omni Commercial Development of New England had approached him during a dock shift a couple of months ago, and Burke had declined the conversation. Afterward the firm doubled its efforts, sending a pair of higher-ups accompanied by an Eaves town hall Building Maintenance Committee member, cornering him at the marina. Pissed off, he'd quietly reaped some satisfaction from watching them flee the pier as the documents they handed him floated in the water. "I'm not going to sell to Omni or anyone."

"But Sofia—"

"Not even to her. Can't do it," he stressed, hating the disappointment that stooped her shoulders now. "I wanted to offer some kind of assurance, but, hell. I feel like I'm on the same level as the vulture tossers."

She reached for her bouquet, and her bracelets—had to

be ten on each wrist—glinted under the sun. Ironic that she snapped pictures of people stripped nude but kept her wrists dressed. She glanced at him, but he didn't hide that he'd been trying damn hard to peer past those bracelets. "Burke, if it were someone else, I'd be angry about the building. But I'm not upset with you. I understand you."

"Yeah?"

"Very much. You might think I'm behind a camera and underground in a bar so much that I'm isolated, but those are excellent vantage points to really see who people are." She tapped the flowers against his arm and smiled as if to whisper *I'm not here to threaten you.* "I see you, Burke. I think there's only one reason you despise that building but cannot let it go. But it's not up to me to judge and make suppositions. If you *do* decide to sell, I hope you'll give your neighbors an exclusive. If not, lower your guard just a little, respect Sofia enough to give her the chance to understand." She stood, brushed off the seat of her pants. "That's more advice than you paid for. Another five, please."

Burke thought she was joking until she wiggled her fingers. "Christ, take it." He slapped the cash into her palm. "But thanks. Expensive as it is, I appreciate the advice."

Laughing, she pocketed the money. "Tariq gives free shots to flirts. I'd better take over if we're to have any liquor left for the night crowd." Then she and her camellias abandoned the tree-canopied sidewalk.

Waning daylight escorted him to the acre of land that held Niall Slattery's old farmhouse. Vehicles lined the sand-dusted curb, and when he climbed out of his truck he could smell charcoal and hear music and hold-nothing-back laughter that probably carried all the way to the nature preserve behind the farm.

Niall wouldn't spend his Saturday any other way. A retired factory worker, he opened his home to folks as generously as he opened the private animal shelter to any stray that needed a spot to rest its head.

The screen door flapped open before Burke made it to the porch. Belly first, Hannah stepped out. He would've thought that at this stage in her pregnancy she would be in maternity clothes, but what did he know? She might be comfortable in jeans and that extra-tight Nike tee.

She grabbed his wrist, making a point of looking at the face of his chronograph watch. "You're late."

"How you doing, Hannah?" he greeted her, obliging when she offered her cheek.

"No complaints, except the guys made me officiate their damn football game and kept me good and distracted while folks ravaged the dessert I brought. We've got a pastry expert on-site, so all's great. C'mon out back. Grandpa's playing poker dealer now."

He followed, his height and the low ceilings of the century-old house compelling him to duck beneath every doorway as they passed rooms papered in faded floral patterns and crowded with antique furniture. Copper pots hung in the kitchen and from the oven wafted an aroma that hit him right in his appetite.

"Apple pie?" he asked the woman scrubbing baking utensils in the sink.

"A summer favorite." Joss Vail wiped her hands on an apron so worn that it might've come with the house when Niall Slattery had bought the place for his bride, Amy, fifty-something years ago. Untying the apron, she revealed a painted-on gold dress.

Burke turned to Hannah. "You told her this was a low-key backyard get-together, didn't you?"

"Grandpa Slattery invited the guests." She twisted her mouth, as if he'd made an asshole misstep. "*I* think you look perfect, Joss. Some guys don't know what to do when a hot woman's in front of them, so they do what's stupid."

Niall must've been a busy man, making his rounds inviting pretty women over for poker around a fire pit and food on the grill.

"Want in on the poker game?" Hannah asked him, heading toward the door.

"Yeah. Tell Niall to save a chair for me. Be right out."

"This isn't traditional apple pie," Joss said, setting the wet utensils on the drying rack. "I didn't have all the ingredients I wanted on hand, but I gave the filling some pizzazz—five spices and lemon. It's part of a ribbon-winning recipe."

Burke waited a beat, gearing up to shut down her segue to the Cape Foods building. But she said, "Sofia's here, in the backyard playing cards."

"How is she?"

"Skilled," she said, smoothly twirling around the meaning behind his question. *Is she feeling all right?* "I think she's cleaning the guys out, so you might want to end this early before it turns into strip. Grandpa Slattery's a charming old guy but I don't want to see him in his shorts."

Hell, he couldn't help it. He burst into laughter and she gave in to a giggle, too, as she reached into the fridge for a pair of long-necked bottles. Apple ale. Nonalcoholic. Niall had stopped stocking the hard shit years ago after his grandsons had gotten fucked up on the contents of the liquor cabinet one too many times. Both Abram and McGuinty had set their drugs of choice aside but neither abstained from alcohol. They trusted themselves to court it casually. Burke couldn't say the same for himself.

"I'm serious," she said, handing him the bottles. "Get

out there. Sofia might like a break from poker hustling and Abram says there's a walking path."

Not inclined to argue, because he'd like nothing more than to take Sofia someplace private, he strode through the house.

"Mind reader," McGuinty praised, swiping one of the ales from Burke's hand when he stepped into the flower- and plant-overrun backyard. "Thanks, guy."

"Wasn't for you, jackass."

"Naw?" The man twisted off the cap and turned up the bottle without apology and scanned the folks scattered throughout the yard and gathered at the card table. "Hannah's spoken for. So's Louisa, Sandy, and Kirsten. Gretchen Pruitt's got a lobsterman *and* she'd smack you with her purse. The ladies from the senior center are more Grandpa's speed, but, hey, if that's what you like…"

"You skipped Sofia Mercer."

"No, I didn't. Just wanted to see what kind of look you'd get on your face when *you* singled her out." He shook his head. "Careful with that. She comes with a lot."

"I'm only bringing her a drink."

"You're a fucking lousy liar, Burke." McGuinty swaggered to the poker table and clapped his grandfather on the shoulder. "Wolf's taking my chair. I lost all the cash in my wallet to the shark."

Sofia smirked up at McGuinty and when her gaze drifted to Burke the smirk transformed into that sexy lopsided smile that threw his libido like a switch. "Hey."

"Hey." He came around to deliver the apple ale and saw an impressive Siberian husky lying at Sofia's feet. "Tish, what's up?"

Ears perked, the dog rose and slapped her front paws to his stomach, panting up at him. Indulging, he scratched her under the chin. "I could skip the card game and spoil the hell out of you all afternoon. What do you say?"

"Oh, no you don't," Sofia interrupted, drawing out the words with a wicked look that gripped him tight. She pointed to a chair. "I want to test your poker skills first."

Indulging Sofia now, he sat beside her and waited for Niall Slattery to deal a fresh round. Chatter crisscrossed the table and he managed not to lose himself completely in the woman's bubble-gum fragrance. Jesus, it was making him crazy not to have the authority to reach right over and kiss her in front of every set of eyes out here.

Somehow he played, lasting as others folded until only Niall and Sofia stood in the way of victory.

"I think," Sofia said solemnly, glancing from Burke to the burly grizzled widower in the flat cap whom she called "Grandpa" as naturally as if it were true, "that you two fellows are ready to fold."

Niall upped his bet, challenging in a gravelly voice, "Nobody bests me three times in a row, no matter how pretty she is." He winked a pale green eye and she beamed across at him.

Burke suddenly didn't care who won; the sooner the game ended, the sooner he could have her to himself. "I'm out," he said, laying down his cards. "Fold."

"All in," Sofia said next to him, nudging her stack of chips forward.

He folded. She was all in. He wasn't ignorant to the symbolism of that.

Sofia and Niall faced off, then she finally revealed a busted hand. Triumphant, Niall stood and pumped a fist as onlookers erupted in cheers at his hard-won victory. Sofia, in a fluttery high-necked dress that stopped barely past her hips, pranced through the grass to throw her arms around Niall in a congratulatory hug.

Burke waited, Tish at his side, as she toasted people with her bottle and laughed, and at last she came to him. "Joss's pies are cooling and Hannah says dinner won't be ready for a bit," she reported. "Want to walk to the pond with me?"

He couldn't remember getting a sweeter, more sincere invitation. He took her hand, leading her away, not allowing himself to get caught up in how the gesture looked or what it meant. Screw all that, because it felt incredible to touch her and even common sense wouldn't deprive him.

Tish followed them as they moved farther from the farmhouse, toward taller grass, thicker trees, and the glimmer of a pond up ahead. He heard Hannah ask, "Where're they sneaking off?"

"I wouldn't worry about it." This from Abram. "Tish won't let them get too naughty."

"Joking, right? She was *Luz's* dog."

Sofia laughed a little but stayed beside him on the dirt path as chaperone Tish trotted behind them.

"I think every man in that yard's got a crush on you," he said, holding a leafy branch out of her way.

She plucked a leaf, then rolled its stem between her fingers. "And which one should I have a crush on?" She traced the point of that damn leaf across her lips.

Hell. Burke closed in, framing her, boxing her in against a tall, arching oak. The bark scraped his palms, but he didn't care when her sugary scent was filling him and she was staring at his mouth with naked anticipation. Lowering his guard, taking a chance, he confessed. "Me," he told her, seizing her mouth. *Hell, hell, hell, this is good.* So hot, pulling his hair, yanking him in closer. Deeper. Rougher... "No-damn-body else, Sofia. Just me."

* * *

"We're closed. Read the sign." Lights glowed and the register hadn't been counted yet, but it was two a.m. on the dot and Bautista wasn't changing his mind. He pointed to the CLOSED sign hanging on the door. The woman on the other side didn't budge.

Whatever Joss Vail had to say, whatever troubles she thought she'd drown at the bottom of a glass, he couldn't take in. Not tonight. The club was preparing to ride out to Florida, and he required a special frame of mind for that. What she brought to his doorstep would heap on complications he didn't want.

When he put his back to the door, she pounded with her fist.

"*¡Qué mierda!*" He disengaged the locks and threw the door open. "Is it worth it, busting glass to get a drink?"

"I'm not here for a drink, and you know it." Joss patted a pocketbook against her hip and the sequins on her short gold dress shimmered. "But yes, I'll humor you. Let's go to the bar. Bourbon neat."

"I'm not going to let you sit here and get wasted when I shouldn't have let you in to start with."

"If you didn't want me here, I wouldn't be here." Her blue stare challenged him, and part of him was glad that the fire in her spirit had come back. The recklessness was back, too, and it rode on the tails of ire. "Bourbon neat, if you didn't hear me before. I had mango sparkling water with dinner. Ask all the people who were at Grandpa Slattery's farmhouse. That's where I was when I got this text." She bounced onto a stool and tapped her phone. "Come here. Read this."

"Do you want me to pour a drink or read a text message? I won't do both."

"The text," she said, swinging a pair of long legs and offering him the stool. "I can get my own drink."

Unless Caro had educated her on the liquor he carried and where he required it all be stored, she wouldn't have an easy time finding her way. Bautista took a seat and read the screen.

OMG!!! Pete was beaten. Did you know? They said some guys tried to mug him. Cops don't know who did it. Crazy times.

Joss had apparently given up the quest for bourbon neat and opened a bottle of Absolut. She took a swallow, shuddered, and when Bautista muttered an obscenity she took another. "I think that text doesn't surprise you. I think you have everything to do with this," she said finally, coming around and pointing the bottle at him. "Look at me."

"Where?" He took the bottle and set it on the bar. "Where do you want me to look? At the bruise next to your eye? Try to cover it all you want, but it's still there. When someone hurts another person, they don't bounce right back."

"Oh my God," she whispered. "It *was* you. You hurt Peter."

"Clean hands." Powerful words, but probably some of the most overused in his vocabulary.

"Then you sent someone else to do it. How dare you interfere in my life?"

"What did you feel when you found out somebody had gotten to that bastard? Did you hurt for him, or were you satisfied even a little? Answer me."

Joss reached for the vodka but he nudged it out of the way. "It—it wasn't fair that he could use me and hit me and walk away. It was unjust and I hated it."

"Answer me, Joss."

"I was relieved. But that was before it sank in and before I suspected what you'd done. Sofia told me about you and your motorcycle club. I know you have no regard for the law."

"The law let Peter Bernard walk away a free man after he abused you."

"Cutting corners does me no favors. My life imploded before and I've been so careful to avoid a repeat. Leave me alone, Bautista. Your duty is to Sofia. Luz was her aunt, not mine. I'm nothing to you."

"You'll do anything to play life safe, even if it means being used? Explain that. Tell me what I don't know. If I'm in the wrong, I'll admit it."

"Admit it?" She didn't appear convinced. "You'd contact the NYPD and turn yourself in for organizing a beating? Somehow I think you're lying."

"Is that what you want, then? Lawful justice for Peter?"

"No." She shuddered again, but it wasn't because of the bite in her vodka. "Why do this?"

"For you. He shouldn't have hit you and turned you inside out."

"They all do, eventually. I can't stop making the same mistake. What is that, insanity?"

"It's insanity if you keep making that same mistake but expect a different outcome. It's possible to get close to a man who's no good for you and still walk away without being crushed."

"Bad men are bad men for a reason. They all crush. They never care."

"That's a generalization and it ain't always the truth, Joss. I'm one of the bad ones. I never said I wasn't. But I don't crush. I care."

Sliding off the stool, because he knew she'd defy his care and probably call him a dick again on her way out the door, he wasn't prepared when she pushed him against the bar.

She didn't use her hands but launched her entire body into him. He tried to step around her and all that golden sparkle, but she gripped his collar and pulled him down to her.

Landing was chaos and bliss. It was too soon to want another woman, yet it seemed as if forever stood between this moment and the last time he'd touched his fiancée. He couldn't lick into Joss's mouth and taste Luz. He couldn't settle his hands at Joss's hips and pretend that he was gripping Luz's curves.

"I know it hurts," Joss said, her lips moving over his. "I lost so much, too. The hurt's so deep. I can't breathe through it."

Gilded and warm, she locked herself around him and he carried her past the bar, past the restrooms.

In his office, she slid to her feet and started for his chair.

"No," he said quietly. Not there. No one else would ride him there.

"Okay." Joss waited a moment, her lips dark and wet, her hair tousled. He thought he could end this now, delicately put a stop to the recklessness, but she peeled down her gold dress and walked naked to him. Her pain lay against his, and then she had his pants open and slipped a hand inside to curl around his stiff flesh. "Thank you."

Thank you.

It'd been too long since someone had meant those words the way she did.

CHAPTER 15

$\mathcal{C}$onsidering what happened the last time Sofia had come to Burke's boat with a proposition, she suggested he meet her on neutral territory. A full week hadn't passed since their kiss in the woods but she was so hard up for another taste of his mouth that she might jump him on sight if she didn't keep her priorities in order.

Eaves's lighthouse, Bellini Beach Light, established in 1821, was small and certainly not the most impressive that East Coast America had to offer, but it and the old, scuffed-up Ferris wheel nearby made for some interesting historical tourist attractions. Closed to tours tonight, it was locked against visitors, but its blinking beam would rest like a comforting hand over the water.

A solemn moon and teardrop stars loomed over her as she pedaled to the parking lot. Unsurprisingly his truck wasn't in the lot. She'd asked him to rent a bike to travel the dunes and meet her at the lighthouse.

Sand dusted the wheels of the ten-speed as she took a

marked trail she hadn't thought about in years. She was instantly reacquainted with it once she found it. The trail appeared private and deserted now, but before the sun dropped it must be crowded with tourists and volunteers.

Caro had mentioned the increasing difficulty in scheduling outdoor sunset boudoir sessions, because everyone wanted to be on Bellini Beach.

Sofia couldn't imagine stripping in front of a camera at all, let alone doing so on the beach in natural light. There were faint silvery marks on her hips from an adolescent growth spurt that'd given her curves. Then there was her scar, currently throbbing and forewarning rain on the horizon.

The sky was clear and the air huffed a chilly breeze, but she trusted her body's barometer and it was beginning to drop.

Pedaling through a pine forest and over a sand dune to the lighthouse would challenge her stamina, but she was invigorated—and very excited about the snacks and blankets piled high in the bike's basket.

Meeting a guy at a lighthouse with a picnic basket and blankets in tow could be construed as a date, but this was an appointment on neutral ground to discuss a business matter. The beach was a beautiful, calm milieu and she hoped levelheadedness would prevail. Since their encounter at Grandpa Slattery's place, from the moment Burke said "*Just me*" in a fierce whisper, she had hunted opportunities to see him, reasons to want him, excuses to pretend he'd stay. That was the unfortunate truth about doing the wrong thing—it was so beautifully *easy*.

As the trees thinned and fireflies winked a game of hide-and-seek, she saw tire tracks pressed into the sand, and her enthusiasm inched up.

Blush was almost ready for the public. The web designer had refreshed the e-commerce site, merchandise was fully stocked, and the people at the stationery store had given them a discount on printed materials.

Those were all classified as the easy parts of taking the reins of a small business. Bautista had agreed to lend Sofia his legal services. The only fly remaining in the ointment was the vacant Cape Foods building. Every day that she passed it, whether jogging with Tish for exercise or pushing a shopping cart of laundry across the street or swinging by Au Naturel to chat about anything and nothing with Caro, the place mocked her. Inside it were memories, but she didn't desire it for nostalgia's sake. An erotic bakery between a sex shop and a boudoir photography studio, and a spacious nightclub underneath them, was brilliant. They could capitalize on cross-promotional efforts and Society Street's central tourist-hub location.

An empty commercial building plunked between two naughty, sex-oriented businesses was so damaging that it'd serve their block better to have it not exist at all.

The most appealing option was to occupy it.

Would Burke meet her partway? They had once been best friends. They were maddeningly attracted to each other now. Did that count for nothing when money and property ownership came into play?

The lighthouse rose into the night from rock and sand with a wildflower gate tracing its brick walkway. It wasn't pristine. Made distinct by its ring of large blue diamond patterns painted over solid white, the lighthouse carried a gentle dullness—a weariness. It watched over the water and seemed to ask for absolutely nothing in return.

Was it a vista like this that slanted people's reality and nudged them toward hasty romances and impossible dreams? Because as Sofia gazed at the small fenced house that stood close by, she thought she could fall in love here.

Salty air tickled her nose as she sped up the last hundred or so yards, focusing on the bike she saw ahead and the man standing beside it.

Burke's leather jacket hung open, offering white cotton and hard muscle beneath. She toed the bike's kickstand and went to him. The breeze ushered his clean scent straight to her and the arrow struck her every vulnerable point. Both her arms reached out, diving into the jacket to wrap around his waist. "Hi."

"Hi." Burke's lips hovered at the top of her head and he dropped a kiss there. "No. Hell, no. That's not good enough."

A hug? A chaste kiss? Who were they lying to?

His hands stroked her, one and then the other, and when she raised her chin he caught her, turning her need into a vicious thing.

"Mmmm." The frustrated sound was part sigh, part growl. Her teeth snapped his lip.

"Was that payback?" he groaned as their mouths slid together in a wet, hot dance. Their first kiss had ended in a bite, but this was different. They'd just begun.

"An accident. I can't strategize right now. I just want you on me. In me." Brazen words, but dragged up from a place of honesty. "Let me tell you something about my bucket list. The first goal is to own a business. I didn't imagine Blush, but sometimes reality modifies dreams for the better."

"What's next on your list?"

"As I wrote it when I was nineteen? 'Trade my V-card for lots of sex.'" She studied him for a reaction but no emotion slipped. "Angry sex, thank-you sex, birthday sex, morning sex, I-just-ate-a-good-piece-of-cake sex—I wanted it all and thought I'd be ready for it if I only got a chance to live. During that first post-transplant year I pushed myself to be strong. I kept at it, past the fifth year, past the tenth year, but yeah, in some ways I withdrew. My cardiologist and psychiatrist insist I'm good to go, and I'm aware of the risks...but I guess I didn't *want* to challenge myself like that."

"What's different now?"

"The man. It's different because it's *you*. At the farmhouse you put your name on me. Why'd you do that?"

"Necessity. You're a need to me, Sofia. Sex? I can give you that." He bent his knees, putting himself at eye level with her. "But if it's tied to promises or commitment or..."

So it was out there. She hadn't imagined it. He'd spoken with a soft graveness, but she and the fireflies heard every syllable. "Promises and commitment aren't on my bucket list." But they sounded nice...felt like a dream. "It's on you now, Burke."

"On me," he repeated, sounding skeptical, his frown unmistakable. He mounted his bike and she followed, down the trail to the wild grass on the sandy shore. Then he hopped off and beckoned her into his arms. "Get in the water. Naked."

Sofia stepped back. *Naked?* "No."

"What's your excuse to withdraw this time?"

"The lighthouse—"

"Is closed." Tugging down her jacket, he kissed her ear, and there was the brush of his scruff and the touch of his tongue on her skin. "Next excuse?"

"A storm's on the way."

"Forecast is for clear skies." He unfastened her jeans, pushed them past her hips. "Try again."

The forecast was wrong, but if she told him her scar said so, he might stop touching her, and she didn't want that. His hard hands, the calluses on the pads of his fingers, thrilled her on contact. "The…" *The fireflies are watching. My undies aren't sexy. You're too good at this.* "The water's cold," she finally said.

Yes, the cold water. What would the shock of sudden submersion into the frigid Atlantic do to her system?

Burke gripped the crotch of her panties, pulling until the fabric put tight pressure directly onto her hypersensitive flesh.

Oh, God. Keep doing that…

He slid the panties down to tangle with her jeans and then his hand was back, stroking her thighs, gliding between them. "I'll be in the water with you, Sofia. Wrap yourself around me if you wanna keep warm. When you get out, I'll take one of those blankets you brought and put it around you."

"An answer for everything," she whispered as his other hand worked beneath her shirt and flicked open her bra. "Let me get it from here."

Granting her privacy, he released her and peeled off his own clothes. Completely, *gloriously* nude, he began his trek through the damp sand to the dark water beyond.

"*This* wasn't on the list." A deep breath, then Sofia stripped and sprinted past him like a streaker, throwing herself into the water with a dramatic splash.

It covered her like ice chips, but it invigorated as she dipped beneath the surface and burst up, laughing. This was crazy, so crazy—

Burke dove, and the ripples carried to her, touching her skin, tickling her someplace deep, and God, she was happy.

Naked at the lighthouse, skinny-dipping in the Atlantic. Overhead the stars and clouds observed, withholding judgment. In front of her was a man who'd been her friend before but was someone entirely new now.

"C'mere," he said, though it was he who swam closer. His

gaze didn't stray south to her scar. "If you say it's okay for me to look, I will."

She thought she could rise out of the water and reveal it, but would it be ungrateful to introduce ugliness on such a beautiful night? Swimming in the ocean naked was enough. So she kept it under the surface, pressing to him, giving him herself but denying him, too.

"Sofia, the question's looping in my head, and I've got to... You said there're added risks. What risks?"

He was her friend, and if he couldn't handle this they both ought to know now. "Pregnancy. My doctors say I'm healthy enough to have sex, but pregnancy may put too much strain on my heart. Also, miscarriages. Preeclampsia." When he frowned, silently asking for clarification, she gave the barest-bones explanation possible. "It spikes blood pressure, can do some nasty things to the kidneys. After my transplant there was a kidney issue, so renal dysfunction's something my doctors don't want to see."

"God."

"Burke, it's not an absolute."

"You'll need to be protected, every time."

"Birth control's not completely effective. Slim odds, but I could get pregnant someday. Slimmer odds, I could carry the baby to full term and survive."

He pushed a hand through his damp, dark hair. "You're not considering that."

"I wouldn't intentionally conceive, no, but if it happened I'd fight for that baby."

"And risk your own life?"

"I beat the odds, Burke. I'm doing it now." She tried to stop here, but the words tumbled out of her. "The average life expectancy of heart transplant recipients past ten years is barely above fifty percent. I'm on year twelve."

The magnitude of it fell on them, pried them apart. He waded a few feet, turned his back to her. A strong, sturdy back, so fit to carry her if only he'd try. She almost asked him to, and started to go after him, but then he spoke.

"Average life expectancy. What's that, an expiration date?" His voice was chipped in places, but it wasn't the interference of wind.

It was fear.

"Every patient's different. Worrying about this won't benefit either of us." How many lovers had seized opportunity in this very spot, beneath a lighthouse that had served as guardian to over a century's worth of souls? Why couldn't she and Burke join that number? "I'm not meant to live forever. No one is. I'm here now, though, and I want to enjoy the life I've got. Okay?"

"You tell me I could lose you at any time and then ask me if I'm okay with that? Really, Sofia?" The fear was prominent now, and her name sounded broken on his lips.

"Yeah. Just as your dangerous career can take you away from me at any time." Still he didn't turn back to her, and she cut through the water to the gritty sand. "It's a risk and I want to try. Because it's you, Burke. Because, damn it, you've always meant something to me."

He caught up to her as she was pulling on her clothes. He snatched a blanket, ran it over his wet skin, and dressed quickly. "I always meant something? How's that, when you went to New York and never picked up a phone to tell me you were all right?"

"You left Eaves, too."

"Not right away. First I almost destroyed myself trying to detox. Then I got on the right track and was finally able to get my GED and get out. Stupid as it sounds, I waited years for just one goddamn call from you."

"I called." The admission took too much energy, and she dropped her shoulders. "Once. Right after the surgery. I called your dad's house. I wanted to tell you...Nobody answered."

"You gave me one chance to fix this. How's that fair?"

"It wasn't," she allowed. "Maybe we needed that time and that space, Burke, to fix ourselves."

"I'm clean and you've got a second heart, but we're not fixed. We're only coping."

"Coping's easier with someone to hold you up," she said, pulling on her jacket and stepping into her shoes. "Sponsors and support groups are great. So is a friend who's got no obligation but just cares and wants to help."

"Don't volunteer, Sofia. You can't handle this."

"Up to me to decide. I'll try, for you. So what can *you* handle?" Gulping in the salt-tinged breeze, she climbed onto her bike.

Burke grabbed the bicycle to hold it still, but her feet were already on the pedals and she crashed into him. He bellowed a swearword.

"Are you okay?" She scrambled off and the bike fell to its side like a tipped cow. "Oh, no, you're bleeding."

Maybe they *were* hazardous to each other's health.

Sofia dug a disinfectant square, a sample-size tube of antibacterial ointment, and a bandage from her tote bag. Carrying first aid supplies was an unbroken habit. Over the years she'd stopping packing masks and hydrogen peroxide, but some items remained handy. "I have painkillers."

"No aspirin." He took over, securing the bandage himself, then he helped her right the bicycle.

"It's an over-the-counter. Nonnarcotic. It won't trigger a relapse."

"Sofia, I once swallowed a bottle's worth of aspirin and chased it with gin."

"That could've killed you."

"I know. I knew it then, too." He paused, and she heard what he didn't say. *I wanted it to kill me.* "But I changed my mind about it, threw up, and whatever was left in my system made me sick as hell for days. So no aspirin for me. Appreciate the gesture, though."

"I'm not an expert on marine careers," she said, "but being a dockworker's strenuous labor. What do you do about aches and sore everything?"

"Grin and bear it. Massage it out. I spent too many years numbing myself with drugs to go back to that."

The fireflies had retreated and now clouds began to gather in the sky.

They should leave Bellini, but she wondered what had drawn him to marijuana and cocaine and whatever else he'd indulged in. "Why'd you start using? It had to hurt your dad to watch you deteriorate like that."

"Don't confuse Deacon with Finnegan. Deacon didn't 'watch' me deteriorate. He prophesied it. I was exactly what my father said I'd be—a mistake."

"Deacon said you were a mistake?"

"Sofia, the word he used is *murderer*, and he started telling me that right after my mom died."

Melody Wolf had died when Burke was five or six years old. Complications from a virus had taken her down. "It was chicken pox."

"I brought the virus home from school, infected her. Deacon snapped when he lost her."

"You lost her, too."

"You wouldn't know that if you read her gravestone. 'Loving wife,'" he quoted. "Not wife *and mother*."

She hadn't realized... "He blamed you?"

"I spread the virus. He told me to stay away from her

while I was sick with it, since she'd never had it. I hated being quarantined away from Mom, bawled every time I couldn't be with her. So she kept being my mom. She took care of me. Then...then, fuck, she was dead." He turned on his heel, put his focus on the lighthouse. "After her memorial, Deacon didn't let a day pass without reminding me what I'd done. I killed her."

You didn't kill her, she wanted to say, but now wasn't the time to interrupt. This talk should've happened ages ago. That's what finding each other in the basement was about— confessions and friendship and understanding.

"When I went to P-town for that first tattoo, it wasn't because I was a bored idiot. Deacon said inking in Mom's favorite Bible verse mocked her. That's not why I did it. I did it to honor her." He gripped his bicep. Under the leather and cotton were the words. "I wanted drugs to take me away."

"Deacon didn't want you to hurt yourself like that. After I told him about the tattoo, he thanked me. He asked me to continue looking after you because he worried."

Whatever my boy does that's not right, you let me know, honey.

Sofia had done her duty for Burke's safety. "Imagine being a father and seeing your kid blitzed—or having him come home bruised up. You'd worry yourself sick and you'd do anything to protect him."

"If my kid *came home* that way, I'd worry." He turned again, facing her. "Why'd you want to meet me here tonight? Does it have something to do with the pastries that bounced out of that picnic basket of yours?"

Once again her plan had derailed. "It's about the Cape Foods building. I asked Joss to make some samples to show you we're serious about the bakery."

He mounted his bike. "The building's not for sale."

"What about renting us the space?"

"No. Sofia, I can't." Cold raindrops pelted them, hesitantly at first, then the sky cracked like a coconut against a rock. "How the hell did you know about the rain?"

Her scar seemed to throb with pride. "Just a hunch." Putting her bike in motion, she pedaled alongside him up the trail, through the dunes, and toward the pines. "There's clothesline inside Blush and a hair dryer to hurry things up. Or we can go to the marina."

Burke sped forward, then took a sharp half turn and was right in her path. She squeaked and managed to stop the momentum in time to avoid T-boning his bike.

"Dangerous much? I could've run into you."

"This is what I can handle." He threw his leg over the bike, strode to her through the rain and the canopy of pine trees, and kissed her. "Compromise. I'll trust you to know your health, and you'll stop asking me about Cape Foods."

She had met him here for the very conversation he wanted her to table. Give up the fight...give up a dream...and gain what?

Will you stay? "Will you take *Colossians 1:14* out of its slip and disappear?"

"No, Sofia. I won't do that to you."

When he settled his mouth on hers again, she nodded and clung a little too long, but he didn't pull away until she was ready to let him go.

CHAPTER 16

𝒞aro brought pink champagne. "Gold balloons and black theater ropes—brilliant! Now instead of wanking on the sidewalk to your mannequins, people can come in and shop. Whoever said sex doesn't sell is a liar."

It was early, two hours before the grand reopening, but Sofia thanked her with a swaying hug, popped the cork, and filled a glass without ceremony.

"Drink." She proffered it to Joss. "You need this."

Joss had been dangling on the edge for weeks, her mood gliding back and forth as if it were a pendulum. "Water a plant with it. I don't want it," she said, striding into Vices, where Paget was neatening their selection of floggers.

"One of our medium-intensities is missing," Paget told them. "Red handle. Has anyone seen it?"

"Sorry, no," Caro replied. "Medium intensity? Aren't they all tails attached to a handle?"

"Intensity deals with the hide used and the length of the tails," Joss said. When the others' gazes darted to her in silent surprise, she smoothed her kohl-colored minidress. They'd agreed on a black-attire dress code but had stepped it up for what they hoped would be a successful first day. "I'll check our shipment boxes out back. I'm sure I can find it."

"Is she all right?" Caro asked when Joss fled through a door marked AUTHORIZED PERSONNEL. "Seems something's irking her."

"The molds she ordered for her chocolate penises were lost in transit, but a replacement shipment's being couriered out this week." Paget shrugged and moved on to arranging the restraints just so. "I know she was hoping for a full treat display."

"Nipple tarts. A vulva cake." Caro listed the items she found in the classic-Hollywood style pastry display. "Are those miniature penises ... with cock rings?"

"Yes." Paget smiled. The shiny black pants and sheer-in-the-back top made her skin and hair appear even paler. "The rings were my idea. I think they add something extra, plus they ought to plant little seeds of curiosity about the full-size ones we carry."

"I'm curious."

"C'mon over here and I'll show you. What size is your man?"

Sofia *had* to know Caro's response to this. The photographer and McGuinty Slattery continued to slink around each other, and it seemed whenever he retreated to lick wounds left by her rejection she reeled him back in.

"I don't currently have one. I was only wondering what they do. Sort of intimidating."

"It doesn't have to be," said Sofia. Props and possibilities beckoned her imagination to dance. Lust, a need to be closer still to Burke, was music that pounded so loud she could hardly hear anything else. "Rings do nothing if no one's wearing them. Whips lie still without someone to hold them."

"Fair enough," Caro agreed. "Let's have a look, Paget."

As Caro went with Paget, Sofia drank the champagne, and saw Joss return with the missing red-handled flogger. "Found it. All's peachy."

Sofia set down her glass, took the flogger, hefted it in her hands, and dragged her fingers along the tails. It didn't sting her skin—nor would it, without someone's fist wrapped around the handle. She put it away and faced her friend. "Caro's concerned. Paget thinks you're miffed about the molds."

"I am miffed about the molds. I planned for white, milk, and dark chocolate. Different lengths and circumferences, too. One was going to be curved."

"Nice diversity," Sofia commented, and it felt surreal that this was a legitimate business-oriented conversation. At Manhattan Greetings, a lively meeting would concern weighing in on the design team's font choices or card stock options. "Edible penises for every preference."

"Strong tag line. I'm going to use that."

"You have my blessing." Sofia tried to return her light smile, but concern hovered. "It's not really the molds, is it? Is this about Peter?"

"What about him?"

"When we were at Grandpa Slattery's, you got that text. Peter hurt you, Joss, so if you're thinking about going back to him—"

"I'm not," her friend assured her, pain and conviction in her voice. "It'll never happen. I don't want to see him again."

"Then why have you been a wreck since that night? I've been trying to allow you space, but it's as if you're barely holding it together."

"It's nothing serious. It's change, that's all. New town, new faces, new job."

"Is there anything I can do to help?"

Joss raised a hand to nibble her thumbnail. Considering that her slate-colored nail varnish was fresh, Sofia's concern deepened. "Sof, when I mess up, I mess up big time."

"Everyone messes up, Joss."

She shook her head the way people do when they're staring at their greatest regret. "Not the way I do."

"What does that mean?"

"Never mind. Oh, they're looking at lube. I know a thing or two about that. Come here."

The shelves offered option after option. Lined neatly were gels, liquids—

"Oil. Water. Silicone." Joss pointed as she spoke. "A few things to consider, ladies," she said, addressing them all. "Oil-based lube is kryptonite to condoms. If you're in water, avoid water-based lube and go for something silicone. For the most part, water-based won't irritate, but if you or your partner has sensitive skin, try"—she plucked from the shelf a bottle marked TESTER and squirted some onto her fingertips—"this gem. It's hypoallergenic and gives the skin a really silky texture. Feel."

The others put out their hands and each received a dollop squirted into her palm.

"Nice, right?" Joss put it back and took down another tube. "The skin on your hand is different than your vagina, of course. It'll take some experimenting, but your guys should like that."

Crickets.

Paget looked around incredulously. "Are we all single? No one in this room is getting any action? There's something very cruel about that."

"Improvise, then. Toys. Fingers. Produce?" They laughed and as Paget and Caro moved on, Joss pressed a bottle into Sofia's hand. "Set this aside for yourself. Your longshoreman should appreciate it. Oh, and since you stocked their flavored line, you're going to want to take some time to taste them."

There went her plans for a yummy gooey cookie for dessert. Lube-sampling after counting out the register and sending the others on their way sounded naughty...and sexy.

Caro left, wishing them many horny customers, and Sofia sneaked upstairs to check on Tish once more.

"Reopening Blush feels like a good thing," she confided, scratching the dog under the chin. "Do you think Luz would approve?"

Tish puffed out a breath through her nostrils, and her all-knowing silver eyes pressed shut, then stared directly into Sofia. Not *at* her, but into her soul, and the dog claimed her place in Sofia's heart.

"This mascara's waterproof, but I'm not going to cry." She sniffled and used the excuse of pet dander to wash her hands and wad a towel that she gently dabbed to her nose and the corners of her eyes. "I miss her so much." Finnegan and Ellen didn't care—Sofia's health problems had run her father off and her mother hadn't even tried. But Luz's love was transparent and had followed Sofia wherever she went.

"I have to go," she told the dog, "but I'll see you at lunch."

She returned to Blush a half hour before opening. A familiar man stood just inside the door.

"Our first customer? Too early, but we won't turn you away," she said, automatically reaching out to pat his arm teasingly. Hesitating at the last moment, she folded her hands.

Javier Bautista could be as closed-off and enigmatically intimidating as Tish. But both were her guardians, her friends, even though neither would admit it.

"I'm not here to buy anything, *querida*." He curled his fingers in a *give me your hand* gesture and surrendered a stone.

"This belonged to Luz?" she asked.

"No, it was my mother's, from a charm bracelet. That's a moonstone. She said the charms gave her good luck." He shrugged. "I don't think they did, but luck's how you perceive it, isn't it? Anyway, the place looks damn good. Luz would raise a toast to you."

She smiled and hugged him before he could dodge her. "That means everything. Thanks."

Not leaving out the others, he tossed a skeleton key to Paget and put a penny in Joss's palm. "*Buena suerte.*"

"A penny. Something tells me it's the least valuable of the three," Joss said, turning it again and again until he laid his hand over hers.

"That's one way to look at it. There's a legend stuck to this penny, says a man was shot but wasn't killed 'cause it was in his breast pocket. I don't believe that, either, but Mom said hanging on to it made her feel safe. If it does that for you, then it's the most valuable."

"Okay." Joss sealed her lips, and for a second it looked like she was holding his hand tightly, but as Sofia approached for closer inspection, he stepped away and sought the door.

When the jingling bell announced his departure, Sofia held up her stone. "Good luck. Think we need it?"

"Well, if you decide you don't want yours, give it to me," Paget said, sliding the skeleton key into the pocket of her tight pants. "I'll take all the luck I can get."

Joss didn't answer. She stood there, gazing at the windows, once again turning the penny.

At nine o'clock sharp, Sofia flipped the sign to OPEN, and the next few hours were an erratic flip-flop between pandemonium when visitors descended—few shopping, some refusing to venture past the tamer front room, most storing tidbits to feed the rumor mill—and frustrating quiet when there was no activity but porn on the television in Vices.

The first pregnant customer to cross the threshold made Sofia do a double take. "Hannah, hi."

"Hi. I was checking to make sure you're treating my friend Paget all right. Of course you are." Smiling, she waved to Paget over the throng of customers and turned a circle in the sunshiny gold-and-white splendor. "Love the upgrades."

"You were a customer?"

Hannah's dark curls tumbled forward as she dropped her chin. "If Luz had offered a loyalty club, I'd be a platinum member from the condom saga alone."

Well, well, well, Abram Slattery. You know my dirty laundry and I'm about to know yours.

"My husband's libido's on Red Bull or something lately," Hannah said. Clearing her throat, she glanced around nervously—*vulnerably*. "He calls me beautiful, but I don't see that when I look in the mirror."

"If intimacy makes you uncomfortable—"

"It's not exactly that. I like that Abram still desires me. I was scared he'd stop, that he'd . . . step out."

Would pregnancy alone plant *that* kind of insecurity in a woman as confident as Hannah? Sofia studied her and detected a slight frown that wasn't quite confirmation but close enough.

But Hannah wasn't searching for consolation or support.

She wanted to shop. "When Abram and I make love, we switch positions a lot, so I want some ideas for late-term pregnancy sex."

"Know what, Hannah? Let's start with you. We don't have much maternity lingerie, but browse and think about what makes you feel sexy." She offered her elbow to the woman, who looked ready to topple forward from the weight of her baby bump.

Later, when Hannah headed to the boutique's exit with a damask-patterned shopping bag, Sofia felt a sense of victory. Not because she'd sold the woman two teddies, a pregnancy porn DVD, and warming massage oil, but rather because laughter touched Hannah's eyes when she ate a nipple tart and hope brightened her smile when she took an Au Naturel business card from the counter and said she'd consider Sofia's suggestion to schedule a consultation with Caro for a maternity boudoir session.

"I'd better see you at the Fourth of July picnic," Hannah said, bumping the door open with her butt. "Hot Dish is catering the barbecue. So come early and eat, and I promise I'll understand if you slip away to watch the fireworks from a certain longshoreman's boat."

Wait. What? "No, no, Hannah, it's not—"

"Later, hon."

Jingle!

"—what you think."

* * *

Curiosity could be detrimental to a man who seemed to find trouble without even searching for it. Aware of this, Burke had only himself to blame for angling his truck on Society Street at the peak of night.

Cape Foods stared down at him like a reproachful parent. Its papers had his signature on them, but the building owned him. If he were to unlock the door and go inside tonight, he'd empty his stomach right in the middle of the gutted space. After Deacon had died and the man's final expenses called Burke home, he'd gotten rid of everything but the structure, but he could close his eyes and see it as it'd been before—three registers, the owner's office on the right, a customer service counter on the left and a stock room in the back.

More familiar with its features than he was with the tats in his skin, he'd never forget the store as long as he remained chained to it through ownership papers. Yet he couldn't let it go.

Torturing himself this way was penance, in the same vein as scrubbing and sweeping the market for no pay had been. What he'd earned in tips he'd pocketed—it was how he'd saved the cash to buy Sofia an iPod for Christmas one year—but he'd never collected a dime from Deacon Wolf.

He'd worked, cooked hot dinners, and escaped when he could. The boarded-up tunnel underneath Cape Foods had been a safe haven for him, a place to hide.

Sofia had been a hornet, gentle to look at but fierce when anyone threatened her colony. And that colony was a tiny one, just her and Luz and Finnegan. He had no colony to protect, and none to protect him—until Sofia.

Eaves made him out to be the monster, but all he'd been was prey—the true monster a man he called *Dad*.

Sofia knew Deacon as the decorated war vet who ran the neighborhood market and had given her peppermint candies from the time she was old enough to come toddling into his store. She didn't know the impact of his fists or that Burke had learned to patch drywall and replace windows by repairing the damage his father left on the house in the wake of his rampages.

The church congregation knew only that choir singer Melody's little boy stopped coming to service and had chosen drugs over the Lord's grace—but not that a Saturday-night beating meant he'd be nursing his own cuts and cracked bones at home on Sunday.

The school knew he had a brain but squandered his potential with petty fights—but not that every brawl featured the same man who put food in Burke's stomach and always paid the bills on time.

The vilest way Deacon destroyed his son was to let him stay alive. So in the solitary instance when Burke had landed a fist on his father's jaw in defense and Deacon had pointed a gun at Burke's forehead, he hadn't pulled the trigger.

You killed Melody. I could empty this chamber into you and send you straight to hell, where you belong.

Burke had pissed his pants, wept for his mother, and the next day he'd taken his first toke of weed. He'd been fourteen then and had made the decision to never raise his hand to his father again. But neither would he let Deacon wreck him. Burke's life was his to wreck, and he'd come mighty damn close to accomplishing that.

Burke shuffled backward on the sidewalk. He could reach down and lob a flowerpot at the window, but the demons would be set free to float in the darkness.

It lay in the past, and he'd managed to hold it there until Sofia started hounding him about selling the building. If she knew, maybe she'd back off. Or maybe she wouldn't if it stood in the way of her ambition—and that would hurt more than he cared to realize.

With a simple "Fuck you, Dad," he set Deacon Wolf aside and started walking again.

Head down, he didn't invite the smiles of strangers or acknowledge the tense regard of people who knew him and
didn't like the man he was.

Remnants of a burst balloon rolled under his boot and
he looked up at Blush. As late as it was, the place must be
closed. Black velvet ropes held with gold posts designated
a short path to the door. Hanging over it was a banner with
GRAND REOPENING printed in a flourish. The mannequin
orgy was slightly different—they were still naked, but all except the one in the white robe wore party hats.

Surrendering to a chuckle, he sought the other window.
Every molecule of his being shot to attention. It was as though
he forgot where he was going and what was important.

On the other side of the glass was Sofia, wearing a
black dress and stockings, standing on a platform arranging strings of golden icicle lights against a midnight backdrop. He'd recognize her slender form and the soft curve
of her ass a continent away. The lights' twinkle reminded
him of fireflies. A pair of mannequins sat side by side under a blanket, and surrounding them were wads of some
white gauzy fabric.

The previous display to scandalize this window had been
hazily familiar. This one brought him back to their night at
the lighthouse.

Was that her intent? Was this a message meant for him?

Sofia turned to pin a string in place, and when she paused
at the sight of him square in front of her, she didn't return
his wave.

Disappearing from the window, she appeared at the door
and he heard the twisting of locks.

"Y'all working late?" he said, stepping inside.

"Just me. We closed at nine. Paget's shift ended well
before that, and Joss is upstairs making fresh treats for to-

morrow. And I'm dressing the windows. There's leftover pink champagne in back. It's all very Zen right now."

"Want me to go? You sound tired."

"No," she insisted, laying her hand on his chest. "Stay. If that's what you want, I mean."

"Are we still doing this, Sofia? You're acting out fantasies with mannequins in your windows and I'm waking up every morning hard with you in my head. For what, though, if we're still dancing around *this*?" He indicated the space between them. It wasn't a lot. If he bent forward just a few inches, he could taste her mouth and he'd have something pure in his life again.

His body had wanted hers—so badly—from the moment he'd spotted her at the cemetery. At the lighthouse she'd gazed at him openly, not blaming him for the guilt hugging his shoulders.

The dumb choices he made to protect her weren't in vain—she'd been worth it all along.

"I'm not tired. It's a mixed-feelings sort of day."

"I want to stay."

"You do?"

He didn't hear the words, just watched her mouth form them. "Yeah."

She led him through to Vices, and he stared at the sway of her hips in that snug, satiny dress the entire way. Hanging out here with hardcore porn on the TV was going to test the mettle of his restraint. Not mind over matter—mind over erection.

"Level with me, Sofia. How can all of this stuff not get to you?"

"It's merchandise. I'm running a business. The creeper we caught trying to use a toy in a dressing room kept everything in perspective." Still, she looked from him to the male-on-female anal sex on-screen and clicked off the TV. "Hope you don't mind."

"I don't need a video to teach me how to get that done."

Sofia's slim neck rippled as she swallowed. "Oh."

"There's some very sexually explicit dessert in that case," he commented. "Your friend Joss have something to do with this?"

"Yeah—help yourself. I was taste testing flavored lube, and I've got to monitor my sweets intake anyway. But you're welcome to it. The Venus piercing's edible."

An edible pierced vulva. Burke had witnessed the northern lights, watched a hurricane nearly capsize his boat, and survived an attempted hijacking at sea—but *now* he'd seen it all.

If that crooked smirk was any indication, his discomfort amused her. "Something funny?"

"All the naughty things are getting to you. It's adorable that you're nervous."

"I'm not nervous."

"You are. So careful. Polite."

Nervous. Careful. Polite. He would erase those words with a single sentence of honesty.

He concentrated on getting to her, on getting nice and close. Flared pupils dominated her brown eyes; the rise and fall of her chest quickened. Grazing her earlobe with his lips, he said frankly, "Sofia, there's only one pussy I want to lick in this place, and it ain't covered with frosting."

She slapped a hand over her mouth, then curled her fingers. "That was filthy."

He nodded. "But you're not telling me to go."

"I'm…" Her arms fell, one then the other, as she walked backward toward a pair of slim doors marked DRESSING. "I'm not."

He tried to remind himself. *Mind over…* What?

Fuck it—the past, the future, and everything in between that made sense. Opening one of the doors to a room with mirrored walls, she offered him a gift—her trust.

Advancing on her and walking into her outstretched arms, he sighed. "Jesus. Sofia, be sure. Are you sure?"

"It's you, Burke, so I'm sure." When she wet her lips, he took the invitation.

Their tongues collided and her heat filled the coldest parts of him. Keeping his mouth occupied, she dragged up his shirt, then broke away to whimper, "Take it off. I need to touch you."

Complying with her desperate command, he stripped it off and pitched it.

She kissed his neck as she hooked her fingers into the waistband of his jeans. Teasing him, pressing along his shape, she unbuttoned the fly and lowered the zipper. "These next. Take them off."

"Nah."

"What?" Confused, on the borderline of crushed, she searched his face. "I thought we—"

"Turn around and hold up your hair."

Sofia spun, and with her back to him she faced a mirror. At every turn, every angle, was their reflection. Hesitant fingers gathered the dark, silky sheet, though some strands managed to slip away.

Beautiful.

Untying the knot at the top of her dress and taking down the zipper, he revealed her pale olive skin. She shivered, letting her hair fall. He kissed her shoulder blades, knew his bristly jaw scoured her.

"It tickles, your beard on me," she said with a halfhearted giggle. In the mirror he could see her hands gripping the front of the dress to her breasts—to her scar.

Moving his mouth to her ear again, he said, "Just because you said you were sure before doesn't mean you can't change your mind. Tell me to stop and I'll take my hands off you. No questions."

She said nothing, seeking him in the mirror and parting her lips as her hands relaxed on the dress.

From behind Burke took both of her wrists and outstretched her arms, and the dress dropped as if it'd fainted from her body.

Oh, hell.

From the freckles on her nose to the ruched tips of her breasts to the slender legs decorated with sheer diamond-patterned stockings, she was incredible.

"It's ugly," she whispered. "It didn't heal great."

From the top of her breastbone to the bottom, the scar was gnarled dark tissue.

His hands demanded her. They cupped her tits, unsnapped her garters, drew down her stockings...

"Listen to me," he said, turning her again and lowering slowly. He tongued the hollow of her throat, each of her nipples. "It's a scar. It's not supposed to be pretty to look at. *You*, damn it, are beautiful. This scar is the reason you're here with me. It's your second chance, Sofia. And you know what? That's what makes it the most beautiful thing about you."

She seemed hopeful yet afraid of that hope. "It is?"

"Yeah." He picked up her hand, kissed it. "Touch it. I want to see you do it."

She bounced her fingertips along the trail, her lips parted as if something he'd said mesmerized her. Had she never known she was a friggin' treasure?

He nudged her until she was flat against the mirror and gazing down at him. On his knees, he peeled down her panties. "Is this underwear or floss?"

Laughing, she ruffled his hair. She held the sides of his face, held his attention. "I can't believe we're doing this. I wanted this."

But there was hesitation in the nervous way she caught her breath and the shyness of her touch.

"What'd you want, Sofia?" He stretched up, licked one nipple and then crossed her scar to the other. "Me to kiss you here?"

"Mm-hmm," she said, melting into a moan when he sucked on her. "I thought about you holding me, putting your mouth on me, tasting me. I don't want to think about it anymore. I want to live it."

Smiling, proud of her for telling him plainly what she expected, he peppered kisses down her abdomen at the same time that he slipped a hand between her thighs. "You touched yourself thinking about me."

She nodded. "A lot."

"Tonight, let me take over."

Another nod. "Okay."

Burke watched her, kissing her belly as he firmly inserted a finger into her damp heat. When she moaned and opened herself further, he withdrew and sat on the floor. "Get over here. Straddle, all right? Keep standing and just put a foot on either side of my legs...I really like how you follow my directions, Sofia."

Trembling, she gulped whatever retort she had ready for him. "Then what?"

"Enjoy." Burke pushed her thighs apart wide and licked her mound. He suckled her, his tongue learning her clit and memorizing her taste. The firmer the pressure, the slicker she became. His index and middle fingers alternated inside her, and her sharp sighs punctuating the wet noises of his feasting had his cock straining ruthlessly in his jeans.

"Put both in," she said eventually. "Take care of that and we can keep going. It'll be easier for you."

"I don't care about what's easy."

"We need to both take away something good from this, Burke. That's fair."

"I don't care about what's fair, either." He looked up at her. She was everything. Redemption, forgiveness, love. Everything he needed but wouldn't dare ask for. "This is about *you* right now. Can you let me show you that?"

Rocking impatiently on his hand, she whispered a swear-word and hell, did it turn him on.

His tongue and fingers worked as a single unit—strumming her, exploring her—and the music of her tense cries fell on him.

"Come." A one-word demand, infused with so much power. He took his mouth away so he could see her eyes, but continued to stroke. "Come, with my finger in you. I want to feel it."

Gripping his hair, she uttered a sharp keening sound and grinded violently on his hand. Her body pulsing around him, clenching him, he felt her take what she wanted.

Burke gathered her on his lap as she continued to ride out the intensity of the orgasm, but suddenly she began flapping her hands and scrambling away.

"Sofia?"

"H-h-help! The hospital." She pressed against her scar; her breath was short. Fear and panic thickened inside him, solidifying the blood in his veins. "Something's wrong."

CHAPTER 17

he nurse said you showed up naked."

Sofia, freshly returned from a battery of tests and a shower, lounged on a hospital bed. The patient gown was uncomfortably crisp and the soap rising from her skin smelled sterile. A blood pressure monitor clipped onto her finger refused to stay put and the IV drip attached to her arm made maneuvering awkward. She forgot all those inconveniences when she saw Joss carrying bundles of balloons and blooms. "That'd be funny if it weren't true. Gretchen and Richard were here earlier. They brought a card and sweats—which don't fit, unfortunately."

"Word travels *fast*." Joss placed the balloons in the corner and set the flowers on a table. "These are from Caro and Evan. They were here this morning, waiting for you to come back from testing, but she had to take off for a client appointment. Evan made me promise to give you this." She retrieved a plush bear from a gift bag.

"Aww." Sofia hugged the stuffed animal and propped it on the pillow beside her. "That kid's ridiculously sweet."

"Isn't he?" Joss emptied a shopping bag. "Outfits. I'm liberating you from that gown. Can't stand the thought of you in hospital chic for three days."

Last night Sofia had been admitted for a seventy-two-hour observation period, accommodating her cardiologist's arrival from New York to consult with the Eaves Community Hospital staff and coordinate treatments. IV fluids were addressing her dehydration. The hypertension and heart palpitations weren't fully under control yet and required further study, though the attending physician's current impression attributed her symptoms to stress.

"Here's your purse. Your meds are inside." Joss gave her a sidelong glance. "I took care of the clothes I found in that dressing room."

"Oh. About that."

"When Burke called to tell me he'd brought you in, he asked me to make sure no customers found your stuff on the floor like that. He's rough around the edges, but chivalrous."

There was *never* a good time to experience a cardiac emergency. But to experience it precisely in the middle of sex? In a dressing room? With a man who was already a hair trigger away from bolting? *Seriously?*

Sofia picked up a pillow and smashed it against her face. "I'm mortified."

"Care to fill in some blanks? Burke calls the apartment, tells me you're in the hospital with chest pain and your stuff's in a dressing room. Then I find out he brought you here naked."

"I wasn't naked," she cried through the pillow.

"The nurse said you were half-naked with a guy's shirt wrapped around you, and that Burke Wolf was half-naked, too. So I figured two half-nakeds may as well make a whole naked."

"Where is he?" She hadn't seen him since she was wheeled away from her emergency-room cubicle for labs and an ECG last night. "Did you see him?"

"Shh. Calm down—your BP's going to soar again." She pointed to the untouched breakfast tray. "Is that a cracker or a hockey puck?" When the quip failed to soften Sofia's frown, she sat at the foot of the bed. "I'm not going to lie. I told him to leave."

"Let me get my phone," she said, dropping the pillow. "I have to call him."

"Sofia, he was exhausted. He paced the waiting room for hours, hassled staff for information they wouldn't provide. So I told him to go to his boat and sleep, that I'd be here. Now please tell me what the hell happened."

"All the test results haven't rolled in and my cardiologist hasn't had his say yet, but the doctors here think the cardiac event and the dehydration are stress related. It all hit while Burke was going down on me. There—blanks filled."

"Holy. Shit." Joss swung her legs up to cross them akimbo. "Why then?"

Sofia shrugged. "Sex is cardio. It triggers all sorts of physiological reactions. You get hot. You sweat. You breathe hard. Your pulse leaps like crazy."

"All pros...except you're in a hospital, and that's a big glaring con." She opened Sofia's purse and thrust out the phone. "Fine, call him."

Dialing with the IV and blood pressure monitor in the way was awkward, but she managed.

"Sofia. You okay?" No greeting, just a gravelly demand.

"Better. The tests are still out, but on first impression it's just dehydration, elevated BP, and mild palpitations."

"Just? It was worse than anything I saw happen to you. You couldn't breathe. You said your chest hurt."

"I'm sorry I scared you."

"Don't apologize. Hell, you're in a hospital because of me and *you're* apologizing." Silence stretched. "Joss told me to take off and rest, but we've got to talk about this. We went too far. I knew this wasn't good for you."

"What about our promise at Bellini Beach?"

"It doesn't matter when being with me put you in the hospital."

"Stop, Burke. You're tired. I can hear it. Rest. Come back later. If you're going to end things with me, okay. But you'll do it face-to-face. Visiting hours are over at eight." She ended the call and dropped the phone onto the mattress.

Joss glanced from the phone to Sofia. "End things?"

"He says he's to blame for this, but I feel he's afraid to get closer. It's more convenient to feed the fear." She uncurled her body and pressed her face into the pillow.

Joss smoothed her hair back in a manner that was motherly and a faint comfort. "Hey, you're preaching to the choir here. It's so hard to trust, to give, and when you think you're with someone who's different and he pulls away, too, it hurts."

Sofia sat up again. "Peter was never different. Same all-polish, no-substance as the others who lifted you up with promises and then dropped you."

"No, you're right. Peter wasn't different," her friend said quietly, and Sofia was momentarily confused. Who besides Peter Bernard had hurt her? "So when this happens, we need to bounce back every time."

How had Sofia managed to bounce back from losing Burke before? She might've been tougher then—loving him, yes, but not *in love* with him.

She was configured to love him. Stubborn despite its vulnerabilities, her heart wanted him. But it was careless, impractical, to reach for a damaged soul who kept a dangerous career and panicked in the face of her ugliness.

This scar is the reason you're here with me. It's your second chance, Sofia. And you know what? That's what makes it the most beautiful thing about you.

She hadn't conjured those words wrapped in a husky voice that tickled her ears the way his beard tickled her skin. Burke had said them, to her, and he'd *meant* them.

"Stop thinking about Burke," Joss said. "Just for a while. A reading popped up on your machine. One forty-three over eighty." Searching for what to say next, she commented, "Nice of the Pruitts to visit."

"Gretchen said they were having breakfast at the general store when someone told her I was brought to the ER. I can't believe a nurse told you I was half-naked. Is patient confidentiality not a thing in Eaves?"

"She didn't tell me directly. She was speaking with a white coat. I eavesdropped at the nurses' station. Stranger circumstances have happened. This would hardly make it on *Untold Stories of the ER*." When Sofia giggled despite herself, Joss exaggerated a *Whew! That was close!* gesture. "Although I think you might end up on a church prayer list."

"Prayers are appreciated."

"Gracious of you. A little too gracious." She eyed the IV pouch. "What's *in* that bag?"

"Fluids." She picked up the teddy bear. "A kid sent me this because he cares about my well-being. Gretchen and Richard visited for the same reason. Yes, there's gossip—tons of it—but some people give a damn."

"And Eaves, does it feel like home again?"

"Not totally, but I was expecting it to feel like the home

it used to be. Changes." She swung her legs over the side of the bed. "I want to go to the windows."

"Careful. Does this BP monitor transport?"

"It's on wheels. C'mon." Slowly, she got to her feet and Joss helped her wheel the IV and monitor across the hospital room. She raised the shades and sighed, looking out past the hospital's grounds to the sun-touched sand and water in the distance. "For the next three days I'm going to be wishing I was out there. Have you swum in the ocean yet, Joss?"

"The ocean? Oh, actually, no. I laid out tanning."

"Swim. It's amazing."

"You sound so sad, Sof. Three days is nothing. It'll go quickly."

"What about Blush? Yesterday was the grand reopening. It's going to be closed for the next three days."

"Paget and I will hold it together. We won't let you down."

What'd she do to deserve friends like this? "Thanks, Joss."

"Well, good morning! Even better to see you up and about," a male announced, knocking, and when they turned to him, he had a smile prepared. She'd met him before. *Aeneas Strayer.*

"Mr. Strayer, hi."

He carried a long-stemmed bouquet. "Call me Aeneas. A word with you ladies?"

"Okay." With Joss's aid, Sofia settled onto the visitor chair. "What can I do for you?"

"Start by accepting these." Settling the flowers across her lap, he reached into his suit jacket for a card. "I'm not aware of the particulars of your illness, Sofia, but it concerned me to know you're not well. So I thought of the best possible way that I can lighten your burden." He handed the card to

Joss, who shared it with her. A figure was written on the back. A sizable figure. "I'm a real estate investor, and my client has authorized me to present their *opening offer* for your property on Society Street. In light of your health issues, we can appreciate that you'd be a motivated seller, but fairness is a virtue—particularly in delicate business transactions such as this."

"Wait, wait." Sofia tried to return the card, but he made no move to accept it. "My property isn't on the market. I have no plans to sell it. I reopened Blush yesterday."

Aeneas Strayer dropped his voice. "And today you're here. Sofia, let me speak plainly. I put my ass on the line to convince my client to offer what's clearly in your financial favor. Don't make an emotional decision. Think it over while you're here eating your Jell-O." His smile had slipped and his words felt like contempt. "Luz was interested in streamlining her obligations, trimming some fat. She wanted Blush off her plate."

"It's on my plate now. Please don't pressure or lecture me, Mr. Strayer."

"Aeneas. We're all friends here."

"Good-bye, Mr. Strayer."

He took his cue to get the hell out. Joss shut the door behind him and set aside the flowers he'd brought. "Creep. I'm seriously regretting that I let him pour me a cup of tea. He's downright insulting."

"Desperate. Not to mention the figure on that card. It's a lot of money with room to negotiate. It's the second generous offer someone laid down for that property. Remember the man from Omni?" Omni Commercial Development of New England. Or, according to Caro, Beelzebub. "I could sell Blush and be wealthy. I could keep it, work my ass off, and still somehow fail."

"Sounds like an easy choice when you put it that way."

It *was* an easy choice. "I'm keeping it."

Joss knelt. "You're the craziest, most badass chick I know."

"Doubt not." Sofia laughed. "People will think I'm a complete idiot for passing up money like this. I could retire early and live a life of leisure in the tropics someplace. I could buy you a new construction."

"It's not their place to judge, but who cares? Caro must be receiving similar offers, and this kind of money could put her son through college a dozen times over. She said no. Burke Wolf said no."

"He said no to me, too."

Although, if their agreement made at the lighthouse was null and void, then she could pursue the Cape Foods building again with a clear conscience.

"Just relax and congratulate yourself on batting away another vulture. I want to remind you, you're not in this alone." Joss went to the breakfast tray, peeled open the cherry Jell-O, and spooned out a dollop. "I'm willing to secure a bank loan to go in on Bautista's bar with you and Caro."

"Joss, no. I'm sitting here turning down huge money and you're putting yourself in debt? It's wrong."

"It's my decision to be part of something, to have something real. I'm tired of being told no and watching doors swing shut on me. Ideally Burke would sell and we can convert the bar into a legit club where people can dance, for God's sake, because this town's suffering a nightlife crisis."

Sofia had no argument. Caro had been spot-on in her early thoughts about opening the basements. Aphrodisiac foods, nude photography, and kink upstairs. Liquor and dirty dancing downstairs. New York was full of similar dens.

"Only, Burke won't sell to me any more than he'll sell to Omni."

"Men can be swayed. It takes the right kind of persuasion."

Sofia cocked her head. "Okay, what's that supposed to mean?"

"You and Burke have more than some teenage memories. If he truly cares about you, he'll want what's best for you. Remind him of that." She started playing with the zipper pull on her purse. Random charms and a tiny plastic container holding a penny clanged together. "I've given it a thought. Men throw the word *care* around too lightly, and sometimes they need to be reminded that care is a commitment, not a group of letters that means nothing."

But it wasn't for Sofia to come from a place of aggression. She wanted Burke to sell the building from a fair business perspective, not under duress.

She was about to express this to her friend, but a nurse entered and Joss departed, saying, "I'll check on Tish, and Paget and I'll manage the store. Need anything at all—call."

Vitals checked and finally updated that this morning's labs had come through but the ECG reading wasn't yet finalized, Sofia watched the nurse hum with dissatisfaction at the information derived from the BP monitor.

With a digital chart in hand, the stout woman dragged over the visitor's chair. "Dr. Engles will be on-site in the morning. In the meantime, as Dr. Cochran informed you last night, we're going to need to administer a different BP drug, since your numbers are still up there. We'll get you a blocker that won't conflict with your current drug therapies." She clicked her tongue. "Yeah, we really don't want to aggravate this creatinine level."

"Creatinine? What is it—Let me see the report."

The nurse's gray eyebrows rose. "Dr. Cochran's making his rounds. He can interpret the data for you—"

"Creatinine levels are used for kidney function eval. I know already." This wasn't her first rodeo. It wasn't her first go-round with renal dysfunction. It *was* her first confrontation with it when she had everything in front of her...so much to lose. "I only want to know the severity of...May I see it—the report?"

"God," the nurse whispered. Empathy bled through her professional composure. "I'll print a copy. Dr. Cochran will be here. Give him a chance to dissect this. I...I'm sorry, Sofia."

She could do nothing but breathe until the nurse delivered the lab report. Alone at a moment when she needed someone's arms around her, she found abnormalities in the glomerular filtration rate from her blood draw and the amount of protein in her urine sample.

Had disease been developing bit by bit for months? Her most recent follow-up hadn't revealed anything alarming. This, the report in her hand, was alarming.

"I'll fight you, too," she whispered to the letters and numbers and symbols that tried to break her. "I can be a bitch, and I'm going to fight like one until I beat you."

* * *

There never seemed to be anything distracting on TV when Sofia was in the hospital. By midafternoon she'd grown exhausted of stalking Food Network programs, had eaten a bland lunch that wasn't nearly as appetizing as what she'd watched chefs prepare on the screen, and was still wearing a patient gown. She wasn't motivated to change into any of the clothes Joss had brought.

She'd almost dialed Burke too many times to remember. She wanted him here. She wanted to explain her prognosis, to gently let him know that there were unknowns and variables in play and nowhere was it written in stone that suggestions of early-stage kidney disease meant he'd lose her tomorrow.

She wanted to make him understand that a mild cardiac event and renal complications didn't mean she no longer had the right to live and love.

I love him and he's not here.

Until, finally, he was. Shuffling into the room, he had the body language of one guiltily sneaking into a place he didn't belong. "Sofia?"

She unclipped the monitor and dragged her IV pole as she ran to him. "I'm sorry."

"You've got to quit apologizing."

"Excuse me," the afternoon-shift nurse said from the doorway, "but the patient needs to be in bed with that monitor on her finger."

Burke reattached her monitor and they sat side by side on the bed. "I drove halfway here four or five times today. Kept telling myself to stay out of your way. But I was going goddamn crazy without you. It's selfish and I know that. But…it's *you*, Sofia. You."

"It's okay." *Because, my God, I love you.*

"I tried not to miss you and need you." His voice shook. "I was spinning out. That's not all right."

"I'm here," she said, consoling him so she could take a break from consoling herself. The report rested in her purse; the Eaves Community docs had a preliminary plan and it was too soon to drop more into his lap. "My BP's in a normal range now and the IV fluids will rehydrate me nicely."

"Stress," he said quietly. "That's what brought this on?"

"Community seems to think so. My cardiologist comes in tomorrow, but so far the plan is to adjust my meds. The drug combo can be tricky, pairing the immunosuppressants and the antivirals."

Tell him the rest...

"The panic attacks, now heart palpitations and high blood pressure and dehydration," Burke listed. "I didn't want this for you, Sofia. It's too much hitting you all at once—losing your aunt Luz and starting a whole new life here. Taking me and all my shit on? I would rather walk away than screw with your health."

"It's a simple fix." A cheap lie. A coward's escape. "New prescription. Fluids. Naps."

"That's all? You sure?"

She nodded. "It's just maintenance. Community's going to keep me for three days for observation, and then I'm back to scandalizing Eaves again. Back in your arms again." She could look at him right now and clearly picture him sitting in front of her with his gray eyes fastened on hers and then his tongue sliding—

"I don't want to hurt you."

"Then don't."

"I need to be doing something. Helping somehow. What if I kept Tish for the next few days?"

"You'd do that?"

"Yeah. She can ride shotgun in the pickup, hang out on the boat. Think she'd be good with running a mile at dawn? 'Cause sometimes I do that to loosen up before chores."

Tish, all fur and muscle and beauty, running at full speed as the morning opened. "She'd love it."

She found his hand resting on his thigh and wove her fingers through his. Once they'd been able to hold hands and wrap themselves around each other and it hadn't meant the beginning and end of the world. But they weren't a couple of teenagers in rip-kneed jeans hanging out at gas station convenience stores or beach bonfires. He raised her hand and kissed her knuckles hard. "I care about you, Sofia. From the beginning I cared."

Except when he and his friends had vilified her in school. But the past didn't sting anymore. She stroked his hand with her thumb. "Do you still sketch?"

"No."

"Why not?"

"I left it behind in rehab. It was something to piss away the time. The sketches were half-finished and ended up thrown out anyway."

"When was the last time you finished one?"

"Before we fought. Before you left." He went still, then, "Why'd that happen? That last day—why'd we have to be that way?"

To answer him, she'd have to let herself remember. Painful it might be, but if she wouldn't tell him about the lab results tucked into her purse, she owed him this. Hurt him with either the past or the present.

She chose the past.

Sofia knew she was an hour late and Burke's dad would be home soon.

Burke wasn't allowed to have girls in the house, and that included her, but what was one more rule to break for each other?

Whatever dinner he'd cooked would be cold. She hoped it'd make him mad at her. Then it wouldn't hurt so badly to cut him out of her life.

Burke was eighteen and had a crappy car that ran if you worked the engine just right. He said he'd visit her after she and Dad moved to New York. She needed to make sure he'd be so mad that he wouldn't think about her again.

Sofia came in through the back door and the Wolfs' house smelled good, like pizza or something.

"Hey." Burke put down the cordless phone in the kitchen and crossed his lanky arms. A purple bruise that resembled a meaty handprint peeked out from beneath his baggy goth band shirt. "Where you been? I was about to call Luz."

"Yeah, smart! Call her and tell her I'm late sneaking to a guy's house."

"Luz doesn't care that we hang out."

"My dad doesn't like it."

"Tell him to fuck off sometime. He wasn't controlling you when he was in jail." He pointed to the spotless table in the spotless kitchen in the spotless house. "Take a seat. I'm gonna have to warm the sauce up some and boil more spaghetti. It got cold. Or I can toss all this and make us sandwiches."

"Won't you get in trouble if your dad sees me here?" She didn't want to think about Burke getting lectured or grounded when she was already aiming to do so much harm.

"I'll tell him you came over for homework or something. Maybe I'll survive. Maybe not."

"What?"

"It was a joke."

Sofia didn't sit down. One big, deep breath, then she did what she had to do. "I wasn't even going to come here, but I thought you should know that when Dad and I move, we're starting over. So don't come to New York to visit me." And because she started to feel really shitty and guilty, she hefted the stock pot of marinara sauce off the stove to take it to the garbage disposal. Yeah, it'd grown cold.

"Why don't you want me to visit?"

"When I move, I don't want to be friends with a stoner. Okay?"

Burke reached for the pot. "Give me that. What the hell is wrong with you?"

Sofia tugged. She wouldn't let go. "Screw you."

"You know what, Sofia? Screw you." And Burke let the pot go, sending her stumbling back with lukewarm sauce sloshing over her.

"The floor!" he growled. "The goddamn floor's a mess."

The floor was what he cared about when she stood covered in spaghetti sauce?

Burke whirled on her, tears in his beautiful gray eyes. "Get out of here, Sofia."

"No problem. You stay out of my life. I don't want to see you ever again." She pushed a hand into her pocket. It'd hurt to give him up when he was her best friend and she loved him. "Here. Take the iPod back. I don't want it."

"Keep it. Now get the hell out."

Sofia couldn't help it; she rested her head against him, then poked her nose into his shirt. Plaid flannel rolled to the elbows, and it held his scent. "I was on a transplant waiting list. It didn't look good. I thought it'd hurt less for you if we weren't friends when I died."

He laughed, and it was a rough, dark sound. "It didn't hurt less, Sofia."

I love you.

"I loved your drawings," she said, editing her thought.

"The drawings were shit."

"They were angry—" Demons. Fanged, dagger-clawed creatures. Death. "But they were yours. I always thought you were trying to say something with those sketches. And I thought you were morbid."

"Had a reason to be."

"Under all of that, you were a good guy, Burke." When he didn't say anything, she held him and let him hold her, and for the first time since her great-aunt's funeral, Sofia caught a glimpse of her old friend.

Turning his face toward hers, she kissed the man he'd become.

CHAPTER 18

he next time Burke got the idea to chastise someone for living in a fantasy, he'd start with himself. Part of him warned that what he had brewing with Sofia wasn't real. But there were plenty of people crawling over one another to re-inforce that warning.

The night she was discharged from Community, he'd cooked dinner on his boat and taken her out on the water. It'd almost felt like absolution for the last time he attempted to fix her a meal, but in a bigger sense those hours were more about the here and now. Yesterday, before they took off to Salisbury for a country-and-western bar, they'd filled his truck and inside the gas station convenience store she'd lost a dozen quarters at the claw machine before charming him into giving it a shot. He'd hit his mark, grabbing a plush lob-ster that had to be more than thirty years old.

They didn't call it dating. They didn't utter the word *re-lationship*. They just were.

Burke and a few others stood back under the hot sun as

Abram's electrical guys wove wiring through the studs in the new framing. Sawdust dotted his sunglasses and he grabbed his work gloves from his back pocket to wipe the lenses.

"It's taking shape. Hannah finally believes it's going to happen," Abram said with pride, swinging up a Coors. "But I don't know what I'm going to do to stop her from sneaking out here to look around. It's dangerous."

"She's excited," Burke commented, recalling how Abram's wife and her melon-shaped belly stalked the yard. She'd even been wearing a hard hat. Where she'd gotten one was beyond him. Goggles and work gloves were the extent of the men's protective gear. "Shouldn't she be busy? The picnic's tomorrow."

Hot Dish was catering Eaves's Fourth of July celebration and Burke knew that unless Hannah was in active labor, she'd be hands-on cooking at the restaurant tonight and on-site at Bellini Beach tomorrow.

"She is—working too hard, in my opinion, but every time I broach the subject she wants to bite my head off. She's on her feet too much. They're more swollen than they ought to be, and now she won't let me rub them because every time I start we end up having sex."

"Yeah, I didn't need to know that."

Abram chuckled, then looked around to see who was in earshot. "Your girl Sofia's partly to blame. She sold Hannah a pregnancy flick."

Burke tucked his gloves into his pocket. "What, you didn't already have one in your garage stash?"

"Very funny." Abram lightly jabbed him on the shoulder. "So, I can't help but point out you didn't object when I called Sofia your girl."

"I'd call bullshit on him if he did," said McGuinty, approaching with his arms folded. He'd shown up late today, having helped old Niall run a pet adoption event at the animal shelter. "One of the shelter volunteers works the graveyard shift at the hospital. The folks at the bank are talking about it, too. That's all I oughtta say."

The bank? Managing money didn't keep them occupied enough?

Abram's mouth dipped at the corners. "Hannah let me know she was laid up at Community. We visited her. Y'all wouldn't believe the way those two dragged me to the nursery and then ignored me as soon as they started oohing and ahhing over the babies." He looked from his brother to Burke. "So is she all right?"

"She's fine. It was a reaction to stress and her medication," Burke said tightly, watching the electrical crew stomp across the scaffolds.

"Glad to hear it. Now what's the rest of the story?"

"Burke brought her to the ER," McGuinty said. "The way the folks at the bank told it, he and Sofia were both missing vital articles of clothing. Damn vital."

"Yeah, I was with her." He glared at his friends through dark lenses. "I don't owe you another word. Abram, you're my sponsor, not my pastor. McGuinty, back off."

"Calm down," McGuinty barked, and silence waved over the yard, broken only by the faint spray of the sprinkler system. "She's a vortex. That's what you need to remember."

She was his salvation. She'd loved him, even when she had sliced into him with brutal words the last time they were together at his father's house. "McGuinty, I swear to God—"

"While you're constructing that pedestal to put her on, take one friggin' minute to remember what happened the last time she cut you to the quick. Abram remembers. I remember. Grandpa does, too." McGuinty shook his head.

"Grandma cried when we brought you home beaten and half out of your mind."

"That was a long time ago. I apologized to Amy for letting her see me like that."

"It's not about the fucking apology! Damn, it, Burke"—McGuinty grabbed his collar—"stop acting like a dick and listen to me."

Burke pushed him off and stalked him into the mudroom. "There's a line. Don't cross it."

"Christ, listen to yourself. You're deaf to any proof that she can cost you everything you set up for yourself. Sofia's sexy and funny and she can be sweet—yeah, I get that. But she blindsided you once. You cut off Courtney Abernathy, were trying to get sober, were doing it all for Sofia. Then what?"

"I backslid. It wasn't on her."

"Backslid? Man, you got stoned and somebody beat your ass. Grandpa loaded Abram and me up to get you, because Deacon said fuck it and you had nowhere to stay."

The order of events was off—the beating had happened first, then he'd sloppily filled his system to assuage the pain—but what good would it do to correct McGuinty when the past couldn't be changed and he was bent on proving a point?

"You were confused, depressed, and it took a farmhouse full of people to get you right. The whole time you kept saying *Sofia*, again and again, like you had no control of your mind. It can happen again. Doesn't matter one fucking iota how long you've been sober. It can all snap in a moment."

McGuinty Slattery was one of the roughest sons of bitches ever made, but he wasn't a liar.

Burke scratched his skin through his shirt. The sweat darkening the collar made him itch. Or maybe it was the pinprick of doubt that told him Sofia was as much a threat to his health as he was to hers. "It was a bad fight. She'd told me she was taking off with her father and not looking back. I couldn't figure out what'd made her snap, aside from Finnegan being forced to uproot her. He couldn't find work after he was collared."

Finnegan Mercer had been arrested for stealing money from Cape Foods when Sofia was sixteen. His months-long sentence for burglary and theft had imploded whatever stability she thought she had. It had rocked this sleepy town awake, that an upstanding bank manager and loving father could be revealed as a common bastard.

Burke and Sofia had become friends when her father was in lockup and she'd come to live with Luz. Even after Finnegan's release, she'd remained with Luz for a year, and she and Burke couldn't be pried apart until she walked out of his life to make one for herself in New York.

"Finnegan was responsible for his own shit. Just as you're responsible for yours," McGuinty said. "Sofia can't protect your sobriety. The freedom to get out of this place when you need to is probably what's holding you together, so make damn sure you know why you're risking what's important."

"I'm not putting my sobriety in her hands. We're taking this easy."

"You kept her dog and were on edge the entire time she was in the hospital. People see how y'all are together. We're on the periphery, though, because you and Sofia have tunnel vision. All she sees is you. All you see is her. There's nothing wrong with that. But there's a whole hell of a lot wrong with pretending it's not true. It insults my goddamn intelligence and I don't appreciate it."

All she sees is you. All you see is her.

"I'm saying this because I'm your friend." His expression

grave, McGuinty appeared decades beyond his age. "I'd expect the same courtesy from anyone who wants to call himself my friend."

"Yeah? Then I need to tell you to take a step back from Caro Jayne. She's got more problems than you and a bunch of flowers can fix."

Self-destructive people could always recognize parts of themselves in one another, and he figured the woman who poured his drinks with a pretty smile on her face and bracelets stacked up her wrists suspected the worst of his damage the same as he suspected hers.

"It's just advice from a friend," he said to McGuinty, turning to leave the house and return to the job he'd come here to do. "It's up to you to take it or piss on it. That works both ways."

* * *

"Anyone who's anyone in this town is supposed to be out at Bellini Beach. Isn't today a holiday?" With his multi-millionaire swagger, Aeneas Strayer—Rooster, among the Dead Men—advanced on the visitor's chair in Bautista's law office.

Nessa, who'd just finished compiling disclosures for an ongoing case, gave the man a flat smile and made an escape to her own office. When Aeneas visited Bautista here, it rarely had anything to do with follow-the-proper-protocol legal matters.

"Mmm, she's a hot one. Feisty." Aeneas swiveled toward the door to attempt another look at Nessa. "A lot of woman, but I can handle her."

"No, you can't." Under different circumstances, Bautista would've laughed out loud at the notion of down-to-earth

Nessa giving top-to-bottom-polished Aeneas the time of day.

"All right, we'll agree to disagree."

Bautista nodded and went to the door to shut it. "Something else we're going to agree to disagree on—you're not getting your hands on Society Street."

"Hey, easy now. No need to be hostile."

"Shut up." Aeneas was his friend, his club brother—but when it came to fork-tongued deception, there was no friendship or brotherhood. "When Luz died, I didn't close my eyes and ears. So I know you approached Sofia Mercer when she was hospitalized, that you tried to lure her to the negotiation table."

"A client was interested in the property. On that client's directive, I presented an offer. That's business. That's craft. That's food on my goddamn table."

After Sofia had shown him a business card, Bautista had scheduled a meeting, without his brother Rooster, at Bottoms Up. It would be the last time he'd host a talk inside the bar. The familiar atmosphere, the advantage of being on his territory, had aided him to put the puzzle together, piece by treacherous piece.

"What about working an angle when Luz was in my ear about putting my bar on the market? What about pulling her strings so you could broker deals to sell the strip to Omni and collect double commission? What's that?"

"Temper, Judge. The person you should be angry with is the woman who was sucking on your cock by night and making plans to get into our club by day."

"I know you preyed on Luz. You dangled the promise of club membership in front of her. Admit it and I won't retaliate."

Aeneas gave the room a cursory scan. No witnesses. No

weapons. "She said you shut her down when she told you she wanted in."

True, but beside the point. He never wanted the two halves of his world—the club and Luz—to collide. It'd pissed him off that she'd asked to join the fold after he'd already decided to retire to protect her. "Don't tell me her sins. We're talking about yours."

"I told her I could get her in."

"No way in fucking hell would the club have allowed it." Bautista had been transparent—Luz was his, and it was understood that she was completely untouchable to the club. He would've killed the membership nomination quickly, before it could bleed out on the voting table.

"Luz didn't know the hierarchy," Aeneas said. "I told her I could do something for her that you wouldn't. All it took was proof that she'd sacrifice for the brotherhood."

Bautista watched him, unblinking. He could stop Aeneas's heart in ten seconds—and he might, depending on the answer to his next question. "Did you touch her?"

"You asking if I fucked your fiancée?" Panic leeched the blood from the man's face. Yes, Bautista could end him here in the luxury of the East Millennium Tower while the town celebrated the birth of a free nation. Or, if Aeneas chose to lie, Bautista could put him down slowly, let him suffer—as any iron-hearted executioner would.

"Did you?" Bautista asked simply.

"No. I didn't touch her."

He believed Aeneas, but there was strategy and advantage in not indicating that he did. "Keep talking."

Testimony of overheard conversations and sales invoices obtained through creative means had offered a clear picture, but Bautista demanded the truth from Aeneas. Brother to brother, the man confessed to ordering a custom-made jacket and putting a bike on loan for Luz. The agreement was she'd sacrifice property in exchange for the Dead Men privilege. Not just her shop—the entire three-building strip.

Except Burke Wolf was a stubborn son of a bitch who'd turned every offer down, and then Luz died...her ring absent from her finger because, according to Aeneas who'd asked her about it when he noticed her bare hand one day, she'd claimed she hadn't deserved it.

Bautista doubted the ring and the love it symbolized were enough for her anyway. She'd wanted inclusion, family that wouldn't leave her.

"Luz is dead. What does it matter now?" Aeneas said. "I need this goddamn deal. I made some bad investments. They turned my accounts upside down. My wife's blowing through money and doesn't know we're living on credit."

Bautista sat at his desk. "So you'd screw over Luz and me to avoid pissing off your wife?"

Swearing viciously, Aeneas slammed out of the chair and let it capsize onto the floor. "You don't want that bar. Jayne can go snap her pictures anyplace else. Wolf would be out of his fucking mind to turn down two million dollars for that store. And the other place—are you shitting me? Sofia Mercer's only here because she followed the money."

"She's not going to sell."

"It's too late for her to start giving a damn, don't you think? Luz wanted in the club because she had no one here to call family. She thought I was the man who could give her what she wanted, who could satisfy her...and I think you envy me that."

Bautista laid his hands flat on the desk instead of letting them curl in violence, because Aeneas Strayer was as wrong as he was right. "You've got three properties on Society Street that aren't for sale. No deal, Aeneas."

"It's Rooster to you."

"Nah, it's Aeneas." He watched the man sputter, unraveling as he stood in an expensive tailored suit. "I'm riding with the Dead Men in some weeks, to retire. I don't want you on that ride."

Unspoken but nevertheless true, the club's loyalty lay with the member carrying higher seniority and influence, meaning Javier Bautista over Aeneas Strayer.

"Get the fuck out of here, Aeneas. Don't disturb Nessa."

When Bautista eventually left the East Millennium Tower, he drove to Society and went to Bottoms Up. Even after he relinquished part of the ownership, it'd still feel like his bar. He could leave Cape Cod, lose himself in the crowds of a metropolitan city somewhere, and this small underground character would still belong to him. The only way to bleed this place out of his system would be to cut himself deep.

Caro, sharp-eyed and ruled by intuition, had known that when she'd refused to buy it cheap. He'd never let it go completely.

The crowd was thin today with so many descended on Bellini Beach for food and fireworks. No words to spare, no patience for pleasantries, he hunted down the solitude of his office but stopped cold inside the door. "Who let you in here?"

"Don't be upset with Tariq," Joss said, standing in front of his desk. "I told him I had Blush business and was leaving you a note. In a way that's true."

Bautista had fucked up, letting his weakness and hers meet at a tragic moment. The sex had been fierce, angry, the kind that pushed his limits, but he wouldn't make the mistake again.

Joss wanted to come back to him, wanted to find something in him that didn't exist. She was meant for someone who could heal and love her the way she deserved.

"What about Blush?"

"Sofia and Caro are game to join you in ownership of Bottoms Up. I am, too. We have plans for this side of the block. It involves cooperation from Burke, but Sofia and I didn't get anywhere by lying down for defeat. Caro's a fighter, too."

"Caroline told me you want to take down walls, make this into a nightclub."

"Did she tell you we named it? We'd want to call it Guilty Pleasures. Bautista, the three of us went to Hot Dish, where men galore were flirting and the food was delicious, but we sat there for hours dreaming and planning and making decisions. We're serious. We're in this together."

"I'm not the man you need to convince. Talk to Wolf."

"Then you're okay with partnering up with me, even though we slept together?"

"My name on the paperwork doesn't mean I'll be down here with you every night. It doesn't mean I won't leave altogether and check in from wherever I end up."

"You'd disappear? Would that be easier than avoiding me the way you do now?"

"Eventually you'll thank me for the distance, when you move on with a man who can give you the love you've been looking for your whole life."

Joss rubbed her temples and came forward. "I don't want to wait. I'm so damn tired of waiting."

"Don't touch me, Joss." He couldn't let infatuation or rebound turn into attachment. "Don't do that to yourself."

She ignored him, reaching to clasp his hand in both of hers. One day a man would cherish her soft skin and soulful blue eyes and vivacious spirit. She was a phoenix—she'd rise again. Getting mixed up with him would only hold her down.

"Bautista." She closed her eyes. "Javier. Hold my hand, okay? Hold me. Please."

He laid his free hand on top of hers and she sobbed so quietly. God. Damn. She thought he was hurting her, but he was sparing her. "Joss."

"Wait. Please…" Sniffling, she moved closer and tipped up her face. "Please."

Bautista kissed her, and she gasped in his air and tightened her hold on his hands. Finally he pulled away from her mouth and she whispered, "No, not yet. Not yet."

"Let me go," he said gently. "You have to."

She unwrapped her fingers and held her hands to her mouth.

"I can't be what you need, Joss. Somebody is going to lead you to everything you're searching for. He's going to love you on every level there is, but it won't be me." He held her shoulders when she pleaded with him with tear-filled eyes. "I wish you the best. Happiness. Safety. Luck. I want that for you. Okay?"

Tears escaped as she nodded, and her voice came out in a croak. "Okay."

She left and he collapsed into his chair before he allowed the first tear to fall. Alone now, he could give himself time to grieve.

CHAPTER 19

$\mathcal{T}$he American flag wasn't meant to cover a woman's crotch, or so Anne Oakley informed Sofia when she and Tish joined the celebration on Bellini Beach.

Patriotic inspired, with a starred top and striped bottom, the bikini was the first Sofia had worn in public without the modesty of a cover-up.

Eyes flocked to the scar gleaming under the spotlight of a cerulean July afternoon. Children wrinkled their noses or stared with perturbed fascination—Caro's son, Evan, asked with precocious curiosity, "Does it hurt?" and then offered her the rest of his dripping watermelon wedge before giving Tish a sticky-fingered hug and hurrying off with Caro to set up a blanket near the water.

In an effort to be tactful, some adults looked away after giving her the briefest of hellos and "Happy Fourth!" greetings. Others inspected the scar with curious glances and flung their attention elsewhere to avoid lingering too long.

And then there were some who noticed that there was a human being attached to the nasty, jagged bolt.

The mixed reaction was expected, but she couldn't pretend she cared much. It was Independence Day and she was breaking free of restraints that'd held her too long.

Maintaining distance between Tish and the barbecue buffet required more muscle and creativity than Sofia had anticipated. Fortunately Caro waved to them from a paisley-print blanket and offered to keep Tish while Sofia hit the buffet. Nearby, Evan was constructing a sand castle...

That looked a great deal like a military tank.

"That's one freakishly accurate tank," Sofia said to Caro over the live bluegrass band when she returned to the blanket with a plate made heavy with barbecue chicken and potato salad.

Caro knocked away an errant curl and her many bracelets jangled. "Evan's a very precise child. If he sets out to do something, he insists on doing it well."

Nice way to sidestep Sofia's emphasis on the subject of the boy's sand castle art. When she'd babysat him on a night when Caro had a late photo session, she'd put him to bed in a room filled with G.I. Joe action figures on the floor, military books on the shelves, and a camouflage comforter on the bed.

"Caro, is Evan's father in the military?"

They had become fast friends and she hoped Caro trusted her with an honest conversation.

The woman worried her lip and stole a square of potato from Sofia's plate. Lying on the blanket, Tish eyed her hopefully but seemed to huff when Caro popped the potato bit in her own mouth. "He's a navy SEAL. He's not a part of Evan's life, or mine. But the military interest is something Evan has in common with him. I didn't encourage it at first, but then a friend suggested that I strengthen my bond with Evan by allowing him to understand his father's life instead of steering him away from anything linked to him."

He and *him*. Caro chose her words carefully, avoiding letting the man's name pass her lips. She smoothed down the hem of her summer dress. "He told me that being a SEAL was in his blood and he couldn't abandon that. I thought it was a load of bollocks, but it seems to be in Evan's blood, too, and how can I fight that?"

"Did you ask him to leave the navy because of the danger?" Sofia asked as they both observed the dark-haired child crouch in the damp sand and mold the tank with a frown set in his eyebrows.

"I never asked. I knew he'd say no anyway. So I let him go."

"But for a man to leave his kid?"

"He left before Evan was born." Pointedly, Caro looked at Sofia as the question sprang up. *Does Evan's father know he's a father?* "I'm not sorry for my choices when it comes to my son. Whether he continues this obsession with the military or moves on to, I don't know, building blocks or something, I'm his mum and that's fine enough."

"Okay."

"Let's choose a new subject, shall we?" Caro scanned the clusters of people gathered at the buffet, surrounding the picnic tables, and walking the shoreline. "No Joss?"

"She's not coming. She said she was tired and might find someplace to watch the fireworks tonight." Sofia let her have her space, though it wasn't like her friend to pass up a social event, particularly one with catered barbecue.

Tish rolled over, offering her belly for a scratch while her nose wiggled at the aromas wafting from Sofia's plate. Caro obliged, tickling the dog's tummy. "Massive turnout today.

People are dancing in the sand. Oh, I dream nightly of the moment customers come to our street for dancing."

"It's a lovely dream, but Caro, that's it. We'll have a say in the bar. That's our reality."

"Luz would wash your mouth out for that, and I'd hand her the soap." The wind combed her fluttering curls as she leaned forward. "She told me that Blush was a dream. It was one she and your mother dreamed together."

"I have a hard time believing that." Sofia licked honeyed barbecue sauce from a knuckle. "Ellen couldn't wait to pop me out of her womb and hit the road."

"As I remember Luz telling it, Ellen stopped believing in their dream when she was pregnant. The boutique wasn't practical and neither were you. Motherhood was a dream for her, too, and I guess sometimes when people end up with what they want, they don't know what to do with it and can't cope with happiness."

Sofia's appetite abandoned her as she stared at her plate. Ellen couldn't cope with having what she wanted? She'd *wanted* Blush and a family of her own? "I was nobody's dream. A burden, yeah. Not a dream."

"I didn't say that to hurt you, love."

She might have nodded, but she felt numb.

Was failure to cope with happiness a blood bond between Sofia and Ellen, as the military was for Evan and his father? Or was she more like Luz, single-mindedly driven to chase what she wanted?

"I dream about Guilty Pleasures, too," she confided. "But it won't come true for very real reasons. Burke won't budge." Even if Burke gift-wrapped the Cape Foods building, Sofia and her friends would have plenty of hurdles to surmount. But she tingled with a craving to have the opportunity.

"Speak of the ridiculously sexy devil," Caro murmured, her eyes widening. "Stage left. Wipe the sauce off your chin."

Sofia snatched the napkin she held on her lap and swiped until her friend gave a thumbs-up and gestured for Sofia to smooth her windblown hair.

Unimpressed, Tish lazed on the blanket, her almond-shaped eyes imploring *You're kidding me, right?*

Sofia was equally ecstatic and bereft when Burke's shadow stretched on top of her. There were no sea or food spices in the air. There was no music from the band and no conversation on the lips of everyone gathered here. There was no July warmth.

Just him.

They had plans for tonight. After dropping Tish off at the apartment, Sofia would watch the fireworks spectacle from *Colossians 1:14.* She saw herself in his arms, mesmerized by bursts of fire in the sky and his heat around her. But a gauzy layer of dismay lay underneath the excitement. Every day she let pass without sharing her medical prognosis, the lie weighed more heavily on her chest. It was unfair that finally they were together but a secret between them deprived her of experiencing him with pure abandon.

"I'm here to steal my girls," he said, and her periphery returned again. The beach was hot with summer and loud with celebration. Tish surged to all four paws, as if she understood perfectly that Burke had claimed her and Sofia as his girls and she was quite okay with that.

Caro pretended to mull this. "Hmm...Oh, I *guess* you deserve them." She summoned Evan to say good-bye and the child had hugs for everyone, leaving sandy fingerprints on Sofia, Burke, and poor Tish.

"Tish agreed to this shindig only for the chance of barbecue," Sofia told Burke, hefting her tote bag and walking with him and Tish. He carried a folded blanket under one arm and gripped the dog's leash. "Everything's covered in seasoning and sauce, so I've had to deny her."

"Then she might appreciate that I asked Hannah to set aside a few pieces of *un*seasoned, *un*sauced, deboned chicken."

She halted in the sand, turned, and laid a smacking kiss on his lips. "You're kind of all right." The burst of heat in his gray eyes singed her deliciously from her wind-teased hair to her patriotic-blue toenails.

Burke's arm wrapped around her waist, guiding her, and surprise registered on faces spying them from under hats and behind sunglasses.

Sofia Mercer, with the transplant scar and tawdry sex shop. Burke Wolf, former junkie and forever badass.

If their relationship hadn't been the subject of whispers before, it would be now.

Richard Pruitt stopped them, peddling raffle tickets for a kids' summer sports program. Burke caved, purchasing twenty just so he wouldn't have to deal with the change, and, overjoyed, the limping man ushered them to the luxury portable dance floor that was set up near the band. Above it was a pergola made of string lights and paper lanterns that only faintly sparkled in the daylight but would glimmer through the shadows tonight.

Apparently it cost money to take a whirl around the dance floor, and since Burke had so generously donated, he and Sofia were entitled to a dance.

"We can't. The dog," Sofia tried to tell Richard. His solution was to hand the leash and blanket off to his wife, Gretchen, and give them a good-natured push toward the floor, where people were already filling the space two by two.

When a town offered no decent place for the masses to

partner up, get close, and shake loose, people took what they could get.

"Dance! Happy Fourth!"

Guilty Pleasures, she thought as Burke led her to the floor under the web of twinkling lights and then drew her to him. *It could be this, every night. No holding back. No restriction. Just indulgence.*

Sofia rested against the hard plane of his body, lying with him while standing. "The music's nice."

"I didn't know you liked bluegrass," he said, the scruff on his jaw grazing her ear.

"I like anything that catches me at the right moment." She tightened her arms around him. His T-shirt, a deeper gray than his eyes, was soft on her skin and her fingers stroked the fabric.

"People keep staring at your ass. I'm tempted to cover it with my hands."

She laughed. "That's just an excuse to cop a feel."

"Can you blame me? I've been wanting to get my hands on you for an eternity."

The moisture dried in her mouth, as if she'd swallowed dandelion fuzz. Burke was barely moving and they were squandering their turn on the sparkling dance floor as one of the musicians took the mic and the band struck up a heart-tugging rendition of "Amazing Grace."

"When we're alone tonight on the boat, you won't have to wait," she finally whispered as a banjo eased the song into its final strains. "Whatever you love and hate about me, it's yours. All of me."

"Put your entire life in my hands? I don't think I'm fit to hold you like that."

"All you have to do is keep wanting me, Burke. Keep caring." *Maybe even love me.*

If he did that, then no matter how many or how few days like this remained for them, he would heal when change struck again. So strong, he was for her—hadn't he always been?

Collecting Tish after their dance, they fed her the barbecue Hannah had put aside and let themselves be waylaid by conversations and flocks of folks rushing over to pet the dog. Finally Tish grew weary of her popularity and Burke hoisted the Siberian husky in his arms. Even more astonishing than the breathtaking ease with which he gathered the large animal was that Tish allowed herself to be swept off her paws.

They walked until the clusters of people thinned. On one side of their path was a line of tangled trees. On the other was the shoreline and miles of water.

"Come in with me," she said on impulse. "*Both* of you!"

"Hey," he protested, chuckling, "you're the only one dressed for a swim. Tish probably doesn't want her harness to get soaked."

"So let's take it off. That's the Atlantic. It's incredible. It's beautiful and we're all here and I just want her to remember swimming in the ocean with me." Rambling, she knew she must sound frantic, but she couldn't resist fighting for this moment. "Please."

Grappling for memories, desperate to capture this hot Cape Cod afternoon, she stepped out of her sandals and unhooked Tish's harness. "Come with me, Tish."

The dog considered her, then her ears perked up as she detected shorebirds.

Encouraged, Sofia patted Tish's rump and they approached the gentle sway of water touching the shoreline. Venturing farther out past a grouping of large rocks, she sighed at the yield of the sand under her feet and the cool wash of the waves against her legs. She knelt and splashed Tish, who immediately shook out her fur in retaliation, pelting Sofia with droplets. More splashing, more fur-shaking, more playing, and soon she and the dog were both drenched.

Catching Burke holding up his phone, she hollered over to him, "You're not taking photos, are you?"

"So what if I am?" He aimed the phone, then paused with a frown. "Let's try that again, this time *without* flipping off the camera."

"Nope. I refuse to cooperate, so you might as well get in the water with us." She splashed Tish, eventually so distracted that she didn't expect Burke to come jogging barefoot to them in just his jeans. She was in his arms before she had time to gasp or dive out of the way.

Seizing her, he dipped her into the water and all she had to do was hold on tight. Ocean water on her skin, salt and sand in her hair, sun caressing her scar, and Burke's lips on hers, Sofia celebrated.

It was almost perfect...

Almost enough to make her forget the lie that breathed inside her.

* * *

At sunset Sofia got Tish settled at home and freshened up, changing into a simple white dress with sandals and putting her hair into a single braid.

"In this area there's no better place to see the fireworks show than on Bellini Beach," she enticed, passing Joss, who sat at the kitchen table engrossed in a recipe book. "Paget's there now. I saw her as I was leaving."

"I still might," Joss said, glancing at her through round-framed reading glasses, but the words were empty of conviction. "Jotting down some recipes to try out. I'll probably need to run to the supermarket. Need anything, if I go?"

"Can't think of anything." She'd completed the shopping for the week already, and they were still fully stocked. "You sure you won't be lonely? It's not like you to spend a holiday alone."

"Probably because when there wasn't a party or a guy to keep me occupied, you were home and we found board games or lame movies to ward off the loneliness. Now you're the one with a guy to keep you occupied." Joss playfully flicked a balled-up sticky note at her, then she made her index finger and thumb into a ring and poked the other index finger through. "Hint, hint."

Sofia flushed. "All this time I've been living with a pervert."

"Says the woman responsible for the erotic mannequin art downstairs. Ten dollars says there's sex paraphernalia in your bag."

A bullet vibrator, condoms, and a bottle of lube. "Shut up."

Joss slapped the recipe book shut, shaking with peals of laughter. "Nice!"

"I carry first aid stuff. I believe in being prepared."

This only made Joss laugh harder as she shooed her out the door.

So where do we go from here, Burke? Sofia wondered, approaching *Colossians 1:14* as people moved around her seeking other slips or heading to the marina parking lot. The darkening sky cast grayish shadows on the boat.

"Lost your way again?" Burke was on the pier, appearing troubled. It was as if his smile from earlier, the lighthearted moments that'd warmed her fully, had been illusions.

"No. I know where I am and why I'm here."

"C'mon," he invited, and when she reached him, he subtly touched the top of her scar and murmured, "You're beautiful. Are you starting to believe that now?"

"*Trying* to."

"Trying's good." He held out a hand and electricity popped at the contact. A spark. He smiled at her surprised gasp. "Aren't the fireworks supposed to be in the sky?"

"Kiss the hell out of me." She yanked his hand and his arms flexed as he gathered her close. Still on the pier with an audience of marina neighbors, he bunched her dress in his hands.

"Careful what you ask for, Sofia," he said, and she felt his knee parting her thighs. Whatever she was going to reply was stolen by a deep, hard kiss that quite possibly did take the living hell out of her. "You could tell me to fuck you on this pier and I wouldn't try to make you rethink it. My cock wants to be in you, and I'm craving another taste of you. Can you handle that?"

"The boat," she said, dizzy. People had paused to stare and mutter complaints. "On the bed, the first time."

His mouth twitched in a smirk. "And after that I'm going to bend you over and ride that soft ass of yours." He pulled her along onto the boat and they thundered down to his cabin.

Impatient, she pushed his shirt up. "Off. Take everything off. I need to touch you. I'm on fire."

When he stripped, she, still fully clothed, lay back on the bed and lifted her hips to take off her panties. "Get on me."

"Wait, Sofia."

If they waited there would be another interruption. Something would interfere—she sensed it. Either she'd blurt the truth or a panic attack would hit or he'd find a reason to pull back.

"I've waited," she said, pleading.

Hurry, Burke. Take me before the truth takes everything away.

He lowered over her and nudged her center, gyrating his hips against her.

Watching him, she fit her hands over the firm muscles of his ass. She loved this man nude, from the hardness of his chest to the crisp pubic hair grazing her mound, to the taut pressure of him stroking into her—

"Protection!" she shrieked. "Burke, we forgot."

Another interruption. Something else to draw them apart.

He swore and rolled off her immediately. "I'm an idiot. I can't believe we almost went that far without a condom."

"I have plenty. It's all right." Sofia scrambled off the bed to locate her purse. If she was fast enough, she could tear one off the strip and hand it to him and slide back into position as though they hadn't missed a beat.

"This happens a lot when we're together," Burke said, sitting on the bed with his feet on the floor. "We forget what's important."

She went to him, condom in hand, and froze as he began to cover that incredible body with his jeans. "Why are you getting dressed? We can get back to where we were."

"We can't, though. I'm heading to port tomorrow, Sofia."

Port? "You're on vacation. How can they call you back all of a sudden? You're a union regular."

"I called the hall—I'm going to handle a crane at the yard, and I'm thinking about getting myself something on location."

"You're *choosing* to up and leave like this?" He was running away—no question about it. "So how was this supposed to play out, Burke? Were you going to sleep with me, slap me on the ass, hand me my underwear, and send me to the pier?"

Her stomach hurt; her neck felt hot. "I—I don't want to know." She flung the condom onto the bed, whirled, and slammed herself into the head, throwing herself against the door.

He knocked on it almost immediately. "Sofia, open the door. Talk to me."

"I can't." *I can't love you if you're going to leave me. I can't tell you the truth about my condition if you're going to run.*

She'd thought they'd have more time to figure out how to make the impossible make sense, but it couldn't happen if one was willing to fight and the other content to surrender.

She opened the door. "I trusted you. I was going to fight for us."

"I need time."

"Ready or not, convenient or not, I was willing to try." She didn't touch him. Her fingers itched to trace the edges of his tattoos; her lips begged permission to lie with his. "When did you contact the hall?"

"After you were discharged from the hospital. Jesus, Sofia, the only thing that'd be worse than losing you would be to stand here knowing I'm to blame for it. That would destroy me. Say I'm scared. A coward."

"It's not hard to love me, Burke. You want this to be complicated."

"Don't bring that word into this."

"Which word?"

"Love. You and me—we're doing this too fucking fast. What are you doing with me? Do you even know?"

Loving you. Why wouldn't the syllables form?

"Silence. Great, Sofia. That's what I thought. You *can't* fight, not for me."

"I don't have a history of chasing violence and brawling, but I fight every single day."

"Survival's a struggle. No dispute. But if you knew me, you wouldn't say I went around looking for violence." He strode to the galley, poured himself a glass of water, and drank it down, not caring when he spilled drops down the front of his shirt. "Fractured bones. A concussion. Bruises. A scar from the time my dad kicked my ass for spilling marinara sauce on the floor."

Marinara sauce? "After I left your house that day, your dad hit you?"

"It was his excuse that time."

"He hit you more than once?"

"Nearly every day. At best it was a fist to the face for too much salt in the potatoes or an unmade bed. At worst it was Deacon putting a gun to my head."

She sagged against a wall. "Oh, God. At the lighthouse you told me what he said, that he blamed you for what happened to your mom. But you didn't tell me he hit you and threatened to shoot you."

"It can't be changed now. It wasn't your war."

Deacon had asked her to report to him any misbehavior Burke was up to, and she'd done so. She'd thought he cared, thought Burke was fortunate to have a father who hadn't abandoned him.

She wanted to go back into the head to retch into the toilet. Drug abuse hadn't been the trigger to his problems—it'd been a symptom of another problem altogether.

"Weed took me away. When the lighter shit didn't get the job done, I went to meth, cocaine, heroin. I didn't want Deacon to have the satisfaction of taking my life away. I wanted the honor."

Sofia had found him unconscious at school once and had called 911. The next time she'd seen him, he was sporting a fresh bruise. Rolling her eyes, she'd been disappointed in him for getting wrapped up in yet another brawl—for not taking care of himself. Had Deacon welcomed him home from the hospital with a beating? "He tried to break you, but he didn't. Not completely. You're clean now and you're strong."

"When I need to sharpen the focus on my sobriety, I leave."

"You've never tried to stay. Try for me."

"You don't need my hell. You said you wanted someone easier, right? Someone stable. That's not me." He smoothed his hands over her hair. "I'm going to port. You just took over Blush. Settle into that. Give me some time to figure this out."

"And what if I can't wait for you to decide what matters?"

"I'm not going to tell you to put your life on hold for me."

"Tell me. I'll do it. You're worth it. To me, you are worth that."

"Sofia, I'm not going to tell you that."

With nothing more to say, he stood there while she gathered her things and left, walking on the pier as color burst in the sky.

CHAPTER 20

"We're all out of chocolate penises."

It was only two thirty in the afternoon, which Sofia pointed out to Paget, who'd announced to the boutique at large that their most popular erotic treat was yet again cleaned out in record time. Joss was collecting the data to see which items on her naughty menu were top sellers.

"The next time one of those town hall suits comes in here to give us a morality lecture, I'm going to alert them to Eaves's voracious appetite for chocolate dicks," Sofia vowed.

"Yeah, we should also alert the media," Joss joked, going to the treat display to remove the empty trays that held her edible penis assortment. "Here's the headline. 'Cape Cod Cock Consumption Crisis.'"

A throng of shoppers at the Vices register chortled. The blond-haired man who'd wandered into the back blanched a little. "Whoa."

Sofia's mouth dropped open. "I didn't recognize you

without your cello case." She smiled at the nice guy who'd given her a gentle kiss outside a coffeehouse in New York City. "Hi, Nathan."

Nathan Swanson came forward and hugged her. "Hi, Sofia."

"Hi," Joss and Paget, and some of the customers, said in unison.

He was a looker, and his startled *What kind of Narnia did I walk into?* expression was charming.

"What are you doing here?" Sofia asked after she introduced him to her coworkers.

"I'm road-tripping with some friends this summer. We're on our way to Wellfleet, but I remembered you said you were moving to Cape Cod and I looked you up. We're checking out the lighthouse and the Ferris wheel, after here." His green eyes caught on a double-ended dildo and he nervously scratched his neck. "So this is really your place, huh? My friends are going to lose their minds in here. I'll make sure they come through before we head out of town."

Then he watched her with uncertainty through a haze of silence.

"Um, so, Nathan, can I help you find anything?"

The nudge appeared to startle him, and he dragged in a sharp breath that made her suspect he was gathering courage. "Look, I had an amazing time at the coffeehouse... Do you want to do that again? Or maybe we can have dinner tonight?"

A date. She was being asked on a date. The last man who'd taken her out was Burke, and she hadn't seen him since the Fourth. The Xs on her desk calendar marked twelve days since his departure.

He wasn't far away, in Boston working the shipyard, but she respected his plea for time to sort out his shit. Waiting was hard, but rejection was bitter. They were two unfortunate sides of the same coin.

In front of her was Nathan Swanson, a man who played the cello and kissed hesitantly and was presenting her with a third option: toss the coin away.

"Dinner tonight." She was in love with someone else. But twelve days ago he'd shut down on her and let her leave the marina in grief. She was free to share a meal with Nathan Swanson, welcome to smile at him under the streetlights, at complete liberty to let him begin to mend the frayed edges of her spirit—something Burke had left in tatters. "There's a little fish-and-chips place that has a dance floor. Practically nowhere to sit, and you're going to have to shower off the smell, but I really feel like dancing."

"If this fish-and-chips dinner and dancing goes well," Nathan said, "what then?"

"When are you leaving Eaves?"

"Depends on the reason I'd have to stick around. What time can I pick you up?"

"Nine thirty." That would allow time to count out the register and muster some enthusiasm. There was a difference between being free to move on and *wanting* to. "So... tonight, then."

The bell announced his exit and moments later Paget moseyed over, wearing a black tank dress and sporting an incredulous glint in her smudge-lined eyes. "Sofia, what are you doing?"

"Changing a bulb in this lamp." Another few screws and the shade filled with light over a selection of panties.

"I mean about that man who was just here. The one you're having dinner with tonight. What about Burke Wolf?"

"Burke Wolf isn't here." But she couldn't stamp his

name on her heart and loan it out to someone else, and she knew Paget was thinking the same thing. "I don't know if Burke…"

"What is it?" Paget gently patted her arm.

"What point is there to loving a man who's not here? It's crazy." Conversation done, she strode to the back to trash the blown bulb and to regroup alone.

The entry bell wailed, the sound so alarming that she immediately flew from the back and rushed through Vices to investigate the commotion as a couple burst into the boutique.

Activity had slowed and the smattering of customers all whirled around.

McGuinty Slattery, his arm flung around Caro's shoulders—*What?*—announced, "Yo, ladies! Hannah's in labor."

"Evan's sleeping over at a friend's tonight, so I'm heading to the hospital with McGuinty," Caro volunteered. Was she oblivious to the three women staring at her with their eyebrows practically kissing their hairlines?

"Abe's already at Community. When he called he said Hannah was freaking out because her water broke at the restaurant."

Yup, Sofia could see why a restaurant owner might be nervous about customers' reaction to embryonic fluid on the floor. "McGuinty, wait." She came forward as Joss and Paget continued to shoot Caro expectant glances. "Hannah told me her due date. The babies are two weeks early."

He nodded, exchanging a concerned look with Caro. "We know. Abe said he's not focusing on what can go wrong. If we want to get caught up in what-ifs, let them be positive ones."

"Mm-hmm," Caro agreed. "Like, what if both babies

are girls and Abram's completely outnumbered?" She smiled at McGuinty, who returned an appreciative grin of his own.

What was this connection? And *when* had it happened? Caro hadn't mentioned that something had changed in their dynamic, hadn't confessed to caving under the temptation of McGuinty's solemn strength, sexy copper-colored beard, and burly smolder.

"You guys mind if I split?" Paget asked, taking inventory of their customers. "I'd love to see Hannah before everyone else descends on the hospital."

"Go," Sofia said. "I'll take care of things here, then I'll be along."

"And I'll hang with you," Joss said. "We can close up shop for an hour or so to visit."

"C'mon with us," McGuinty offered to Paget. "Save that tin can with a steering wheel some gas."

"Quit knocking my ride. It's a classic." Paget pretended to deck him, but he simply secured his other arm around her and gave both women a squeeze.

When they left, Sofia and Joss handled the remaining customers before flipping the sign to CLOSED.

With no eavesdroppers within earshot, Sofia turned to her friend. "Not that Caro's obligated to keep us updated on her sexy-times status, but..."

Joss smirked. "Think she's given up playing Penelope?"

"Penelope?"

"A character in Homer's *The Odyssey*. She kept her honeypot locked, a no-fuck zone, until her one true man, Odysseus, found his way back to her." She tilted her head. "What? You look puzzled."

"Nope, I remember *The Odyssey* from high school English. It's just that I've never heard anyone sum up

Penelope's story like *that*." Sofia gave it a thought. "Who do you think Caro's holding out for? Or *was* holding out for?"

"Anyone's guess. But who's without secrets? We should respect hers."

Sofia grabbed their purses from the back, considering the almost defensive note in Joss's voice. *But who's without secrets?*

What were hers?

* * *

They picked up several coffees on the way to Community. The little shop was already abuzz with chatter about Hannah Slattery making a splash in the kitchen of her fancy restaurant. Thankful to collect the order without the barista engaging her in *You heard the chef at Hot Dish broke her water while she was cooking, didn't you?* gossip, Sofia reached the hospital in great time to get in, say hello, and scoot before Hannah's large family arrived from the mainland and things became *really* chaotic.

In the labor-and-delivery waiting area, people swooped down on the drinks Sofia and Joss held, leaving the carriers empty before Abram reached them.

"Eight was supposed to be plenty," Sofia said, baffled.

The man must have been six-plus feet of taut nervousness, but he laughed easily, issuing one-armed hugs to her and Joss. "It's all right. Thanks, though."

"How're you holding up?" she asked when Joss took the carriers to dump them. "How's the wife?"

"Hannah's fantastic. The OB says she's doing great and the babies are, too." He casually scanned the room. "C'mere for a sec."

"Sure." They stopped in a wide hall that was surprisingly

sedate for a hospital section that housed at least one patient in active labor.

"Hannah didn't want to know the sex of the babies early, begged me to promise I wouldn't go poking around to find out, either. A nurse was talking...Girls. Daughters."

Sofia squealed, then pinched her lips. "Sorry."

"Don't be. I'm just...It's unreal. But it is real. And I'm not making a damn bit of sense."

"Congratulations, Abram." The tears—well, they had to be from a place of overwhelming joy, though something inside her sighed wistfully as it sometimes did when she watched Caro with her son or other mommies and daddies with their children. Curiosity and envy could imitate each other if they caught a person at the right moment. "I think your girls are going to be lucky to have you and Hannah. Is it fine if I pop in to say hi?"

After visiting a sweaty and tense Hannah, who appeared remarkably tiny wrapped in tubes and attached to monitors, she slipped to the waiting room and sat beside a familiar friend. "Hey, Grandpa. Or should we start calling you Great-Grandpa?"

Niall Slattery squeezed her hand. "Still Grandpa." He glanced at her with fatigued eyes and released a forlorn sigh. "Thinking about my Amy, and the boys' parents. I picked out chairs for them. John and Luna would sit there by the pop machine. Amy would sit where you're sitting, next to me."

Sofia wasn't his Amy, but she rested her head against his arm the way she imagined his late wife might've. He'd endured so much loss, yet seemed to have immeasurable love and goodwill in reserve. "I like to think they're here, even if they're not sitting in these chairs. You're going to spoil those babies, aren't you?"

Chuckling, Niall didn't answer and she knew she'd pegged him exactly right.

As more visitors began to fill the room, Sofia called Nathan the cellist to cancel dinner, then she drifted from one conversation to another, and when McGuinty stepped out to drive Paget back to the boutique, Sofia snatched an opportunity to ask Caro a question: "What's going on with McGuinty?"

"What?"

"Are you guys in a good place now, or...?"

"He brought me camellias, to the bar." She shrugged. "There was a time when all a man like him would have to do is smile at me and I'd sit on his face. Now there's every reason to pass him up."

"Uh, first, you gave me a super-inappropriate visual, considering we're in a hospital waiting for two precious babies to be born. Second, if you want to be with him, then be with him."

"Sofia, it's not that simple."

"It is."

"Oh?" Caro shrugged. "All right, then, love. Tell *him* that." She turned around. *Burke.*

He was here, and her pulse rushed faster the longer she stared at his lean muscle and messy brown hair and that scruffy jaw she'd missed touching.

"Hey, Sofia. Caro." So nonchalant, as if he'd forgotten he reflected everything she loved and hated about herself, as if he didn't know that missing him was breaking the heart that had saved her life.

Caro acknowledged him with a smile and disappeared around a corner. Where was she going? Where was Joss? Weren't friends supposed to back each other up in times of man-crisis?

"I came through to see Abe and Hannah, but it's go time." Staff had cleared the room of visitors, save for Hannah's mother and husband. "I'm going to take off." But there was hesitation as he patted his pockets, and she tried to capture it.

"Uh—um—" she stammered, struggling for something to say that would keep him here, with her. "Are you searching for something?"

He plucked out his keys from those criminally perfect-fitting jeans, and his muscles moved in cruelly sexy harmony as he freed his phone. "I found it already."

Why couldn't he put the phone down instead of walking away, gesturing that he was headed to a cell-friendly part of the building?

Why didn't he know by now that no one loved him the way she did? Other women might make him laugh harder or burn hotter, but *no one* could love him better.

"We should get going," Joss said, approaching. "What's the matter? Is Hannah—"

"Burke's here. I mean, I don't know where he is this minute, but I saw him."

"And did you two talk?"

Talk led them in circles, provoked them to sidestep each other. So they wouldn't talk. Sofia started for the corridor. "It wasn't the right time before, but it's going to happen."

* * *

Entering Blush with a pounding heart but not a hint of anxiety inside her, Sofia shopped. Midnight-blue bustier with white piping. Matching V-string panty. Sheer stockings.

"One other thing," she said to Paget, who stood at the register with saucerlike amber-green eyes, frozen when she was supposed to be scanning the items and laying them in a shopping bag. She set down a smooth plastic bottle. Champagne-flavored lube.

After closing the boutique for the night, she settled Tish in the apartment, changed and freshened up, and when she still hadn't second-guessed herself, she cinched her long white sweater, slid into the driver's seat of the Lexus, and set course for the marina.

There were no fireworks in the sky entertaining the pier tonight. Only thick shadowed clouds lazing over dark water as she dialed Burke's phone number.

"Sofia?"

"Hi, Burke. The reception's not the best here on the marina, is it?"

"You're here?"

She hung up and dropped the phone into her purse. The hem of the sweater brushed her thighs and her stiletto heels struck the planks with determination.

Burke emerged from his boat, alarmed. "Are you okay?"

"I have a question. May I?" She gestured to the boat. *May I step on board? May I ride you until dawn? May I have a place in your life forever?*

"Yeah." He guided her to the main saloon. "What's your question?"

"Can we last one night without hurting each other?" She loosened her sweater and the soft white fabric slipped over her shoulders and down her arms.

Burke's lips parted, and, frowning, he let his gaze sweep her from elegantly bunned hair to bustier to sheer stockings— pausing below her waist. The V-string was sheer, too.

"I can fuck you senseless—and Jesus, do I want to," he said, his harsh voice scraping the air, "but I can't promise it'd fix anything. Odds are it'll stir up more complications."

"Sex isn't about fixing stuff, not for us. It's about telling

each other things we deserve to hear," she said wearily. "A
one-night truce. If we can't keep the hell away for just one
night, then we're weaker together than we are apart. If we
can make it through, though, then that means everything."

"Truce."

Truce. It was going to happen, now, and anticipation
slammed her.

He knocked the bunched sweater from her wrists and the
thing soundlessly hit the floor.

She thought she might loop her arms around him, but he
spun her and grinded his hips against her. She felt his stiffen-
ing cock through his jeans and all the lights went on inside her.

Wake up, her body chimed. *Now's the time. It's him. It's
always been him.*

With certainty, he turned her again and began unlacing
her bustier.

"I missed you," she whispered as the garment became
slack around her and started to slip.

The interior light caught the glint of emotion brightening
in his eyes. "I missed you every damn day. At the hospital,
when I said I found what I was searching for? It was you."

A hard tug, and the bustier joined her white sweater.
Burke lifted her; she locked her legs around his waist and the
next thing she knew, her bare skin was encountering the cool
softness of his bed.

Standing at the foot of the bed, he shed his clothes and let
her take in the details. On closer inspection she noticed his
markings—not the collection of tattoos but faded scars.

She held out her hand and when his fingers linked with
hers, she pulled him down. In stockings and the V-string, she
was almost naked, but she wanted total nudity. Nothing hidden, nothing enhanced.

Honesty.

"Last time we forgot a condom, Sofia."

"This time I didn't. There's one in each of my stockings, more in my purse. There's also lube, but I think right now you can see for yourself that I'm ready for this."

"This?"

"You. I'm ready for you to"—she pried off one stocking—"fuck"—then the other—"me"—then the V-string—"sense-less."

He leaned over her, kissing her, spiraling his gifted tongue the way she liked, nipping her bottom lip the way she needed him to. He worked his way downward, playing with her breasts, oh-so-gently fastening his teeth around her nipples. Each zing of pleasure had her gripping anything she could find—his hair, his biceps, the sheets.

"Oh…" she moaned from somewhere deep when he teased. "Oh my…*hell*!"

He pushed her knees apart wide.

"I have flavored stuff in my bag," she offered.

"I want to taste this, right here where it's wet."

"Okay."

"Yeah?"

"Yes."

"Tell me you want me to lick you. Tell me how hard you want me to taste you." He grazed her inner thigh with his teeth. "Mmm, I've got time."

She didn't. She'd lose her mind any moment now. "Remember this when I have your dick in my hands. I might make you tell me exactly how you want me to take you."

He chuckled and she felt his warm breath on her center. So close he was. Maybe if she lifted herself upward…

Burke murmured, "I think I know what you want, Sofia. I think I know you now." Then he spread her intimately and the flat of his tongue met her.

Ohhhhhh...

If oral was a talent, then he deserved medals.

"Good, Sofia?"

"Mm-hmm." He kissed her but somehow made his lips fasten onto her clit, drawing it away from her body, then releasing it.

Trophies. He deserved solid gold and platinum trophies for working her with intuition she would never be able to explain.

Sliding a finger into her, he continued to kiss her and she came, pushing against the intensity but unable to squirm away from it.

"You survived it," he said, opening one of the condoms, pinching the tip, and rolling it on. He stretched to kiss her mouth as his body fit over hers.

Sofia held his shoulders, her fingers sinking in when they slipped on the sweat-slicked surface of his skin. "It was always you, for me."

Burke took one of her hands and kissed the knuckles. "Look at me." Then he released her hand, held himself steady, and pumped into her deeply.

Her body's impulse was to tighten, to lock up, and that amplified the snap of pain.

Wincing, she gasped in air through clenched teeth.

"Open your eyes, Sofia..." His whisper sounded so close. She'd shut her eyes but opened them again to the concern and heat at war on his face. "Hi."

"Hi."

"You've gotta relax your grip, babe. Your thighs are crushing me a little." Kissing her, massaging a hip, he began to work loose her tension as he continued a deliberate game of drive-deep-and-retreat into her. "The truce's still on, in case you're wondering if tightening up like a vise on me violated that."

A giggle escaped. And it was okay. Completely okay to laugh, to figure this out, to listen to each other as they took for themselves.

Stroking his shoulders, she sank into the bed and accepted the fluid rhythm of his thrusts.

He cradled her, reversed their positions and she was on top, rocking onto him at her pleasure. Then his hands snared her hips and the force of her grinding against the drive of his body pushed him deeper, pushed her further.

Palms on his chest, she dropped her head forward and her hair swept him as she rode out a brutal orgasm that grabbed him tightly and tantalized him to follow.

Sated, she was exhausted and sore, but she had to tell him something.

Sofia fell asleep sprawled on his hard, comforting chest before a single word of *I love you, Burke* could escape her lips.

*   *   *

Could sheer force of will make a person materialize in front of you? Burke had to wonder as he radioed a reply to his dock boss that once he finished transporting his current container he'd come straight to the office.

"No prob. Iz can keep her entertained," his boss's hoarse smoker's voice said over the radio, speaking of Iz Rosetta, the dock office secretary. "Wolf, she's a good-looking one. You're a lucky sumbitch."

Burke squeezed a quick smile before returning his focus to the container his crane was unloading from the docked ship that'd come in from Singapore two days ago. He'd been assigned to the first of two gangs pulled for this gig, and this was his third day of waking up extra early to drive in to the harbor and work the ship.

He was in a good mood because this morning, when he'd gotten up at four, Sofia had been with him, her warm and supple body ready for him. Problem was, the wake-up fuck had him aching for her all day.

Now she was here on the dock, and it felt like an eternity before his container was unloaded and he could relinquish the crane to another operator while he headed to the office.

In gear, he stepped inside the blessedly air-conditioned building with his hard hat, goggles, and safety vest still on.

"Hi," Sofia said, getting up from a creaky visitor's chair in front of Iz's desk and kissing him hello.

Oh, damn, can you make yourself scarce, Iz?

Iz relaxed in her chair and feigned fanning herself.

"You taste like cherry cough drops," he said to Sofia, drawing off his hard hat and raking back his hair.

"Your boss gave me one while I waited. I don't have a sore throat, but I was afraid to decline."

His supervisor was a *my dock, my crew, my rules* kind of man who did his job superbly but had the people skills of a rabid beast.

"He thinks cough drops are preventative," Iz supplied. "When he's passing out Halls, he's in a happy mood." She picked up a tablet from an overcrowded desktop and a near-empty carafe from a table near the door. "I'll take care of the coffee crisis. The blinds stay open, so use your discretion."

When Iz slipped out the door, Burke banded his arms around Sofia. Kissing her freckle-speckled nose, her cherry lips, he said, "I've been half-hard most of my shift, thinking about you."

"I won't feel sorry for you. I put a cock ring on a dildo and simulated a hand job for a customer this morning, and I've been half out of my mind thinking about *you*." Returning his kiss, she cupped him through his jeans. "We could be quick—"

"Discretion," Iz reminded, breezing back into the office. "Forgot my phone." With a succession of *tsk*s, she left again.

Sofia blushed. So damn cute she was when little moments like this overwhelmed her or took her by surprise. They'd been together for a few weeks now, rolling into August as an official "item," as Hannah Slattery christened them when she conceded her quest to play matchmaker for him.

Regular rotation day shifts had him twisted up by the end of the workday, pining to hear Sofia's voice, catch a whiff of her hair, touch her skin. Coming to her at Blush or meeting her on the marina in the evening was the highlight of each day, but it wasn't enough.

Time was precious. He wouldn't ask her to cut back on her hours at the sex shop; he couldn't chance distancing himself from the line of work that saved him when he needed to escape himself. But too many miles lay between Society Street and the Eaves Marina, and to go on like this when all he wanted was to love her seemed like punishment.

Loving her was his redemption, but penciling in that love around two separate lives was retribution.

If they could each give a little...

"I know you need to get back, so I won't keep you long," she said. "I want to show you something and I figured I'd come here, since historically every time I attempt to present business matters in private we get off track."

Burke chilled, suspecting what lay inside the portfolio she retrieved from her bag. "Don't give me that."

"You don't know what it is. Here, sit with me and take a look." Sofia nudged him to lower onto the chair and she knelt beside him as he opened the portfolio. "I consulted with Bautista on this start to finish, but feel free to have your lawyer review it."

The business proposal was black print on white paper—harmless, but the meaning behind it wasn't.

"This is our plan for a club, spanning across all three basements. You already know about the entry between Blush and Cape Foods. I told you before that Cape Foods connects to Bottoms Up, though Bautista had the entry sealed when he set up the bar. He's restless. Caro and Joss and I are buying in." She glanced at him. "Burke, if you're concerned about his involvement, don't be. I trust him."

Bautista had respected Burke's refusal to sell Cape Foods when he'd asked before Luz's death—but Sofia couldn't do the same: respect him.

"He's not my concern. You are."

"Burke, this is solid. Flip to the back and you'll see our offer. Joss and I have each secured the money and we're willing to negotiate finer points. We've comped it out and this agreement's very fair."

An agreement. She'd gone ahead and had an agreement drawn up. Papers that would take away the one thing his father left him that didn't hurt.

"It's not for sale."

"But you told me Deacon treated you horribly. He didn't love you."

"No, he didn't love me. Do you?" What was she feeling when he was moving inside her and it seemed their souls were entwined? What did she want from him when he'd already given her all of himself?

Right, the Cape Foods building.

"Burke, we've been through so much. Don't you know me, how I feel?"

"I told you from the beginning that I won't read your mind."

"This isn't a one-way street. You never said *you* love *me*."

"Damn it, Sofia, I love you. Just you, from square one." The truth sliced his vocal cords on its way up. "I loved you when I couldn't stand you."

"You love me?"

"Every goddamn thing about you. How does that affect this agreement you put in my hands?"

"I—This is my dream. It's a vision and purpose. It's home." Her voice caught, and she approached from a different angle. "Why hold on to that building, Burke? Deacon abused you, and by keeping that link alive, it's as if you're keeping that abuse alive. How can you want it when your father was a bastard?"

"You're using that as leverage?" he cried. Then, just as he'd taught her, he said *Fuck it* and set the truth loose. "The thing is, Sofia, folks with bastards for fathers shouldn't throw stones."

"What does that mean? Is that an insult to my dad?"

"Finnegan's got you terrified of being left behind. You're with me, but you're shutting me out. Don't think I don't notice, Sofia, that you're trying to be a carbon copy of Luz."

"Luz grabbed her dream. What's wrong with that? And yes, Finnegan left me and it scarred, but I can be grateful that he tried to be a good father. I was sick for a long time and it wore him down."

"Wore *him* down? It almost killed you. His daughter should've been the most important thing in his life. As I see it, Finnegan's no better than Ellen."

"I'm not defending him. I'm explaining that the stress got to him. It builds up—God, I know that. Stealing money from your dad's store was stupid, but it was one mistake and

Eaves vilified him for it. Trauma like that can change a person's composition."

"If those excuses help you deal, okay. But he's a bastard for cutting you out." Burke stood and slapped open the portfolio on Iz's desk blotter. He snatched a pen from a Red Sox mug. "And Sofia, it wasn't one mistake. I can't remember how many times I caught him stealing from the store, can't count how many ass-kickings I took so you wouldn't lose your father."

As he clicked the pen and began to scribble his signature on the documents, she grabbed his arm. "Burke, stop!"

"Here." He tossed the pen, put the portfolio in her hands. "The fucking building's yours. Any other papers, have Bautista send them to me."

"I don't want it this way."

"Does how you get it even matter, as long as you end up with that building?"

She bristled. "My dad—Finnegan—he stole money from Cape Foods before that incident?"

"Yes. The first time I caught him, he asked me not to tell you or Deacon. He said your medical bills were bleeding him dry. But he kept coming back and taking more, and I tried to make up the difference with tips and some side construction jobs around town. Deacon thought I was cleaning out registers and he beat me every time the drawer came up short."

"Oh, God." She shook her head. "I thought you hated me."

"I told you I never did. I felt sorry for you. All I've ever tried to do is protect you." He pointed to the portfolio. "Good luck with your dream. I'm not a part of that, and, fuck, it's probably better this way."

"What are you saying?"

"That I have a ship to unload. Go get started on your life and let me live mine."

"Running, Burke, really?"

"Yeah." He opened the office door. "This time I'll take a page from your father's book and won't look back. Maybe then you'll respect me."

CHAPTER 21

*S*of, you need to see this."

In the musty stock room of the former Cape Foods building, Sofia excused herself from a conversation with the contractors who'd come out to prepare a bid estimate for the complete renovation that would turn Eaves's modest Society Street market into an erotic treatery.

Even with the windows open and industrial-size fans running, the building was still stuffy, and she jogged down the basement steps with trepidation. The muggy August heat made for an uncomfortable several days of organizing Joss's takeover of the space.

When Sofia had turned in the paperwork to her lawyer, Bautista had said quietly, "You look like you went through a lot of pain to make this happen."

"He's gone," she'd said, and left him to handle the legal matters. The treatery and Guilty Pleasures would happen, but she and Burke were over, strange as that sounded now that she'd become so used to having him around. One dream was coming true at the cost of another.

She and Joss hadn't celebrated. Instead they'd immediately gotten to work because they intended to open Lust Desserts for business in the fall.

Joss waited at the bottom of the stairs. She jerked her thumb behind her and said, "I'm blown away."

They ventured into the basement, which was now cleared of everything but old building materials and produce cartons cluttered with miscellany.

"I found this in one of the cartons," Joss said, giving her a cobwebby sketchbook. Page after page offered creatures that appeared to be conjured from the devil's nightmares.

"Burke's old drawings. He had a thing for horror."

"Keep turning," her friend said.

A vampire; a Transformer-type monster with metallic fangs; a tree with serpents for branches and reptilian eyes carved into the bark.

Then something different. It appeared to have been drawn with an unsteady hand, the shading clearly done with fingers, as faded prints smudged the pencil stain. A boy in baggy clothes with dark hair flopping over his brow sat holding an iPod in one hand and a book—no, a drawing pad—on his lap. In the background a thin girl with long hair and a frowning mouth stood leaning toward him, as if spying over his shoulder.

Sweet God…

"That's you, isn't it?" Joss asked. "You and Burke in that passageway."

She nodded, and a tear fell. "Oh, no, I'm going to ruin it."

"If you're crying now, maybe don't look at the next page just yet."

The warning only encouraged her to flip the page.

Another pencil drawing, of shaggy-haired Burke wearing a fierce expression and some kind of formfitting superhero getup complete with a billowing cape. One hand was in a fist pointed straight ahead and in the other was the hand of a girl. The same girl from before, but she was smiling and her eyes crinkled. On her T-shirt was a robust, shiny heart colored with red ink.

A healthy heart, and Burke her hero.

Was she dragging him down in this sketch? No, she realized, she was flying away with him.

Sofia couldn't see, and rubbing tears out of her eyes only introduced irritating dust. "I—I can't."

Joss was quiet as she took the sketchpad and closed it, then it was apparent that she, too, was crying. "He loved you back then."

"I know. Now I do."

Why hadn't she told him before that she loved him? To protect her pride she'd held herself back from saying it first. What had that mattered?

"I need some time in the apartment, okay, Joss? I have to be by myself for a few. Can you deal with the contractors?"

"Yeah." Joss sniffled and handed her the sketchpad. "You should hold on to this," she said, walking out of the room.

Sofia accepted it but it remained closed as she went next door, entered her apartment, and set the sketchpad on the kitchen table. She heard Tish's toenails click on the floor.

"Tish, I want you to listen to something." She pulled out her phone and loaded her saved voice mail messages. Sitting on the floor, she hit the PLAY button.

"Niece—see, I said 'niece,' so you know I mean business. Anyway, are you still driving up for Christmas? If you are, you owe a backlog of presents. I wear a size six. I'm kidding... I got everything for the peach cobbler. You can

take it back to New York... Okay, well, call me back or I'll just see you on Christmas. Okay... All right, bye-bye."

Sofia set down the phone, swiped ruthlessly at unstoppable tears. She'd stayed in the city that Christmas and sent Luz a Happy New Year card she'd gotten free from Manhattan Greetings. She'd signed it *Love, Sofia* and addressed it, but she hadn't sent another card and had been planning to finally drive out to see her great-aunt for her birthday.

Planning, procrastinating, putting off the woman who'd been her mom when no one else would...

The pages of the calendar had turned so quickly, it seemed, from December to May of the following year. There'd been other voice mail messages from Luz, other one-sided conversations decorated in her Argentine accent, but Sofia had tried to conserve storage on her phone and had deleted most. She'd managed to skip this one, somehow.

Thank God, because she had Luz's voice at comfortingly easy access. The recording added dimension to Sofia's memory of a woman with long black hair, a smirk on her lips, and ambition in her eyes.

She played the message again, then once more, and she cried in her hands. "I love you so much, Aunt Luz. Thanks for this life." Only, it was *her* life. The heart in her chest was *hers* to protect. It was time to own both fully, and she couldn't without letting love in. She had somebody, loved him savagely, and he needed to know it.

She rose up on her knees and wrapped her arms around Tish. "I'll be a good mom to you, Tish. And Luz's keeping an eye on things."

Tish's rear end met the floor and her thick, furry tail thumped the hardwood. She didn't howl or snap, but there was a tiny whimper from the large, intimidating beast.

Sofia kissed Tish's cold nose. "She knows you miss her.

Until we see her again, let's have a good life and get into heaps of trouble, and I'll let you know every day that I love you. Can we give that a shot?"

Tish inclined her snout, and Sofia chose to interpret that as *Okay*.

She ruffled the dog's gorgeous fur, then whispered, "I love you, Tish."

* * *

Sofia didn't have a shopping cart of soiled laundry or a friend carrying cupcakes, but the following afternoon she went to The Dirty Bastards anyway—and she wasn't leaving until Abram Slattery gave her answers.

"I understand that he's pissed," she reasoned with the man, "but it's been weeks." Yesterday she'd broken down and started trying to make contact, but the phone calls, texts, and emails to Burke remained unanswered. Her number and email address might be blocked, but how would she know if he'd taken such a severe step?

Grunting a swearword, Abram came around the counter and hollered out to one of his staff to man reception for a few minutes. "Let's walk, Sofia."

They left the laundromat and passed the stationery store with its chalkboard advertisement for back-to-school printing specials out front and pastel flowerpots circling its lampposts. She thought he was heading to the public bench the next block over that stretched below a wrought-iron street clock, but he stopped and pointed at Blush.

"What about it?"

"That window display might seem to some to be selling underwear, but you're not fooling me."

Gone was the firefly-inspired dressing. She'd replaced it

with a lone female mannequin in a black lace-edged hooded dress on her knees, stretching forward as if reaching out for something. Strips of tulle crisscrossed over her head and filled the backdrop.

"What are you trying to tell him that you couldn't seem to say face-to-face?"

The display, she admitted to herself, could be described as nothing but *lost*. She was productive at the boutique and putting in extra effort with the upcoming bakery and the underground club, but her heart couldn't seem to regain direction.

"I can't find him," she interpreted. "There's so much that needs to be said. There's so much I know now."

"Damn," he muttered. "I should've laid money on this. I told him to hang back and give you time before he took off."

Abram had months ago regarded her as a risk to Burke's sobriety. A friendship had uncurled between Sofia and Abram, but that didn't erase the conversation.

"You thought I was a threat to him."

"Sofia, I thought he'd be a threat to *himself*. He'd been unhappy so long I figured he wouldn't trust that shit was finally good for him. That he'd panic and lose out on—"

"Happiness?" she supplied, leaping to what Caro had said on the Fourth of July about Sofia's mother.

"Not even that. Redemption. He's strong, tough as hell, but he's human. He's not a fan of his own weaknesses, but that's life, ain't it?" Abram clasped her hand and gave it a squeeze. "Look, Sofia, don't rely on your storefront windows to speak for you. Tell him."

"I'm trying to. I've been reaching out since yesterday."

Abram averted his gaze, as if debating something. "He probably hasn't seen any of that. He's on a mariner run, working cargo on *Viking Five*. The ship's on a storm delay outside Canada. When weather stuff hits the fan those folks can hardly get access to any decent communication."

Storm delay. "Why didn't you tell me?"

"It's too early to start worrying, Sofia. Don't let yourself get worked up. If he found out you wound up in the hospital over this, he'd probably swim home to you. I'm asking you not to put him in that position."

"He wouldn't do that."

"He would, if it meant rescuing you."

And that was true. Burke had endangered himself and fought monsters for her protection, because that's what love meant to him. He wasn't a superhero, just *her* hero. "It's my fault that he's out there."

"Don't start blaming yourself."

He'd taken an onboard assignment out of the United States to get away from her, and now he was on the water, left stranded in a storm? Of course she'd worry; of course she'd blame herself.

"Sofia, you and Burke are so effing afraid to hurt each other that you end up doing exactly that. I almost lost Hannah that way. I messed up, and it's a miracle that she's mine and we've got two girls now." His voice gentled. "Love's not perfect, and the longer y'all go on thinking it ought to be, the bigger your chances are of losing each other. Stay put and wait for word to come through from the ship. That's all I'm going to say about it."

But as she sprinted across to her side of Society Street, something clutched her. Not panic, but a plan. Not a dream, but a future.

Taking hold of both, she hoped Abram wouldn't mind too much that she ignored his advice: *Stay put and wait.* She couldn't do that. Letting love call the shots, she closed Blush in the middle of the afternoon, searched *Viking Five* on an online vessel tracker database, packed a bag, and loaded Tish into the SUV for a road trip.

* * *

He didn't manage more than a couple of hours of sleep, patched together over the course of forty-six hours, and whenever he did drift, he dreamed of Sofia.

Throwing himself into dock work hadn't led Burke far enough away from her and all the love that surged through him beneath the anger. Putting himself on board and crossing international waters had done nothing but make him think about being on *Colossians 1:14* with her in his arms.

The hurricane that had battered the side of his ship even in shallow sea waters and left it stalled spurred rumors of estimated tens of millions of dollars in damaged cargo should the steel snap and the vessel capsize. Men had their eyes on lifeboats and flotation rings even as they threw every ounce of energy and skill into manning the ship, and the Coast Guard had been enlisted for a search and rescue mission during the period when they had dropped off radar. Waves spurred by high winds rose like an opaque whitish-gray wall against an eerily blue sky. The shipboard crew tried to contact loved ones but the onboard computer system and wireless communication had failed them. The storm, the threat, was only a category two and could be called mild in comparison to crises Burke had witnessed when a ship on a tight schedule and a storm crossed on the water, but this was an invisible shove that'd hit with more force than the wind-powered waves against the ship.

He didn't want to restore himself. He wanted Sofia to know he loved her and would until his last minute on this earth.

And then, when the storm had relented enough for the

craft to be anchored at the nearest open port, and lines of communication reopened somewhat, the correspondence had come through in a batch.

Sofia, with the same message, over and over, repeating in text and voice mail messages and emails: *I'm sorry. Come home.*

She *was* home, his home.

And he was coming back to her.

Burke intended to drive into Eaves the moment he got a decent shower and put on some clean clothes, but protocol held him up once the ship reached port in Brooklyn, New York. Activity erupted as the harbor crew descended for inventory and transfer. Freight vehicles, medical teams, security, and media personnel clogged the roadway and docks.

Detained for over an hour, he was impatient for the medic performing a cursory examination to wrap things up, let him sign his papers and go home. Questions and the beam of a penlight aggravated him further, because his repeated "I wasn't hurt—just sprayed with water" went ignored in favor of liability procedures.

Dirty and wind-beaten, he finally made it to the parking lot. He thought he heard a woman calling his name and figured he'd double back to one of the emergency vehicles for another once-over, because he either had a strange-ass case of tinnitus or had lost his friggin' mind. But then a dog barked and he saw headlights flash under the gray New York sky.

"Sofia!" Tugging off his baseball cap, rubbing his eyes to make sure he was seeing her right, he began to run. His body ached but adrenaline fueled him. She threw herself from her Lexus and crashed into him, wrapping her arms around his neck and her legs around his hips. "You're crazy! It's chaos here. You should be home—"

"We had to find you," she cried, nestling against his

sweaty skin, kissing his wind-chapped lips. "We're your girls. We had to see that you were safe."

Burke peered through the windshield, but Tish poked her head out the driver's window and barked, demanding attention. "Honey," he halfheartedly admonished the dog, "you're supposed to talk her out of stuff like this."

But, with Sofia still in his arms, he went over and ruffled the scruff of Tish's neck. Then he kissed his woman. "I love you, Sofia, but you can't put this kind of stress on yourself."

"Knowing your ship was trapped in a hurricane probably should've crumpled me, but I didn't let it. I fought, and I took Tish and we found you."

No one had greeted him at port before. Friends checked in, considered his safety, but none had tracked him across state lines and waited for God knew how long just to see his face.

Sofia unwound herself. "Now that I know you're safe, I'm going back. Get your truck and do what you've got to, but we have to talk, Burke. Come home, okay?"

Burke hated that he had to watch her drive off, but he was downright pissed when crew carpool hit a delay and delivered him to Boston late that night. He'd intended to shower at a motel and get on the road. In actuality, he was so exhausted that he'd ended up sprawled on a bed with nothing but a towel around his ass and slept for damn near fifteen hours.

But rested, with his path so clear now, he aimed his truck down Society Street and parked in the first available spot on Sofia's block.

In front of his father's grocery market.

It wasn't that anymore, though. Getting out, he hesitantly approached and read a banner hanging overhead: LUST DESSERTS—COMING SOON!

Damn him, but he smiled at that. Sofia and her friend were going for it—a dream—full force.

As if turning the pages of an album, he saw himself as a kid in the shopping cart practicing kindergarten vocabulary words while his mother, Melody, pushed it along and coached him with a smile on her face as she shopped; as a teenager bagging groceries and staring sometimes at a dark-haired girl he didn't talk to in school but thought about; as a sullen man finally coming back to Eaves in the wake of Deacon's death and bawling on the floor, grieving someone who'd despised him but whom Burke had inexplicably loved in a way that a son couldn't help but love his father.

The building wasn't his—he'd let it go. The memories wouldn't disappear because of a transfer of ownership, but standing here now he felt no rage for something that was now a part of Sofia.

Love and hatred, side by side, lying together inside him. But he was changing, letting her in, and she was beginning to heal him. Making a choice, Burke walked away from the past and toward the future.

He swung open the door to Blush, searching for the woman represented by a lone window mannequin being swallowed up by some frilly material.

"So you really did escape a hurricane in one piece," Paget said, and it was the first time he'd seen her smile—at least at him. It was also kind of nice that she didn't greet him with *Hello, you ass.*

"I've survived worse. Is Sofia around?"

"Oh, sorry."

Damn, was he too late?

"I'm not going to tell you to put your life on hold for me."

"Tell me. I'll do it. You're worth it. To me, you are worth that."

"Sofia, I'm not going to tell you that."

"I've been a real dick."

According to Paget's startled expression, he'd said that aloud.

A woman holding a pair of patent leather spiked heels glanced at him; a guy with gauges in his ears and a dog collar around his neck snickered.

"Relax, guy," Paget said. "There'll be plenty of time to get into all of this with Sofia. She's out on errands. The bookstore, then the post office and probably the taffy place."

Thanking her, he whirled, darted out the door, and collided with a bicycle.

"Ahhhh!" the rider cried out.

In a tangle, they almost spilled onto the sidewalk, but he gripped the handlebars and steadied...

Her. Sofia.

"Burke." Her laugh was part shriek and she scrambled off the bike. It tipped this time, falling onto its side with the wheels spinning. "You're here."

He rushed her, trying to touch her everywhere all at once. "I'm checking you for injuries."

"Oh? It feels like you're fondling me very thoroughly."

"That, too."

She looked at his mouth and he wanted to dive in, but she spun out of his arms and righted the bike. "I need to take this behind the building. Coming upstairs?"

"Yeah." As if there was any doubt.

She walked ahead of him and he stared way too long at her backside. Her ass was a thing of wonder, but decorated in metallic black pants... *Mmm.*

She parked the bicycle and when she led him up to the apartment, he said, "The bakery and the club are happening for you. Are you happy?"

She turned on the light above the kitchen sink and a translucent halo beamed over her. "Excited. It's not the same as happy."

Out of nowhere Tish came slinking between them and settled near the refrigerator.

"She's going to stick close and listen to me grovel?"

"You're going to grovel, Burke?"

"Apologize. It's my turn to say sorry."

Sofia went to the dog and murmured, "I love you, Tish. But I love him, too, and I need to spend some time telling him all about it."

I love him.

Tish turned, pointed her nose in the air as if assessing things, then trotted out.

"Did you just tell Tish that you love me?"

"She's the entitled type. She appreciates knowing things first." Playfully, Sofia dragged her knuckles up his body until she was lightly grazing his jaw. "I've loved you for a friggin' ridiculously long time. But I was scared of being rejected, left behind, and I didn't own what I felt. I should've."

"It sounds like you're apologizing to me again, when you're supposed to just say you love me and then let me prove to you that I deserve it."

"What you deserve is the truth." She appeared to debate and when she spoke again, her voice was nearly as soft as a whisper. "When I was in the hospital, the lab found abnormalities."

Christ. No, not again. "Your heart?"

"Kidneys. Burke, wait, don't react before I tell you where things stand." She sighed, holding him. "The transplant, the side effects from my meds, the hypertension, they made me vulnerable to chronic kidney disease, it turns out. The docs looked into things further, and I'm at stage two."

"Can it be treated?"

"Progression can be slowed, with diet changes, my BP meds and some close monitoring, but no, babe, the damage can't be undone."

"And when it progresses?"

"Dialysis. Maybe a transplant. Those are end-stage options, could be years away." Sofia stared at him, silently begging him for something he wasn't sure he'd be able to provide: understanding. "I'm going to fight. But the quality of my life counts. I want to *enjoy* this life, every day with you and Tish and my friends."

"Joss and Caro. Bautista. Do they know?"

She nodded. "I sat them down after I finalized a treatment plan with my nephrologist. He's in Boston."

"I want to meet him, ask some questions."

"Okay, of course. Everyone's in agreement. The girls and I are still going for our dream. It's going to be tough, after a while. If this . . . If *I'm* not for you—"

"Hell, yeah, you are." Deliberately, he slid his thumbs over her cheeks and down her neck. She needed him to help carry this burden, and it was devastatingly natural to share his strength with her. "I'm in this with you, Sofia. I was fucking wrong to leave. You matter. Your dream matters."

"My dream's here—all of it's here. The businesses downstairs. You. If you think you won't push me away, Burke, let me love you. I'm good at it."

The best, but . . . "I'm fucked up, Sofia."

"You are." Openly, she searched his eyes. "You're fucked up and broken and afraid to let your guard slip. But so am I, and neither of us is asking for a perfect love."

"We're going to piss each other off."

"Guaranteed."

"We remind each other of every screwed-up thing in our past."

"Then there are no lies and no reason to pretend. That makes us free."

They were free. Free to love her, he secured his arms around her. "So damn beautiful... You're not good at loving me. You're the best."

"I've had some time to get it right. Know what I found in the basement next door? Your sketches. I didn't know you loved me from the start of us."

"It wouldn't have been enough then."

She nodded. "No, but I hate regret. It feels like a stain I can't wash off, like a tattoo." She stroked up his sleeve to expose his ink. "Are there any regrets here?"

He'd been beaten within an inch of his life for the Colossians tattoo, but he couldn't say he regretted it. "No. The thing I regret is setting you aside. I won't make that fuckup again. So let's agree to be messed up and in love, because I've been wanting to kiss you since Brooklyn—"

She slanted her mouth over his. Swaying her backward, he lifted her ass and set her on the edge of the counter.

She braced herself so he could rid her of those shimmery pants. And when he had her naked, haloed under the light, he parted her thighs and kissed her. She was wet and primed for him, made for him.

Burke picked her up, carried her to the bedroom, and saw two faded drawings in frames dominating her nightstand. She'd made space for him in her body, and was now making space for him in her life.

"Burke, we're okay, aren't we?"

"Very." Stripping, baring himself to the love of his damaged, patched-up life, he sent one of her thighs east and the other west.

CHAPTER 22

They're going to give this town hell." Bautista knew he'd get no response through the swell of music and noise. In a bar full of folks, yet somehow still alone, he considered the contents of his glass.

In the center of the bar, Caro, Joss, and Sofia danced on the pool table with their arms up and hips shaking. This place was theirs now—he'd cleaned it carefully, extracting the traces of his past he didn't want them to inherit—and they could do what they pleased. They appeared to be three carefree, skating-through-life girls, but were the most scarred women he'd ever met—and he'd met a lot of women.

Eaves needed some hell. Either he was going to regret partnering up with them, or he'd die knowing Guilty Pleasures was the abso-fucking-lutely best decision of his life.

Allowing himself a few more minutes to observe, he eventually set his drink aside, shook Tariq's hand, and started walking. The racket ushered him out the door and up the steep steps to the sweltering summer evening.

His chopper gleamed as stubborn tails of sunlight pinged off the chrome. Reunited with it, he threw his leg over the bike and put on his sunglasses.

"Bautista, hold up!" Sofia, with Joss and Caro sticking close, pranced up to him holding something. A tiny gift box. "It's time you got this back."

Wordlessly he opened it. Inside was a ring. Luz's ring—and a pink sticky note dressed in Sofia's handwriting.

Don't ever forget you loved her.

He crushed the note in his fist. He couldn't forget his love for Luz if he tried. Nor would he ever forget that behind his back she'd schemed to join his motorcycle club and had been ready to cut him to the quick to do it.

All for the semblance of a family, because unlike him she couldn't tolerate solitude. And his love, this ring, hadn't been enough for her.

Sofia didn't know that. She wouldn't.

Bright, so beautiful, she'd come into the bar flushed and sated-looking, with Burke Wolf close behind wearing the rumpled look of a man who'd just fucked with nasty abandon—each of them marking what's theirs.

Yeah, he'd seen *that* coming.

"When are you coming back?" Caro asked him, and the others edged closer to absorb his answer.

Tonight he was riding out with his club brothers, but he'd make no promises as to when he would put Eaves's sand and gravel under his wheels again. "When I need to."

Caro sighed her frustration, but he was watching Joss, who remained silent, hugging herself. Then she took a step back, tapped Caro's arm, and they both sought the stairwell.

Sofia touched the motorcycle's handlebars, smudging them, but he had no complaint. It was a damn shame the way cards were dealt for some people. What kind of fucked-up déjà vu was it that he'd care about someone only to lose her?

But Sofia was resilient. Her spirit was tough and he had nothing but faith in her.

She hugged him and he was surprised the force didn't tumble the chopper. "What if I start missing you?"

"If you need me, Sofia, I'll come back. *Dios te bendiga, querida.*" Finally he patted her back, then urged her safely away so he could crank and ride. "Hold it down, okay?"

"Bye, Bautista."

* * *

The first sign of autumn in Eaves was room to stretch your arms on the downtown sidewalks. Tourists departed and the town began to settle. As Sofia pedaled her great-aunt's bicycle, she took her hands off the handlebars and let the September breeze flap against her sweater and play with her hair.

She had miles to go before she reached Gingham Road, but the Pruitts weren't expecting her at the cottage for a while and she could tour the scenic streets. The trees edging the sidewalks were still full and flower bushes maintained their bloom—Eaves had always been loath to let go of its summer-peak luster.

Stopping at the closet-size wine shop, she chose a bottle of bold zinfandel to pair with the catch-of-the-day lobster from Richard's boat. When Gretchen had called to invite Sofia over for dinner, she'd said it wasn't necessary to bring anything, but considering that the Pruitts had brought her sweats when she was in the hospital, she reasoned a bottle of booze dressed in an elegant red bow should make them even.

Gingham sat on one of the highest peaks in the area, and Sofia rose off the bicycle seat, taking on the incline as she headed for the old metal mailbox and half-rotted birdhouse on the curb. Past rows of tall, thick shrubbery she would find a derelict but inhabitable little cottage and some of the best views in Barnstable County. Though the place was rarely occupied, the Pruitts should get around to sprucing it up. She'd volunteer to help.

As she approached, she stopped abruptly and gravity began to pull the bicycle backward. Catching herself, she turned onto the wide drive and stared with her mouth open at a sight that was both simple and spectacular.

The trees were golden. The hedges, too. And the flowerpots and bushes. Tiny dots of winking light tangled and crisscrossed and danced together from one high tree to the other, creating a whimsical cave.

Grabbing her purse and the zinfandel, she dismounted. She missed the kickstand but was only vaguely aware of the bike collapsing onto grass. Wandering forward, she found a candle burning on a scratched white table underneath the twinkling ceiling.

Luz's table.

"Oh my God." As much worse for wear as the table was, she couldn't imagine the Pruitts buying it and setting it outside like this.

She turned to race to the cottage for an explanation, but the answer was a Ford with the tailgate down and a man reaching inside for a pair of chairs.

"Luz's table," she hollered across. "It's here."

Burke turned and winced as he nodded. "It was supposed to be a surprise. Gretchen said you'd get here at eight."

"Gretchen and Richard aren't here, are they?"

"Nope." He brought the chairs over, setting them opposite each other, with the candle-topped table between.

"Then there's no lobster."

He laughed. "Nope, but we'll go anywhere you want for dinner. In the meantime, there're pears on some of the trees and you're welcome to whatever's in that bottle you're holding." He took the zinfandel and guided her to the golden canopy.

"What's going on, Burke?"

"I was thinking of putting up a gazebo right here—you could sit and look out over the cranberry bog. The house should have an upstairs balcony, so you could walk out with your taffy and look at the lighthouse."

What? "The Pruitts' cottage doesn't have an upstairs, and...What are you saying anyway?"

"This isn't the Pruitts' cottage anymore. I came into some money recently—sold a building to a couple of women who want to open a naughty bakery"—he winked—"so I made an investment in something permanent here." Burke sat on one of the chairs and she numbly claimed the other, the candle burning between them. "Eaves looks good from up here. There's plenty of room for Tish to run around. The new house can be anything we want it to be."

"You bought this property for us?" Tears surfaced, blurring Sofia's vision. *Permanent*, he'd said. In the face of her diagnosis, he wasn't running. He was stepping closer, holding her tighter. "You're making plans?"

"Yeah, Sofia. It doesn't mean giving up your apartment or my boat tomorrow. But our future can happen here."

A house. A home with Burke Wolf. Pictures on the walls, a cozy quilt on the bed, maybe a fireplace for the wintertime and a sofa in front of towering windows where she'd sit with him and watch the lighthouse guard the water. It'd be a damn strong house, equipped to handle the ebb and flow of their life together.

Make plans. Live this life. Love him.

"I want this," she said, reaching across the table, and he met her halfway, taking her hand. "We're going to laugh and fight here. We're going to have sex here."

"Crazy-hot sex. You know, we don't have to wait for the house to go up." Burke came around the table, pulled her chair out, and straddled her lap. "Choose, the laughing or fighting or crazy-hot sex."

"Crazy-hot sex," she said automatically, sliding her gaze from the heat in his gray eyes to the belt buckle that was front and center and *such* easy access. She pushed his shirt up, too impatient to bother with buttons, and then unfastened the belt. Stroking him, kissing him, she whispered, "No one will love you better than I do, Burke. No one can outdo me there."

"Damn right." Stepping back, he pulled her upright and began to strip her for their audience of pear trees and golden lights. "When I put my name on you, you put yours on me."

Finally, he held her face and she knew as he studied her that he was storing this memory in a safe place where he'd be able to call it up to get him through someday. And then he kissed her mouth, and as giddy as she was for a future with him, the here and now was pretty freaking great, too.

Whipping off his shirt, Burke took the candle from the table and handed it to her. "C'mere, Sofia…" He led her deeper into the sparkling cave and she realized he'd spread a comforter there. "That candle's pure paraffin. I know a dirty little shop on Society Street that carries them."

Her eyes widened, fastening on the flickering candle and the liquid wax pooling in its jar. He'd bought a candle from Blush.

And that made him hotter than the molten wax she held in her hand.

"You sure, Burke?" she asked, watching him lie on the

blanket and roll to offer her his naked back. God, she loved his back.

"I trust you. You trust me?"

"So much." Turned on beyond reason, Sofia tested the heat, then sank to her knees and sat astride him. As she raised the jar high, she whispered, *"I'm so glad I love you,"* before the first shimmering drop dripped.

Joss Vail knows how to play by the rules *and* how to break them. But when her erotic bakery lands her in serious trouble, she must depend on her sinfully delicious handyman... who's not exactly the angel he seems.

A preview of *Yours to Take* follows.

CHAPTER 1

$\mathscr{S}$tarting over sure hurt like hell.

Joss Vail managed to dump the hammer a safe distance from her fuzzy-socked feet before squeezing her thumb and screaming like a vulgar-mouthed banshee. Pain throbbed in time with her pulse, and when she scraped together enough courage to investigate the damage, she was surprised that one, the digit was still attached to her hand, and two, it wasn't a mass of bloodied flesh and crushed bone. After all, she'd been picturing her exes while swinging the hammer— so many men that no one would blame her if she forgot a name or a face here and there, even though each had left behind a scar that she'd remember forever—and she hadn't exactly been gentle.

Some ice, an aspirin, and she'd be fine. Nope, make that a pint of whiskey. There was a bottle of JD in the pantry and she wasn't driving tonight. A short back-alley trek to the sex shop next door and a flight of stairs to the apartment above it and she'd be home. She would be more than ready to dilute frustration and jar loose some stress after she put the bakery to bed tonight.

Dine-in hours were seven a.m. to four p.m., Monday through Saturday, yet Joss couldn't remember coming in later than five in the morning or leaving before midnight since Lust Desserts' grand opening last month. The sit-down bakery, specializing in erotic treats—or what her mother's most recent ranty email had christened "perverted pastries"—was her baby. At less than a month old, the bakery was still merely an infant and she had every right to be a cautious parent.

A step from crazy it might seem, but she would give this place the care, protection, and love she'd been denied all her twenty-nine years.

Thirty, she amended the thought. Thirty years ago today she'd been scooped right out of Matisse Vail's porcelain belly and set loose on the world. From that first cesarean section incision, her mother had known Joss would be trouble.

She'd tried to forget today was her birthday. Everyone who knew her apparently had. She was still getting her bearings here in Eaves, Massachusetts—Cape Cod was day to New York City's night—but Sofia, her best friend and the owner of the erotic boutique on her left, and Caro, who owned the boudoir photography studio on her right, probably should've remembered. Each had popped in earlier for treats, but neither had uttered the word *birthday* even though today's special was the Birthday Suit, a nude caramel cake dessert. The caterers, clients, and colleagues Joss had known in New York, where she'd worked for eternity and a day as a chef's assistant, had for all intents and purposes severed acquaintance with her when she'd moved to the Cape this past summer. No one in Stamp, New Jersey, had forgotten the scandal that had compelled her parents to send her off with a one-way ticket anywhere but home.

The last correspondence from her parents' joint email account had been her mother's all-caps message: YOUR FATHER AND I CAN'T LOOK OUR CLIENTS IN THE EYE...WE'RE FORCED TO EXPLAIN THAT OUR KID IS SELLING EDIBLE PORN...WHEN YOUR LITTLE BAKERY FAILS—AND IT WILL—WE'RE NOT BAILING YOU OUT. WE MADE THAT MISTAKE ONCE AND WON'T DO IT AGAIN!

Joss had deleted that one promptly, then restored it to draft an all-caps reply: FUCK YOU, TOO, MOM. Then she deleted it, along with Matisse's email, and tried to ignore the fresh hurt cloaking her like new-fallen snow.

There'd be plenty to follow once Let There Be Light electricians Hendrix and Matisse Vail found out about Guilty Pleasures. Joss hoped the news of her coownership of a nightclub—or an underground sinners' playground, depending on who you talked to—wouldn't reach her family for another couple of weeks yet. That way the Vails could have something significant to bemoan at the Thanksgiving dinner table or the Stamp Baptist Church winter social.

Not that Joss would overexert herself trying to gather any give-a-damns. Guilty Pleasures was a place to belong, and it belonged to her, just as it belonged to her friends.

Just as it still belonged to the man who'd owned it when it had been a claustrophobic dive bar called Bottoms Up.

Can't forget that *nugget of reality...*

"Guess it doesn't matter how far you've come when you screw up everywhere you go," she murmured, trying to pry loose the smashed wall anchor with a festive ginger-polished fingernail.

Joss Vail, who'd once had potential to be her parents'

prayers come true, was committed to proving herself the hell neither Hendrix nor Matisse had expected to come from the sperm of an honest hardworking man and the egg of his by-the-Good-Book wife.

When they wanted to scale social ladders with every high-profile client and commercial account they won, all she did was pull them down with her scandals and errors and scrapes. Even after they'd flicked her away as one would a gnat, she managed to disappoint them from afar.

And they *always* managed to make sure she knew.

Thinking about her parents only intensified the pain radiating from her thumb, and she found herself glaring at the hammer she'd tossed into the toolbox on the floor. Wasn't this how it tended to play out? Concentrating on people who hurt her, whether picturing their faces attached to a wall anchor or recalling a shitty email, only led her to hurt herself.

The pattern ended here, in this bakery. It wasn't a glamorous Manhattan hot spot, didn't boast the highest-grade equipment, and wouldn't likely ever serve celebrity clientele, but she'd utilized her limited start-up funds creatively, secured a reasonable bank loan, and now she was a culinary artist who had something to be proud of.

For the first time in her life she was okay with herself. She'd survived worse than a sore thumb to get to this point.

Damn her if it all hadn't been worth it.

Joss crept back to study the wall. She'd intended to hang a series of erotic paintings, from her dirty mind straight to the canvas. And okay, she was proud of that, too—her penchant for naughty art.

The wall anchor was cracked, but the worse damage was the numerous ugly cavities where the hammer's face had busted the drywall. The brand-new, expensively finished and painted drywall.

"Fuck. Me." DIY-ing the menu board with photo-framed chalkboards affixed to a rustic ladder and adding her paintings to the sensual violet accent wall behind the counter had been last-minute, off-design decisions. The carpenters, already visibly annoyed with her previous last-minute, off-design changes, had provided a hefty quote with their offer to put her on the calendar for art hanging, but she'd insisted she could handle wall mounts and a T-square just fine. Holes in the wall and cracked anchors weren't testimonials to *just fine*.

She was tired. Overly tired. It was taking its toll. She couldn't allow it to affect the quality of her baking, the training of her already time-strapped part-time assistant, or the management of her business.

Nor could she let customers find the place filthy with marred walls and chalky dust on the wood floors.

Turning her wrist to gauge her watch, she noted it was approaching nine p.m. She figured she could go home now, put an early end to this day, and come in at two or three in the morning to patch holes and scrub floors before diving into food prep. She wouldn't be bright-eyed and bushy-tailed—more like sluggish and cranky—but all would be taken care of without the added expense of paying a professional to swing a hammer.

Joss's purse and the high heels she'd traded for comfy socks after locking up for the evening were in the back, so she started shutting things down in the eatery, cutting the music and turning off some of the lights.

When she stepped outside to bring in the Word of the Day dry-erase easel—the word nerd in her couldn't resist, and today's word was one of her favorites: *partake*—a snap of cold sneaked through her clothes. Black leggings and a pale gold dress that shimmered like champagne might look great on a crowded New York street where there was body heat aplenty to warm her, but this was November in a small Cape Cod town that was next-door neighbor to the Atlantic Ocean.

The easel was heavy. The antiques dealer who'd sold her the piece had to have been mistaken when he claimed it was made of bronze. The thing had to be a hundred percent cast iron. It scraped on the sidewalk as she struggled to drag it toward the door. Not that she was too fragile to manage—her sore thumb complicated things. Around her, people walked briskly, carrying on their conversations and journeys as their scarves flapped in the wind.

"Thought y'all were closed," someone said from inside a car on the street.

The words—that voice, actually, like the murmur of thunder stirring up havoc on a calm night, was meant for her. It could be a threat or a comfort, and it was up to her to decide which she wanted it to be.

Curious, she traced the voice to a shined-up Lincoln. Perfectly fine vehicles were parked on either side of it, but somehow it eclipsed them, made them appear inferior. The ride looked like a fantasy and must drive like a dream. Jealousy threatened, but hey, its owner might be overcompensating for some unfortunate shortcoming.

"We *are* closed. I'm tucking everything in for the night," she said, aiming her response at the crossover. Lamps and the lights strung around them cast golden beams over the streets, but she wasn't trying to get a close look at the driver. She didn't want the intimacy of eye contact, not with someone whose voice had her feeling as if she'd slipped into a hot, fragrant bath.

Joss was trying to be different now. Not new, but improved in her own little way. Relationships left her bruised and torn. Just-because sex was always hot and fun in the moment, but it was a temporary remedy, kind of like a square of gauze on a gaping wound.

No more men until next year. It was a promise, a personal challenge to mend herself. What she'd done a few months ago... The man she'd done it all with... The lies she still carried long after they'd showered away their mistakes and he'd let her go...

Something must be wrong with her, and she had the rest of this year to make the proper adjustments before allowing anyone else to get close.

It didn't mean that come 12:01 a.m. New Year's Day she'd pounce on the nearest guy, but it also didn't mean she *wouldn't.*

A smooth click, then the Lincoln's driver-side door opened as the window rose and the interior lit. Not that Joss had been paying all that much attention to a man who'd hollered at her from an open window.

Hyperawareness was to blame for the pleasant sensation across her skin and how her ears twitched the way her friend's dog's did whenever she heard a noise but was too lazy to get her rump up to investigate.

Sex was primal instinct to Joss, and denying herself the act didn't suppress her appetite for it. Temptation was everywhere: the erotic treatery that made her hungry for more than sweets, the sex boutique that enticed her to collect every toy in stock, the boudoir photography studio that teased her to get naked in front of a lens because she was a sexual being and she wanted everyone to know it. And, of course, Guilty Pleasures, a club beneath her feet that piped in sultry music, kept quality booze on tap, and encouraged nightly dry-grinding.

Celibacy was a shock to her system, healing her in some ways but breaking her in others. That was the point of this study of self, wasn't it? To take away the fundamental element that made her Joss Vail and find out what remained?

She continued to lug the easel, but the man's voice interrupted, holding her still like strong hands clasping her wrists high over her head.

"Can I give you some help with that?"

"I can handle it—" Joss began to say, before her gaze tripped over him. Dark skin, darker eyes, a face whose angles and hollows held light and shadow with devastating perfection.

She ignored his body, refused to be impressed or intimidated. Plenty of men did unfathomably amazing things to a simple sweater and jeans.

He reached for the easel and she almost cried, *Hey, who do you think you are, some damn modern-day gladiator?*

Then he lifted it with beautiful effortlessness and instead she shut up and admired the view.

When she held open the door and then followed him inside the half-lit Lust Desserts, not for the first time tonight she whispered two soft syllables. "Fuck me."

The sigh of the door drifting shut swallowed her plea, rescuing her from that horribly awkward embarrassment, but now he was in her bakery and things were awfully quiet and the air was becoming tight.

"Thanks for bringing it in. You didn't have to go out of your way," she said, adopting stoic professionalism that was promptly unwound the moment he glanced down at the Fraggles on her feet.

"Are those—Is that—" He shifted this way, pivoted that way, as though figuring out how to approach the question. "Are you wearing *Fraggle Rock* socks?"

Yes.

"I'm not sure I know what you mean."

Yes, she did.

His face eased into a grin—great, it had to be a *gorgeous* dimpled one—but his eyes blatantly conveyed that he detected the liar in her.

So he knew she could lie in a heartbeat and she knew he possessed staggering strength.

"Can I have the name of my knight in faded jeans, please?" What was with the everyman clothes, anyway? Men who drove luxury Lincolns stepped out in tailored suits, not plain sweaters that were the color of the sky just before dawn. She knew that color well. It greeted her when she slid out of bed to start her workday.

"Aaron North."

Aaron, a solid name. A Biblical name. She wouldn't have harped on that detail had the chain around his neck not held a simple gold cross.

No. Nope. No way. Not a man who attended church on Sundays while she painted carnal oils. Not a man who'd try to save her soul until he ultimately surrendered and dismissed her the same way her parents had.

"Thanks again for bringing in the easel, Aaron," she said politely, she and her Fraggles going to the door. "I won't hold you up."

"You're not holding me up. I was hoping to catch you, Joss."

She hadn't given him her name. "We've met?"

"No, but I'm here about the ads." He pointed, but she already knew he referred to the HELP WANTED and APARTMENT FOR RENT signs taped to the front window. Running a dine-in plus offering specialty catering across the Cape, Joss needed more help than only one assistant could provide. She hoped to rent out the upstairs apartment to offset the expense of bringing another set of hands on board.

"Which are you inquiring about?" she asked. "The job or the apartment?"

"Both."

"You have baking experience?" Imagining his hands working fondant wasn't a great idea, so she stopped—eventually.

"I used to bake for church and charity functions."

"Are you any good? Be honest."

"I'm a lot good." He paused long enough for her to apply all sorts of meanings to that. "I came in earlier asking about the ads, but someone persuaded me to buy one of those pudding cups and told me to talk to the owner, Joss Vail."

"Little Deaths," she said, naming the caramelized fruit and frosted coffee cake crumble samplers. "That's what they're called."

"It was delicious as hell—Hold on. Isn't a 'little death' an orgasm?"

Yes, yes, oh God yes. "Uh-huh. I call this bakery Lust Desserts for a reason."

The tension that tightened his shoulders and settled in his dark-lashed eyes probably had plenty to do with all this *little death* talk and nothing to do with dessert.

"Um, so why'd you assume I'm Joss?"

"Y'all closed a few hours ago but you're still here. The mark of somebody looking after what's theirs."

Reasonable enough, but . . . "If you came here earlier and knew when we closed, why were you waiting outside just now? So you're aware, if you say it's because you were hoping for the chance to bring in my easel for me and show off your muscles, you're better off leaving."

The grin returned, accompanied by a laugh, and she struggled to find some immediate flaw, some turnoff besides the cross he wore, which only reflected her own faults and wrongness. Maybe his virility wasn't all it ought to be. Could be his spelling was atrocious and he ran screaming from a game of Scrabble.

Then she found it, a flaw in his smile, a chip at the corner of a bottom tooth.

Crap. The discovery only made him humanly imperfect, and it heightened his appeal because Joss *liked* this imperfection.

"I was checking out the area. Heard there's a club around here. What kind of trouble comes with that?"

"The club's downstairs."

His brows drew together, as if leaning close to share a secret. "Quiet as a library."

Library... ooh, one of my trigger words. She was no great scholar, but the written word was a magical thing. When everything else in her world was fiery shit, she could break out the reading glasses, stick her nose in anything from a pastry cookbook to a dictionary, and calm the hell down.

"Guilty Pleasures opens at nine." She raised her wrist, looked at her watch. "We've got a few more minutes before the revelry begins. Actually, the noise doesn't carry to the apartments. Cross my heart. I live with my friend in the one above the boutique next door."

"What happened to your thumb?" Aaron laid her hand in his. She was pale on top of him—cream poured over cocoa—and his heat seemed to penetrate every cold crevice of her. If he swirled his fingers over her palm just right, chances were she'd shatter in a little death of her own right in front of him. "Somebody took a mallet to it?"

"Not a mallet. A hammer. I was hanging art." She took her swollen-thumbed hand away to turn on the rest of the lights and indicated the accent wall she'd ravaged. "It didn't go well."

"Put something cold on it."

"I intend to." A frigid shower ought to suffice. "Well, since we're both here, and if my ineptness with a hammer hasn't turned you off, would you like a look at the apartment?"

"Yeah, if you feel up to giving me a tour."

She led him out the rear door and up a set of stairs that ushered them to a welcome mat and a pair of ceramic pots—chrysanthemums in one and pathetically wilted basil in the other. She'd been so preoccupied with sprucing up the interior that she'd forgotten to freshen up the small sort-of porch for potential tenants.

Aaron made no comment and strode easily into the apartment.

"Aside from the appliances, it's not furnished," she said, just to fill the air with something more than the smell of paint and the rush of her horny heartbeat. She trailed him from one neutral-colored room to the other. The open living room/kitchen tapered into a hall that introduced two bedrooms and a pair of closets and a four-piece bathroom.

"This room's kind of furnished." Aaron leaned against the doorjamb of a room with stormy-gray walls and gestured to the king-size bed, rumpled sheets, and stack of books on the floor. Library finds, probably overdue now.

Shit, she'd forgotten to clear it all out. "That's my stuff," she admitted. "I sometimes crash here when I want to give my roommate and her guy some privacy." Though Sofia was lately spending more nights at the Eaves Marina on her man's boat. "I won't do that once you move in. You know, if things check out and you sign the lease."

"Why don't you live here, if your roommate needs that kind of privacy?"

"These walls aren't so thin." Thin enough that she sometimes heard the bump of bucking bodies and grunts of sex, but Aaron North didn't need to know that. "It's not an every-night thing. Besides, maybe I want a house and a fence and flamingos in the yard next."

He made a concerned face at *flamingos* and she snorted, but she was only half kidding.

So greedy, she couldn't help but crave more. A bakery, part ownership of a club, and now she wanted a home. Put down stakes, plant roots—she would do that here because New York had disappointed her and New Jersey didn't want her.

She wasn't in a hurry to flee the place she shared with her best friend, though. She and Sofia Mercer, a marketing exec who'd recently inherited the erotic boutique next door and inspired Joss to move to the Cape and confront her dreams, had been roomies for eons in Manhattan. They'd survived their twenties together, years of screwups and fails and angst, and were as close as Joss imagined sisters were.

"My sights are set on a fixer-upper," she found herself telling him. "Something with a past. Something I can make new again." That's what the bakery was. Formerly a grocery market owned by a real son of a bitch who died some years ago, the structure had been reconfigured and given a second chance. It was what Joss wanted for herself.

"I saw the holes in the wall in your bakery, and that thumb's got to be hurting like hell. Sure you're ready for a project that'll demand something more dangerous than a hammer?"

"Funny, not funny," she said, but she didn't take real offense. This was banter, light teasing, how people figured each other out. "I'm fine with a hammer. I'm just having an off night."

What Joss didn't—and wouldn't—tell Aaron was that she

was terrified to live alone. She had trouble sleeping without a weapon handy or the protection of the silver-eyed beast Sofia insisted was a Siberian husky but might actually be a wolf.

Aaron sat down on the bed. Was this how he carried on, going around doing what he wanted without waiting for invitation?

But, more important...Could he smell her on the sheets? Was he picturing her stretched out on the mattress, wondering if she slept naked?

She *wanted* him to, because at the ripe age of thirty she'd lost her mind.

"I don't think I know anybody who owns one of these," he said, pressing his hands into the memory-foam mattress.

She'd financed it when she had a stable list of wealthy Manhattan clients and a Wall Street whiz of a boyfriend who'd lavished her with luxuries before abusing and dumping her.

Another life, she reminded herself.

"It's comfortable," she blurted, plunking down beside him. The movement didn't jostle him. "Want to know something neat about this set? The sales guy had me lie flat on one side, then he went to the other and started jumping up and down. I live to tell you I wasn't catapulted into the air."

"If I said I didn't believe you, would you demonstrate to prove me wrong?"

Ask him to lie flat while she bounced around him on the mattress? He was using her words as weapons of flirtation.

Crafty bastard, wasn't he?

"Think I weigh enough to catapult you into the air?"

"Not even close. The question's still there. Would you demonstrate?"

"Only if I were selling you my bed. Which I'm not.

Although..." She tapped a fingertip to the dimple in her chin, pretending to contemplate. "I *might* consider including it in the lease."

Good business was sparing herself the migraine of relocating the massive bed and instead presenting it as a fabulous feature to a potential tenant.

"About the lease," he said. "Would you reconsider the one-year lease—agree to month-to-month?"

"As far as the bakery goes, I'm looking for someone to stay on for a while. Preferably full-time, but we could work something out. I was thinking if we work well together, maybe I won't want to let you go so quickly."

"I can't give you permanent. If you need help in the bakery for the next few months, I can do that, but I'm passing through."

"Passing through? That's what I thought when I first came here. Eaves has a certain charm, though. Don't underestimate it."

"Charm's not always enough to convince somebody to stay."

Stranger to stranger, blue eyes to brown, she saw something extraordinarily familiar in him. She saw herself, rootless, searching for something to embrace her. "What are you running from in that fancy car of yours, Aaron?"

"The Lincoln," he said, rolling a set of shoulders that would feel like carved stone under her hands, "gets me from place to place. Nothing more to it than that."

"Vehicles aren't *vehicles* where I come from. They're status symbols. Calling cards."

"Is that why you're here instead of where you come from?" he challenged, making so much sense that she might've kissed him if she were still the reckless type.

"You sidestepped my question."

"I don't have a criminal record, and I'm not looking to earn one here. Call it sidestepping if you want, but that's all the answer I owe you at the moment."

Fair enough. Though she could practically see his solemnity as a dam barricading a flood of some abstract pain.

"Eaves is home for me now, but I don't expect it to be yours. If you want month-to-month, I'll consider it," she decided. "If we don't mesh downstairs, don't worry too much. I came in when tourist numbers were at their peak, and all that's mellowed out, but plenty of shops are hiring for the holidays."

"We're getting along all right, don't you think?"

"Yes, but we haven't worked together. Maybe a place called Lust Desserts will turn out to be too sexual for a guy who wears a cross around his neck."

"I'm good with it. Thanks for the warning, just the same."

"Optimism's great, but you should still be prepared, Aaron. You'll need income to pay the rent. Guilty Pleasures used to be a tiny hellhole of a bar, so the old clientele remember it and it gets okay traffic. By summer, though, it'll be *the* naughtiest hot spot on the Cape. Point is, I don't handle the hiring, but I can put in a word."

"You're going out of your way for a man you don't know."

"I know you need a reason to stop for a second and get your crap together." Leaving out the confession that she was a lousy judge of men and most used the fact to take vicious advantage of her, she patted the mattress. "About this. I bought it brand-new. I've had it almost a year and always use sheets and a mattress protector." She leaned across him to peel the fitted sheet from a corner of the mattress and almost fell in his lap. "Actually, you've got a better angle."

Aaron laughed and she did, too. Nervously. Giddily. Quite possibly stupidly.

"Told you I was having an off night," she attempted to explain, but he didn't appear all that inconvenienced. "Before this gets any weirder, we should step out of this bedroom."

"It's not weird. Not to me."

"Oh." *Take me, take me, take me.* "Okay."

"How's the heat up here?" he asked, pointing to the radiator. "I'm from Florida. Didn't expect the kind of cold that'd freeze a man's balls off. Not in November."

She very much hoped his balls were in excellent working order. "Poor you. We're right up against the ocean, so you'd expect it to be a touch warmer, but the wind's having its say. Where in Florida?"

"Pensacola."

"What's Cape Cod have that you couldn't find in Florida?"

"A change of scenery. Different opportunities. Somebody new to look at." Aaron leaned forward, his hands braced on his thighs.

If she reached, tucked his cross beneath his collar, and tasted the curve of his mouth as if experimenting with a new recipe, he would retract what he said about this not being weird. He'd haul his sexy ass out of here and she'd lose a potential tenant and a damn fine set of helping hands.

So Joss kept *her* hands to herself. "Nothing wrong with a fresh beginning. A do-over." She held a finger to her lips. "Shh...Hear any noise?"

"Nah."

"It's past nine, the club's open, and we're not being disturbed. Told you so."

"You get an unusual amount of joy out of being right, don't you?"

"Sure do." Because it didn't often happen. Her parents would passionately attest to that. "What do you think of the apartment?"

"Suits my needs. The rent posted on the sign is good, but I want the bed."

"Why would I just throw in this expensive bed?" And why would a guy who drove a lust-worthy Lincoln shake her down for a freebie?

"I don't doubt it was expensive when you bought it, but you said it's about a year old and, come on, I don't know what kind of mileage it has."

Oh, really? Feigning insult, she let her mouth drop open. "I can't believe you just said that."

"Which lie do you want me to believe—that you're offended by it or that you'd be doing me a favor to throw the bed in?"

He had her. "The second one. All right, the truth is this set doesn't fit in my room next door. I have nowhere else to store it."

"Include it in the rental agreement."

"This isn't a done deal, Aaron. All I know is you're from Pensacola and have a nice ass—I mean, you're strong. You lifted that easel with zero effort. So yeah, all I know is you're from Pensacola and you're strong." Water. She needed water, or to tie her tongue in a knot to keep from screwing herself with it. "Résumé, background check, references, rental history—I intend to work you over very thoroughly."

"Cool." Aaron pulled out his cell phone. "I can email you whatever you need, or I can bring it tomorrow and maybe help you hang your art. I'm qualified—construction and plumbing."

Construction and plumbing explained the ride. When you

knew how to optimize body and brain power, the money could be nice in those trades. She'd learned the foundations of small business from watching her blue-collar laborer parents turn Let There Be Light into a countywide success.

What she had here was a handyman named Aaron who baked for charity and wore a cross around his neck. Had her parents prayed him into existence just to come to her and rescue her from herself?

"How much would you charge to help hang the art?" she asked him.

"I don't want your money."

"You'd do it for free?"

"Not exactly free. I still want this memory foam to sweeten the rental deal, but my services are going to cost you. Fixing that wall and hanging your art...A half dozen Little Deaths ought to cover it."

A half dozen treats—or orgasms? And why was she even considering pulling his sweater over his head, unzipping his jeans, and acrobatically accomplishing the latter? "Desserts," she said, because she was a reasonable adult after all. "Six of them."

"Mm-hmm. Want to do that for me?"

She caved, smiling and nodding. That was always her problem. She was so easy that even an utter stranger detected it. "Come early."

"What're you thinking? Seven?"

"Earlier." She stood and gestured for him to leave the apartment with her.

"Six?" he asked on the stairs.

"Five."

"Damn."

Downstairs in the bakery, she wrote her cell number on a business card. Now they could feel the low vibration of bass and hear the muffled swell of music. "Guilty Pleasures closes at two. Go down and have a drink. Dance a little. There's no cover charge tonight."

"Where are you going?"

"Home. I can head over there and drink and dance whenever, but that, sir, is a perk of being part owner."

"You sound sad about that."

"I'm not. Not about that, anyway. It's an off night."

Aaron turned the business card a few times before tucking it in his pocket. "You said that a couple of times. Why's it an off night?"

"Today's my birthday. It's been a very boring one."

"Oh. Well, Joss, happy—"

"That's not necessary, Aaron," she interrupted. She went to the door. Thankfully he didn't put up any argument. "I've got more tidying to do. So I'll see you in the morning?"

"Yeah. Five."

"Okay. Good night."

Alone again, she sighed. She couldn't refuse a tenant or employee simply on grounds of ridiculous attraction, but she was courting complications.

Cleaning away the debris from her earlier art-hanging debacle, Joss washed her hands, then wrapped a few ice cubes in a towel and held it to her thumb. After a while she liberated a cube, popped it into her mouth, and was crunching gracelessly when she heard her phone chime.

"Hey, Sof," she answered. "What's up?"

"Can you come down to the club? Quickly? We've got a problem."

Oh, screw. A fight? Drugs? Cops?

"On my way." Joss snatched off her socks, stepped into her high heels, and grabbed her purse. She locked up, then blindly twisted her dark blond hair into a knot as she hurried down the sidewalk, took a sharp turn around the corner of Au Naturel, the photography studio, and thundered down the building's side steps to Guilty Pleasures.

She flung open the door.

And was immediately assaulted with confetti.

"What the—" It tangled in her hair, clung to her skin and sparkled on her clothes under the teal and gold club lights. "Huh...Uh..."

"Surprise!"

Fall in Love with Forever Romance

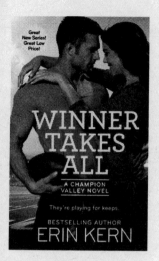

WINNER TAKES ALL
By Erin Kern

The first book in Erin Kern's brand-new Champion Valley series, perfect for fans of *Friday Night Lights*! Former football player Blake Carpenter is determined to rebuild his life as the new coach of his Colorado hometown's high school team. Annabelle Turner, the team's physical therapist, will be damned if the scandal that cost Blake his NFL career hurts *her* team. But what she doesn't count on is their intense attraction that turns every heated run-in into wildly erotic competition…

LAST KISS OF SUMMER
By Marina Adair

Kennedy Sinclair, pie shop and orchard owner extraordinaire, is all that stands between Luke Callahan and the success of his hard cider business. But when the negotiations start heating up, will they lose their hearts? Or seal the deal? Fans of Rachel Gibson, Kristan Higgins, and Jill Shalvis will gobble up the latest sexy contemporary from Marina Adair.

Fall in Love with Forever Romance

MEANT TO BE MINE
By Lisa Marie Perry

In the tradition of Jessica Lemmon and Marie Force, comes a contemporary romance about a former bad boy seeking redemption. After years apart, Sofia Mercer and Burke Wolf reunite in Cape Cod. Their wounds may be deep, but their sizzling attraction is as hot as ever.

RUN TO YOU
By Rachel Lacey

The first book in Rachel Lacey's new contemporary romance series will appeal to fans of Kristan Higgins, Rachel Gibson, and Jill Shalvis! Ethan Hunter's grandmother, Haven, North Carolina's resident matchmaker, is convinced Gabby Winter and her grandson are meant to be together. Rather than break her heart, Ethan and Gabby fake a relationship, but if they continue, they won't just fool the town—they might fool themselves, too...

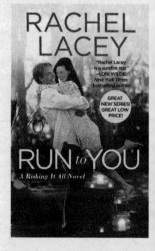

Fall in Love with Forever Romance

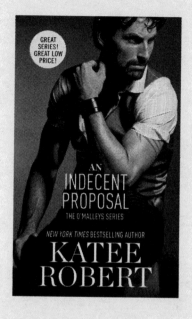

AN INDECENT PROPOSAL
By Katee Robert

New York Times and *USA Today* bestselling author Katee Robert continues her smoking-hot series about the O'Malleys—wealthy, powerful, and full of scandalous family secrets. Olivia Rashidi left behind her Russian mob family for the sake of her daughter. When she meets Cillian O'Malley, she recognizes his family name, but can't help falling for the smoldering, tortured man. Cillian knows that there is no escape from the life, but Olivia is worth trying—and dying—for...